THE PROFANE

TRISTAN VICK

REGOLITH
PUBLICATIONS

A REGOLITH PUBLICATIONS BOOK

THE PROFANE NOVELIZATION
Based on the comic book "The Profane" by Regolith Comics.
Published by Regolith Publications
First Edition, copyright © April 16, 2024.

Published initially on Kindle Vella, January 24, 2024
https://www.amazon.com/kindle-vella/story/B0CVZLZHJT

Edited by Tristan Vick
Cover design by: Christian Bentulan
Chapter plates & interior art are paid stock images via
Adobe Stock Images © 2024-2025

ISBN-13: ISBN: 978-1-950106-10-3
ISBN-10: 1-950106-10-3

"Fear...is the relinquishment of logic, the willing
relinquishing of reasonable patterns. We yield to it
or we fight it, but we cannot meet it halfway."
—Shirley Jackson, "The Haunting of Hill House"

"You are not cursed–you are a reaper. You are the
night incarnate, the ferrier of souls. You are the
bridge between the living and dead..."
— Adalyn Grace, "Belladonna"

CONTENTS

PROLOGUE

THE DINER AND THE STORM

LIGHTNING LIT UP THE dark and dusty sky in blinding candescent flashes. For a moment, the world came into technicolor focus, and then it disappeared into the murky gloom of the stormy night, as if devoured by a great darkness.

The neon sign of Mel's Diner, a small roadside diner that sat along the old Wood River County highway, lit up the four-way intersection with an almost soothing pink glow that rippled across the patchwork of quickly forming puddles in the parking lot.

It looked like a severe storm was brewing, thought Lacey as she prepared a fresh pot of coffee. The rain would be good for the crops, but the summer thunderstorms could be intimidating, like anywhere else in the Midwest. Still, the diner provided a safe oasis amongst the cornfields and cattle. It was an oasis at the end of every backwater highway that ran through the county. A place where truckers could grab a bite to eat and weary travelers could stop by for refreshments and a nice, hot cup of coffee.

Lacey liked working at Mel's Diner. She'd worked here for the past seven and a half years and hadn't missed more than a few shifts. Work was easy when there wasn't a boyfriend or any kids to hold her back. Having a social life in the middle of *Nowheresville, USA,* wasn't much of an option, so she put off her dream of meeting her Prince Charming and starting a family. Besides, she believed that if it were in her destiny to find those things, they'd come into her life naturally. Why stress out over it?

Besides, she wasn't lonely. Not by a long shot. Every day, she came to work knowing she'd learn all the exciting news and gossip from the regulars as they aired everyone else's laundry. She'd hear the stories of those just passing through, from drifters to families on vacation to the odd couple taking a trek across the great United States as if on a pilgrimage from one end to the other. Perhaps she was on the unusual side of things, but she enjoyed conversing with customers and learning their stories. And everyone, regardless of their background, whether young or old, had a story to tell.

As she wiped down the countertops, the jingle of the diner doors swinging open caused her to glance up. She always greeted the customers with a smile and a "What can I get you, hon?" Given the terrible weather, she wasn't surprised to see a woman, drenched from head to foot, standing at the entrance.

"It's pouring out there, sweetie. Get yourself inside and set her down anywhere you'd like. I'll get you a fresh cup of piping hot coffee."

It wasn't uncommon for weary travelers to stop in and take

shelter from the storm on a night like this. Perhaps while stranded here, they could enjoy the comfort of freshly cooked food and hot drinks as they waited out the worst of it. But if she was being honest, she hadn't seen a storm this bad since the twister of 2018.

Luckily, it missed the diner by about a quarter mile, but it tore the roof off Farmer Johnson's barn and, consequently, destroyed his fence too, which allowed his two hundred head of startled cattle to disperse across the valley.

Another surge of hot, white veins, made up of Zeus's divine fury, crackled through the ionized air, crawling across the sky like the tendrils of some nefarious vine. For a split second, the woman standing in the doorway of Mel's Diner was fully illuminated. A beautiful blonde wearing a formal blouse and skirt stood at the entrance, breathing heavily.

A slow, rolling clap of thunder soon followed her arrival, breaking up the pitter-patter of relentless raindrops that battered the black asphalt of the parking area outside. The pink glow of the neon emanating from the Diner's sign hanging above her bathed the mysterious woman in its rouge hues.

Lacey brushed down her white apron and smacked her gum as she spoke, "You're lettin' a draft in, darlin'. Would you mind coming in out of the rain and closing the door behind you?" She nodded toward one of the stools in front of the counter, gesturing for the woman to take a seat.

Another jingle alerted the patrons that the woman had passed beneath the threshold. As she slowly approached the counter, the regulars looked up from their plates to see an attractive blonde with sopping wet hair. She strolled over to the counter and sat on the stool in the center.

"Oh, you poor thing," Lacey said, genuine concern for the

woman's condition evident in her soft-spoken words. "You're drenched to the bone."

Lacey glanced down momentarily and noted that the woman's white blouse top was now a flesh-toned gossamer that left little to the imagination. Even so, the woman didn't seem to mind. At least bashfulness wasn't on the menu, Lacey mused.

Noticing her guest was as white as a sheet, Lacey added, "Let me get you that hot coffee to help warm you and maybe bring some color back to you, darlin'. Do you take cream or sugar with it?"

With a single fluid motion, Lacey grabbed the coffee pot off the hotplate with her left hand and, turning as she went, like a ballet dancer turning a pirouette, pulled out a coffee cup balanced on a saucer with her right.

For her grand finale, she added another spin just as a flourish and promptly set the cup and saucer down on the counter in front of the woman with the palest skin she'd ever seen. The wet sheen gave the woman's skin a porcelain quality, and Lacey couldn't help but lean in, as she always did when trying to be friendly with a new customer.

Pouring a freshly brewed pot of coffee, she topped off the cup and said, "You're more drenched than a tabby in a typhoon. This will warm you right up, darlin'. And don't worry, this one is on the house.

She drew up a handful of pink sugar packets and little beige creamer cups and slid them across the counter, giving her customer a generous amount just in case. Better safe than sorry, she felt. It never hurts to leave a little extra. Most folks appreciated the small things, and Lacey was happy to do a little extra if it meant seeing another smiling face.

At the other end of the counter sat a trucker with a thick

black beard that covered his dark skin, which contrasted with his ultra-bright smile. He nodded at his mug, tapping the rim with his index finger. Lacey smiled back and brought the coffee pot over to him. "Coming right up, Dale," she said, using his name.

The regulars appreciated it when you remembered them by name, so she always called people by their proper names once she'd learned them.

She topped Dale off, stopping just as the coffee threatened to overflow past the lip of the cup. Dale took the cup in his thick hands and sipped it, his eyes shifting to the blonde woman who sat at the counter, seemingly in shock. Her blonde hair dripped onto the diner floor, creating fresh new puddles.

Dale wasn't the only patron who'd taken an interest in the young blonde, fresh from the rain. An elderly couple in a booth beside the window shot her disgusted glances and uttered unnecessarily loud groans to alert everyone in earshot of their obvious displeasure regarding the woman's immodesty.

"Young people, these days, Harold, don't respect anything. They lack propriety. You can practically see her nipples through that soaking blouse top. You'd think she'd have more common sense than that. At least put on a bra." The old woman smacked her teeth and looked away.

When Esther swiveled her head back toward Harold, she noticed him staring at the woman's chest. "Stop ogling her breasts, Harold," Esther scolded, her brow furrowing in equal parts jealousy and loathing as she glared at her husband. "For God's sake, have some decency."

Harold blushed, shrugged, and returned to cutting his country-fried steak slathered in white gravy sauce.

The cook leaned down, appearing in the service window,

and beckoned Lacey to come over to him. She went over and leaned in, her head glancing back toward the woman several times as he whispered something to her. Lacey nodded, smiled, and strolled back over to the blonde, who, Lacey noted, still hadn't touched her complimentary coffee.

"Jake, the line cook, said he'll whip you up anything you want to eat, completely on the house. Considering your state, it's the least he could do."

The woman sat silently, her vacant stare not wavering for a second as she leaned forward on her little perch. Both arms rested at her side as if numb from the cold. At the same time, her purple lips parted as if to whisper something, but nothing apart from a soft breath of air passed over them.

Lacey started to grow concerned. Drawing close to the counter, she leaned forward and waved her hand in front of the woman's face. "Miss, excuse me, but are you all right?" The woman still didn't respond, and Lacey stood upright, looking back over her shoulder at Jake. "I think this poor thing might be in shock, Jake. What should we do?"

Wiping his hands off on his apron, Jake stepped out of the kitchen and went over to the payphone on the back wall. It sat between the ladies' restroom and the rear exit. "She's obviously in worse shape than we thought. I'll call 911 and see if we can get anyone to come out here in this storm. Although I wouldn't be surprised if they closed the roads."

"Thirsty."

"What was that, darlin'?" Lacey asked, turning toward the woman's barely audible whisper. "I didn't quite catch that."

"Thirsty," the blonde repeated. Her low, husky whisper had an unnerving quality that could raise the hair on the back of one's neck. There wasn't anything particularly wrong with her voice. It evoked a sense of dread.

Shaking off the eerie feeling, Lacey glanced down at the now lukewarm cup of coffee and then at the woman. "If coffee ain't your thing, love, I can get you some hot tea. We also have sweet tea, soda, and sparkling water."

Without warning, the blonde's arm shot forward and clutched Lacey's apron. Startled by the sudden and aggressive movement, Lacey screamed and drew back. The tension drew taut on her apron, and, with surprising force, the blonde jerked hard, pulling Lacey into her.

Grabbing Lacey's face with her entire hand, her fingers stretched across Lacey's nose and cheeks like the legs of a spider, the blonde drew her close and hissed, "THIRSTY!"

Taken by surprise, Lacey struggled to break free, clawing at the woman's cold wrist with both hands as she tried to pry her off, but the blonde's grip was too tight. "What the fuck, lady?"

Before Lacey could tear herself free, the woman hoisted her into the air, pulling her up onto the countertop, and just as quickly pinned her down again. Lacey's shoulder blades met the counter's hard top, coaxing a pain-filled chirp as the woman's icy-cold grip clamped down on her.

The woman's fingernails dug into Lacey's face, and she squirmed and kicked her legs to try to break free, but it was no use. The woman's grip was too tight.

Opening her mouth wide, the blonde woman bared a set of long fangs. Not teeth, but actual razor-sharp fangs like those of a predatory beast. She threw her head back and hissed so loudly it sent shivers down everyone's spines.

"W-what are you?" Lacey asked, finally giving up the struggle in a bout of exhaustion.

Another flash of lightning lit up the sky outside, followed by another clap of thunder. This time, the boom rattled the diner's windows as the storm bore down on the small diner and its terrified customers.

A shriek pierced the air as the blonde tore into Lacey's throat. Lacey continued squirming, hoping to break free, but the woman bit down harder, causing a needle-like pain that caused Lacey to start crying. "Please," she whispered, "I don't want to die."

Finally, having had enough of this freak show, Dale slid off his stool and pulled up his sleeves. He quickly arrived at the blonde who was tearing into Lacey's neck with her teeth and reached up, grabbed the blonde's shoulder, and pulled her off. She came off with a chunk of Lacey's flesh in her teeth while pieces of tethered skin stretched from Lacey's wound to the woman's mouth before snapping like rubber bands pulled too tight.

A blood-curdling scream tore out of Lacey's chest and rattled the diner as her blood splashed out across the countertops. Harold and Esther sat frozen in their booth, watching the horrific scene unfold.

The blonde looked down at Dale's hand on her shoulder, his oil-stained fingers gripping down tight. "Now, listen here–"

Suddenly, there was a resounding snap, and Dale yelped like a wounded dog. He looked down at his forearm to find his wrist pointing upward and his fingers pointing back at him in the wrong direction. "The crazy bitch broke my arm!" he howled as he staggered back.

The blonde relinquished her impossibly firm grip, and Dale stumbled, backing up and falling against the counter. Still clutching his broken arm, he leaned on the counter but quickly pushed himself off when he saw Lacey's blood seeping out and spilling toward him like a slow-moving lava flow. Sadly, she'd gone silent, and her breathing was shallow.

Seeing how Lacey and Dale had both been viciously attacked, Jake reached behind the entrance to the kitchen and drew out a shotgun that he kept on the back wall next to the fire extinguisher. Aiming it at the blonde woman, he said sternly, "Easy now, lady." We don't want any trouble. Just let Lacey go and kindly get the fuck out of my diner."

The woman's head abruptly turned towards Jake, her icy blue eyes locking onto his. She let out another carnal hiss, which startled him, causing him to flinch and inadvertently squeeze down on the trigger. The blast of the shotgun rang out, and Esther screamed as the shot shattered the diner window in the booth directly behind her head.

Determined not to let Lacey bleed out, Jake cocked the shotgun and pointed it at the woman again. "I'm not in the habit of repeating myself, but I'll say it one last time. Get out, or the next shot goes through that pretty head of yours." Although he tried to make it sound menacing, it merely sounded to him as if he were reciting a bad line from a movie.

Harold chimed in, "Stop your chitter-chatter and shoot her already. Can't you see the Devil possesses her?" Harold made the sign of the cross on his chest, as any good Catholic would do, and reached over to grab the fork on his table.

Jake glanced around the room, taking in the fearful looks plastered on everyone's faces, and tightened his grip on the shotgun. "Devil or not, it doesn't matter...I gave fair warning."

He fired off a shot aimed directly at the blonde. The muzzle flash temporarily blinded him, but he could feel blood splatter across his face. Jake opened one eye, still squinting, and wiped the blood splatter from his face with his good arm. Dale, who was standing off to the side, did the same.

Harold gasped when he saw that the blonde had used Lacey's body as a shield. Lacey's back had taken the brunt of the gunshot, which chewed through her uniform and flesh, leaving only a bloody mark of carnage. If her breathing had been shallow before, it was now practically non-existent.

"Shit," Jake cried, realizing that he had just killed Lacey. "Shit, shit, shit."

"What the fuck, man? You fucking killed her." Dale shouted across the restaurant, glaring at Jake.

"Shit. I'm sorry... I didn't mean to–"

The blonde woman dropped Lacey's dead body onto the counter, but it hit awkwardly and slipped off, falling to the floor. Everyone glanced down at Lacey's lifeless form, everyone in a state of shock, when the blonde leaped over the counter with the agility of an Olympic gymnast and pounced on top of Jake.

"For fuck's sake!" Dale shouted, stumbling back further, startled by the full-body takedown he'd just witnessed.

With a clamor, Jake and the blonde disappeared behind the countertop. The room fell silent as everyone held their breath. Their eyes were fixed on the counter and where they'd gone down.

"Hey, man," Dale called out as he leaned over the counter, craning his neck to see better what was happening on the other side. "Are you all right?"

Motivated by fear and adrenaline, Harold moved like a twenty-year-old and swiftly rose from his seat. He shuffled over to the diner's front entrance, leaving Esther stunned and unaware of what was happening. Grabbing hold of the door handle, he pushed down and gave it the good ole heave-ho, but it wouldn't budge. He leaned into it, ramming his shoulder into the thick glass, but it was useless. He might as well be smashing into a brick wall for all the good it did.

"Oh, no," he mumbled, facing the others. All color drained from his face, and he opened his mouth to speak again but was too befuddled to think of anything worth saying.

"What is it, old timer?" Dale asked, nervous sweat dappling his brow.

"It's locked," Harold informed him. "She must have jammed it somehow when she was standing here." He wagged his finger at the spot where the blonde had first appeared earlier that evening.

"Shit," Dale said, still cradling his wounded arm, "that means we only have one way out of here." He nodded at the back entrance, and Harold looked in that direction only to have a sinking feeling in his chest that they wouldn't be able to make it.

The exit was at the back of the diner, but more importantly, it ran past the other end of the counter. They'd have to cross paths with that ravenous woman to escape this bloody nightmare.

Both men scrounged up the courage to make a break for it. As they moved toward the back, keeping as close to the wall as they could, the blonde slowly stood up, appearing on the other side of the counter. She looked directly at them, and they came to a halt.

Blood stained her lips and chin and ran down like a crimson waterfall. Pink streaks of sweat and blood trailed down her sternum and meandered like branching tributaries, only to gather again as they seeped down into the crevice of her cleavage. Her see-through blouse was soaking wet, and under her breath, she muttered, "Thirsty."

Harold shuffled over to his wife of thirty-two years and shook her shoulder. "Esther! Esther," he whispered urgently, "We must go. Snap out of it, Esther. We've got to go now."

As Harold attempted to break his wife out of her trance, the blonde turned her gaze upon them, giving Dale the opportunity he desperately needed. While she was distracted by the old couple, Dale pushed past them and made a beeline for the rear exit. Just as he was about to reach the hallway, the blonde stepped out before him, cutting him off.

Her head slumped, she gazed out the broken window behind Esther, but her face slowly turned toward Dale until her eyes met his. Her wet, blood-stained hair hung across her sunken shoulders like tendrils of a terrible Medusa. *"Thirsssty,"* she repeated.

"Look, lady. I don't want any more trouble." Dale, deciding he'd rather stay alive than get dead, knew he'd need to fight his way out of the diner.

Even though she possessed superior strength, she seemed sluggish and slow to respond—almost zombie-like. Reaching behind his back, he drew a knife tucked away inside his belt. Brandishing the knife, he waved it threateningly in front of the woman's face. "Stay back. I'm warning you."

The woman took a step forward and mumbled, "Thirsty."

"Nah, bitch," he said, "I ain't gonna go out like that." He held the knife out straight, pointing its tip directly at her. To his astonishment, she stepped forward, letting the tip of the blade dig into her left breast.

"Thirsty," she muttered, oblivious to the cut opening on her chest. Blood dribbled down from the fresh wound, but she either didn't feel it or didn't give a fig and kept pushing forward.

Dale looked down at his hand, holding the blade as she

leaned into it. When he felt it hit bone, he cringed and let go. As soon as he relinquished his grip, the woman reached up with her slender, white arm, clutched Dale by the thick of his neck, and picked him up off the ground—two twenty-five and all.

His mangled left arm dangling at his side, he reached up with his right and clasped onto the woman's forearm to steady himself lest he twist his neck out of shape. Through a crushed larynx, he wheezed, "You crazy bitch."

He had scarcely muttered the insult when the harsh crack of bone grinding on bone abruptly silenced him. His head fell limp to the side, and the woman cocked her head, like a curious puppy, before tossing his body to the side.

Harold thought it was impossible. A slender woman like her shouldn't be able to lift a two-hundred-and-twenty-pound man off the ground under normal circumstances. But to do it with just one arm—that was inhuman.

"Come, Esther. We're going now."

Esther was still catatonic when Harold pulled her out of her seat and ushered her toward the back. As he used his wife of thirty-two years as a human shield, he kept her between him and the monster. As they approached the woman, the knife still lodged in her left breast, Harold shoved his wife forward and made a mad dash toward the exit.

Esther fell forward, reaching out reflexively and grasping onto something to hold. She caught herself and looked up to see the blonde woman's gaping maw slowly twist into a grin. Esther gasped in fright and let go of the blonde, staggering back. As she looked up and glanced over the woman's shoulder, she saw Harold slip on the blood of the line cook and fall out of view as he crashed to the hardwood floor.

Turning back to the woman, they came nose to nose. A

strange stillness settled over her, and knowing this was her timely end, Esther closed her eyes and took one last breath. She tried to embrace the searing pain of the razor-sharp fangs slicing into her neck, but it grew too unbearable, and she let out a terrible shriek.

Harold, who used a nearby stool to pull himself up, watched in horror as his wife sank to her knees and tottered momentarily before falling onto her side with a lifeless thud. Her throat had been torn clean out of her neck, and blood spurted out in pulses from her severed carotid artery.

With tears in his eyes, Harold slipped on the crimson floor, his feet going out from under him a second time. Too feeble to spring to his feet, he dragged himself backward using only his elbows. Smeared lines appeared on the floor as he carved trails in the freshly spilled blood. "Please, no," he pleaded as the woman turned her darkly gaze toward him.

Another white-hot flash of lightning lit up the diner, revealing a red tapestry of blood that painted every surface. Like wet red paint, the blood had splashed across the countertops and floors and spackled the walls, covering everything along with the victims with a crimson blanket of death.

"I beg you. Please. Let me live." He looked over in time to see Jake's shotgun lying no more than four or five feet out of reach.

Mustering up his remaining courage, Harold rolled onto his side and reached behind the counter, daring to retrieve the weapon. His fingers danced across the stock of the gun, but just when he gained enough leverage and traction to clasp onto it, something yanked him from behind and dragged him back. Clawing and screaming, he made sounds no man should ever have to make. Dreadful sounds.

Rolling onto his back, Harold looked up to find the woman standing over him. She looked down at him and, reaching up with a pallid hand, wiped the blood from her mouth. With a groan, she plucked the knife from her breast and discarded it. It rattled on the floor just a few feet away from Harold, but he was too afraid to contemplate retrieving it, let alone pull it off.

No, he thought. It would take a miracle to get out of this godforsaken pickle. Remembering his Catholic upbringing, Harold began to recite Psalm 23 under his breath. "Though I walk through the valley of the shadow of death, I will fear no evil."

The woman stomped down onto Harold's neck with her foot, crushing his windpipe. Unable to finish the prayer, only gurgles came out as Harold slowly choked to death on his blood and spit. As the life drained from him, his last thought was of his wife and how he'd betrayed her. If Hell were a place, he was confident that Satan was heating his pokers for him.

A resounding silence settled across the room. The diner almost seemed calm, except for the buzz of a solitary, flickering fluorescent light in the back kitchen and the rumbling storm outside.

After a moment of blood-fueled revelry, the woman calmly returned to her seat at the counter and sat down as though nothing unusual had transpired. She picked up the cup of chilled coffee and drew it to her blood-encrusted lips. She paused as if to reflect on her handiwork and took a long sip.

Inside, another flash of lightning revealed the blood splatter coating every surface of the diner. Outside, the bolts of lightning striking from the heavens hit a tree in the nearby forest. It caused an electrical surge that upset the breaker and sent up a spray of sparks that slowly faded into the darkness like dimming fireflies. The neon sign to Mel's Diner flickered and came back on more potent than before, illuminating the entire parking lot with its radiant glow before exploding in a spray of sparks.

As the lights and embers all faded, consumed by the indomitable storm's black void, the diner went completely dark. With the electrical grid down, Mel's Diner, a once bright beacon for all the tired and weary souls who roamed the backroads, was a beacon no more. That bustling oasis pit stop had become a lifeless tomb.

Pulling the diner door open, it swung freely as if it had never been stuck in the first place, and the blonde stepped out into the rain. The storm raged on, and another ear-shattering boom followed another flash of lightning. She walked across the parking area, leaving pink footprints behind her as the rain washed the blood from her body.

Leaving the carnage of her misdeeds behind her, she came to the roadside and let the freezing rain cleanse her. While the blood baptism had brought on the demon, the rain seemed to wash away her sins and bring her back to some semblance of humanity. The bloodthirst had subsided, and her fangs finally retracted. The feral creature she'd unwillingly become gradually receded into the confines of her psyche, and her true self began to awaken.

She stepped into the center of the old highway and, with a deep breath, paused and looked up into the night sky. It was a black starless void, as vast and terrible as anything imaginable.

"Jaclyn," a voice said. The woman shook her head and snapped out of her deep trance. No longer a feral beast mad with bloodlust, Jaclyn reached up and touched her blood-stained lips.

"No, no, no," she muttered to herself. "Not again."

Jaclyn looked back over her shoulder at the diner and felt

the pit of her stomach drop. Dreading what she might find there, she decided it was in her best interests to keep moving forward.

She turned around to face the road again and noticed the sign to her left. Although barely visible in the darkness of the dreadful night, it gave her the indication she needed—she was approaching civilization.

As she walked past it, another flash of light illuminated the white letters on the green sign, allowing her to read the words. The sign said, "Welcome to Wood River. Population: 18,000."

XVIII

1

WOOD RIVER BRIDGE

WOOD RIVER, IOWA, WAS situated sixty-three miles east of Sioux City. Wood River was slightly larger than most rural farm towns but about as forgettable. Nobody ever moved to Wood River to move there. Jobs were sparse enough as they were. Unless you were a farmer, there was little to do in Wood River—except pay taxes and die.

Detective Jaclyn Benoit was concerned with the latter point—death. Truthfully, she hadn't expected to be investigating a homicide so soon after relocating to Wood River roughly three years ago. But here she was, investigating the murder of a Jane Doe, dumped at the foot of the Wood River bridge.

Born and raised in Brunswick, Maine, Jaclyn had joined the police force to make a difference. After eighteen years in Maine, however, she needed a change of scenery. In trading one small town for another, she discovered that Wood River was like

Brunswick—small, quiet, quaint, and everyone knew everyone's business.

At heart, she was a simple country girl who felt more at home in contemporary America's Star Hollows, Capeside, Riverdale-styled rural hamlets, and small Midwestern towns tucked away in some nondescript part of the nation.

Wood River was reasonably pleasant compared to other rural towns. It was big enough to have a few nice apartments, a couple of clothing boutiques, a coffee shop, a community college, and far too many fast-food establishments. There was a choice bowling alley at the edge of town that made a mean burger and great waffle fries. And like most Midwestern towns, it had a pretty decent fair every year.

Not that she'd gone out of her way to count, but she estimated that there were about as many bars as churches in the town, and you could choose to go to confession or drown away your worries in the microbrew and bar of your choice. Meanwhile, the rural folk seemed to worship two things with equal devotion—Jesus and American Football.

While Jaclyn didn't care much for either, as getting sloshed and screaming at the television to support one's favorite sports team was entirely unappealing for her, she understood that such things were a soothing balm for the mind-numbing boredom most Midwesterners faced. There was no ocean to sail, no winding rivers to kayak, and no mountains to climb. It was all flatland and cornfields as far as the eye could see. Her partner always joked that when someone's dog ran away from home, they could watch it leave for three days in any direction.

Like any significant change in life, she had her fair share of gripes but kept such thoughts to herself. She didn't want to ruffle anyone's feathers lest she make a wrong impression. First impressions were everything, and she hoped this new community would accept her for who she was—namely, a badass bitch good at her job. She had worked hard to establish herself in her previous role, building a reputation she was proud of, closing cases, and being the best detective she could be. Each day felt like a balancing act between showcasing her skills and fitting in with the team, but she was ready to rise to the challenge.

Feeling the chilly night air prick her skin with its frigid bite, Jaclyn rubbed her hands together and shoved them in her jacket pockets. She stood atop a hill that sloped down to a rocky riverbank and watched a team of forensic scientists in white suits scuttle about like a flock of seagulls looking for hermit crabs to eat. They were busy cordoning off a boundary around a Jane Doe that had washed up on shore a few hours ago. It was not the sort of thing she wanted to be investigating at 2 AM, but she was the only detective on call for the evening.

Floodlights set upon large tripods illuminated the tall grass around the basin, creating the illusion of a couple of full moons floating over the white suits. If you'd stumbled upon the scene, you might mistake them for Blue Book spooks investigating a UFO crash at this godforsaken hour in the morning.

Jaclyn zipped up her burgundy leather jacket to block the cold as she walked down the grassy hill to the riverside. The air was chilled to the temperature of a refrigerator, and the temperature difference between the water and the land created a mist over the river, giving the peaceful morning an ethereal quality.

Her boots crunched down onto the pebbles of the embankment, and she made a sharp right turn as she headed toward the cluster of forensic officers working diligently beneath the giant, glowing orbs. Drawing nearer, she could make out that the body lying in the grass was that of a *Jane Doe*. She guessed the victim was in her early to mid-twenties and wore a white t-shirt and blue jeans.

It was highly probable that the body had been dumped. Maybe even tossed over the bridge. Of course, it might have been dumped somewhere further upstream.

Jaclyn squatted down next to the body to get a closer look as the on-scene forensic officer, Scott Harding, stood over her shoulder and jotted down notes on a yellow legal pad. "So, what do you think?" asked Jaclyn.

Deep in thought, he tapped his pencil contemplatively, not registering Detective Benoit's question.

"Earth to Scott," she said, waving her hand in front of his face.

He looked up and smiled. "Oh, hi, Jackie," he said, still tapping the pencil on the side of the clipboard.

She answered with a friendly smile and asked, "So, what have you got for me?"

Before he could answer her, a bright set of headlights flashed across the riverbed, blinding them. Using their hands to shield the light, they watched a squad car come to a stop at the crest of the hill.

Jaclyn squinted at the figure that stepped out of the car, using her other hand to shield her eyes from the direct beam of light that shone upon her. Recognizing her partner, she smiled and spoke up so he could hear her from his vantage point halfway up the hill. "Don't tell me the captain got you out of bed for this, Michaelson?"

Michaelson shrugged. "Nowhere I'd rather be than freezing my balls off with you on a beautiful crisp morning such as this," he said, rubbing his hands together as he made his way over to them.

She nodded and sarcastically replied, "Don't blow steam up my ass, Michaelson. You're not that good of an actor."

"Yeah, well, I get all fired up for that union pay," he said, with a chuckle.

"One of these days, you might grow a pair and tell the captain that I don't need any hand-holding. I've been on the force for five years now."

I'd tell him if I thought it'd make a difference. But believe me, Jackie, it's a lost cause. He's set in his ways, and in his mind, you're still just a rookie detective."

"Fucking hell," Jaclyn cursed. She didn't mind the captain so much, but he could be a stubborn old goat when he wanted to be. "That old wanker is going to be the death of me, I'll tell you that much."

Michaelson chuckled. "Madeline says hi, by the way. Oh, and she told me to tell you the next time you drop by not to forget the strawberries.

"Ha-ha, very funny, smartass."

"Hey, I'm not bullshitting you. She said that. I swear on my mother's grave." Michaelson made the sign of the Holy Cross like a good Catholic and added, "God bless her soul."

"You asshat," Jaclyn said, her brow hardening into a frown. "Using your own mother's hallowed name against me. That's low. Even for you."

"Hey, I'm only the messenger. Strawberries, Jackie. Two boxes full!" He held out his hands, gesturing to the exact size of the produce box he was referring to.

Jaclyn couldn't help but blush. "Two whole boxes, huh? "That's..." she paused to gulp down and suppress a hot, bothered breath, "a lot."

"Yeah, I think she misses the sweet taste of your…"

"Don't even say it!" Jaclyn warned. She punched Michaelson in the arm hard enough to make it hurt.

"Dang," he said, rubbing the sting out of his arm. "You hit like the goddamn She-Hulk."

"And don't you forget it," she replied, wagging a finger at him.

Scott raised his hand and cleared his throat, interrupting their little banter. "I hate to break up whatever this is," he informed, pointing the eraser end of his pencil at Jackie and then Michaelson, "but this body isn't getting any more alive."

"So, Scotty, what did you fish up for us tonight?" Michaelson turned toward the body of Jane Doe, who was lying halfway up in the tall grass as if someone had dragged her from the riverbank and set her there.

"No identification was found on her person, but she has a couple of tattoos I could ask about. If she had them done locally, it shouldn't be too hard to track down the artist and sift through his records to find a name."

"We'll likely need a warrant for that, but I can probably get one in the morning," Jaclyn said, pressing her hands onto her hips as she surveyed the scene.

"Shit," Michaelson said, taking a closer look at the deceased woman. His voice sank to a low, almost sorrowful tone. "That won't be necessary," he said. "I think I know her."

Jaclyn shot him a surprised look, raising her eyebrows at him. "Come again?"

"I know her. Her name is Danielle Pruette. The one I was telling you about."

"Oh, shit. Your babysitter," Jaclyn gasped.

"She started college a year ago. I think she was accepted into Duke University."

"Duke. Wow. That's prestigious as fuck," Jaclyn replied. "But it doesn't make any sense. Who'd want to kill your babysitter?"

"That's just the thing. Nobody would want to kill Danielle. To the best of my knowledge, she has no enemies and is the sweetest girl. *Was* the sweetest girl," he corrected. "I heard through the grapevine that she was back in town for spring break, visiting her family and working part-time to save some money."

Jaclyn turned her attention toward the misty river, which ran so calmly that it scarcely made a sound. The full moon's reflection danced across the river's surface in the small patches where the mist hadn't yet fully invaded.

"Penny for your thoughts," Michaelson said, gently nudging Jaclyn with his elbow as they stood before the body.

"Doesn't this remind you of another case from a few years back? The one where those nine teenage girls were murdered."

"I know just the one you mean. The Blood Drive Murders, as the locals called it. The name was derived from the fact that all the victims had had their blood drained, leaving a procession of porcelain-skinned, doll-like corpses."

Jaclyn nodded along as Michaelson recapped all the pertinent details. "That's not all, though," he continued. "All of the girls had just celebrated their sweet sixteenth birthdays. I was still a rookie on the force back then, so I only assisted the detectives in some canvassing. But I remember it like yesterday, and not just because it was the first serial killing ever to hit Wood River. It stuck with me because the killer was never caught. You don't forget something like that."

"Sounds like you went through the wringer your first year."

"Their faces still haunt me to this day. I saw them lying there like that. Their bodies were all placed alongside the riverside as if on display, not so unlike Danielle. The only difference was that they all wore summer dresses and were posed like dolls, their arms crossed over their chests."

"As far-fetched as it might seem, do you think this may be related somehow?" Jaclyn threw her hands onto her hips and looked down at the body. Danielle's skin was white as a sheet as she lay there, staring at the stars.

"I don't know. Danielle is much older than the original killer's M.O. The original nine were barely teens. And our victim hasn't been posed or dressed up. She's just as she was at the last instant of her life. Out of curiosity, what makes you say that?"

"Because it looks like Danielle Pruette has been drained of her blood as well."

"Good eye, detective," Scott Harding said, crouching down and pointing at the neck. "If I may draw your attention to her neck, there are a couple of puncture wounds where the killer likely put a needle in her to draw the blood."

Rising back to his feet, Scott looked over at Michaelson. "As outlandish as it sounds, Detective Benoit isn't wrong. This woman has been drained of roughly five quarts of blood. That's about ninety percent of the human body's overall blood storage, give or take a couple of quarts, which is why she doesn't look like a shriveled-up mummy. She still has enough remaining in her system to maintain a normal appearance, apart from her sunken cheeks and the bags under her eyes.

"Fuck," Michaelson said under his breath.

"What is it?" Jaclyn asked.

In contemplation, he rubbed his coarse chin with its 3 AM shadow. "I just realized I'm going to have to break the bad news to her family."

"You need me to ride along?"

"Nah. It's okay, Jackie. Your shift is about to end. I'll handle this one. Go home and get some rest. You look like shit." Michaelson made sure to emphasize the 'look like shit' part and winked at her.

As he turned up the hill to return to his car, she raised her hand and flipped him the bird. "Fuck you. And tell your wife I said hi."

Michaelson merely raised his arm above his head and waved a silent 'will do' before getting into his squad car and heading off to tell the Pruette family the awful news about their daughter's untimely death.

Jaclyn turned back toward Scott and crammed her hands into her pockets. "Bring me up to speed on everything you've found so far. Don't spare the details. No matter how insignificant it might seem, I want to know everything. And I mean, goddamn everything."

"Right. But I warn you, detective, there's something you need to know first."

Jaclyn gazed down at Danielle Pruette's face. It almost looked as though she was sleeping peacefully. "Let me guess. There are signs of assault."

"Once the medical examiner looks her over, we'll be more certain. But she does have defensive bruises on her forearms and here on the back of her neck."

"Well, shit," Jaclyn said, letting out a disappointed sigh. Why did all the pretty young girls have to be abused, too? It wasn't fair. Now, a rage burning inside her, she wanted to catch whoever did this more than ever.

Scott kneeled again and, with his pencil, gently moved a tuft of Danielle's hair to reveal bruising on the back of her neck.

"It seems she was held down here from behind. And then there's this…" He pulled out a small blacklight wand from his utility belt and flicked it on. Waving it across her groin region, a hideous patch of splatter lit up with phosphorus clarity.

"My god," Jaclyn gasped, covering her mouth with her hand.

"Of course, we'll run the lab tests to confirm, but I'll bet you my last dollar that it comes back as blood and semen residue."

Scott turned back toward Jaclyn and switched off the light, letting the grisly scene fade behind a shroud of darkness.

"We've seen sexual assaults like this before. Whoever raped this poor woman forced her to face away from him as he assaulted her. I also suspect that she didn't die from drowning. The bruises on the back of her skull suggest she may have been bludgeoned before the killer dumped her body in the river." Scott paused and tapped his pencil on his pad as he mulled over any details he missed.

"So why go through the trouble of draining all her blood then? It's a bit much, even for a sadistic rapist," Jackie pondered to herself aloud. Even though her question was only rhetorical, Scott had an idea.

"My best guess," Scott said, rubbing the back of his head, "is that they wanted to throw us off." And by making it look like a serial killing from the 90s, they'd have us chasing zebras of deceased ghosts instead of looking for sexual predators walking among us."

"You would make a fine detective, Mr. Harding," Jacklyn answered, agreeing with his assessment.

I appreciate the nod of confidence, but I prefer forensic

science. The science never lies."

"Well, I'd say you're on the right track. But I'd be lying if I didn't admit that something doesn't feel right about all this. It's like a giant puzzle piece is missing.

Still, she'd have to wait for the medical examiner's reports in the morning before making any further assumptions about the demise of Danielle Pruette. In her gut, though, Jaclyn felt this was only the beginning of something far more sinister.

At the same time, however, a killer rapist didn't sound right, either. Most rapists leave their victims alive because they're habitual abusers. They want to keep their victims so that they can abuse them again. Even if they were driven to murder out of a jealous rage from the mere thought of having to share their victim with someone else, this level of instability wouldn't go unnoticed. There'd be records of previous domestic disputes or neighbors calling in noise complaints due to incessant shouting and fighting. Records she'd undoubtedly have to track down in the morning.

She yawned, covering her mouth, as the lack of sleep caught up with her. "Have a good evening, Mr. Harding," she said. Scott merely waved goodbye. "I'm going to call it a night. Look at things with fresh eyes in the morning."

"You bet," Scott answered. "Have a good one, Jackie." He waved goodbye, returned to his clipboard, and resumed scribbling his notes.

Jaclyn waved back as she turned and slowly climbed back up the hill. Her breath formed small vapor clouds as she huffed to the top. At the same time, her mind raced a million miles per second. She began weaving together the morbid threads of a sickening tapestry of what might have gone wrong in the small community of Wood River.

Was the Blood Drive killer back? Was it a copycat? Or was it, as Mr. Harding had suggested, a red herring meant to send them on a wild goose chase while the real killer hid behind the cover of a cold case turned urban legend, only to go unpunished?

She had more questions than answers, but Jaclyn was determined to investigate. The phrase 'cold case' was not in her vocabulary.

She knew that whatever this gruesome murder was, it was different than anything she'd ever worked on before. It was something dark and disturbing. Something profane.

2

MADDIE

THE KNOB OF THE old shower faucet screeched in protest as Jaclyn turned on the hot water. Sadly, she couldn't take the nice shower she'd been hoping for the night before. After getting home, she made herself a sandwich, sat on the sofa, took a few bites, and then went out like a light.

Smelling of yesterday's dirt and grime, Jaclyn stripped off her clothes one layer at a time. Like anyone living alone, she didn't bother tidying her place unless she knew she was having company. She dropped her jacket to the floor, peeled off her slacks, and unbuttoned her blouse. Soon enough, she was standing in her underwear as steam began to fill her small bathroom, fogging up her mirror.

Bending her arms around her back, she unfastened her bra, a tacky beige thing that didn't match her skin tone. But, hey, it was comfortable. Ugly but comfortable seemed to be the secret of all women's underwear. Beware of sexy and sleek, for that way lies heaps of discomfort.

Once freed from her undergarments, she stepped into the shower and shut the glass door. Steam slowly filled the shower stall, and she was thankful that her walk-in standing shower had a glass door. Being overly paranoid, she needed the glass door to see her surroundings. If she didn't have a glass door, she'd grow even more paranoid, and every little sound would frighten her.

She was the type of person who wanted to see the monster coming. She wanted to know the thing. So many others, if pressed with the choice, would prefer the curtain to be pulled shut. They wouldn't want to know about the thing lurking on the other side. They'd wallow in dread, knowing it might be there but never entirely sure. No, she needed to know. She needed to see the monster coming. That way, she'd be ready for it.

Her neurosis aside, she couldn't wait to get to work and crack this case. It also meant she'd need to re-open the cold case for *The Blood Drive* murders. With any luck, she might kill two birds with one stone. Her partner would call her too ambitious, but she liked to think of herself as determined. And she was determined to solve this mystery. Just then, her cell phone began ringing.

"Shit," Jaclyn cursed, looking over at her phone that sat on the top of the bathroom sink. She saw that Michaelson was calling her, probably to ask what kind of coffee she wanted. She slid open her shower door, leaned out, and, dripping all over her shower mat, fetched her phone. Swiping the green answer button, she put the phone to her ear and asked in a curt tone,

"What?"

"Am I catching you at a bad time?"

"I'm in the shower, so make it quick."

"Oh, really?" he chuckled.

"Wait… why are you calling me at…" Jackie paused, glanced briefly at her phone, and returned it to her ear. "One forty-two in the afternoon?"

"Oh, no reason. Did you want some Dunkin, as this is technically your morning?"

"You know my answer is yes. Always yes to free coffee and sugar."

"Iced or hot?" he asked, knowing that she enjoyed both and often mixed it up—one day preferring hot, the next day cold.

"Surprise me."

Michaelson began to say something more, but she hung up on him. With another sigh, she pressed her forehead against the tile and let the water stream down her back and shoulders. Jaclyn took a deep breath and decided all her hair needed was a quick shampoo; she could condition it tomorrow.

Swiping her phone with her thumb, she opened a photo album and found a pretty risqué photo of Madeline. It was Maddie in some veneer lingerie and striking a sexy pose.

Reaching up with her free hand, she unfastened the showerhead from its hook and changed the steady pulsing jets to a gentle stream. With the shower head pressed between her thighs, her entire body tightened as she let out a sensual moan.

Her neck taut, veins bulging, face red, she held the massaging stream of water precisely where it maximized her pleasure until she couldn't take it anymore. She gasped loudly and began panting lightly, staring deep into Madeline's brown eyes, her phone's screen fogging up and obscuring the image.

As shitty as it was of her, she had developed a rather large crush on Maddie and had been flirting with her unashamedly for the past six months. Entertaining the idea of a secret liaison, Maddie had even sent her some more risqué images that caused her to gush just thinking about them.

Madeline and her little dalliance began last year's barbeque. They had made out like a couple of horny teenagers in the laundry room amongst the mismatched socks and the fresh spring scent of fabric softener.

The whole thing happened so unexpectedly. Jackie was standing in her bra, wringing the spilled beer out of her shirt— a victim of a little prank by her co-workers who thought it would be funny to shake up her drink and watch it drench her.

She had just tossed the shirt into their dryer and turned it on when Maddie came in to grab some paper towels off the back shelf. The laundry room was barely wide enough for two adults to pass, so as Maddie pressed up against Jaclyn, leaning in as she reached for the top shelf, Jackie misread the signs and thought Maddie was leaning in for a kiss. Maddie's body pressed into hers as Jaclyn placed her hand on Maddie's waist and kissed her squarely on the mouth.

This caused them both to step back as they stared at one another with eyes full of pleasant surprises. The funny thing, however, was that the accident didn't feel like an accident. There was no awkwardness to it whatsoever. Kissing Maddie in that laundry room that day felt like the most natural thing to her. It maybe shouldn't have. But it did.

Something else existed in that kiss: a spark, an urge, a

longing. Did she feel it, too? Jaclyn's concerns were quickly put to rest when, to her utmost surprise, Maddie dropped the paper towels and threw herself into Jacklyn's arms. They stumbled back into the dryer as their lips met again, and that spark of unspoken longing exploded into a heated, passionate make-out session.

Their chests heaving and their hearts pounding as they shared the most resounding, most sultry kiss imaginable, Jaclyn had her hand up Maddie's shirt while Madeline was busy unfastening Jaclyn's jeans when, without warning, the door flew wide open.

Michaelson, Maddie's husband, and Jacklyn's partner walked in on them tongue-deep in each other's faces. He was searching for Madeline to ask her where the wine opener was when he stumbled on them, lightly buzzed from the afternoon beers making out like a couple of horny teenagers. Mortified, they peeled themselves away from their heated embrace and stared at him with stunned doe eyes. But to their surprise, Michaelson took it inexplicably well.

The sheepish grin plastered across his face spoke volumes. Forgetting what he'd even come down for, he winked at them both and said, "As you were, ladies," before shutting the door on his way out and giving them their privacy and a hearty chuckle.

She and Maddie had laughed so hard their ribs hurt. *What the hell were they thinking?*

After fixing their melted mascara and makeup, they made themselves presentable again before returning to the party. Nobody, except for Michaelson, was any the wiser.

The barbeque continued without a hitch, and Jaclyn, still smelling like beer, leaned across the picnic table, whispering to Maddie, "I thought for sure he'd kill me."

Maddie only laughed. "My husband? No way. He's the most open-minded man I've ever met. That's why I married him. I'm free to be myself around him, and we accept each other for who we are. Simple as that."

"Are you sure? I mean, this, whatever this is," she said, gesturing at Maddie and herself, "must bother him on some level. He is a guy, after all."

"Mike's not like that," Maddie assured her. "If something is bothering us, we talk about it. It's called being in an adult relationship."

"Ah, communication. That's a skill I haven't yet mastered. "Which," she added with a sigh, "is probably why I haven't had a relationship that lasts more than a few months."

Maddie laughed and brushed a tuft of her brunette hair behind her ear as she smiled at Jackie, her mind still reeling from the thought of them being back in the laundry room, kissing like it was their prom night.

"You're lucky. Not everyone finds someone who accepts them for everything they are, no matter what sort of skeletons they have tucked away in their closet. Shit, now I feel like a huge bitch. I'm sorry if I've made this weird for you, Maddie. It wasn't my intent to–"

"Let me stop you there," Maddie said, raising a finger and pressing it upon Jaclyn's lips. "If I thought it would send my marriage into a downward spiral only to crash and burn, I would have never done any of that with you. Everyone's fine with it. I'm fine with it. My husband is fine with it." She pointed at the barbecue, where her husband, fully clad in his cooking apron, waved the tongs and gave them another sheepish grin. "Just take the win, Jackie."

Later that week, during a stakeout, Michaelson grilled Jaclyn on the incident. He wanted to know how serious their relationship was. She knew he knew it was more than innocent flirting, but was it more than a fling? She didn't even know the answer to that question, but she wanted to reassure him that he wasn't losing his wife.

"I hope the thing with Maddie and me doesn't bother you. I guess I didn't realize I was bi until I met your wife. Still, I realize, there is no excuse for what I did. I went behind your back, which is shitty of me, I get it. But I just wanted you to know you have nothing to worry about. Maddie told me how much she loves you and how accepting you are of her. Does any of this make sense? Maybe I should stop talking."

She glanced at Michaelson, but his face remained expressionless. Eventually, he shrugged, and she felt relieved he wasn't upset with her. Still, she thought it was a little weird that he wasn't upset with her.

"Okay. I've got to ask," Jackie said, turning toward her partner, who was halfway into a Rob's Deli turkey club sandwich. "Are you guys poly?"

"Poly?" he asked, raising an eyebrow.

"Yeah. As in polyamorous."

"What is that, like a Pokémon or something?" he asked.

She was about to correct him when she saw him try to mask a grin.

"Oh, you shit-head." She stuck her tongue out at him and folded her arms across her chest as she shifted in her seat, gazing back out the front windshield. "Why doesn't it bother you, though? Most men are too insecure to consider a more open relationship model. Especially with their wives."

"Not all men," he chuckled. "Everything is hunky-dory in marriage land," he assured her. "I don't know. Ultimately, I suppose I want her to be happy. What kind of husband would I be if I prevented her from enjoying the only life she had and being who she was meant to be? She's not my property. She's my partner." After a short pause, he added, "But if Maddie ever did leave me for someone else, I sure as hell hope it would be you."

"Oh, shut up," Jackie laughed.

"I mean it, Jackie. You're the most level-headed, smart, and honest woman I know. I get why you two are attracted to each other. You're like a match made in heaven. I just happened to meet her first. Otherwise, I'm almost certain you two would be together now."

She brushed a blonde tuft of her hair behind her ear and sank into her seat. The more she thought about it, the more she couldn't shake the feeling that maybe she secretly did want to break them up. Perhaps that would explain why she continued to do it. To push that boundary. Or perhaps it was because she was fucking lonely. *A sad, single woman with no real life outside of work,* she thought about herself and her pathetic life. *Get your shit together, Jackie.*

Just then, her phone chimed, snapping her out of her memory. She glanced down at a new text that had just come through and tapped the display to open it. A photo loaded only to have Madeline's face appear with her tongue slipping between her fingers as she threw up a reverse peace sign. That was the universal symbol for sugar, spice, and all things cunnilingus. Jaclyn laughed.

Perfect timing, too, because she was on her second orgasm. *Thank God for shower head settings,* she thought. She placed the showerhead back on the wall and, legs quivering, replied on her phone, writing a quick *'LOL. Love you, babe.'*

She hit send before she realized what she'd done.

"Oh, shit," she said, almost letting the phone slip out of her hands. She opened the chat back up and frantically tried to delete the message, but it was too late. The message was sent. Then the little icon popped up saying that it had been read.

Screwed, she thought as she stood there staring at her phone. Admitting she was in love with Maddie was a huge step in their relationship. It meant something, and she was terrified of what Maddie would think. After all, Maddie was not obligated to reciprocate any of Jackie's feelings. Maddie was a married woman. Jackie was just the third wheel in someone else's relationship.

A chime alerted her that a reply was being written, and she looked down, waiting for the dreaded three pulsating dots to reveal the message. She was almost too scared to check Maddie's reply when the text popped up. She looked away briefly before she could read it, took a deep breath, and looked down at the message.

"I love you, too," it read.

Jaclyn let out a massive sigh of relief and placed her head on her forearm as she leaned against her shower tiles. She smiled to herself as the warm feeling bubbled up inside her. Maddie loved her, which seemed to make the entire world right again.

After her shower, Jaclyn quickly dressed, grabbed her sidearm and jacket, which were hanging off the back of the kitchen chair, and ran out of her apartment with wet hair. Usually, she'd blow dry it, straighten it, the whole nine yards. But today, she wanted to get in early and tackle this case.

Her hair was still glistening when she met Michaelson outside. He leaned on the side of his car, eating a donut. When she saw him, she tensed up slightly and blushed. How much did he know? Were they always completely open and honest with each other? He already knew about her and Maddie's little dates, but did he know that Maddie filled her every waking thought and was in her dreams? She'd grown obsessed with Madeline over the past couple of months. The way she smelled. The way she tasted. Jaclyn couldn't get her out of her mind.

"Rocking that 90s Jennifer Aniston wet hair look, I see."

Jaclyn paused and then flipped him the bird. "Get fucked, dick-breath," she quipped.

He laughed and then handed her a cup of Dunkin's famous iced coffee, which she gladly took from him.

Cradling the coffee in both hands, she said, "Thanks."

"You look surprisingly chipper," he said. "You get some good sleep?" Finishing off his donut in one bite, he grabbed his coffee off the car's hood, walked around to the driver's side, and waited for her answer.

"A few solid hours." She raised her coffee as a gesture of thanks and then took a long sip, watching him over the rim of her cup with her striking blue eyes.

Before getting into the car, he looked at her and said, "So, Madeline sent me a text, but I think it was meant for you." He pulled out his phone, opened his photos, and held up the picture of his wife for her to see. As she predicted, it was the same image she'd just received a few minutes earlier.

"Shit. Busted," Jaclyn said with a twinge of embarrassment.

"I guess it was a good shower." Michaelson laughed as he slipped his phone back into his pocket and got in the car. Jaclyn took another sip of her coffee and opened the car door as the engine roared.

During the car ride, an awkward silence lingered between them. Finally, much to her relief, Michaelson broke the silence. "Do you know why my wife and I hired Danielle as our babysitter?"

Jaclyn looked at him and shook her head. Michaelson never spilled personal details with her like this, but she lent him her ear and continued to listen to what he had to say. It was the least she could do, seeing as she was probably going to be the subject of his future marriage counseling sessions.

"It's because, in every marriage, a million different stresses test your bond and patience. Kids can be a blessing, but they can also be a curse. When we had our second daughter, Katie, we implemented Operation Date Night."

"Of course, you'd phrase it that way," Jaclyn chuckled. He smiled at her and continued speaking.

"Madeline and I like to keep the romance in our marriage. And, as shocking as this may come to you, she has been entirely upfront about her crush on you. I even know about the incident with the strawberry."

"Oh, shit. She told you about that?" Jacklyn found herself blushing, her cheeks turning rosy with embarrassment. She looked away, feeling vulnerable, knowing he was aware of her and Maddie's most intimate encounter.

"Yes. But that's what I'm trying to convey to you, Jackie. We share everything because we love each other enough not to let anything threaten our relationship.

"I can't believe she told you that. More importantly, I can't believe you're not more pissed off about it."

"Why should I be? I love her and want her to be happy. Demanding that she only loves me and nobody else, to fly into a jealous rage anytime she so much as looks at another man or woman is *not* love. It's obsession. It's possession. Jealousy is an ugly emotion that ruins everything it touches, and I'll have no part of it."

"No hints of jealousy at all?" she probed, her skeptical gaze narrowing as she lightly bit her bottom lip.

"Look, we evolved to be jealous of those who threaten to steal our mate." Reproductive instinct is a huge part of being a primate. When silverback gorillas fight, they fight to win. They get all the wives, all the children, and all the responsibility of leading the troop."

"Did you just compare me to a silverback gorilla?"

"If it looks like a duck and talks like a duck," he said, stifling a laugh.

"Fucking asshole," she chirped in mock offense, letting out an exasperated sigh and rolling her eyes.

"All I'm saying is that men and women co-evolved, but some of us have never gotten over the caveman attitude of bashing the woman over the head and dragging her back to the cave. These individuals are slaves to the primitive, reptilian part of their brains. But where does all the chest-thumping get them? I'll tell you where. Nowhere. Ultimately, the green-eyed monster makes everyone who comes across it miserable. And you can quote me on that."

As she sat thinking, she couldn't help but suppress her feelings. She knew, deep down, that she was falling madly in love with Madeline. "Madeline is the luckiest woman in the world to have such an understanding husband. I mean that. I do."

"I'll tell her you said that," he replied. He was about to say something else when, suddenly, he gripped the steering wheel tight and shouted, "Shit!"

Metal scraped metal as the brakes squealed, and Michaelson's squad car lurched to a stop in front of the Wood River County Police Department parking lot, barely missing a kid on a bike.

"Fucking hell," Jaclyn cursed as the car lurched to a halt. She jerked forward in her seat and, just as quickly, slammed back again, only for her coffee to splash across her chest. "Goddammit."

Michaelson flashed his red and blues, releasing a siren chirp at the kid who had rudely cut them off. When it was safe, Michaelson pulled the rest of the way into the car lot.

Shifting the car into park, Michaelson leaned over, opened the glove box, and pulled out a small packet of tissues. He peeled back the sticky cover and offered Jaclyn a few. She plucked out a couple of tissues and began dabbing her cleavage. The coffee made her shirt transparent enough to see her black bra as she cleaned herself. *Of all the days to wear a white top,* she thought.

Jaclyn finished cleaning herself up and noted that this was the second time she'd had a drink spilled all over her chest in as many months. Either she was accident-prone, or she had stumbled upon a different meaning for the "law of attraction."

Satisfied she wasn't a sopping mess any longer, Jacklyn opened her door and climbed out of the squad car. She looked over at her partner, who was rising out of the driver's side, and nodded when he made eye contact with her. He nodded back, and they slammed their doors simultaneously, as if perfectly in sync, and headed into the police station.

26

3

INTERROGATION

PULLING DOWN THE COWL of his green hoodie, Darius Reid unfastened his bike chain, wrapped it around the front wheel and frame, and locked it to the bike rack with a padlock. Wiping some chain oil from his hands onto his jeans, he turned and went inside the police station to report a missing person.

When Danielle Pruette hadn't turned up for her afternoon shift at the Westside bowling alley, he had grown concerned. When he called her number, there was no answer. He tried several times before realizing her phone was turned off, or, more likely, had run out of battery. Either way, it didn't bode well for Danielle.

After his morning shift, he closed the bowling alley early and went straight to the Wood River Police Department to report her missing.

He hoped she was sick, but he didn't know her parents' number, and they weren't in any listings. Better to be safe than sorry, he thought.

Approaching the front desk, Darius saw a black female police officer with a darker complexion than his, sitting behind thick bulletproof glass and motioning him to come forward. "How may I help you, hon'?"

"Uh, yeah. I'd, um, like to report a missing person." The woman officer reached beneath the desktop, drew a clipboard, and attached some paperwork. She slid it under the slot at the bottom of the glass and asked who he thought was missing. He replied, "My co-worker, Danielle Pruette."

"Just fill out the forms," the woman said plainly, gesturing for him to move aside so the next person in line could come up.

He took the clipboard from her and was about to sit down when he saw a blonde woman standing across the hall with long, flowing hair draped over her shoulders. She wore a white blouse top and the tightest-fitting brown skirt he'd ever seen. She was staring at him quite intensely, and he would have almost been flattered that someone as attractive as she would notice him—that is, until he saw the badge prominently displayed on her hip.

Shit. She's a cop. He sighed disappointedly and gave her a bashful wave. "What's up?" Darius said, feeling his cheeks flush with embarrassment as she gave him a curious glance.

She held a small paper cup filled with hot coffee, and as they made eye contact, she drank it all in one go, tipping her head back to get every last drop. Finishing it off, she met his gaze again, crumpled the cup in her hand without ever breaking eye contact, and tossed it in a nearby garbage bin. It went in even though she hadn't looked away for a moment.

"Excuse me, but did you say that you're looking for Danielle Pruette?" she asked, her intense gaze still fixed on him.

He looked around to see if she was talking to him and not somebody else.

The hot cop approached him, took the clipboard from his hands, and leaned over to put it back behind the safety glass. As she leaned forward, her chest brushed against his arm, and he suddenly became light-headed. The blonde cop looked at the woman officer behind the desk and said, "I've got this one, Maya."

The officer, a voluptuous black woman slightly dark-skinned than he was, nodded and turned her attention to the next person in line, waving her hand to signal them to move up the queue and approach the window.

When the blonde detective turned back around, she caught Darius eyeing her ass, and he quickly looked away.

"Um, so," he stammered, running his fingers through his curly hair, "do I report her disappearance to you? Or...?"

"Follow me," she said, slipping past him and moving toward the back cubicles and offices where the detectives and higher-ranking officers worked.

"Uh, yeah, okay," he answered, looking down at her ass again as she stepped out in front of him. *Idiot!* he thought. Don't act like a creep. But he couldn't help it. She was the finest cop he'd ever seen.

He followed her into the precinct's inner sanctum and made a sharp left at the water cooler. Then, they moved down a long corridor that passed by a breakroom with vending machines, a sink, a couple of pots of coffee brewing, and a microwave oven.

After exiting the hallway, they entered a bullpen-style office area. Several desks lined the wall with windows, while a cluster of cubicles occupied the other half of the room. They cut through the office clutter and walked over to the two desks facing each other near the windows.

Darius noted that the green paint on the windowsill was chipping. He reached up and peeled a piece off. He watched it flake off and flutter to the ground. The sound of a chair scraping on the floor snapped him back to the present, and he refocused his gaze, watching as "hot and on duty," who, in his opinion, could be a supermodel, pulled out a chair and beckoned him to sit down.

"Take a seat," she said, closing a file folder on the table and perching herself on the corner of the desk. She waited for him to be fully seated and then reached over and touched his shoulder. He looked at her hand and then back into her crystal blue eyes. Her eyes were the purest blue he'd ever seen and sparkled like gems.

"I'm afraid I have some bad news, Darius. Danielle Pruette's body was found this morning just outside of town, near the Wood River bridge."

"What?" Darius asked, half laughing, thinking it might be some joke. "That's impossible. I just saw her yesterday. She might be missing. But dead? You've gotta be messing with me."

"I'm sorry," Jaclyn said, tossing her hair as she leaned over her desk and plucked a business card from a cardholder. "I wish I had better news for you, kid. I wish your friend were just a missing person. But I'm afraid she's gone." She paused to let him process things before speaking again. "Please, take my card," Jaclyn said, handing it to him between her slender fingers.

Darius slowly reached up and took the card. Inspecting the gold-foil stamped lettering, he spoke in a hushed voice, "You're not joking, are you?"

"I'm afraid not," she answered, leaning back on the edge of her desk again and folding her arms under her chest.

Darius raised his head and looked at her. "Out of curiosity, how'd you know my name?"

Jaclyn looked at Darius and smiled. "You're Darius Mitchel Reid, yes?"

"Are you like a mind reader or something?" he asked.

She laughed. "No, Darius. I'm no mind reader. I'm a detective. Remember? I saw your name on the missing person's form you were filling out."

"Oh, yeah," he said awkwardly, feeling like an idiot. "Right."

She smiled again and leaned forward, her right arm reaching out to steady herself on the desk. As she leaned close, he realized that the top couple of buttons on her blouse were undone, and it was hanging open enough to allow him to see her cleavage. Feeling guilty for sneaking a peek, he looked back at the card.

"Nice to meet you, Darius," she said with a playful laugh, extending her hand directly in front of his face. After a brief hesitation, Darius looked up, took her hand in his, and greeted her with a proper handshake.

"Same," he answered.

Being able to touch her soft, white skin sent tingling up and down his spine. Something about her scared and enticed him all at the same time. He couldn't remember feeling this attracted to anyone before. He felt as though he'd do anything for this woman. And he'd literally just met her.

"Darius, if you don't mind my asking, how do you know Danielle Pruette?" she asked.

"I, uh, guess from work. But we did go to high school together. She was a grade above me. But I don't think she ever noticed me back then."

"I see. If you wouldn't mind, I'd like to ask some questions about Danielle's last known whereabouts. Would you be willing to hang out here for another hour and help clear some things up for me?"

Darius realized she was being deliberately vague. But he only wanted to help Dani, and more importantly, he wanted to help Jaclyn, so he nodded along. "Anything I can do to help," he said. "You name it."

"Good. Excellent," she chirped spritely, sitting back up. "Before we get into the details, might I suggest we head to the interrogation room? "Not that you're in trouble or anything," she added, noticing that mentioning the interrogation room made the kid nervous, "It's just a precaution." Some of the things I need to share with you are sensitive.

She ushered him to a room and opened the door for him. She gestured for him to sit in the metal fold-out chair at a nondescript white table in the interrogation room.

"Make yourself comfortable while I go fetch my partner. Do you want some coffee, tea, or soda?"

"A Pepsi will be perfect. Wild cherry, if they have it."

Darius watched Detective Benoit sashay out of the room, her hips swiveling gracefully, and then took his seat as requested.

As Darius sat waiting for his Pepsi, he leaned back in his chair and studied the interrogation room. It was as Spartan as they came. Virtually empty, apart from a solid walnut table with four chairs at its center and a two-way glass mirror, similar to the kind seen on detective shows, it was also home to a speaker on the wall, a circular clock on the opposite wall, and some ventilation ducts and piping hung overhead. That was about it.

The entire room had an unfinished industrial vibe. Also, he was reasonably certain the clock wasn't keeping proper time, as the second hand moved one tick forward and two ticks back.

He sat in one of the available chairs, jammed his hands in his front hoodie pocket, and waited for Detective Benoit to return. He sat for about five minutes, give or take, before Jaclyn returned with a soda and her partner.

"Sorry that took so long," she apologized as she entered the room. Gesturing to the tall man behind her, she added, "This is my partner, Detective Mike Michaelson." She set the Pepsi can down on the table and slid it over to him. "Oh, and they only had regular Pepsi. I hope that's okay."

Darius reached out and caught the can of cola, which skidded precisely at the correct distance. Looking down at the can of regular Pepsi in his hand, he accepted her offering and cracked it open.

It released a hiss of carbonated air, raising it to his lips, and he replied, "Yeah, it's fine."

Darius took a big, long swig of soda before smacking his teeth and sighing with satisfaction. Still holding the can in his hand, Darius looked up at Michaelson and noted how well-kept his beard was. It was downright immaculate. It also had a hint of gray to it, hinting at his age.

"So, let me get this straight. Your first and last names are both Michael?"

"Do you have a problem with that?" Michaelson asked sternly, shutting down any further inquiries and causing Darius to sit back in his seat.

"No, sir," Darius replied, shaking his head. Growing anxious from how Michaelson was still eyeballing him, he took a long swig of cola to mask his nerves.

Jaclyn sat on the edge of the table, crossed her left leg over her right knee, and brushed down her skirt so it wouldn't ride too high. She looked down at Darius and took a breath to compose herself.

"Darius, remember when I told you we found Danielle Pruette's body early this morning near the Wood River bridge? I didn't want to mention it openly, but we saw signs of foul play.

"You mean she was...murdered?" The very idea of someone taking her life was absurd. She was too nice a person to be the victim of some random psycho-killer.

"We're looking into it," Jaclyn replied, anticipating his question. We'd appreciate it if you could keep this information confidential until we have completed our interviews and collected our preliminary evidence.

"What I need from you, Darius," Jaclyn said softly, "is to paint a picture of that night for us." Was there anything unusual? Anything out of the ordinary that you might have noticed? Was Danielle perhaps acting differently in some way?"

"I mean, we work together," Darius informed her, pausing when he realized his mistake. "Worked," he corrected, clearing his throat to mask the break in his voice. It took a lot not to break down sobbing. Danielle was too pure a soul to be murdered.

"Where did you both work?" Michaelson asked from the back of the room, arms folded across his chest as he maintained an intimidating posture, never relaxing, never smiling.

"Westside Bowling Lanes." Darius looked at Michaelson as he answered, but his gaze slowly settled back onto Jaclyn. She was more attractive than the noir detective wannabe off in the corner of the room.

Jaclyn leaned forward and touched Darius's shoulder. He gulped and slowly raised his gaze to meet her crystal blue eyes. "I know what I'm about to ask may be of a sensitive or personal nature. But I need you to answer me as truthfully as you can."

Darius nodded again. "Uh, yeah. Of course. Why wouldn't I? I've got nothing to hide."

"Were you and Danielle, by any chance, sexual partners?"

"What?" Darius choked on the next sip of his cola and began coughing. The question had caught him off guard. Gathering himself, he replied, "No way, man. I mean, I wouldn't have said no, you know? If that's what she wanted. Dani was a dime girl if you understand my meaning. But, no way, we never slept together. Dani and I were just friends. I swear to God."

"I believe you," Jaclyn said in a gentle tone that was somehow both disarming and arresting at the same time.

The more she smiled at him, the more she felt drawn to her. The more she held his gaze with her sparkling blue eyes, the more he fell under her spell.

Darius pinched the bridge of his nose and tried to shake the invasive thoughts. What was it with this woman? Why was he so attracted to her? He'd never lusted over anyone before. So why her? It almost felt as though a spell had been cast over him.

"Well, how about you walk us through that night at the bowling alley and the last time you saw her?"

"We had finished the late shift out at Westside Lanes. It was my turn to lock up for the evening when I heard her drop her car keys. I turned around and asked if she was all right. She smiled and said she was glad I was with her because parking lots always spooked her at night."

He paused mid-story and looked at both detectives, scanning them for signs of prejudice. He wasn't sure if they were taking notes or making a case against him. "Do I need a lawyer or anything?" Darius asked.

"Why? Do you think you need a lawyer?" asked Michaelson, eyeing Darius with a skeptical look.

Jaclyn raised a finger, gesturing for her partner to back off.

"No," she answered. "You don't need a lawyer, Darius. You're not under arrest, and this isn't an official interrogation. If you feel uncomfortable, you're welcome to excuse yourself."

Darius nodded.

"You were saying?" Jaclyn asked, prompting him to continue his account of the events of that terrible night.

"So, anyway, I told her to be safe, and we got in our cars and drove off."

"Would it surprise you to learn that her car never left the bowling alley's parking lot?" Michaelson asked. He unfolded and refolded his arms, shooting Darius another prying glance.

"Wait, what are you saying? That she was killed after I left her there? That's..." Darius's voice grew weak as he realized the shocking fact that he may have been able to prevent her death. "Wait a minute," he said, his eyes darting from one detective to the other, "you don't think I killed her, do you?"

"Darius," Jaclyn said, pulling his gaze back into hers. She drew him into her with an alluring charisma—the kind you couldn't resist. "We're not saying that. However, you may have seen or heard something that could tell us about her final moments. Something that could shed light on these events and maybe help us find justice for your friend."

"I don't know," Darius replied, pausing briefly to consider the answer. He wanted justice for Dani. But he really didn't know anything. At least, nothing important to the case. "All I know is that it was storming for most of the evening. The rain had just stopped, and the air smelled fresh. I remember Danielle's perfume. It was green tea-scented."

While Michaelson was a by-the-book cop who'd write a ticket to a jaywalker because the law is the law, Jaclyn Benoit was different. Darius could tell she was the kind of person who might occasionally bend the rules and maybe cut you some slack. She wasn't as concerned with the letter of the law as she was with the principles of justice.

Even Darius knew that the law could be wrong sometimes, especially when crooked men in power wrote crooked laws to punish innocent people for invented crimes.

An unexpected knock at the door diverted all their attention to the entrance, and a woman officer poked her head into the room. It was Maya, the officer from earlier. Scanning all the faces looking back at her, Maya addressed Detective Benoit. "Pardon the interruption, y'all, but Danielle's parents are here to complete the paperwork."

"Your turn to shine, partner," Jaclyn said, gesturing for him to attend to their needs. Michaelson nodded and stepped out of the room, leaving the door ajar as he left.

"So, am I, like, free to go?"

"I have just one last question if you don't mind."

"Shoot," Darius said, catching his poor choice of words. "I mean, don't shoot, but go ahead. Ask away."

"Nice save," she said with a light-hearted chuckle.

"Thanks," he replied, laughing nervously along with her.

Darius watched as she sat down at the end of the table again. But this time, he remained well-mannered and behaved.

Changing the subject, Jaclyn brought her fist to her mouth and cleared her throat. "I need you to look me in the eyes, Darius. Do you think you can do that?"

"Your eyes?" he asked incredulously. Before he realized it, though, his eyes met hers and, without intending to, became locked in her gaze.

"It's all right. Just let yourself relax. Don't fight it. "I don't bite, I swear." She laughed at her little joke and asked, "What color blue do you see, Darius? What color are my eyes? Describe them to me."

As he gazed into her blue eyes, a strange sensation began to overwhelm him. "They're light blue. There's a touch of teal. They look like the ocean. They're..." As he tried to describe them, he suddenly felt a strange wave of energy pass through him. "W-what is happening? Why do I feel so–"

"Relax," she said in a consoling voice. "It's nothing to worry about." She leaned in gradually. Darius mimicked her movements as if controlled like a marionette on strings. His movements were no longer his own. He was a slave to her supernatural-like influence.

"Now, I want you to think back to that evening, Darius. After you said goodbye to Danielle, did you notice anything strange? Anything at all?"

"Maybe," Darius replied, his voice settling into a strange monotone. It was as though he had to answer no matter what. He felt compelled to answer her. He'd tell her his deepest, darkest secrets if she asked him. What was going on?

"You can tell me, Darius. You can tell me anything. You know that, right?" Jaclyn placed her hand on his but never broke her gaze. Instead, it only grew more intense.

Her blue eyes grew even more radiant, becoming dizzying—hypnotic even—and he fell into them like someone crashing into the deep blue ocean.

Finally, he felt his barrier fall and answered her without reservation. Without thinking, for that matter. She could ask him anything, no matter how intimate or personal, and he'd be willing to answer her.

"You wouldn't believe me even if I told you."

Leaning closer than before, her lips practically brushing Darius's ear, she whispered, "Try me."

Darius nodded slowly, his eyes never diverting from hers. Not even for an instant.

"After leaving Dani at the Westside parking lot, about a mile down the road, I saw a woman. A naked woman was standing in the middle of the road. She was standing in the darkness beneath the wine-dark rain."

"What color were her eyes, Darius? The woman was standing beneath the rain. Do you remember what color her eyes were?"

"Blue, like the sea," Darius replied.

Jaclyn held her powerful gaze, and Darius grew scared when he realized that he couldn't look away or, for that matter, move a single muscle. He was frozen. As she held his gaze, he was ensnared in her spell.

Jaclyn Benoit raised her hand and snapped her fingers. This broke Darius's trance, and he clutched his chest as he gasped for breath.

It felt like he'd been swimming underwater, holding his breath for hours, even though he was sure it'd only been a minute or two. His chest heaving and his head filled with questions, he glanced at Detective Benoit.

"That will be all, Darius," she said, standing up and gesturing with a wave toward the entrance. "You're free to go now."

"Really?" he asked, still panting and holding his chest.

"It's fine. I've got everything I need from you."

Darius grabbed his backpack and stood up. This may seem a little inappropriate, all things considered. But would you like to get coffee with me sometime?"

"Me?" Jaclyn asked, raising an eyebrow.

"Yeah," Darius replied, chuckling softly.

"Oh, you're sweet, kid," she answered, "But I can't. I have a girlfriend."

"Oh," Darius said, rubbing the back of his neck nervously. He turned to leave, looking back one last time to find her staring at him with that hollow grin and ocean-blue eyes that masked a hunger, a lust, a longing that frightened him to his core.

"What a weird fucking day," Darius muttered to himself as he slung his bag over his shoulder and headed into the hallway.

On his way out of the building, he passed by a conference room and saw Danielle's parents sitting with Officer Maya. Danielle's mother was bent over the table, sobbing into her hands, and Danielle's father was drying his eyes with his sleeve. Darius noted that Maya was offering them a box of tissues, but Detective Michaelson was nowhere to be found.

Didn't Jaclyn mention that he'd be taking care of things? Apparently, he had more important things to do than console the Pruette family, thought Darius.

Realizing he was late for class, Darius tucked his bag under his arm and raced out of the police station. Getting his bike from the bike rack, he hopped on and figured that going around the back of the police station would let him cut across the parking lot and would be much faster than going all the way around.

As he peddled around to the back of the building, he passed a narrow alleyway between the main building and what seemed to be the police car barn and auto repair shop. Unintentionally, his eyes glanced into the narrow wedge, past the air conditioning units, and spied something moving in the shadows.

With a screech of his brakes, he skidded to a halt. Unsure of what he'd just seen, he slowly backed his bike up and peered into the narrow opening. His eyes widened with spine-tingling terror when he realized what he was looking at.

As his stomach dropped out and his extremities began to tremble, Darius began to push his bike away, hoping he wouldn't be noticed. However, his bike wheels squeaked in protest, and he stopped dead in his tracks.

Slowly, reluctantly, Darius turned back toward the thing in the alley. The creature spun around and looked at him with hungry, carnivorous red eyes. This prompted a long, drawn-out *"Fuuuck"* to pass across Darius's trembling lips.

Frozen in terror, he gulped loudly as the monster's blood-thirsty eyes locked onto him. Swaths of glistening crimson painted its gaping maw as shredded meat dangled between the creature's razor-sharp teeth. When it caught him staring, it threw out its blood-soaked claws and hissed at him.

"HISSSSSSSK!"

Jaclyn Benoit opened her claws and let Michaelson's lifeless body slip from her clutches. His body fell to the ground with a thump, and she wiped the blood from her chin with the back of her hand, but all she managed to do was smear more blood across her face.

With a lamentable sigh, she gazed at Darius, her eyes now filled with lethal intentions. Her eyes were no longer the safe and calming color of the deep blue ocean he remembered. Now, they glowed ruby red, sparkling like her soul was on fire, and he was somehow glimpsing the torment broiling inside of her.

"Darius... I really wish you hadn't seen this."

That was a big NOPE for him, and he promptly "NOPED" his way out of there.

Leaping onto his bike, Darius took off, pedaling as furiously as his legs would allow.

4

SCARLET FEVER

"SHIT, SHIT, SHIT," DARIUS groused as he pedaled furiously as he could, doing his best to get away from the hideous thing in the alley. He still couldn't shake the lingering fear that had filled him when those ruby-red eyes had locked onto him. They were spellbinding, and he'd felt the same feeling earlier, when she peered into his eyes during the interrogation.

Along with the loss of self, for that was the only way he could describe it, he'd felt a sense of being subjected to a power far greater than anything he'd ever known. It was overwhelming. In that moment, he realized he was her puppet and would do anything for her. Anything she asked of him. Those dreadful, piercing blue eyes. He was powerless to resist them.

It took everything he had to break away from the creature's

ruby-red gaze that held him in its influence—the creature's will overriding his own. The deep blue sea eyes were no more. They were filled with blood lust and sparkled crimson. But Darius wasn't about to be the token black character who died in the movie's first act. *Fuck that shit,* he thought as he tore himself away from her terrible influence.

Managing to break free, he raced up the middle of the street, peddling as fast as his feet would allow. All he cared about now was putting as much distance as possible between him and her.

Some streetlamps began buzzing and flickering as they grudgingly came to life. As they lit up, one by one, Darius rode past them, his legs burning with fatigue as he pushed through the pain. Even though he felt he'd put a good distance between her and himself, he didn't dare look back lest that godforsaken creature be trailing after him.

What had he just witnessed? He shook his head in disbelief as the scene from moments earlier replayed in his mind. The image of Michaelson spitting up blood and gasping for air as his throat was being ripped out of his neck—the look on his face filled with both dread and confusion.

Michaelson's eyes turned to Darius in his last moments as if to beg for help. Help that Darius couldn't provide. Michaelson raised his hand and mouthed a warning to Darius. And it rang loud and clear in the silence. *Run.*

Even though Michaelson was a total prick, as far as Darius was concerned, he didn't think the guy deserved to die that way. Not like that. He didn't deserve to have his fucking throat ripped out. Darius shuddered, the haunting memory still fresh in his mind.

More haunting than the gore, though, were her eyes. They were glazed over with a thin veil of blood. When the moonlight touched them, they glowed a deep red, giving them an almost demonic appearance.

Perhaps more shocking than all of this was the razor-sharp fangs protruding from Detective Jaclyn Benoit's mouth, painted crimson with the fresh blood of her victim, Detective Michaelson. Darius did not want to be next on the menu.

Racing on his bike at a brisk pace, he contemplated ditching the road and cutting across lawns or alleyways. But from experience, since he must have taken this route to school a thousand times before, he knew cutting across the softball park would be much faster if he wanted to get to school in one piece.

Right now, getting to campus was his best bet. His home was twice as far away, and he didn't want to risk staying out in the open that much longer if she was stalking him.

Skidding to a stop in front of the park entrance, Darius paused and looked over his shoulder. He sighed a massive sigh of relief when he saw that nothing was pursuing him.

The street was empty, illuminated by a dozen or so street lamps. Surprisingly, the rhythmic buzz of the halogen lamps and their dim glow provided a sense of comfort, as if they were warding off the darkness. But now, a new concern plagued his thoughts. Where had she gone? Where had Jaclyn Benoit—or whatever the fuck she was—disappeared to?

Maybe he'd lost her. Perhaps she had lost interest in him and returned to feeding on Michaelson. That's when Darius remembered something. The underpass to the ticket and concessions building cut under most of the parking lot. If he went through the tunnel, he'd come out less than four blocks from the college. It was the mother of all shortcuts.

The campus would be lit up bright as day until midnight, and he knew that he'd be safe there. If Jaclyn, or whatever she was, followed him, people would see her—they'd see what she really was. It was the perfect example of safety in numbers. The herd could fend off predators, while the unlucky one separated from the herd was likely doomed.

Popping a wheelie, Darius used a cement parking stopper like a ramp to catapult his bike into the air and jumped over a row of bushes, landing safely on the other side. He skidded back onto the sidewalk on the other side and rode to the top of the stairs.

Skidding to a stop, Darius reached the top of the underpass and glanced back to ensure he wasn't being followed. *Good,* he thought, finding the street behind him empty. Not a single trace of the fanged detective vampire cop.

Darius began descending the stairs, his bike jittering so violently that he nearly lost his grip. Riding down steps was always a death-defying act. He just held on tight for dear life and said a little prayer to himself, just in case.

Hitting the first landing, he paused and then took a deep breath before starting the second leg of his journey. From here, he could see the tunnel and make out one of the busted lights flickering sporadically in the distance. It couldn't be more than thirty yards off.

There was only one more landing before the final descent to the bottom. However, halfway down the second set of steps, his front tire hit something wrong, and his handlebars twisted out of his hands. As his front tire caught on the landing, his momentum carried him forward, and he went head-first over the bars.

"SHIIIT!" yelled Darius as he and his bike tumbled down the final set of stairs.

"Oomph...ow....oomph...!" he groaned with every hit as he

plunged the whole way down the unforgiving cement stairs.

Both he and the bike landed in a heap at the bottom, where a trash bin broke his fall. Scraped, battered, and bruised, Darius grunted as he pushed himself to his feet, the trash can rattling as he nudged it out of the way.

Still sluggish, he stumbled over the spilled garbage and reached down to get his bike. When he pulled it back up, he found it bent out of shape and grumbled, "Fuck my life."

The front wheel was folded at a ninety-degree angle. The back wheel hadn't fared much better and now had an "S" shaped wobble. It became painfully clear to him that he wouldn't be riding out of there on his bike in this busted-up condition.

"For Christ's sake," he grumbled. "This whole day has been nothing but one giant shit show." He kicked the rocks on the ground in frustration and then froze in his tracks. Staring at the ground, he noticed an additional shadow lined up with his.

Darius stood frozen with dread, and the hair on the back of his neck bristled. His skin rippled with goosebumps as he stared at the shadow next to his, praying it didn't move. Darius slowly raised his head and glanced over his shoulder to find Jaclyn Benoit standing at the top of the stairs.

"*DARIUSSS...*" she hissed in a strangely resonant voice that didn't seem her own. Her voice sent shivers down his spine and made his skin crawl. It was deep and layered as if another voice was talking beneath hers simultaneously, matching her every utterance word for word.

As she stood atop the stairs, Darius noticed she was plastered in blood, and it dripped down her neck and chest and trailed into her cleavage.

"Oh, god," he gasped when he saw her hands. Her hands—they'd become deformed somehow. Her fingers were long; her nails were even longer, forming hideous claws. And they glistened with the fresh blood of her slain partner.

Darius knew there was no way Michaelson was walking away from that level of mutilation. Whatever was left of him was sure to resemble shredded beef more than it did a person.

"Stay away from me, you blood-sucking bitch! I saw what you did to Detective Michaelson. I'm not going to let that be me."

Darius turned and ran toward the tunnel. The entrance light still flickered sporadically, briefly illuminating the area, only to fade out, allowing the darkness to reclaim the space once more. He could hear Jaclyn's reply to his callous taunt from over his shoulder.

"*Tsk, tsk,*" she scolded. "Is that any way to talk to a lady, Darius?"

He wished she'd stop using his name. How she said it so casually, as though there was a sense of familiarity between them, made his skin crawl, as if maggots were squirming just beneath the surface, trying to wriggle their way out. He looked down at his arms and found himself unconsciously scratching claw marks into them, trying to dispel the awful feeling.

"Run all you want, Darius," Jaclyn said, her red eyes watching him run into the dark mouth of the tunnel. The light temporarily lit up his fear-stricken face every time he glanced back to see if she was stalking him.

Peering over his shoulder, he saw her standing at the top of the steps, holding back her pursuit. He looked forward and back again, gasping when she'd somehow moved from the top to the bottom steps of nearly three flights of stairs in a hair-raising second. No, she was not standing on them; instead, she hovered menacingly above them.

Her toes were pointed downward, yet her feet were raised about a foot off the ground. Before he could react, however, he rolled his ankle on a large rock that, for some fucking reason, was planted directly in his path.

Crashing to the ground, he hit the ground hard. Gravel and dirt got into Darius's mouth, and he scraped his chin. But it was his ankle that hurt the most. Pain shot into his foot like a thousand white-hot needles as he pushed himself back up. He hobbled forward, collapsing onto his hands and knees again, unable to put any weight on his sprained ankle.

It was no use. He'd twisted it badly and wasn't going anywhere fast. That's when the hair on the back of his neck began to stand on end. He could sense her standing directly behind him.

Darius, still on his hands and knees, slowly turned around to find the crimson-eyed vampire grinning at him. A terrifying grin of white teeth and fangs appeared from behind the curtain of blood-stained lips.

To his dismay, she had moved from the top of the stairs to the bottom with inhuman speed. And now, a split second later, she had closed the gap between them and was practically hovering over him like a specter of death.

"You can't hide from me. Never from me, Darius."

Throwing up his hands, he pleaded with her. "Please, listen to me. You don't have to do this. I won't say anything. I promise you. My lips are sealed."

"Oh, Darius. Don't worry. I promise to make it painless." She hovered toward him, and he fell back onto his ass.

Tears welled up in his eyes, and his voice began to quiver. "I swear, I didn't see shit."

"You didn't see me feeding on my partner? Because I could have sworn that I saw you standing in that alley, staring at me in abject shock with your jaw hanging between your feet."

She reached out with a long, slender index finger and delicately ran her sharp claw over his lips. Then, shoving her finger in his mouth, she reached inside and invaded his personal space with an oddly sensual kind of foreplay.

"That wasn't you, my pet?" She pulled her glistening finger out of his mouth and brought it to her lips. Sucking it clean, she looked down and smiled at him, waiting for his answer.

"Please, don't do this. I don't want to die."

"Die?" she laughed. "I'm not going to kill you, my pet. I'm going to drink you up. Don't worry, though, my darling. You'll wake up in the morning and won't remember anything that transpired here this evening. It will seem as if it was all just a bad dream."

Her foot gently touched the pavement, and as her weight settled onto her two legs, a blurred motion just behind her back slowed, revealing two giant bat-like wings attached to her back. They'd been moving so quickly, like the wings of a hummingbird from hell, that he hadn't noticed them until now.

"Please..." he begged her, unable to finish his sentence due to his voice cracking under the crushing stress of the life-and-death situation. He slowly sank to his knees, and she sat beside him, wrapping her arm around him as if he were a lover.

"This may pinch a little," she warned, clutching him by the nape of his neck and drawing him into her open mouth and lacerating fangs.

Darius groaned in discomfort as her fangs penetrated his

flesh. He squirmed to get free, but she held his neck so tightly he thought it might snap if he twisted it wrong. Once the initial sting of her needle-like fangs subsided, however, he began to feel warm and fuzzy. It was almost as if his system had become flooded with painkillers or anesthesia of some kind.

Lightheaded, he fell back into her arms as she fed. The faint, suckling sound, accompanied by an occasional squelch or slurp, almost felt soothing. He felt his heartbeat slow, and his vision began to blur.

No, he thought, *don't you dare give up.* But the more he wanted to resist her, the more he fell under her spell.

As she sucked the life out of him, her silvery hair brushed up against his face. Her scent was intoxicating. She smelled like wildflowers and sun-kissed skin, with a hint of mango butter.

"I-I..." He tried to speak, but he couldn't get the words out. He was too weak to talk and was growing weaker with every passing second.

She paused her drinking and looked down at him, gently stroking his hair. "Did you say something, my pet?"

Darius reached up and touched her face, his thumb brushing her cheek. Then, mustering up all his strength, he sat up and kissed her. As his lips met hers, he felt her kiss him back, her embrace tightening.

As an immeasurable feeling of bliss came over him, his eyelids grew heavy, and he slowly began to fade. The fringes of his vision grew dark, and the black vignette of what he could only assume was death closed all around him until the darkness was all that was left.

Darius, wake up. Darius... you need to wake up now.

Darius struggled to open his sleepy eyes. "Darius," a voice called. He wiped the sleep out of his eyes and opened them. He found himself lying in a parking lot. Sitting up, a thick fog surrounded him. Slowly, he rose to his feet.

"Darius," the voice called to him again. He spun around to see where it was coming from. Astonishingly, he found Danielle Pruette standing directly across from him. She looked angelic in the moonlight and the white glow of the fog.

It took him a moment to realize he was back at the bowling alley parking lot. But how could this be? Was he dreaming? Was any of this real? Was she?

"It's all right, Darius. I'm in a better place," Dani said, reaching out and touching his face. He closed his eyes and reached up, taking her hand in his. "But your time has not come. You must wake up, Darius."

Tears began flooding his eyelids, and his lips quivered. "Can't I stay here with you?" he asked, his eyes peering into her beautiful hazel ones. She smiled, took his hand, and drew it away from his face.

"I'm afraid that's not possible. I'm only here as a messenger," she informed him, still holding his hand.

"A message from where?" he asked.

She smiled again. "I think you know. Deep down inside, you know, Darius."

He sobbed even more when she pulled him into her arms, embracing him. At that moment, all he felt was pure joy and love. "It's going to be all right, Darius." All you need to do is wake up now."

He pulled his head off her shoulder and looked into her stormy gray eyes. "I was going to ask you out," he said, sharing his wish to date her.

"I know," she replied, tenderly touching his face like a mother would her baby's. "But sometimes things don't work out the way we expect them to."

"I'm sorry I let you die. I should have waited with you longer. I should have ensured you got safely into your car and were a mile down the road before I left."

"It wasn't your fault, Darius. There's no way you could have known."

"But I was right there. I could have..." his voice trailed off. She smiled at him again, and he looked around the parking area. As he scanned the area, he noticed that the fog had grown thicker and whiter during their conversation. When he turned back around, Danielle Pruette was gone.

"Dani?" he whispered, calling out for her. His voice growing to an audible level, he called her name again. "Dani?!"

Darius stood in the bowling alley parking lot, head lowered, shoulders slumped, a hollow feeling coming over him. He missed Danielle so much that it hurt. But she was gone. Forever.

"Goodbye, Dani," he whispered, eyes brimming with tears. His voice cracked as he struggled to get the words out, but he finally managed to get the words out. "I'll miss you, Dani."

DEET!

DEET!!

DEET!!!

DEET!

DEET!!

DEET!!!

DEET!

DEET!!

DEET!!!

Half-asleep, Darius rolled over in bed, slapped the top of his alarm clock to silence it, and rolled back over again. It hadn't even felt like a minute when the snooze alarm went off.

"All right, all right. I'm up," he grumbled. Slowly, he sat up in bed, his shirt and hoodie discarded beside him and piled on the floor.

Rubbing the back of his neck, which was sore, as was the rest of his body, he yawned and looked at the clock again. It was seven-thirty AM on Saturday, and in an hour, he'd need to go open Westside Bowling Lanes for their 9:00 AM opening. It would be the first time he worked there since the death of Danielle Pruette.

That reminded him that a letter had arrived in the mail. He hadn't had time to read it amid all the madness that had been going on. With a huff, he stood up and stretched. Damn, he thought. Why is my body so sore?

Darius ignored the strange pain in his body, picked up the envelope, and opened it, revealing a card inviting him to Danielle's funeral. Inside was a lovely photo of her. He held it up and studied her beauty for a long time, getting lost in the memory of her. He gazed at Danielle Pruette until the pain became too much and gently placed her picture on his dresser. He missed her desperately. She was the only girl who ever laughed at his jokes and truly made him feel understood.

Although Darius wished they could have been more, he was okay with settling for being her friend, even just a work friend, as it was sufficient in the presence of someone as amazing as Danielle. Knowing her at all had been a huge privilege.

He rubbed his neck as he went into the bathroom. It fucking

hurt. It wasn't like a strain but more like a bee sting or pinprick. Looking at himself in the mirror, he checked for a bee sting or a spider bite. Something. He turned his head to one side and then the other, checking both sides for signs of red bumps or inflammation, but couldn't find anything.

With a shrug, he grabbed his toothbrush, picked up a tube of Crest extra-whitening toothpaste, and squeezed some out. He put the toothbrush in his mouth and stood staring at himself for the longest time. It felt as though he were looking at a stranger.

"Darius, are you awake? Darius... you need to get up now. Breakfast is ready. And you don't want to be late!"

His mom called him from the kitchen, and he plucked his toothbrush back out and hollered, "I'll be down in a minute!"

After brushing, he gargled and spit, rinsed his mouth again, and fetched a t-shirt off the floor. He sniffed the shirt and determined it was odorless enough to be considered clean. If not clean, it was at least wearable. He slipped it on and grabbed a pair of cargo pants out of his dresser drawer.

Dressed, he raced out of his room, grabbing his school bag off the back of his chair. Darting into the hallway, Darius practically skipped every other step, traversing the stairs before landing on the ground floor. Hooking a right at the bottom of the staircase, he burst into the kitchen with a vitality that was out of character since, most days, he was groggy and barely able to move. His mother always called him the "morning sloth."

With his bag slung across his shoulder, he grabbed a glass from the cupboard, took the milk out of the fridge, poured a healthy glass, and put the milk back.

"You got in late last night," his mom said, setting a plate with two eggs over easy, three slices of crisp bacon, and a waffle.

"I did?" Darius asked, mouth full, as he sat at the table and took several bites of real food. "I guess I lost track of time. Sorry, ma'. It won't happen again." He took another bite of bacon.

"Pish-posh!" his mother said. "You're young. You need to have fun, make friends, and get into some trouble."

"Oh, I stopped by the police station yesterday."

"Police station?" his mom asked in a surprised tone. "That's not the kind of trouble I was referring to."

Darius reassured her that it wasn't like that. "Nah, ma', it's not what you think. I wanted to report Dani's disappearance. But..." he paused, "But I guess you heard the news by now?"

"I'm sorry, Dari. I heard it on Channel Twelve's morning report. They found her body by the old bridge. The one out towards that diner where all those other murders were. What's it called? Oh, that's right. Mel's Diner."

"Mel's Diner, yeah. I'd almost forgotten about that place. They had the best milkshakes. Dad used to take me there before..." he caught himself and looked at his mom. "Sorry, Mom. I didn't mean to–"

"It's okay. Your father is in a better place. And he'd be so proud of you—the first Reid to ever go to college." She lovingly ruffled up his hair and then slapped him on the back of his head.

"You stay out of trouble, yah' hear?"

"Yes, ma'am," Darius answered.

"Good. Now, you'd better get a move on if you don't want to be late for work."

"Right," Darius said, placing the second slice of toast in his mouth. He grabbed his green hoodie off the back of the kitchen chair and snatched the car keys off the wall. As he hurried out the door, he heard his mom shouting out to him.

"Don't scratch that car, you hear me? It's the only one we've got. You take good care of her like she were your girl."

"Hey, I'm an excellent driver," he replied, turning back and saluting his mom.

She stood in the doorway, folding her arms. "Uh-huh," she mumbled unenthusiastically. "I think your bike would disagree."

She nodded toward the side of the garage, and Darius looked over to discover his bike was utterly mangled, as if it had been in a terrible car accident.

"My bike!" he yelped, grabbing his head in distress.

"Told yah'," his mother said, wagging a finger and letting out a chuckle before turning back inside.

"Well, shit," Darius said, throwing his hands onto his hips as he stared at the wreckage. It was little more than scrap now. Checking his watch, he realized he didn't have time to investigate the matter further, at least not until after his shift at the bowling alley.

Getting into the baby blue 1984 Buick Regal that his father had lovingly restored before he'd passed away, he started it and looked up to adjust the rearview mirror. His stomach dropped, and every fiber in his body tensed with fright when he noticed the blonde detective standing directly behind his car.
Was it her? What did she want?

"What the fuck?" Darius reached up and adjusted the mirror, but by the time he got it positioned just right, she was gone.

Tearing his eyes away from the mirror, Darius spun around and looked over his shoulder to make sure his mind wasn't playing tricks on him. Peering out the rear glass window of the sedan, he was relieved when he didn't find anything or anyone standing there. He scanned the street in every direction, but there was no trace of her.

Relieved it was all in his mind, he mumbled to himself, "Get a grip, dude. It was just your imagination." He squeezed the steering wheel tightly with both hands and backed out of the driveway.

Upon reaching the middle of the street, he hit the brakes, jerked the gearstick into drive, and slammed on the gas again.

The car's tires chirped as they struggled to find purchase. Biting down, the rubber squealed, and Darius sped off, a plume of gray exhaust billowing behind him.

5

A Crime of Passion

I GOT YOUR CALL, JACKIE." Maddie stood in the open entrance to her house, wearing her silk kimono-style nightgown, and stared at Jaclyn with groggy eyes. She muffled a yawn with her hand and then rubbed her arms to try and stay warm. "What's so urgent that you needed to wake me up at one in the morning?"

She was already nipping through the thin veil of silk and didn't want to stand in the open entrance longer than needed. She yawned again and ran her hand through her hair. When she brought her arm back down, Jaclyn couldn't help but notice that her kimono had slipped open a little too liberally, but Maddie was tired and didn't seem to notice or, for that matter, care.

Jaclyn stood on the top step of the porch and stared at Maddie, framed by the warm glow emanating from the lamp on the console table behind her.

Maddie pulled her kimono shut and tightened her sash as Jaclyn contemplated whether she should divulge her dark secret and tell Maddie everything, including the heinous act she committed against those in the diner. She wanted to come clean about everything, including the harm she inflicted upon Michaelson and the fact that she fed on a teenage kid.

No, she told herself. *It was too soon for that.* Sure, Maddie might feel like she's falling in love with her right now, but the fact of the matter was that Jaclyn's secret was too terrible for a real love to flourish. What's more, if Maddie discovered the truth about Michaelson and Jaclyn's role in his death, she'd downright come to despise her. And Jaclyn didn't think she could handle being hated at the moment. She needed someone to hold her, not interrogate her, and ask questions for which she had no answers. She needed a friend.

In the end, though, she decided against divulging anything about her darker nature. She knew Maddie wouldn't be able to comprehend the bloodthirsty impulses deep within her. A bloodthirst that boiled to the surface every few weeks. A thirst that she was unable to quench until it was satisfied.

This curse made her into something she didn't want to be. It didn't matter that the Red Rage, as she called it, caused her to black out. It didn't matter that something else took her over— she knew what evil looked like. She knew what it made her—a bloody monster.

She thought she could tame the beast inside if she tried hard enough. But right now, all she could do was stand on Maddie's porch and have a complete emotional breakdown.

Jaclyn buried her face in her palms and began sobbing.

"Oh, sweetie," Maddie said, her tone quickly changing from

annoyance to compassion. She reached out, grabbed Jaclyn by her shoulders, and drew her into her breast, embracing her warmly.

"It's been a shit week," Jaclyn said, her words muffled by Maddie's body as she threw her arms around Jackie and squeezed her into her bosom.

Jaclyn wanted to melt into her and forget the world even existed. She tried to forget that she was a vampire and could hear Maddie's heartbeat pick up a tic as they embraced. She tried to ignore the fact that she could detect the sweet scent of Jaclyn's cycle emanating out of her like an intoxicating perfume. And she tried to ignore the fact that the vampire inside her wanted to rip Maddeline's kimono wide open, throw her back onto the stairs, and eat her out—quite literally.

"Please come in," Maddie said, gently nudging Jaclyn inside her home and closing the door behind them. Maddie noticed the mascara stains on Jaclyn's face and smiled warmly at her. She reached up and touched Jackie's face, wiping tears from her cheek with her thumb.

Jaclyn closed her eyes, leaning into the warmth of Maddie's hand. She took a deep breath and looked at Maddie, who had never broken their gaze the entire time she'd been standing there. Maddie smiled and brushed a loose tuft of hair behind Jaclyn's ear. "Would you like some tea?"

"Tea would be great," Jaclyn replied.

Jaclyn was lucky to have a friend like Maddie. She enjoyed every minute with her. She felt she could confide in her. Everything but the darkest parts of her, that is. They sat at the kitchen table, drinking tea and talking until three in the morning. Eventually, Maddie yawned and stretched her arms high above her head.

"You can sleep in my bed if you'd like."

Jaclyn waved her hands in protest. *"Nooo, no, no, no,"* she answered. "If your husband came home and found us in bed together, I'd never hear the end of it."

Maddie gestured toward the sofa and said, "Feel free to take the couch then. That's the best I can do on such short notice. But you're not going home in your condition. And Mike won't be home until around noon after his shift. So, feel free to sleep in as long as you'd like. Maddie placed her hands upon Jaclyn's arms and gently squeezed. "I mean it. My home is always open to you, Jackie."

"I appreciate you, Maddie. I do." Jaclyn hated that she couldn't tell her that Mike wasn't coming home, that something terrible had happened to him.

"You're my best friend," Maddie laughed. Of course, I'll be here for you. No matter what."

Don't make me laugh, Jaclyn thought. If Maddie knew the half of it, she wouldn't say such things. Jaclyn wrapped her arms around Maddie's waist and drew her in. "If you knew the real me, you'd run screaming."

"What are you talking about?" Maddie laughed again. "This is the real you," she said, reaching up and giving her a little *boop* on the nose.

When Maddie leaned in to steal a kiss, Jaclyn raised her hand and pressed it against Maddie's chest, stopping her from getting too close. Maddie drew back in surprise and shot her a hurt look. It was the first time she'd ever felt rejected by Jackie. But she knew something more was going on here. Tonight, Jackie was all over the emotional map.

"I'm serious, Maddie. I'm a selfish bitch. I always have been. I only think of myself first. Hell, I haven't even been able to keep a real relationship for more than a few weeks. I hurt people, Maddie. I rip hearts out, and they-they don't ever come back."

Maddie touched Jaclyn's lips, silencing her. "That's enough. You're here now. You're with me. We've known each other for five years and have grown closer with each passing year. I'd call you my sister, but it doesn't seem appropriate because we've been together. You're my second soul mate. And that makes me feel undeserving. Most people go their whole lives without finding the perfect partner. I found Michaelson. And now I've found you. Just know, Jaclyn Benoit, I love you with every fiber of my being. You're my girl—and you'll always be my girl."

Jaclyn's eyes welled up with tears, and she looked away. "I'm fucking poison, Maddie. You'd be wise to get as far away from me as possible."

Reaching up and touching Jaclyn's face, Maddie drew her gaze back toward her. There was a long silence after their eyes met, their chests rising and falling with each heated breath. In that silence, a yearning grew to the point that one of them had to do something lest they both explode with unrequited desire.

When it seemed like the tension couldn't be any more unbearable, their lips came crashing together in a sloppy, wet kiss.

"Mmm..." Maddie moaned as their lips smacked together and their bodies pressed into one another.

Jaclyn reached down and slipped her hand inside Maddie's loose-fitting kimono, found her breast, and squeezed. This prompted another moan to pass over her lips, and Maddie, clutching Jacklyn's wrist, pulled away, gasping for breath. "Are you sure?"

"I'm more than sure," Jaclyn answered.

"My bed...now," Maddie insisted. She turned to head up the

stairs and, holding Jacklyn's hand, towed her behind her the whole way to her bedroom.

Stumbling into the room, they were tearing each other's clothes off before they'd even made it to the bed. Stripped down to their underwear, legs and arms wrapped around each other, they fell into bed, kissing passionately.

Jaclyn was tongue-deep in Maddie's face when she slipped her fingers beneath Maddie's panties. Maddie caught her wrist, stopping her prematurely. "Wait. I feel like a slimy, greasy-haired mess. Let me freshen up, and I'll be right back. Then you can do whatever you want to me."

"Promise?"

"You won't even know that I was gone," Maddie teased as she slipped off the bed and sprang up. She practically skipped into the adjoining bathroom.

"Don't be too long," Jaclyn said, noticing that Maddie left the bathroom door open a crack so that Jaclyn could watch her. Maddie peeled off her undergarments and turned on the shower, glancing back over her shoulder to shoot Jackie a wink.

Jaclyn blew a kiss at Maddie from the bed, rolled onto her back, and stared up at the ceiling fan. She watched it spin slowly, then let out a long sigh.

What was she doing? Was she fucking nuts? She'd just ripped this woman's husband's throat out of his body. She had literally eaten him alive, and here she was, about to have his widowed wife eat her out so she could get fucking high on a much-needed orgasm and forget tonight ever fucking happened.

Jaclyn hated herself so much right now that she wanted to die. But she knew that the monster inside her wouldn't allow it. Death no longer held any meaning to her because, as far as she knew, the worst part of this curse was that she'd probably live forever.

If she tried to die by committing suicide, such as hurting herself or starving herself to death, the Red Rage would seize her, and she'd wake up amid another massacre, fully rejuvenated. She could never stop killing because the cold, hard truth of the matter was that killing had become a part of her now. She was no longer human—she was a vampire.

When she'd first been turned, she'd resented being a vampire. She viewed it as a terrible curse. Over the years, though, she'd warmed up to the idea. Now, she viewed it as a necessary evil—a means to an end. Although she still had to feed, she could also use her powers for good.

Nothing in the rule book stated that vampires couldn't be honorable, noble, and occasionally kind. They might be soulless creatures of the night, but that didn't mean they were ultimately destined for evil things. Being soulless just meant you were without God, not that you were without compassion. Besides, the religious didn't have a monopoly on love and compassion.

So, she set out to break the stereotype and chose to fight to make the world a better place. Justice, for her, wasn't just about punishing evil. Justice meant righting the wrongs and correcting the injustices that had been done. Of course, it wasn't always possible.

Sometimes, the crimes were so heinous that no amount of good could ever erase the damage wrought by evil. In these rare cases, where all seemed lost, Jaclyn knew that sometimes it took more than just a badge to fight evil. Sometimes, it took evil to fight evil.

But she never wanted to cross that line. Not unless she needed to.

As she lay in Maddie's bed, listening to the steam of hot

water and the steam billowing out of the bathroom door in wisps that quickly faded in the coolness of the air, she began to nod off.

Sex would have to wait. She was exhausted and only wanted to sleep. Grabbing a corner of the blanket, she rolled over, wrapping herself up like a burrito. She placed her face on Maddie's pillow and took a deep whiff of her scent. Maddie's sweat was instantly salty and sweet, like the ocean breeze.

Maddie's smell filled her with a warmth and calmness she hadn't experienced in a long time. She felt at peace. Then, closing her eyes, she let herself drift off to sleep.

Sunlight broke through the shades and lit up Jaclyn's face, causing her to groan and roll over. She turned her face away from the excruciating light and slowly emerged from a deep slumber.

Last night had been one of the best sleeps she'd had in ages. She opened her eyes and looked over to find Maddie sleeping soundly beside her in the king-size bed.

Curious, Jaclyn gently lifted the bed sheet and peeked inside to see whether they were naked or had on their pajamas.

"What are you doing?" a dreary voice asked.

There was a yawn, and Jaclyn put the sheet down, looking up to find Maddie's grinning face staring back at her.

"You're naked," Jaclyn said, raising the sheet one more time and taking another peek. "Very naked."

Maddie laughed. "So are you, hot stuff."

"I'm in my underwear," Jaclyn corrected.

"Well, we shall remedy that right now." Maddie scooted

close and reached behind Jaclyn's back to unfasten her bra with a swift flick of her fingers. Jaclyn's bra fell to the bed, and both women glanced down at one another as they took in the view.

"You're gorgeous," Maddie said.

"So are you," Jaclyn replied, volleying the compliment back to her. The ball was in Maddie's court, so Jaclyn sat there waiting for her to make her move.

They stared at each other for another few seconds, although it seemed like eons, and then came together in a heated embrace. Falling back into the covers, they kissed more passionately than a couple of newlyweds on their honeymoon night.

Jaclyn began dappling Maddie's chest with kisses and slowly worked her way down to her stomach. Maddie touched Jackie's shoulder, enticing her to look up.

"Are you sure?"

"I'm sure," Jaclyn replied, and then, sliding down between Maddie's thighs, she went down on her. Maddie threw her head back and arched her back, letting out a licentious moan that filled the entire house.

Forty-five minutes later, Jaclyn stood by Maddie's bed, getting dressed. She put on her skirt without bothering to put on her underwear. They were too wet to wear anyway, so she ditched them in a pile with Maddie's things.

"Aren't you forgetting something?" Maddie asked, nodding at Jaclyn's panties.

"Oh, God. This is embarrassing to admit. But while I was going down on you, the floodgates may have opened, and they're sopping wet."

"Yeah, they are," Maddie laughed. She propped herself on her elbow and sat in bed, watching Jaclyn dress. "Is it too bold of me to say that I think your tongue is a miracle from God?"

Jaclyn laughed as she fastened her bra. "You taste good, too," she said, winking at Maddie. "It was a delight."

"Me? What about you? You taste amazing. Like mango butter and cherry blossoms."

"That's because I lather myself in mango moisturizer. Every inch of my body is covered in the stuff."

Maddie laughed. "Well, that would explain it."

The truth was, without her warm-blooded circulatory system to properly hydrate her, Jaclyn needed the lotion to prevent her undead skin from cracking and flaking. But that was the part of her she had to keep hidden from Maddie. If not to spare her the terrible truth, then to keep her safe from Jaclyn's monstrous nature and horrendous crimes.

The less Maddie knew, the better off she'd be.

Slipping into her blouse, Jaclyn looked up at Maddie as she buttoned up, pausing midway as a concerned look settled across her face.

"What is it?" asked Maddie, scanning Jackie's face for clues as to what might be wrong.

"Please, don't tell Michaelson. I'm not ready for him to know that we've taken the next step in, whatever this is."

Maddie smiled and nodded reassuringly. "My lips are sealed."

"I'm deadly serious, Maddie. It could mean my partnership. Even my job."

The face Maddie made seemed to be one of confusion and hurt. "I won't," she reiterated more bitingly. "You have my word, Jackie."

"Thank you," Jaclyn answered as she planted an arm onto the bed, leaned down, and kissed Maddeline's lips one last time.

Maddie's grin grew large as she watched Jaclyn finish

buttoning her blouse. She let the euphoria of their lovemaking flood over her. She basked in its afterglow, her fingers gently stroking her bottom lip in a sensuous manner.

Jaclyn was a good lay, as far as Maddie was concerned. She had managed to make her cum five times. That's four times more than anyone has ever made her cum before. She couldn't explain it, but making love to Jackie made her feel young again. She had never felt like this after making love to Michael.

It wasn't bad. Sex with him was fine. But with Jackie, she felt as though she were supercharged. She felt as though lightning coursed through her veins, lighting her up, making her feel like a new woman. Her soul was glowing like a lighthouse, and she didn't care who saw it. She was happy to love both Mike and Jackie. They were—*both of them*—her soulmates.

Jaclyn left the bedroom and headed into the hall. From behind her, she could hear Maddie squeal with glee as she thrashed around, kicking her legs with giddiness and bunching up all the sheets. Jaclyn just smiled to herself and skipped down the stairs.

As she reached the front door, Jaclyn turned and looked back up to find Maddie standing, wrapped in a bed sheet, at the top of the stairs, beaming with joy.

"Jaclyn Benoit," Maddie said. "I *love* you."

Jaclyn blew Maddie a kiss in reply. But as much as she adored her, she couldn't bring herself to say "I love you" back. So, she smiled and winked at her, pulling herself away from the only thing that gave her any sense of peace.

But as desperately as she wanted to call in and stay in this haven, making love to Maddie all day, Jaclyn had a lot of work to do. Even if most of that work entailed covering her tracks and making sure none of the recent string of murders came back to haunt her.

The Danielle Pruette case, however, wasn't her doing. This bothered her because that meant there was a natural killer on the loose. Not a ravenous animal or bloodthirst-quenching vampire, but a cold and calculating psychopath.

She'd count herself lucky if she could spare Maddie the pain of learning this sobering truth. Not everyone was ready to know that the monsters under their beds were all too real.

Perhaps more unsettling than getting found out, however, would be having to explain to Maddie why she did it. Why she had slaughtered Michaelson in the alley that night.

But to explain that, she'd need to explain how Michaelson had left her with no choice—she'd need to go back to the beginning and explain what she'd seen on the road that night after Darius had passed her by when she was coming out of her fugue state as she stood naked and drenched on the side of the road. But she couldn't burden Madelin with any of that right now. She wouldn't understand.

Jaclyn felt it would be better to let things play out naturally. The truth would become known in due time. And as much as that terrified her, she'd face that obstacle when she came to it.

Not that Maddie would ever forgive her if she knew the truth. That's why she opted to keep Maddie in the dark. Jaclyn knew their relationship wouldn't survive the fallout if she revealed it all. And, sure, maybe she was being selfish. But right now, Maddie made her happy. She was fairly positive that she made Maddie happy, too.

So, maybe they could endure the lie a little longer if it meant being happy together.

Shutting the front door behind her, Jaclyn stood on the front porch of Maddie's house and let out a pent-up sigh, releasing all the stress and tension she'd been keeping inside for no good reason.

Why, oh, why did you have to go and eat your partner, Jaclyn? That was perhaps the stupidest move in the history of stupid moves. She knew that there was already a full investigation underway at the precinct where she'd unceremoniously left the body.

That wasn't her only sin, either. Poor Darius, she thought. That poor kid was terrified out of his mind. But halfway through drinking him like a frat girl drinking a blood orange daiquiri, her thirst was wholly satiated. And she had one of two options—let him die from his wounds and blood loss, or make him a vampire, like herself. She chose to turn him, perchance to save him from a premature death brought on by another bout of her uncontrollable Red Rage.

In the coming days, Darius was about to undergo a painful physical transformation. However, once he made it through, he would emerge as something new—fierce, powerful, and primal. After the transformation was complete, she would guide him just as her Master had guided her when she was turned 183 years ago.

72

6

VELMA AND THE SLAYERS

VELMA AND THE SLAYERS were a local girl punk rock band with the most attractive lead singer Darius had ever seen. The lead singer, Velma Lorren Chadwick, had spiky black hair with purple highlights. Her head was shaved on either side, and she had several piercings, including a nose ridge spike and a diamond stud in her left nostril.

Along with these embellishments, she wore a tartan miniskirt with fishnet leggings and had two full sleeves of tattoos, primarily skulls and roses. Even through her black tank top, he could see the studs of her pierced nipples. Darius was in love.

Velma leaned on the counter as she smacked on some gum. After blowing a bubble, she took it out and stuck it under the counter in front of Darius.

"Hey, D," she said. She got a kick out of calling him the "Big D," and he didn't mind so much. There were worse nicknames. "When's the goddamn bar open?"

Darius looked over at the darkened corner where the bar was and then back to Velma. "Usually at five thirty when the bartender gets here."

"It's not that skank, Abby Lockhart, is it?"

"I think Roy is on duty tonight."

"Fuck, yeah. Roy is hot. I'd totally sit on his face and let him squirm."

Darius raised an eyebrow and laughed. "You can sit on whoever's face you want. It's still a free country. But the bar won't be open until five thirty."

"Damn right, it's a free country," she said, smiling at him. Then, leaning in, she gave him a peck on the cheek and whispered into his ear. "If you get me a beer right now, I'll suck your dick."

"Ah, uh...um..." Darius stammered and looked around nervously. Realizing that she was serious caused him to blush, his cheek red-hot from where she had kissed him.

After conducting another survey of the bowling alley, she found that, aside from a few regulars and her band members, there was nobody else around.

"Fuck it," he said and ducked under his counter, then went over to the bar to fetch her a beer. Opening a small fridge under the counter, he pulled out an ice-cold Corona and handed it to her.

"You're the best, D," she said, taking the bottle from him. In one smooth motion, she set the edge of the lid on the counter and then slapped it with the palm of her hand. With a hiss, the cap popped off, and she quickly chugged it all down in one sitting. Wiping her mouth with the back of her hand, she let out a loud belch. "That hit the spot."

"Wait," Darius asked, realizing he didn't know her age, "how old are you?"

"Sixteen. Why?"

The color drained from his face, and he stared at her, a look of mortification on his face. That's when she burst out laughing.

"The look on your face, D., it's priceless!"

He sighed in relief, realizing she was messing with him. Velma tossed her hair and sauntered off, her skirt swishing back and forth over the back of her thighs as she went. "A rain check on that, BJ, okay." Oh, and I'm only eighteen," she added, glancing back at him and winking.

Well, idiot, he thought. You just served a minor because you wanted a blow job that you're probably not going to get. Good going, Einstein.

It wasn't clear whether she was eighteen or not. Velma enjoyed being an unreliable narrator in her own life and frequently made random decisions. She lied to see others' reactions to her outrageous statements. Her personality was unpredictable and edgy, but that's what made her fun, in his opinion.

Darius checked the clock and saw that it was a quarter to five. He only worked until seven thirty, but knowing that Velma and the Slayers were playing tonight, he decided to stay and watch their set.

When Roy finally arrived, about twenty minutes later, Darius saw Velma coerce an extra beer out of him, too. She got a round of beers for all the girls, so either she was older than eighteen or promised Roy the same treat as Darius if he was a good boy.

The following two hours crept by at a snail's pace, but finally, Jesse, one of Velma's ex-boyfriends, relieved Darius of his shift, which mostly involved cleaning shoes and polishing balls.

"She's hot, ain't she?" Jesse asked, nodding toward Velma and the Slayers.

Darius looked over at the group of girls and noticed that every time Velma brushed her hair back, she smiled back at him. "Yeah," he said, his tone completely infatuated with her.

"So, you gonna hit that?" Jesse asked. "You've been pining over her for weeks. Heck, the only thing holding you back was that Danielle chick. But she's out of the picture now, so why not go for it, man?" Jesse hit Darius in the arm, and Darius laughed nervously.

"What makes you think I haven't already?" he asked, pulling off his work shirt and grabbing his hoodie from the stool behind the counter, a devious smile spreading across his face.

"You dog!" Jesse said, snapping his fingers and giving Darius a fist bump.

Jesse wasn't a bad guy, but he was shallow and only cared about wetting his dick. Practically everything that came out of his mouth was smut talk, which was amusing for the first few minutes but got old fast.

Darius turned around to look at Velma again. She wasn't Danielle Pruette, but she had her own set of charms. Danielle Pruette was a veritable angel, whereas Velma was a badass right out of hell. Darius couldn't help but wonder if the stereotype was true: *good girls are good to you, but bad girls do it better.*

Realizing Darius wasn't even paying attention to his profound exposé on the finer side of seducing women, Jesse shrugged and returned to the shoe bin to spray Lysol disinfectant on the soles.

Beads of sweat gathered around Darius's temple and crown, and his stomach churned like a tumbler washing machine. He wondered if something he'd eaten didn't agree with him. But other than his mom's cooking, he hadn't gone out or eaten anything out of the ordinary.

Suddenly, he felt unusually hot, as if he was growing feverish. That's when the urge to vomit hit him with the force of a freight train, and, holding it back, he ran to the bathroom.

He rushed into the men's room, slamming the door behind him as he staggered to a stall. Clutching his stomach, he groaned in pain, feeling it twist into tight knots.

Ducking into the stall, he collapsed to his knees and bent over the bowl. Vomit mixed with his breakfast, lunch, and dinner all came out. More than this, he began heaving and puking up blood. Then more blood. Followed by a steady stream of blood that spurted out of him as though he were a fountain statue.

It seemed that he was throwing up his internal organs as if they had all seemingly liquified inside of him. It was, in his opinion, beyond gross. Once it died down, he wiped the corner of his mouth with the back of his hand and murmured, "What the fuck?"

The water in the toilet went from a chunky pink to a deep crimson color. Having puked half his guts out, he flushed and slowly rose to his feet. Walking over to the sink, he looked up into the mirror and almost gave himself a heart attack.

His reflection was staring back at him—but not. His eyes were black with a red halo around his pupils. "What the—?" he stopped mid-sentence when he noticed two sharp protrusions sticking out of his mouth. Pulling his lip back with a finger, he saw two fangs.

"You've got to be shittin' me," he said in shock. Turning on the cold water, he splashed his face and drank directly from the faucet. He looked back in the mirror again, wondering what was going on. Should he call an ambulance?

His body was burning up, and his skin felt as though it was on fire. He splashed himself with more water, and although it seemed to help mitigate the unbearable burning sensation, the relief was only temporary.

That's when he noticed steam rising off his skin. He slapped the areas that were steaming, trying to put out the invisible flames. But it was no good. He was just too damn hot and was—quite literally—burning up.

"What's happening to me?" he asked, staring at his reflection in the mirror. He had to squint to see it because, for some reason, it seemed to be fading away—as if it were disappearing.

That's when the door opened, and he spun around to find Velma hovering in the doorway, her third beer in hand.

"Holy fuck," Velma said, standing in the doorway.

"What?" Darius asked, feeling bashful enough to try to cover himself. He fumbled awkwardly with his arms before giving up and just standing there.

"I didn't know you were so damn hot. I would have fucked you a long time ago if I knew you had a body like that under all those baggy clothes."

She walked into the men's restroom without hesitation and approached him. Throwing her arm around his neck, she pulled him in close, almost as if she was going to kiss him, but stopped herself short. Looking at his fangs, she reached up and touched them with her fingertips.

"Also, since when did you get into the goth scene?" Gazing

into his eyes, she grasped his face and twisted his head from side to side, inspecting him in an almost scientific manner. "And those contacts are badass."

"Thanks, I guess?" he said in an uncertain voice. He reached down, took the beer out of her hand, and took a long swig. She watched him with amusement and went back to examining his fangs when she accidentally pricked her finger.

"Ow," she yelped as the needle-like prick of his fang stuck her thumb. A single drop of blood bubbled up on the tip of her skin, and she began to suck it.

Seeing this, Darius's eyes dilated with excitement, forming a red halo that expanded into a large ring and then shrank back down.

As Velma sucked on her thumb, she maintained eye contact with Darius the whole time. Pretty soon, she was making a lewd demonstration with her fingers, showing him that she knew exactly how to use her mouth.

Feeling an uncontrollable urge to have her, he picked her up and set her on the bathroom counter next to the sink. Her thighs slapped on the smooth surface, and she chirped excitedly.

"*Yessss,*" she sighed, rubbing her hand down her neck and chest, caressing her breasts. "I like where this is going. Just make it as rough as you can, okay, D? I don't want to be able to walk in the morning if you get my meaning."

"You're a little bit of a freak, aren't you?" he asked her.

"You have no idea," she said, her smile devious. She bit her bottom lip and spread her legs wide, drawing him into her.

As they came together, she grabbed his broad shoulders and pulled him tight, her fingernails digging into his skin. "I want you to bite me," she said, exposing her neck to him.

Usually, Darius would shy away from such brazen acts,

especially PDA. But suddenly, a voracious hunger filled him. It was carnal and lustful, and he didn't care about being the good guy anymore. All he wanted was her.

Not only did he feel more sexually charged than he ever had in his entire life, but he also felt an uncontrollable bloodlust. He wanted to feed. He needed to feed...*on her.*

Darius obliged her wish and sank his fangs deep into her neck. Velma let out a sensual gasp and reached up, grabbing him by the scruff of his neck. She held him tight, locking him in place, and forced him to imbibe her crimson nectar until she was satisfied.

The red rings in his eyes flared again as he drank from her. Blood dribbled down her neck and chest, and as he continued to feed, Velma reached down and peeled off his boxers, her thighs exposed, inviting him into her inner sanctum.

After she'd freed him, she slid her thumbs under her panties' waistband, slipped them off, and readied herself for the ride of her life.

The sound of bowling pins crashing together echoed up and down the eight lanes, and Jesse looked around for Velma. Strange, he thought. Velma had gone into the men's restroom about forty minutes ago. What was she doing in there?

Of course, his mind went straight into the gutter. Who was he kidding? He knew exactly what she was doing in there. She was doing Darius.

The band stood off to the side of the room, tapping their feet impatiently and fiddling with their hair as they waited for their lead singer to hurry up and finish fucking around.

One of the Slayers, a girl with blonde spiky hair and hot pink bangs, approached the counter. "We're going live in five," she said. "Do you think you can fetch our salacious queen for us and tell her to hurry it along?"

Why do I have to be the errand boy, he wondered. But she was hot, so he caved in as he always did whenever a pretty girl asked him for a favor. He nodded and walked around the counter to head to the restroom. The men's bathroom door drew open before he made it around the counter, and Velma stepped out. He looked back at the blonde, who shrugged and returned to her drums.

Velma wiped the corners of her mouth with a licentious smile and brushed down her ruffled-up skirt. When she saw everyone staring at her, she laughed and said, "Let's get this mother-fucking party started!"

She glided over to where the band waited for her and grabbed her guitar. Standing by the amp, she turned it on and strummed a few chords as the other two girls got ready. The blonde got on bass, and a redheaded girl with a leather jacket with nothing underneath who, for whatever reason, also wore cowboy chaps over bikini bottoms sat at the drums.

The bowling alley was filled with punk rock music when Darius exited the men's restroom. He stood in the doorway holding his shirt in his hands. Jesse strolled over and punched him in the arm.

"You a dog! You hit that, didn't you?" He glanced at Velma, who merely stared at Darius as she continued to sing. She couldn't help but smile, and her entire face was a grin from start to finish during the song.

Darius just ignored him, walked over to the bar, and sat

down. Swiveling on the stool, he turned and watched Velma jumping up and down as she screamed what he assumed were lyrics into the mic.

Roy slammed a cold pink lemonade Smirnoff in front of him and said, "On the house. It's not every day you get your cherry popped." Darius looked over at Roy, who winked at him before turning around to help another customer at the far end of the counter.

Darius sipped his drink, trying to look as cool as possible. Leaning back against the bar, Darius stared at Velma as she sang her song, soaking up her words. Words that very well could have summed up their encounter in the men's room quite nicely.

WE WERE YOUNG, WE WERE STUPID. WE DID ALL THE THINGS WE SHOULDN'T HAVE. BUT THE MOMENT YOU LOOKED AT ME WITH THOSE DOE EYES, I KNEW...

YOU WERE THE ONE, YOU WERE THE ONE, YOU WERE THE ONE FOR MEEE!

AND I WAS THE ONE, I WAS THE ONE, I WAS THE ONE FOR YOUUU!

SEVENTEEN AND RECKLESS, YOU WERE MY PLAN A, SO I NEVER NEEDED PLAN B. YOU WERE MY FIRST TIME, BECAUSE FROM THAT DAY, I KNEWWW...

YOU WERE THE ONE, YOU WERE THE ONE, YOU WERE THE ONE FOR ME!

After his fifth vodka cooler, the rest of the night was mostly a blur. All he remembered was the song finishing and Velma coming up to him, laughing and leaning in to talk into his ear. She invited him to hang out with her and the other girls after their performance, and he agreed. Why wouldn't he?

Several drunken hours later, he figured that he must have blacked out at some point during their partying from drinking too much. Because when he awoke, he found himself in bed with all three Slayers. Darius had never been with a woman before today. And now he had been with three? At the same time?! He could scarcely believe his luck.

He looked over at the three girls sleeping next to him. All three of the Slayers had multiple bite marks on their bodies. Marks covered their necks, breasts, and thighs.

For a moment, Darius thought he'd gone too far. He'd drunk until they passed out from blood loss. Stopping himself there, he gazed upon their naked bodies as they slept peacefully next to him, all still breathing – thank God.

Darius got up and walked to the standing mirror in the corner of Velma's studio apartment. Darius nearly shit himself when he looked and couldn't see his reflection.

"What in the world is going on?" he whispered to himself. He touched his face to ensure he wasn't dreaming this bizarro-world version of himself.

"You're a vampire," a voice answered.

He turned to see Velma sitting up in bed, the other two girls still fast asleep beside her.

"And now we are, too," she informed him, exposing her wrist and showing the dark bruising where he'd bitten her hard. He looked down at his wrists to find the same discoloration.

"What have I done?" he asked, staring down at his hands.

Velma grabbed a robe from the end of the bed and slipped it on. She strolled across the oriental rug and over to Darius, her bare feet making a padded sound as she approached him. Wrapping her arms around him, they both turned toward the mirror and stared at the reflection of an empty bed on the other side of the room.

There was no sign of any of them. Not him. Not Velma. None of the Slayers. It was as if they didn't exist.

"Is this really happening?" he asked.

Velma rested her head on his shoulder and answered. "Yes, baby. It's all real. It's happening."

"That's what I was afraid of," he answered in a monotone voice that was neither glad about it nor necessarily all that bummed out either.

She rubbed her hands down his chest, sliding them down his body. She sank to her knees. Looking up, she smiled and said, "I think I'll cash in that rain check now."

Darius closed his eyes and let the waves of pleasure wash over him. He didn't know if one got baptized into being a vampire, but this was as good as any baptism. Not only had he become a real man, but he'd become something so much more.

Darius had Detective Jaclyn Benoit to thank for this great gift, his newfound strength and stamina, and for getting laid. He made a note to thank her later. Right now, he only wanted to enjoy his time with his harem.

Velma brought him to the brink of climax, and he did everything in his power not to let go. But she was relentless, and her mouth was so wet and inviting. Darius groaned loudly from holding back the urge to release his life-giving nectar. He wondered, could vampires even impregnate human women?

"Ugh!" he grunted, unable to hold back anymore.

Velma smiled, swallowed, and continued to move down on him, not missing a beat. He squirmed with a yearning for it to be over but forced himself to accept both the pleasure and the pain that came in the aftermath of such a pounding orgasm.

Amber and Sophie roused and joined them. Velma and Sophie began making out as Amber took over for Velma.

Darius settled onto the bed and watched, a smile forming on his face. Reaching up, he grabbed Velma's hips and forced her to sit on his face. It was his turn to reciprocate the pleasure she'd given him.

She let out a ribald moan as his tongue sank deep into her crotch, passing her soft, pink drapery and into her inner sanctum.

After Velma came all over his face, Darius ran his tongue over his lips and wiped them clean. He kissed her on the mouth, and they fell back into bed together, her head falling gently onto his chest as she drifted off to sleep.

Beyond the bond of blood, they felt a genuine connection. She was his, and he was hers. As he began to nod off, Sophie and Amber snuggled up on either side of them, sandwiching them in between their naked bodies, and joined them in sleep's embrace.

86

IN 1941, EDGAR ALAN POE wrote the first tale of ratiocination or the first detective story. *The Murders in the Rue Morgue* had fascinated Jaclyn Benoit to no end and sparked her interest in becoming an investigator of macabre crimes. But that was back when she was still a warm-blooded woman and still human.

Now, 183 years later, she wasn't the same woman she once was. She was something else—something wicked—something profane. Deep in her gut, she knew that she had lost her human soul when the vampire's kiss cursed her. And here, in this present, she'd done the unthinkable. She'd performed the vampire's kiss herself and made her first progeny—her first vampire.

It wasn't supposed to have happened like this. Darius was never supposed to catch her in the middle of a Red Rage, blood-induced feeding frenzy. He was never supposed to have known about her dark side, let alone become her first creation.

Usually, she tried to plan out her feeding cycles. She calculated them to be twenty-two days apart. If she hadn't fed before now, she would have lost herself to the Red Rage, and her carnal instinct to feed would overwhelm her. It hit her once a month like clockwork.

Ironic, she thought, now that she no longer had her period, the Red Rage caused her to lust for blood with the same predictability as her bloody menstruation.

She found that when she fed in small increments, she could fend off the monstrous hunger pangs until the need to feed became so overwhelming that it consumed her. While she was a victim of this terrible curse, she also became a victimizer. Her instinct to do good made it exceptionally difficult for her to pick her victims. She hated hurting people, and she hated killing.

But if she ignored the monster inside of her, it would steadily grow in hunger and in power until it was able to take control—and then the number of victims she'd hurt would be immeasurable.

All she could do was mitigate it and try to reduce the death and carnage the monster would inevitably leave in its wake by appeasing it and satiating its hunger. Of course, this meant she'd have to offer up the occasional sacrifices. As such, she typically preyed on criminals and evil-doers such as rapists and murderers.

The truth was that it was better to satiate the monster inside and not let him out of his cage than risk letting him escape, because it would wreak havoc on the world. Sometimes, though, even if she were extremely diligent in maintaining a steady feeding cycle where she only needed to imbibe a small amount of blood to get her through the next week, the uncontrollable cravings would still hit.

The first time it had happened, she had tried feeding on livestock. Although it seemed to work, the effects wore off twice as quickly, meaning she had to feed weekly—and sometimes biweekly. Livestock, such as cattle, horses, sheep, and goats, were a temporary fix and not a very good one. No, she needed human blood. That was the only way she could stay normal for more extended periods.

Human blood was the only thing that worked. And when there weren't any criminals around, she'd feed on drifters, hitchhikers, and the occasional homeless person. But only as a last resort.

However, finding such free-range humans had been proving increasingly difficult recently. Wood River had developed a reputation for people disappearing, and the recent string of murders didn't help things much either.

While it was true that the massacre at Mel's diner had been her doing, Danielle Pruette's death was most certainly not her doing.

If all this wasn't a big enough concern, she'd recently been undergoing some changes of her own. None of them good ones either.

The sunlight had increasingly begun to grow painful. Not only did it sting her eyes and cause migraine headaches, but it also gave her skin nasty rashes, which is why she constantly over-moisturized. The silver lining, if there was one concerning her curse, was that she wasn't self-combusting and burning up in flames like in the movies. No, it wasn't like that. It was more of a mild irritant.

With as much coconut-scented sunscreen and mango butter lotion as she used, she was beginning to smell like a goddamned pina colada. Not that anybody seemed to mind. She got more compliments than anything. But it was just one more thing she needed to contend with. And what if it got worse? It wasn't a consideration she had time for, though. Right now, she stood by her desk, watching Captain Raymond Ackhurst nervously pace back and forth in his office.

Jaclyn took a deep breath and braced herself for the bad news she knew he would share with her. She walked up to the entrance of Captain Ackhurst's office and wrapped her knuckles around the door. "Captain," she asked, "You wanted to see me?"

"Jackie," he said, motioning for her to join him in his office. "Good. Come in. And please shut the door behind you."

She did as asked, sat down, and watched him pace the room more. Finally, he went to the corner of his office and looked through the slats of his blinds at the other officers working out in the bullpen.

Captain Ackhurst brushed his bushy mustache down as he contemplated how best to start. As for his mustache, Jaclyn thought it looked good on him. If he were a few years younger, he might even resemble the actor Danny Glover in his prime.

"I've been worried out of my mind about you, Jackie," he informed her. "You weren't answering my calls, and your home line just kept ringing with no answer."

"I spent the night at a friend's," she replied. Not that he needed to know about her affair with Michaelson's wife. Given what she suspected he was about to tell her, that would only complicate things. She crossed her legs and sat patiently, waiting for him to get what he wanted to say off his chest.

"I'm afraid I have some bad news. It's Michaelson. Jackie, he was..." Ackhurst cleared his throat to regain his composure as he was viscerally upset over the news. "He was found dead this morning right here on our goddamn very own back porch."

"I heard on the police scanner," she replied.

"Then I don't need to tell you that he was found with his throat torn out. His throat, Jackie! It's like a wild beast had brutally mauled him. Hell, I'm still having trouble processing what I saw. The amount of blood, Jackie. My God. It was horrific."

"I'm just worried about his wife, Madeline. Do you need me to break the bad news to her?"

"That won't be necessary, Jackie. I sent two officers to the house to do it already."

"I see." Jacklyn felt heartbroken knowing that Madeline would find out about Michaelson this way. But maybe it was for the best. Handle it formally and treat it like any other homicide. Knowing how devastated Madeline would be, Jackie would head over to the house after her shift and do her best to console Maddie.

The captain closed the office blinds as prying eyes began looking into the office from the bullpen. Clearing his throat, he turned around and looked at Jackie with a grave expression.

"What is it, captain?" she asked softly, sensing he had more to say.

"With the Pruette murder, I must ask you something, Jackie. You're the best at seeing connections where others only see happenstance. So, do you think Michaelson's murder is connected to the Pruette case somehow?"

Jaclyn shrugged. "It's too early to tell. However, captain, you'll be the first to know if and when I find any connection between these two cases. You have my word."

"Good. Good." Ackhurst linked his hands behind his back and resumed pacing. "There's one more thing. Something I need to tell you about Danielle Pruette's homicide."

This got Jaclyn's attention. Uncrossing her legs, she sat up in the chair and leaned forward, resting her forearms on her thighs. "What about it?" she asked, tossing her hair and cocking her head curiously.

"It seems that Danielle Pruette wasn't Danielle Pruette."

Jaclyn raised an eyebrow. "Come again?"

"There's no use keeping this information from you since you're bound to find out sooner than later, but I received a phone call today from Homeland Security."

"Homeland Security? What did they want?"

"They wanted to inform us about Danielle Pruette's real identity."

"Real identity? I don't follow. What are you trying to say, captain?"

"Her real name was Sarah Richtman. She transferred here during her freshman year of high school when she was fifteen. Before she'd become Danielle Pruette, she was a regular high school girl in El Paso, Texas, where she'd witnessed the Cartel murder three people on American soil. She and her family were whisked away by the U.S. Marshals the very next day and put into protective custody so that when the time came, she could testify in a court of law. She has been in hiding ever since.

"Well, shit," Jaclyn cursed. "That throws a wrench into things." What had begun as a local murder in a rural town nobody cared about suddenly became a high-profile case that was bound to bring the Federal Marshals into it.

"Oh, it gets better. The U.S. Marshals are sending one of their own to investigate the circumstances of Danielle Pruette's death. They want to determine if it's tied to the cartel in some way.

"Of course they are," she said blithely.

"The Special Agent is arriving today. Please bring her up to speed on everything you've gathered so far. Whether or not she keeps you on the case is her call."

"What?" Jaclyn asked, her head snapping back around to face the captain. "You're taking me off the case?"

"You know me better than that, Jackie. But, as I said, my hands are tied. If the Marshals want to retain you and keep you on this case, they can. If not, I'll have no choice but to reassign you to another case."

Jaclyn stood up and slammed a palm down on the captain's desk. "This is bullshit, and you know it."

Ackhurst stopped pacing and looked right at her.

"It's protocol, Jackie," he growled, putting her back in her place. She backed off. "I suggest you make nice with the Marshals and kiss ass. Butter her up and make her think you're her best friend. Because, realistically, that's the only way you will continue with this case."

"But Captain–" she began, still wanting to complain about how unfair this was.

"Dismissed," he said, cutting her off. He knew exactly what she was thinking because he was thinking the same thing. But there was no reason to let her work herself up any more than she already was. It didn't serve either of them. Instead, he needed his best investigator out there doing what she did best – solving cases and catching bad guys.

Jacklyn nodded and spun around, storming out of the room. Captain Ackhurst watched her leave and counted his lucky stars that she took it as well as she did.

As Jaclyn marched furiously down the hall, an Arabic-looking woman in a burnt orange designer suit came around the corner, and they collided. Staggering back, Jaclyn glared at the woman and growled, "Watch where you're going."

She didn't stick around for any apologies and quickly stormed off.

"Excuse you," the woman said, letting out an exasperated laugh. The laugh people make when they're so offended they can hardly believe their ears.

Shaking off the bad encounter, the woman turned around and marched into Captain Ackhurst's office. She extended her hand and said, "Hi, I'm Special Agent Layla Harker with the U.S. Marshals Office. I believe my boss called you?"

Ackhurst shook her hand and smiled welcomingly. "Indeed, they did, Special Agent Harker. We've been expecting you."

Layla took a step back, throwing her hands on her hips, and looked back at Jaclyn, who was storming out of the bullpen.

"Don't mind her," Ackhurst said. "She just found out that her partner was murdered."

"Oh shit," Harker said, turning back toward the captain. "That's terrible news."

"Full transparency: It may or may not be related to the Pruette case. But that ball of indignation you just met is the one you'll be working with. All I ask is that you give her a chance. She's the best I've got, and she'll take you further on this case than anyone else.

"Glad to know. And I want you to know that I have full discretion to pick whoever I want to work with on this case. If we work well together, I'll have no problem accepting your detective as my partner. "If she continues to act out," Harker said, jutting a thumb over her shoulder to indicate the direction Jaclyn had taken, "I'll have no choice but to remove her from the case."

"Fair enough," Ackhurst said. This time, it was his turn to extend his hand. They shook again, and he motioned for Jannet Rodriguez, who was passing by, to come over.

"Yes, Captain?" asked Jannet as she poked her head into the office.

"Will you see that Special Agent Harker gets her own workspace?"

"Sure thing," Jannet replied before a puzzled look came over her face. "But where? We're at full capacity out here."

"I can work anywhere. A janitorial closet. Maybe a dark records room in the basement..." Harker suggested.

"No, that won't be necessary," Ackhurst said, turning down Harker's suggestions. Turning to Jannet, he said, "Give her Michaelson's desk. Everything needs to be cleared up and checked into evidence anyway. I know Jackie won't like it, but finding Michaelson's killer takes precedence over her preference of who sits across from her."

Layla Harker nodded graciously, to which Ackhurst replied in kind. She followed Jannet to the bullpen and watched as a forensic team cleaned out Michaelson's desk and logged everything into evidence.

"I'm sorry for your loss," said Layla as she followed Jannet's lead. "I can tell by how people talk about him that he meant a lot to everyone here."

"He sure did. May God rest his soul."

"You say that as if it were a good thing," Harker said, noticing the distinct sound of relief in Jannet's voice.

"Did you hear about how he suffered?" Jannet asked, leaning

in to talk in a more hushed tone. "They found his body mutilated."

"That's rough."

"Sure. But he was a teddy bear compared to her. She's, how do I put this lightly, a stone-cold bitch. Is she a good detective? Yes. She gets the job done. But if you were hoping for people skills, well, she must have missed that class in primary school."

"I've dealt with her kind before. But, the truth is, I'm probably twice the bitch she'll ever be."

"It's not her icy personality that ever bothered me. It's her strange relationship with Michaelson that weirded me out."

"By the look on your face, I can tell you don't seem to approve of them. Were they having a workplace affair or something?"

"Oh, God no," replied Jannet, shaking her head. "It's nothing like that."

Harker let out a sigh of relief.

"It was more scandalous than that, if you can believe it."

Harker raised an eyebrow as Jannet continued feeding her the juiciest gossip. She really didn't care about her co-workers' interpersonal relationships, but she realized that in most small-town stations like this one, everybody knew everybody else's business. That's just how small towns were.

"Jaclyn and Detective Michaelson's wife were...well, let's just say it's the big secret around here that everyone is in on."

"She was sleeping with her own partner's wife right under his nose?"

"No, no. He knew about it. From what I can tell, he even encouraged them to do it. Anyway, all I know is that whatever it was...open marriage or some weird threesome thing...it made a lot of people around here uncomfortable."

"I don't doubt it."

"This is a Christian town, and they were living in a world of sin. It was the kind of thing that would make Jesus weep."

It sounded as though Jannet was preaching to the choir. Layla merely nodded along and accepted the news with a healthy dose of skepticism. "I see," she said, being grateful for the information. Although it didn't reveal much, if true, it provided her with some insight into Jaclyn Benoit's character.

Office gossip, even if based on actual events, never tells the whole picture. She didn't want to jump to conclusions and judge Detective Benoit wrongly. She prided herself on always giving everyone a fair chance, regardless of their race, gender, or sexual orientation. "I'll keep that in mind," she added.

Satisfied with her answer, Jannet smiled and returned to the front desk to start her afternoon shift. She paused and turned around before making more than a couple of steps. She checked her watch and said, "You may want to take an early lunch and give them time to finish clearing out Michaelson's things. After it's cleaned out, the desk is all yours."

Harker nodded. "Thanks. I think I'll have lunch. She glanced at the clock on the wall. It was only 10:45 AM, but she knew she could take an extra hour today and visit some of the crime scenes. She always liked to be on-site whenever she began constructing the jigsaw of events.

Layla Harker watched her leave and felt that she was picking up homophobic undertones from Jannet. Layla could hear the masked disgust in her voice when she talked about Jaclyn being in an intimate relationship with Michaelson's wife. It wasn't the affair that bothered her. The notion that two women might love one another got under her skin.

Prejudice wasn't new to her. Layla had dealt with it her

whole life. Being raised in a strict Muslim family was hard enough when you were a young girl of immigrant parents. Getting into the U.S. Marshals Service after 9/11 was doubly tricky as a Middle Eastern-looking woman, even though she was born in the good ole U.S. of A. If it hadn't been for her language skills in speaking Arabic, she probably would have been forced to wash out of the academy.

Still, she worked her ass off and beat the odds, getting promoted to work on numerous anti-terrorist task teams with both the FBI and CIA, but being a gay Arabic woman with a Muslim background? Forget about it. That shit was rough.

Coming out to her father, an Imam in a newly established mosque in Detroit, was hands down the hardest thing she'd ever had to do. Even though he loved her dearly, he considered her to be tainted by sin and, therefore, an apostate to her faith.

Until she came back to Allah and gave up her sinful ways of daring to love whom she loved, he had forbidden her from ever returning home. She wasn't so much disowned as she was, well, told not to come back until she stopped liking women as if it were a choice rather than an instinct.

What her father didn't understand was that it wasn't about indulging in some sexual kink where she liked fucking women. No. It wasn't a kink. It was just who she was. She'd known that she was gay for a long, long time. Regardless of what her father and those who thought like him felt about the "gay agenda" that was ruining their youth, she'd known from the time she was a little girl that she liked women.

Her first school crush was on her third-grade English teacher, Mrs. Danvers. She was eight years old and told a boy beside her that she was in love with Mrs. Danvers. This revelation, of course, solicited an unexpected response. The boy scrunched up his face and said, "Ew. Gross." He told her, "Girls can't like other girls."

She knew that wasn't true because she liked other girls. What he found to be a grotesque anomaly felt like the most natural thing in the world to her. To the extent that she began dating other girls in high school. She kept that side of her a secret from her parents because she knew their old-fashioned values wouldn't allow them to understand. But what use are values if they only cause you to devalue others? Those aren't values. They're prejudices.

As a senior in high school, she had a two-month-long affair with one of the student teachers...which, yes, in retrospect, was wrong. An eighteen-year-old girl was dating a twenty-three-year-old woman. However, it was the hottest and most passionate love affair of her life. All of this, of course, only reinforced the point that from the very beginning, she preferred women and *only* women.

After high school graduation, she came out to her parents. Her mother burst into tears, sobbing uncontrollably as if her very own daughter had passed away. Her father grew irate. He began to yell, flailing his arms as he stomped around the house, muttering phrases in Arabic that she'd never heard before.

The very next morning, she packed up her things, hopped into her friend's car, and drove off. They didn't stop until they arrived at Duke University, North Carolina. Her father just sat at the table reading the paper, ignoring her. He didn't even look up at her once to say goodbye.

After revealing her true self, Layla was dismayed that her mother had reacted worse than her father. Although her mother tried to hug her, she pulled away at the last moment and started crying again. Layla's spirit would have been crushed if it were not for the fact that she felt sadder for her parents than for herself. After all, their beliefs had made them scared, angry, and bigoted people. A far cry from the loving and supportive parents she'd grown up knowing.

In her opinion, her parents had been brainwashed by their religion to hate anything different than what the Qur'an deemed acceptable—and this is why Layla felt that any faith that taught you to hate your own family wasn't a religion of peace—it was the exact opposite.

Layla tried to be strong as she left in her car, but couldn't hold back her tears. It was heartbreaking for her that the people she loved the most in the world and who were supposed to love her back didn't accept her for who she truly was.

Layla Harker checked her watch and decided to find a local diner to eat at. That's when she recalled that five-star diner just outside of town. What was it called again? Ah, yes—*Mel's Diner.*

A short drive later, she pulled her Camry into an empty parking lot. The diner's windows were boarded up, and the sign was dark. She pulled out her phone and double-checked the location. Sure enough, it was the right place. The Internet even said they were open. Obviously, that wasn't the case.

Mel's Diner looked like it had been abandoned for years. The sign above the entrance had been struck by lightning and had scorch marks, while yellow police tape blocked the 50-style swinging glass doors. Everything appeared badly damaged. Similarly, all the windows had been shattered, and debris, including paper napkins and a couple of flyers advertising their Wednesday special, littered the parking lot.

As Special Agent Layla Harker stepped out of her car, she looked around the deserted parking lot and exclaimed, "What on earth happened here?"

102

8
DARK REVELATIONS

MADELINE DIDN'T TALK TO Jackie throughout the entire funeral. Although the sky was overcast, luckily, it didn't rain. Outdoor funerals were always a nice sentiment, but they could be highly miserable for the guests.

After Maddie's eulogy, guests were invited to place flowers on the casket, which had been lowered. This marked the end of the funeral and the end of Detective Mike Michaelson—full stop.

Jackie looked over at Maddie, who Captain Ackhurst consoled the best he could. She recognized many of the faces from the police department, but realized how little she knew about Michaelson's family.

She debated going up to Maddie and giving her condolences, but she already knew the rumors in the precinct were rampant. Instead, she decided to keep her distance and began the long walk through the cemetery back to her car parked on the hill under the shade of cottonwood trees.

Reaching into her pocket, she pulled out her keys and unlocked her matte black Challenger Hellcat, featuring carbon stripes, orange Brembo brake calipers, and a Laguna red leather interior. With a cheerful *bleep-bloop* that seemed out of place at a venue such as this, she began to reach for the car door when a voice called out from behind her.

"Did you know?"

Jackie turned around to find Maddie staring at her with a subdued rage behind her eyes. Jackie looked at her in silence. She knew if she feigned ignorance, Maddie would see right through her. If she told the truth, Maddie would hate her forever. So, she bit her lip.

"Did you know that his body was lying cold on the medical examiner's table as you were fucking my brains out?"

Jackie walked right up to Maddie and hugged her. Maddie drew back and, fighting through her tears, slammed her fists down onto Jackie's chest. Jacklyn moved in again, wrapping her arms even more tightly around Maddie.

Maddie broke down and began sobbing right into Jackie's shoulder. Jacklyn could see everyone staring at them from beyond the cottonwood trees, but she didn't care. Maddie was both her friend and her lover.

After she managed to compose herself, Madeline stood up straight, brushed her black dress down, and slapped Jackie across the face without warning.

"Don't contact me again. I don't ever want to see you. Not in this life, not in the next." Madeline turned around and stormed back toward the gravesite to talk with the priest. As she went, she let out a harsh and deliberately audible *"Bitch."*

Jacklyn looked around, and everyone who had stayed to watch the show grew disinterested and continued on their way. Jackie got into her car and casually drove off, the engine rumbling softly with its supercharged V-8. As much as she wanted to gun it and tear out of there, she knew better than to let herself lose control. Now wasn't the time to make a scene.

"Don't fucking say I didn't tell you so, Jackie," she said under her breath as she drove away from the cemetery. And just like that, she'd lost the only woman she'd ever loved with all her heart. Right now, she only wanted to go home, change into her pajamas, and curl up in a mint chocolate chip ice cream tub, but that would have to wait. She was late for her meeting with the U.S. Marshal, Special Agent Layla Harker.

And, no, Ms. Harker's namesake wasn't lost on her. Jacklyn had read Bram Stoker before. Heck, she'd read the first edition the year it came out. By then, she was already a vampire and knew that he had to have gotten his ideas from somewhere. Vampires had been walking among humans for centuries, whether people realized it or not.

Even so, her kind was still far and few between. She'd only ever met two other vamps in her lifetime. Her master was a mad, feral creature whom the Salem's townsfolk hunted down and killed in 1877.

Although the witch trials were a couple of hundred years earlier, she could still sense a close kinship with the twenty-five women who were drowned, burned alive, and stoned to death in 1692. If she'd been alive then, her perpetual youth would have drawn attention to her infernal state as a vampire. She, too, would have been tortured and killed.

Yes, she, too, could be killed. Technically speaking. But it wasn't easy killing a purebred vampire. Decapitating the head was necessary. You needed to cauterize the neck wound so the head wouldn't reattach itself later.

Additionally, Christian crosses and holy water didn't do anything. That was all just religious superstition. A stake through the heart, however, would prevent her lethargic pulse from pumping any of the victim's blood through her decrepit circulatory system. She wouldn't be able to regenerate. But she could regenerate instantaneously when it was plucked from her chest.

Of course, it was always wise to bury the head separately from the body. There were rare cases when a vampire was able to return to his undead state after having been chopped up and dumped in a burial site. Vampires could heal.

However, none of that concerned her back then. She was a simple farm girl, and stories about vampires were just that, stories. As far as she was concerned, such creatures didn't exist.

One morning, she stumbled upon something terrifying as she headed out to the barn to milk the cows. Sitting in the darkness of the barn was a dark and deformed shape. It looked like a man, but it wasn't. Thinking it may be a wounded animal, she rushed over to help it.

Long story short, young Jaclyn's good nature proved to be her downfall. What had started as another typical day on the farm suddenly turned into a case of young Jaclyn finding herself in the wrong place at the wrong time.

In that barn, that day, she would become yet another victim of that God-forsaken creature. However, it didn't kill her. But it took pity on her. So, instead of killing her, it turned her.

However, keeping her secret from Layla Harker would prove to be the real challenge moving forward. She'd read over the woman's rather impressive resume. She was an anti-terrorist specialist. She'd broken up more terrorist cells and arrested more bad men than Jackie could hope to do in the same lifetime. Luckily for her, her lifetime stretched eons—perhaps more.

If that wasn't impressive enough, the woman wore designer suits because, as the saying goes, she knew how to invest appropriately, and her trading skills on the stock market netted her double her salary.

This meant she was smart. Real smart. And that's just what Jackie didn't need right now —a woman prodigy who could make a thousand calculations in her mind and who, like a pit bull, never backed down.

Jackie drove out to the bowling lanes as requested and stopped next to the pearl-white Toyota Camry hybrid rental that Special Agent Harker had driven. Shit, the bitch was environmentally conscious too.

Getting out of her car, Jackie spotted Layla squatting down and looking at an oil mark in the middle of the parking lot. As she approached from behind, she noticed Harker's pants were riding low-slung because she was squatting low. The top of a purple thong presented itself and perfectly complemented her orange suit.

Hot, thought Jackie. And no tan lines on her dark skin either. "Hey," Jackie said, alerting Harker to her presence.

Layla glanced back over her shoulder. "Hey," she answered.

Jackie stood in awkward silence, waiting for Layla to say something else. She just sat there hunched over the swirls of oil. After thirty seconds, Layla stood up and turned to Jackie.

"How was the funeral?"

"Oh, the funeral was nice. I mean, as nice as any funeral

could be."

"How are you doing?"

"I'm..." Jackie paused, thinking about the harsh words Maddie had said to her earlier. "Honestly, I could be better."

Layla nodded and turned around to survey the parking lot some more.

Jaclyn wondered what was with this woman. What was she even looking for? She seemed distant and detached.

"There were three people here on the night of the murder," Layla said.

"How on Earth do you know that from just looking at the parking lot?"

Layla pointed. "Nobody has been allowed behind the police tape. If they were, their tracks would be uniform. As you can see here, we find Pruette's footprints as she got into her car. Over there are her co-worker's tracks. But if you look over here," she said, pointing at an area of about five feet behind Danielle's tracks, "we have someone else's tracks."

"All I see is gravel," Jaclyn said, looking at the dirt parking area with a touch of incredulity.

"It could be nothing," Layla admitted as she turned to face Jaclyn. "Or it could be something."

"Right," Jaclyn said, trying her best not to sound sarcastic. "So, about yesterday," she said, changing the subject. "I owe you an apology."

"Perfectly understandable. You'd just found out your partner had died. You weren't in the best state of mind. And, I admit, my timing could have been better, too."

Jaclyn stared at her for another moment and corrected her. "Murdered. My partner was murdered."

"I thought that was implied," Layla said. She turned around

again and walked over to Jaclyn's car. "Is this your car?"

"Yes," Jaclyn answered, confused about where she was going with this.

"Why this car?" she asked, turning back to Jackie, and brushing a tuft of dark curly hair behind her ear. Even though she had shoulder-length hair, it was still long enough for a tassel of mahogany hair to dislodge and fall across her face.

"I like muscle cars. Is that wrong?"

"My high school girlfriend drove an old Pontiac Firebird. It was a gaudy gold color, and it had that raw, untamed V-8 animal-like charisma, just like her. God, we had some good times in that car."

Jaclyn raised an eyebrow. "So, you're...?"

"Gay?" Layla said, finishing her sentence for her. "Yes. As sure as Sappho hailed from the island of Lesbo."

"I beg your pardon?"

"Yes, I like women. I just wanted to make that clear going forward."

"Ah," Jaclyn said with a laugh. She looked away, her eyes scanning the road. "You heard about me and the widow, Mrs. Michaelson."

"So, they're not rumors?"

"I'm afraid not. We've been seeing each other for roughly six months. Well, I guess we were. Until today."

Layla gave her a curious look.

"Shit. I don't know why I'm telling you this, but I got dumped today. So, there's that."

"I appreciate your honesty," Layla said, reaching out her hand and touching Jacklyn's arm.

Jackie looked down briefly as Layla initiated contact. She had thick eyebrows, full lips, and an aquiline nose that gave her a regal appearance. Her chestnut-colored skin was smooth and unmarred, with no trace of a scar, and she had medium-length, dark, curly hair.

"So, do you want to get lunch?" Layla asked. "Partners can have lunch together, right?"

Jaclyn laughed. "Yeah, sure."

"All right, it's a date." Layla squinted in embarrassment as she realized she'd made a poor choice of words. "Sorry, I didn't mean it like that."

"It's fine," Jackie assured her. "So, are we taking your car or mine?"

"Yours," Layla said, smiling at Jackie with the brightest smile she'd ever seen.

As they approached the blacked-out Challenger, Jackie looked over at Layla and asked her a question she had never asked anyone. "You want to drive her?"

"Are you serious?" Layla said, growing excited. Jaclyn tossed the keys to her, and she fumbled to catch them but made a quick save.

"By all means," Jaclyn said, motioning for her to go ahead.

Less than a minute later, they were making donuts in the parking lot, tires squealing as burnt rubber kicked up smoke.

With the engine rumbling, Layla shifted it from first to second gear and floored it, and they peeled out of the parking lot. Jaclyn braced herself in the passenger seat and looked over at Layla, who, still beaming ear to ear, seemed to be having the time of her life.

They raced down the old highway in that beast of a car, and Jacklyn asked, "I know you're new to Wood River, but the town is back that way. Where are you taking me?"

"You'll see," she said in a coy voice.

A few minutes later, they pulled into the parking area of Mel's Diner. Jaclyn almost gasped when she saw it. It had been repaired, and a whole parking lot already existed.

"What in the Seven Wonders...?" Jaclyn's jaw hung open. "When? How?" She could hardly get the words out.

"I called in a few favors and had it fixed up."

"You called in some favors to fix a random diner in the middle of nowhere?"

"It's not a random diner," she said, stopping the car at the front entrance. It's mine. I bought it."

"You're yanking my chain."

"Nope," Layla said, turning to Jaclyn. I signed the papers two days ago, flew a crew in to make the necessary repairs, and hired a new line cook and two servers."

"For fuck's sake," Jaclyn said, half impressed but still completely baffled. "So, do you often buy up properties in rural towns?"

Layla laughed. "No. This is the first one. But it's necessary."

"I hate to ask. But necessary for what?"

"For drawing out the killer."

"Come again?"

"The massacre that happened here. The five people that died here, I'm not going to have that be their legacy. Victims of a serial killer. No. Instead, I'm going to show this psycho that he can't destroy the spirits of these people. Their memories will live on, and he'll fade away until he's a forgotten nobody."

"So, your goal is to piss off a killer?"

"Precisely," she said, smiling. One of the things you learn in your time with a counterterrorism task force is how to goad the enemy into revealing their hand. If the killer prides himself on death and destruction, erasing everything they did to get noticed is a slap in the face to their ego. Essentially, it's erasing their life's work."

"Are you so sure this will work?"

"I'm not a hundred percent," she admitted. "But it's worth a shot. And if it doesn't work, we'll catch them the usual way." She pointed to the temple of her head. "Using good old-fashioned brainpower."

Jaclyn laughed. "You're an odd duck, aren't you?"

Layla looked at her with a smile and answered, "Quack."

Opening the doors simultaneously, they both got out and looked at one another across the car's roof. "I think I might have been wrong about you," Jaclyn informed.

"Oh?"

"Yeah. You're not a bitch after all."

"Unlike you, you mean?"

Jaclyn gasped dramatically and laughed. *"Touche."*

"Of course, I'm just teasing," Layla said, the corner of her mouth twisting into a coy grin. Come on," she said, gesturing for Jackie to follow her into the restaurant. I'll buy you a burger and a shake."

"Now you're talking my language," Jaclyn replied, following Layla into the refurbished and revitalized Mel's Diner.

It felt weird to her to be back here, of all places. But, at the same time, she had divorced that memory from her mind. When the Red Rage consumed her, she receded into her subconscious and hid there until it was over. So, although she knew she was the cause of the Mel's Diner massacre, it never felt like she was the one who had done it.

This is why she was able to fool everyone around her. She wasn't feigning ignorance when she said that someone else had done this because someone else had. The Hyde to her Doctor

Jekyll, so to speak.

Resting her elbows on the table and her chin on her palms, Jaclyn looked over at Special Agent Layla Harker, who sat directly across from her, and said, "So, Harker, can you tell me a bit about yourself?"

"What would you like to know?" asked Layla.

Jaclyn's grin widened as she replied, "Everything."

114

9

THE VAMPIRE KING'S REQUIEM

HOT PINK RAYS BURST through Darius's bedroom window. He reached up to block the sting of the daylight with his hand and glanced over at his alarm clock. He was late. It was already 7:15 AM, and he was supposed to leave for class in five minutes.

Throwing off his covers, he flew out of bed and quickly got dressed. Running down the stairs, he flew past his mom, who was doing a crossword puzzle at the kitchen table. Darius darted out the door without pausing long enough to hear his mom was yelling at him. All he cared about was getting to class on time.

With everything that had been happening lately, he'd skipped too many classes. He was already falling behind in his finance class and didn't want to have to take a W. Everyone would be disappointed in him if he dropped out of school. He was the first Reid to attend college. He couldn't let them down.

Luckily for him, the new bicycle wheels he'd ordered arrived last night, and he'd already swapped out the old, busted-up ones. Hopping on his bike, he pedaled furiously as he raced to school. He took the long way around today and avoided the police station at all costs.

He wouldn't know what to do if he were ever to meet Detective Jaclyn Benoit again. He imagined it wouldn't be very pleasant or all that legal, for that matter.

Fifteen and a half minutes later, he skidded to a stop in front of Wood River Community College about four and a half minutes ahead of schedule. Usually, a bike ride like that would have winded him, but today, he didn't feel the least bit fatigued. He felt fucking invincible.

Darius parked his bike at the bike rack and walked towards the school's main entrance. Before he could even make it a few steps, he was hit by a sudden and intense spell of vertigo. He felt as if the world was spinning around him, and he stumbled to the side.

Luckily, he braced himself against a support pillar that held up the overhanging eaves of the roof and tried to steady himself. His vision blurred in and out, and he rubbed his temples, trying to stop the spinning. Soon enough, other students began to gather around him, asking if he was okay.

He stumbled forward and managed to reach the front doors. His vision started to turn red, and a feeling of extreme hunger overtook him. Darius tried to steady himself and took a few more steps into the lobby, but had to stop in the middle of the room to avoid falling. Both vertigo and hunger pangs made him clutch his stomach and double over in pain.

He sank to his knees so as not to do a face-plant in the

middle of the school in front of everyone. The sudden urge to drink blood became overwhelming, overpowering all his other senses. The instinct to feed was irresistible, and it felt as though if he didn't satisfy his animalistic impulses, his insides would twist and turn like writhing worms inside his gut, and he would surely die.

A cute black girl with platinum-frosted cornrows walked up to him, reached out a delicate hand, and touched his shoulder. "Darius? It's me, Sondra. I'm in your finance class. Are you okay? You don't look well."

Darius looked up at her, and she gasped, covering her mouth to silence herself. Drawing back from Darius, she began to tremble with fear.

His ears fixated on her heartbeat, and he could hear her pulse change with the shock of fear. What was a slow thump, steady like the beating drum, became a pitter-patter of exasperated beats that pumped so furiously inside her chest he swore her heart might explode.

Before her eyes, he felt his fangs grow, a red veil of blood washed over his eyes, and his fingernails extended three inches, turning into black-talon-like claws. He knew how terrifying it must be for her because when he first saw it happen with Jaclyn Benoit, it had terrified him, too.

"Well, I guess the secret is out," he said. Just then, he was struck by an intense hunger pang. It felt like he had been thirsty his entire life. His mouth was parched, and his lips were dry. He felt as though he had been lost in the scorching desert heat for decades and was dying of thirst.

But it wasn't water that his body craved. It was the elixir of life itself, blood. Sondra looked down to find Darius's arm buried into her torso up to his elbow, her bowels spilling out of her gut.

"What the actual fuck–" she mouthed, her voice barely rising to a whisper.

Darius had punched clean through her body, his bloody fist protruding out of her backside. She looked up at him, tears welling up in her eyes, and when she was about to scream out for help, he smothered her mouth with his free hand.

"Shhh," he hushed, pulling his hand out of her abdomen with a wet-sounding *schlock.* Other students who witnessed this spectacle felt the terror sink in and began to panic. But Darius wasn't concerned. Nobody here would be making it out alive today.

Reaching up, Darius grabbed Sondra by her face and twisted her head so violently that her neck snapped. She crumbled to the ground, and Darius leaped over her bloody corpse.

Flying across the room, he pounced onto a large man wearing a San Francisco 49ers football jersey and bit into his trapezius. The man yelped like a wounded dog before crashing to the floor with Darius clinging to his back. Although the guy was twice Darius's size, none of his thrashing around seemed to do any good. His vampire strength was far superior, and he held the man pinned to the floor as he tore a stringy chunk of flesh from his neck.

Darius slowly rose with pieces of meat hanging from his mouth like raw, shredded beef. This elicited more screams and panic, and suddenly, pandemonium broke out all over the first floor.

Moving so fast that his motions practically blurred, Darius tore off a blonde girl's right arm, sliced a black-haired girl's throat clean open, then pounced onto a fat red-headed kid, ripped open his stomach, pulled out his entrails, and tossed them to the floor with a sloppy wet slosh.

Pools of blood began to mingle as the death toll grew and grew. Thick, sticky blood dripped from Darius's hands as he scanned the remaining faces. All of them looked terrified, and all were desperately wanting to be somewhere else. The screaming continued as Darius's face grew thick with large chunks of red gore, blood, and guts staining his mouth and chin like strawberry jam.

Standing over his latest kill, a malicious grin slowly formed on his mouth. He licked the blood from his glossy white fangs and sighed with a deep-felt satisfaction. He was actually having fun.

A chubby girl at the other end of the hall let out a shriek, and he charged toward her, chasing after her and five other college kids who had decided to try to make a break for it.

As he came up behind them, he slashed his claws and tore into their flesh. Men, women, young and old, black or white, it didn't matter. All were fair game.

Red painted the walls as Darius continued his blood-fueled rampage. Carving a path of carnage through the hallway, he finally came to the main lecture hall and kicked the doors wide open. This solicited screams from a couple of Asian girls sitting at their desks and their teacher, Miss Anderson.

Upon seeing Darius standing in the doorway, covered in more blood than Carry on her Prom night, the two Asian girls leaped up and made a B-line straight for the side exit. A blonde kid on the other side of the class ran out the back, but Darius ignored their departure and fixed his sights on Miss Anderson. She was in her early forties and rocked the librarian-MILF-vibe pretty hard.

She had dark curly hair, thick-framed forest green

eyeglasses, and was slender but with a secret white girl full caboose in the back. He leaped into the air, landing on top of her desk, and smiled down at her.

Sliding back in her chair, she kicked hard and rolled backward, slamming up against the back wall. Miss Anderson glanced left and then right but realized that the moment she made any attempt to move, he'd instantly be on top of her. Looking up at him, she whispered, "What are you?"

"I'm whatever you want me to be," Darius replied, shooting her a bloody smile. "But I know what you are."

She made the sign of the cross and gulped hard. Darius reached out his hand for her to take. This initially confused her, but she hesitantly extended her hand and gently placed it in his. He drew her into him, and she chirped out of fright as he hoisted her onto the desk. But she didn't try to escape.

Together, they stood on the desktop, Darius wrapping his arms around her waist as if he were a lover. He drew her close, and she chirped with fear but didn't resist. He gently grabbed her head and tilted it to the side, forcing her to reveal her neck to him. Brushing her hair aside, he bent down and sank his fangs into Anderson's carotid artery. She moaned in agony as he tapped her like a maple tree, but she didn't dare resist him.

Halfway through draining her, he pulled out and looked at her, her blood staining his lips and chin. "You taste better than the rest."

Why is that, he wondered. Perhaps different blood types were like different flavors to a vampire. Possibly, vampires had a preference for other blood types. He was new to the game, so he couldn't be sure. But it was as good an explanation as he could come up with.

"A-are you going to kill me?" she asked, silent tears trickling down her cheeks.

"Probably. Yes," he answered. "Is that a bad thing?"

"I don't want to die," she replied.

Slowly, he took her three-tone brown layered shirt in his hands and then ripped her garments wide open. Her breasts were exposed, and she didn't try to fight or resist him, knowing that she would tempt his wrath.

Darius licked his fangs as he eyed her wantonly. Her taste was so intoxicating that he had to drink her in, but he needed to take his time. If he drank her too fast, then he'd be left wanting. Slowly, he reached forward, taking a supple breast in his hand, and gently squeezed. She let out a light, almost pleasurable moan.

He could smell her pheromones, her scent thick with lust, as he leaned down and slowly sank his teeth into her right bosom, drawing blood. This elicited another pleasurable chirp when a side entrance door to the lecture room burst open, and a security guard appeared in the doorway, gun drawn. "Step back and put your hands above your head," he ordered.

Darius pulled out, and Anderson let out an orgasmic-sounding moan. Brushing the trickle of blood away from her breast with his hand, he slowly turned toward the entrance and faced the guard. A crooked grin spread across his lips, and without looking at her, maintaining his gaze with the guard, he said to her, "Run."

She looked at him to be sure he was talking to her, and when it was clear to her that he was giving her an out, she quickly covered her chest, then turned and ran as fast as she could toward the back exit.

"Now, get down on your knees, hands where I can see them," the guard said. "I don't want to hurt you, kid."

Darius could hear the trembling in his speech and smiled. "Oh, believe me, friend. You can't hurt me, even if you tried."

The guard took a cautious step forward, holding his gun steady and maintaining a solid lock on the perpetrator. "I said get down," he reiterated.

Darius hopped down from the desk, unafraid, and looked back up at the guard with his black eyes.

"I warned you, you freak," the guard said, slowly squeezing down on the trigger.

In the blink of an eye, Darius had practically teleported himself across the room and stood directly in front of the security guard. The man gasped in fright and squeezed down on the trigger. Before the shot could ring out, Darius reached up with lightning speed and caught the slide of the gun, preventing it from going off in his chest.

The guard looked down at his gun in shock as Darius effortlessly ripped the weapon out of his grasp. Darius had crumpled the gun in his hands, showing his immense strength, and tossed the pieces to the ground. It caused a metallic sound as it skidded across the floor.

With vitriol dripping from every word, Darius dusted off his hands and asked, "Now, where were we?"

Drawing out a bottle of pepper spray, the guard maced Darius right in his eyes.

"*GRAAAH!*" screamed Darius, his eyes on fire. He rubbed them with his hands, but the burning only got worse. "*What the fuck, man?!*"

It was the first time he'd felt any pain since his transformation. The burning sensation reminded him that he wasn't invincible.

Keeping his eyes closed, Darius focused on the man's

heartbeat. In the blackness, Darius could visualize a circulatory system. All the veins and blood vessels appeared in blue, mingled with red. With his super sense of smell and keen hearing, he could see the man's vascular system pulsating in full color.

Cool, he thought. He wasn't expecting superpowers to come with his newfound gifts. For what else would he call them? He was faster than any athlete and more powerful than any bodybuilder, and his senses of sight, smell, and hearing were vastly improved. Perhaps being a vampire wasn't so bad after all?

And the sex. God. The sex was good. Women's panties were practically falling at his feet. Before he'd been changed, no woman would pay him the time of day. After being made a vampire, though, even his victims, like Miss Anderson, had this basic instinct to be with him on a more carnal level.

When Darius regained his focus, the guard had reached the rear exit. No longer distracted, he raced up the stairs, chasing after his victim. The guard looked over his shoulder and screamed out in terror as the black figure bore down on him.

Darius wasn't polite about it either. The mother-fucker had maced him. So, Darius began by jamming his thumbs in the guard's eye sockets. As Darius forced his thumbs into the man's skull, his eyeballs popped like juicy grapes, prompting him to let out an even louder scream.

The guard staggered back, hitting the exit door, and fell. As he pushed himself back up, he looked at Darius, the jelly in his eye sockets dripping out and down his cheeks in coagulated chunks.

Playing with his food, Darius let the blind guard fumble about the hallway, bumping into walls, lounge sofas, and a few support pillars. Although daylight flooded through the windows, the man might as well have been fumbling in the dark.

Tripping over a dead body, the guard crashed to the floor and smacked his head. He groaned and tried to get up, but his hand slipped in a puddle of blood, and his face planted onto the hard marble floor a second time.

Rolling onto his back, the guard shouted, "Where are you?" He drew out his mace again and started spraying wildly in every direction. After spending the entire cartridge, he tossed the container and rolled away before the toxic dust could settle onto him.

Pushing through the sludge of blood and body parts, he flopped over and began crawling away, feeling his way out by patting the ground in front of him.

Darius casually strode up to the man, reached down, and clasped onto a full head of hair without stopping. Dragging the man by his head, Darius pulled him over to the front entrance and then hoisted him to his feet.

"W-wait! What are you going to do?"

Darius didn't. Instead, he shoved the man so hard that the guard flew through the first plate of glass at the entrance and through the foyer glass. He crashed to the ground hard outside the main entrance and moaned in pain. Sitting up with a groan, shards of glass peppering his skin, the guard tried to stand but lost his balance and fell. He hit his shoulder and rolled onto his back.

Determined not to die, he forced himself to his feet with a grunt, and fueled by pure adrenaline, he limped away, clutching his left arm, which felt dislocated from where he landed on his shoulder.

In the distance, he heard sirens. Somebody had called 911. From where he stood, Darius scanned the entire campus and watched Miss Anderson step out of a phone booth on the opposite side of the campus grounds.

Darius merely raised a single finger to his lips and hushed her. *"Shhhh."*

She nodded and sank to her knees. While it was clear she was relieved to be spared by him, at the same time, she couldn't stop trembling. Darius watched her clasp her hands together as she tried to stop herself from shaking, but it was no use. The fear she felt was palpable. Darius's eyes locked onto hers, and as she trembled, cowering before him, her pants grew wet.

Darius pulled up his hoodie and glanced at the security guard, who was pacing in the courtyard. Before the cavalry arrived, he approached the guard with a twisted grin and reached out to grab him. His vampire claws grew into long, razor-blade-like talons, and a twisted, fanged grin spread across his face.

126

FLUORESCENT LIGHTS BUZZED OVERHEAD as Jaclyn leaned back in her office chair, feet up on her desk, staring at the text that had just come through on her phone. It had been a whole week since the funeral, and Maddie hadn't reached out to her once. But now, here she was, asking to meet.

It was a big enough surprise to her that she swung her legs off her desk and planted them on the floor. Leaning forward, she rested her elbows on her knees and tried to guess the meaning behind the text.

Maddie wanted Jackie to come over for dinner. She felt awkward being invited to the house of the man she'd eaten, and the woman whom she'd also eaten, but in an entirely different context.

She felt overwhelmed by the raw emotions swirling in her

head. Sometimes, she wished that human emotions wouldn't be so draining. Ironic, she mused, this thought coming from a fucking vampire.

"What is it?" Layla asked, looking up from her laptop in time to catch the worried look on Jaclyn's face. Very rarely did anything upset Jaclyn Benoit, but whatever she looked at on her phone made her skin bristle.

"I'm not sure yet. Maddie wants me to come over."

Layla leaned back in her chair. "Isn't that a good thing?"

"One would hope," Jaclyn said, not sounding confident.

"I'm afraid I'm not the best at giving advice," Layla informed. "With that in mind, I would just ask her. The best policy among couples, I say, is honesty.

"Uh-huh," Jaclyn said dryly. "Anyway, I appreciate the moral support. I get too caught up in my head about what it could mean."

"Don't we all?" Layla replied, sighing as she reflected on her last failed relationship. "My last relationship blew up when I found out my girlfriend was seeing her ex-husband behind my back. Or so I thought. As it turned out, I had misread some old texts from their marriage and jumped to conclusions. It said a whole lot more about my insecurities than it did hers."

"Ouch," Jackie said, sympathizing with Layla. "That must have been rough."

Layla sighed. "Yeah. You'd best reply to that woman before she thinks you've lost interest."

"I will, I will," Jackie said, throwing her hands up defensively. Jaclyn grabbed her jacket and scrambled back in her chair, the wooden legs chirping on the smooth floor. "Wish me luck."

"Good luck," Layla said. She smiled at Jackie, prompting a

subtle yet noticeably nervous grin.

Jackie slipped on her jacket and waved goodbye over her shoulder as she left Layla at the station.

The drive to Maddie's house was short—she lived only ten minutes away. Jaclyn didn't know what to expect as she exited her car and approached Maddie's front door, but her stomach fluttered. She was still head over heels for Maddie and prayed to God for Maddie to still feel the same way about her.

Before she could even reach out and push the doorbell, the door swung inward, and Maddie manifested in the doorway. There was a brief pause, and then Maddie practically threw herself at Jackie, latching onto her like a koala bear, arms and legs curled around her, nothing touching the ground.

Jackie walked Maddie inside and set her feet first on the ornate Persian rug decorating her entrance. When Maddie looked up, she burst into tears. "I'm so sorry, Jackie. I was just so angry. I'm so angry at everything and everyone. I wanted the whole fucking world to burn for it taking Michael away from me."

"I know," Jackie said, taking Maddie's hands in hers and drawing her close. "I know."

Maddie pulled back and looked Jackie straight in the eyes. "But you didn't kill him," she insisted. "Some psycho killer who's seen one too many slasher films did. And I hate that I took it all out on you. That was a shitty thing for me to do. Can you ever forgive me, Jackie?"

Jaclyn laughed. "Of course, I forgive you, Maddie. I love you. I love you more than life itself. I just wanted to give you the time you needed to grieve. To heal."

"I'm still in the thick of it, I'm afraid," she replied, taking Jaclyn's hand in hers and drawing her inside, letting the front door latch behind them. "But I'd rather be fucking miserable with my best friend by my side than wallow alone in my misery."

Jaclyn smiled but didn't say anything. There was no psycho killer on the loose. Just her and her fucking bloodlust. But Maddie could never, ever find out about Michaelson's actual murder. If she found out it was Jackie, everything they'd worked so hard to build would be snuffed out instantly, like a candle in the wind.

As Maddie led her up the stairs, Jaclyn pulled back. "What's going on, Maddie?"

"I want you to fuck me like you did that night."

Jaclyn stood midway up the stairs, looking at Maddie with sad eyes. "I don't think that will help things."

"It will help me feel good. Even if it's just for a few fleeting seconds."

"I want to, Maddie. God knows I do. But you're..." Jaclyn trailed off as she searched for the gentlest way to put it.

"But I'm a hot mess right now? I know."

"As long as you're aware," Jackie laughed. Maddie laughed, too. "Maddie," Jaclyn said, reaching up and touching her face. "I will never say no to you."

"I just want you," Maddie replied. "I want you in my arms. I want you to—"

Jaclyn's phone began ringing. She swiped it off without looking. "Sorry about that. You were saying?"

Before Maddie could speak up, Jaclyn's phone began ringing again. Again, Jaclyn hung up without giving it a second thought. Right now, Maddie was what was most important to her.

"I think we—" Jaclyn was cut off by a third attempt to call her, and she begrudgingly answered.

"What?!" she snapped. But the anger that had boiled to the

surface quickly dissipated. "Slow down, Harker; I can barely catch what you're saying."

"Jackie," Layla's voice came over the line, distressed. There was an urgency to her words. "You need to turn on the TV."

Holding the phone to her ear, Jackie looked over at Maddie, who stared back at her. "The TV?" Jackie asked. "What channel?"

"Any channel," Layla replied.

Maddie motioned for Jackie to follow her into the primary bedroom. Once there, she fetched the remote from the bed stand and turned on the television. Wood River Central College popped onto the screen, and both women stood and watched in shock at what they saw next. The entire campus was surrounded by fire trucks, ambulances, and at least seven or eight squad cars.

"Fifteen people dead, Jackie," Layla said over the phone. Her voice was shaken but not defeated. She was going to tackle this head-on. "It was a massacre."

"I'll meet you there," Jaclyn said. She then hung up and turned to look at Maddie. "I'm sorry, but I've gotta—"

"Go save the world? Yeah. I was married to a cop for eighteen years, remember? I know the drill."

"I'll come back here when I can step away. I promise."

"I'll be waiting," Maddie replied. She felt as though she'd burst into tears at any moment. But, to her pleasant surprise, Jackie reeled her in and kissed her.

It was almost impossible to tear herself away. Finally, Jackie pulled back and looked Maddie in the eyes. "I'll always come back to you."

They let the moment linger for as long as they could, and then, once it seemed like they might never part ways again, Jaclyn spun around, dashed down the stairs, and out the front door.

Maddie slowly descended the stairs and watched as Jackie slid across the hood of her Challenger and then got inside. She waved goodbye as the car peeled out, kicking up smoke as it burned rubber.

"Be safe," Maddie whispered. Then she shut the door and locked it.

Special Agent Layla Harker arrived on the scene long before Jaclyn. Flashing her U.S. Marshal's badge, the police officer at the safety barrier raised the yellow tape for her, and she ducked under the police line and crossed into the active crime scene.

She walked across the campus and then passed two additional officers stationed at the front doors as if they were a couple of sentries. The foray was smashed to bits, and broken shards of glass lay everywhere. She looked up to her right and saw a firefighter on a firetruck ladder pulling a man's body off the flagpole. She squinted and looked more closely to confirm what she had seen. The man's eyes were missing. Only two gaping bloody sockets where eyes should have been.

Entering the college, the grisliest crime scene Layla had ever encountered greeted her. And that's saying a lot because she'd seen skinned bodies placed on pikes outside Kandahar when she went in with the Marines to retrieve an asset. She'd even seen the aftermath of a suicide bomber more than once, but this...this was on a whole new level.

Blood dripped from the walls and ceiling. The floor glistened like a crimson lake at sunset. Students' bodies lay scattered about in disarray, most of them disemboweled and or dismembered. Several didn't even have heads. This wasn't a serial killer who did this. She knew the work of an actual fucking monster when she saw it.

"Jesus H. Christ," a voice from behind her said.

Layla glanced back to see Jackie standing over her shoulder. "I'm afraid Jesus had nothing to do with this, Detective Benoit."

"I think I'm going to be sick," Jackie said, placing her hand on her stomach. And she wasn't lying. It took a lot to make her feel wheezy, but this did the trick. Meanwhile, Layla seemed as cool as a cucumber.

This doesn't resemble any serial killer's modus operandi that I've ever seen. This looks like a statement. It looks like a bear tore through here, mauling with abandon. But there aren't bears out here, are there?"

"In the Midwest?" Jacke answered, "Not so much."

"So other than a fucking bomb going off, what on God's green Earth do you think caused all this?" Layla gestured to the gore coating the floors, walls, and ceiling.

"Maybe the Cartel is trying to send a message?"

"By killing random college kids? No, I don't think this is the Cartel's work. If they were behind Danielle Pruette's death, that was a one-and-done. This is something different. Something much more sinister."

"I'm not arguing with that," Jackie said, pushing her jacket back as she rested her hands on her hips. "But I don't get it. Why hack everyone up like you're in a 1980s slasher film and disappear?"

"It's not a slasher film. It's a vampire film," Layla added, reaching for any hypothesis that made any sense.

"What did you say?" Jackie's eyes fixed on Layla with an intensity she hadn't exhibited since the Darius interrogation.

What did Layla know about vampires? Had she encountered them before, or was she throwing out wild theories?

"You know, old vampire films. Blood. Gore. That sort of thing."

"Most vampire films are about sex," Jackie corrected.

"I'll take your word for it. I haven't watched that many horror films. Life is horrific enough. I just thought, blood plus monsters equals vampires."

"Vampires aren't real, though," Jackie said skeptically, still staring at Layla with a bemused smirk on her face. She found Layla's way of thinking cute.

Layla smiled at her. "That we know of."

With a shrug, Jackie laughed out loud and turned back toward the crime scene. If Layla felt it was vampires, then so be it. Who was Jackie to gaslight her? That would only raise her suspicions. If there was anything Jackie knew about Layla, it was that she was as sharp as a tack.

"What did Maddie want?" Layla asked, butting into Jackie's business.

"Aren't we curious?" Jackie said, her eyes meeting Layla's.

"I'm sorry, I'm being intrusive again."

"No, it's okay. You're my partner now, and I need to get used to being more open with you. I'm just a little nervous because you're so fucking intimidating."

"Me?" Layla laughed. "You're the one who's intimidating."

"Shut up," Jackie quipped, her cheeks blushing. "You're so accomplished that you've won awards. All I've managed to do is watch bodies pile up all around my town. It has been a week since Michaelson's funeral, and all I've managed to fucking turn up is zip, zero, zilch, nada."

"Don't blame yourself, Jackie," Layla consoled. "Whatever

we're facing, it's not your stereotypical mass murderer. We're facing something much more dangerous."

"You're still thinking it's a vampire, right?"

"It's most definitely a vampire," she said, slipping on a couple of light blue latex gloves that she had drawn from her inner jacket pocket. Crouching down, she brushed a black girl's braided hair back and gestured with her hand at a couple of bite marks on her neck. "See? Bite marks."

"I see needle marks. Kids in college experiment with crazy shit all the time," Jacklyn said. "Sex. Drugs. All the rest of it. You know how it is?"

"Are you trying to tell me that these don't look like bite marks to you?"

"No, I mean, they're too narrow. Aren't they? I've seen bite marks on plenty of my fellow officers as they brought in meth heads. A bunch of biters, that lot. But it never looked like that."

"We will be sure to check every possibility off the list as we consider it. But I have a gut feeling that we will end up right back here with the theory that best fits the facts."

"Vampires?"

"You guessed it. Vampires." Layla pointed her blue-gloved finger at Jacie as if she were aiming an imaginary gun.

"I'm sorry, Layla, but I'm having a hard time accepting that you, of all people, believe vampires walk amongst us."

"Are you a fan of Sherlock Holmes?"

"Sherlock Holmes?" asked Jackie, growing even more perplexed.

It was clear to Jackie that Layla's mind worked differently. When you reached the first-mile marker, she was already a hundred miles down the road. She could see links between seemingly unrelated events. Her mind spun through the

Rolodex of possibilities faster than most people could form coherent thoughts.

This made Jackie extremely nervous. The fact that Layla's gut instinct was spot on downright scared her. Jackie decided to back off, lest she appear to be protesting too much.

"Once you eliminate the impossible, whatever remains, no matter how improbable, must be the truth," Layla informed, quoting Sherlock Holmes from memory.

"Ah, yes. The detective's adage. I'm familiar with it. Still, vampires are rather far-fetched if you ask me."

"I guess time will tell," Layla said, still squatting beside the body.

Jackie glanced down and caught a glimpse of Layla's purple thong again. When she met Layla's gaze, she found her staring right back at her, a coy grin already on her lips.

"I like your underwear," Jackie said. I love that color. Where did you get them?"

"Victoria's Secret," Layla answered without hesitating. Layla slowly stood up, not bothering to pull up her pants so that the strings of her thong continued to show—a little tease to mess with Jackie.

Layla couldn't put her finger on it, but something about Jackie felt dangerous. But that excited her.

"Nice dodge, by the way," she said, laughing at Jackie's embarrassment.

"Fine," Jackie said, raising her hands in mock surrender. "You caught me. I was checking you out."

"So, what did Maddie want?" Layla asked again, reminding her of the other woman in her life. She knew she was still prying into Jackie's business, but she was still trying to figure this woman out. The more she could learn about her and those she held dear, the better a read she could get on her.

"Guilty conscience, I guess. She gave me her apology, which I appreciated." Jackie sighed and looked down at the ground, trying to ignore the red puddles everywhere.

"That's a start toward mending fences. Or heartstrings, whichever you prefer."

"Yeah."

"So, are you going back to see her after this?"

"I want to, but I don't know if it's such a good idea."

"Why is that?"

"Because I have fucking issues. I was checking out your ass a couple seconds ago. How can I show up on Maddie's doorstep and give her what she wants when I don't even know what I want myself?"

"Yeah. It sounds like you have a lot on your plate. My advice? Be with your girlfriend. Because I sure as hell ain't sleeping with you." Layla smiled at Jackie one last time and then stood up, walking over to the entrance of the main lecture hall.

An officer was consoling a woman who had a police jacket draped over her shoulders to help keep her warm and conceal the damage done to her clothes.

"I understand you were an eyewitness to these horrific events. Is that correct?"

"Y-yes," she said, holding her arms, one cradling the other.

Jackie stood behind Layla and let her do all the talking.

"Can you tell us anything about the perpetrator?"

"I'll do my best."

Jackie stepped forward and addressed the woman. "I know this will be difficult, Miss...?"

"Anderson," the woman replied. "Stacy Anderson."

"All right, Stacy. This is going to be difficult, I'm sure. But I was hoping you could reflect on your attacker's face. Can you tell us what he looked like?"

"He was a black kid. Maybe early twenties. Wore a green hoodie and brown jeans."

Shit, Jackie thought. Please don't be Darius Reid. If it turned out to be him, she was in a world of hurt. After all, she fucking made him. And if Darius did all this, he was out of control, and she'd be forced to put him down.

"Is there anything else you can remember?" Layla asked Stacy, who was still in shock from it all. "Any detail, no matter how small, could help us catch this guy."

"Yeah. He had fangs. You, know, like a–"

"Vampire?" Layla asked, glancing over at Jackie, who responded with an epic eye-roll.

"I don't know how else to put it, detective."

"Actually, I'm a Special Agent with the Marshals Service. She's the detective." As she gestured toward Jackie, another officer in blue came up and handed her an iPad. She looked down at it and raised an eyebrow.

"Security footage caught our perpetrator, but I'm afraid it's of no use," the officer informed them. "There's too much distortion."

Jackie leaned over and looked at the image caught by the security feed. All it showed was a motion blur in the vague shape of a human—a human moving at inhuman speeds.

"Thank you, officer," Layla said, handing the iPad back to him. As he returned to his duties of taking the evidence back to the station to be logged, Layla turned her attention back to Miss Anderson.

"Stacy, would you be willing to come to the station later and describe your attacker to one of our sketch artists?"

"Sure. I'd be glad to. I mean...yes. Anything I can do to help."

"You're appreciated," Layla said, taking Anderson's hands in hers and giving them a comforting squeeze.

Layla turned and walked back outside and took a deep breath of fresh air.

"What is it?" Jackie inquired, noticing that Layla was rattled.

"Nothing I can't handle," she said. After a pause, she added, "I don't drink often. But if there were any reason to get smashed out of my mind, this would be at the top of the list."

"Are you inviting me to drinks?" Jackie asked, folding her arms across her chest, a slight grin forming on her lips. Honestly, getting her drink on with Layla was rather enticing.

"I mean, don't you have that thing with Maddie?"

"I suppose I do, yes." She looked back at the crime scene and watched as her fellow officers made way for a team of white suits with gurneys and body bags.

"Don't worry about me, Jackie. I'll be fine. Besides, the forensics team just arrived, so there won't be much to learn until they've finished going over everything with a fine-tooth comb. You go and console your girlfriend. She's been through hell and back again, and I'm sure she could use your company."

Jackie nodded, agreeing with Layla's assessment of things. She glanced back once to find Layla Harker talking to a medic. After Jackie had turned to leave the building, Layla glanced over her shoulder, too, and found herself checking out Jackie in return.

In Layla's opinion, Jackie was one of those people who was too beautiful to be a cop. She could have just as easily been a supermodel. Not that she was complaining. Having a gorgeous partner was always a nice distraction. But she knew she had to tread cautiously with Jackie. She had a girlfriend, and from everything else she could gather, there was a lot of mystery surrounding her relationship with her ex-now-deceased partner.

Using the spare key that Madeline Michaelson had given her a few months back for such an occasion, Jaclyn let herself inside Maddie's home and then shut the door behind her.

Slipping off her shoes, she tiptoed up the stairs and quietly padded down the hall to the main bedroom. She gently twisted the doorknob, doing her best not to let it squeak, and then slowly opened the door. Peeking inside, she found Maddie fast asleep on the covers with the TV still on.

Jaclyn turned off the television and set her shoes at the foot of the king-sized bed. Then, as stealthily as a leopard crossing a mossy branch in the jungle, she crawled onto the bed. Lying beside Maddie, she edged up to her and settled into the big spoon position, wrapping her arms around Maddie's waist.

She pressed her face against Maddie's neck and took a deep breath, inhaling her scent. She smelled like sandalwood and cherry blossoms—a distinct mixture of her husband's shampoo and her conditioner.

Jaclyn felt her fangs starting to grow, and she forced herself not to think about anything other than how madly in love she was with this woman.

"I'm sorry," she whispered. "I'm sorry for everything."

"Hmmm?" Maddie murmured, briefly rousing from her slumber. Her eyes opened just a crack, and she smiled when she saw Jaclyn's face.

"Nothing," Jaclyn said. "I'm home now."

Maddie rolled over and held Jaclyn tight. She gave her a quick peck on the lips and then drifted back to sleep.

Jaclyn pulled her lover close and touched Maddie's forehead with her own. Then, taking in one final whiff of Maddie's scent, she drifted off to sleep.

142

11

THINE OWN SELF BE TRUE

COVERED IN BLOOD, DARIUS returned to the bowling alley where Velma and the Slayers greeted him. West Side Lanes had become their base of operations, but business had all but died out due to the horrific event that had transpired at Wood River Community College.

Wood River was no longer safe, and most people had decided to stay home instead of going out to restaurants or bowling alleys. Passing through the town, one would be forgiven for thinking it was a ghost town. It felt empty. Dead. And Darius, by some miraculous means, was able to walk through town and return to the bowling alley without being detected.

When he arrived, Velma and the slayers were waiting for him. Darius strode up to Velma, reached around her waist, and drew her close for a kiss. Before he could kiss her, though, she raised a finger, blocking his lips.

"What is it?" he asked. "What's the matter?"

"There were a couple of detectives here earlier snooping about."

"Did they give you any trouble?"

"No, my love," Velma replied. "They just poked around the parking lot for a while."

Darius smiled. "It's probably nothing. They're just investigating Danielle's murder."

"Who?" Velma asked.

"Danielle Pruette," he said, looking at her but not finding any trace of recognition on her face.

Velma shrugged. "I'm sorry, babe. But I don't know who that is."

"You know," he said, his tone growing defensive. The woman who worked with me here. The one who died."

Velma's eyes lit up. "Oh, yeah. I heard about her. She wasn't..."

"Wasn't what?"

"Wasn't she one of your kills?"

Darius shoved Velma aside. "No," he growled, upset that she'd even suggest such a thing. He stormed past her and into the bowling alley, leaving all three girls looking confused at the entrance.

Velma looked at the other girls with a perplexed look but merely received a couple of shrugs. They didn't know any more than she did. Velma let out a sigh and then turned and followed Darius inside.

"Hey, babe," she asked, catching up to him, "why are you covered in blood?"

Darius paused and looked down at himself. His head had finally cleared up, and he wasn't feeling as savage as earlier. The monster was going back into hibernation. But she was right. His clothes were soaked through and through with the blood of the Wood River Community College victims.

"Fuck," he said. "My mom is going to throw a fit when she finds out I ruined another set of clothes."

"Your mom doesn't need to find out," Velma said, slowly lifting his hood and pulling it over his arms as she undressed him. Once she'd freed him from the first few layers, her slender fingers began working his belt buckle. Soon enough, Darius found himself standing naked in front of all three women.

Velma licked her fangs and, snapping her fingers to get everyone's attention, addressed the rest of the Slayers. "Ladies, humble yourselves before your Master."

All three women got on their knees and looked up to the ceiling. Darius stood over them and held out his wrist. They slowly opened their mouths, their long, slender fangs protruding. Darius slit open his wrist with a sharp thumb claw, and a deep burgundy liquid began to pour out of him and drizzle into their mouths.

Bathing in his blood, they drank and began to rub their hands sensually across their bodies. Velma even reached into her pants and began pleasuring herself, blood dribbling down her face and neck.

As the Slayers drank, the memories of the victims flashed before their eyes. Every kill of Darius's was a kill of theirs. He was their Master, and they would do anything for him. They would even die for him. Losing control, Amber, the redhead, clasped onto Darius's arm and began sucking directly from his wrist.

"No!" he yelled and slapped her so hard across the face that she slid halfway across the room.

The blonde girl, Sophie, lowered her gaze and scooted back, showing subservience to Darius, their Master.

Velma quickly stood up and bowed like a servant would. "Apologies, my lord. She'll be disciplined."

Darius looked at Amber, his black eyes locking onto her green ones. "Don't worry about her punishment," he said as though it wasn't a big deal. "Consider it a warning. But overstep your bounds again, my pet, and I won't hesitate to tear the pretty little head from your shoulders and drink from the fountain of your neck."

"Yes, milord," Amer said, prostrating and lying flat on the ground.

She licked spilled drops of his blood right off the floor, which caused Velma to turn around in disgust. "For Christ's sake, Amber," Velma said. "Get a hold of yourself."

Darius walked up to Amber, reached down, and clutched a handful of her red hair in his hand. Drawing her face upward, she slowly rose to her knees. When she tried to stand, he held her down at knee level. Looking down at her, he smiled.

Catching on to his meaning, she smiled back up at him. His dark eyes peered deep into her soul, and the fire she felt in her loins drove her mad with desire. She knew she had to have him, and she had to have him now.

She couldn't wait to taste his lips on hers, but first, she did what any suitable vampire consort would do—she attended to her Master. Lowering her gaze to his manhood, Amber took him in her hands and opened her mouth wide. Sophie and Velma merely watched with unblushing delectation. Their turn would come soon.

Stacy Ingrid Anderson couldn't stop thinking about her attacker. That young man had seemed so familiar to her. Was he one of her students? What had happened to him? And if he were a vampire, why did he spare her life? She had so many questions that she needed answers to.

Mythology wasn't Miss Anderson's area of expertise. She taught business and finance. Even so, back when she was an undergrad, she learned about various folklore from around the world and how each had its own vampire lore.

She recalled reading about the numerous kinds of Romanian vampires. There were the *moroi*, your standard blood-suckers, and the *pricolici*, a type of vampire that could shapeshift into wolves. This coincided with the Greek *vrykolakas*, which were classical werewolves from which the term vampire originated.

Mesopotamian legend talked of *Lilitu*, the great mother of monsters, who created the vampire race. The Babylonians knew her as *Lilith*. She was the mother of monsters, including the forest god Pan, and the mother of traditional vampires and werewolves.

Lilith's precursor was the demon goddess *Lamashtu*, who feasted on newborn babies. Like Lamashtu, Lilith and her daughters, the Lilu, were said to feast on mothers and their newborn babies, both male and female.

The Romani people believed that female vampires were so sexually active that they would exhaust their human husbands. At the same time, the male vampires could mate with human women and give birth to *dhampirs*, half-breeds who were often in high demand for their ability to seek out and detect vampires.

Most dhampirs were said to have been employed as vampire hunters.

Vampires that weren't simply ancient myths from bygone eras, but existed in the real world, gave Anderson pause. She didn't know what to think. Yet, she had bite marks on her neck and a sudden urge to seek out the vampire who'd bitten her. She didn't know what she'd do if she ever found him. Still, she couldn't help but desire to be in his presence again. Deep down, something primal compelled her to seek him out.

This is how she found herself standing in the West Side Bowling Lanes parking lot. For some inexplicable reason, she was drawn to this place.

Slowly, she opened the door. The parking lot was empty, but she didn't expect the bowling alley to be packed at midday anyway. Although the police and the medics all told her to go home and get some rest, she couldn't rest—not now, not after everything that had happened.

Entering the dark building, she adjusted her eyes to the dim light and noticed a group of young people gathered by the second-to-last lane. They lounged on the bent chairs and conversed while drinking a few beers.

She strolled over to them, clasping her hands together to steady her trembling nerves. She was so scared that it took everything she had not to tremble and quake like a frightened animal.

As she approached, three girls stood up and turned to face her. They looked at her, bearing their fangs to warn her of the danger she was walking into. The group leader, a girl in a plaid skirt and fishnets, a leather jacket, spiked bracelets, and many piercings, including a cute nose stud with a diamond insert, said, "Well, well. What do we have here, ladies?"

A red-headed girl licked her fangs and said, "Maybe lunch has delivered itself?"

The blonde girl of the group walked up to Anderson and slowly circled her. Anderson ignored their posturing as her eyes fixed themselves on the dark face of the young man who'd attacked her earlier on campus. "I knew I'd find you here," she said, her voice quaking with nervousness.

"She smells like cinnamon." Sophie turned toward Darius and asked, "Can I eat her? Please? Pretty please?"

Darius smiled and then waved Anderson to come over. She moved over to him, the three girls hovering over her shoulder and making light hissing noises.

"What are you doing here, Miss Anderson?

"You know this skank?" hissed Velma, the green-eyed monster of envy taking hold of her.

"Manners," Darius said. "And yes. She's my finance instructor at college."

"Honestly," Anderson began, her voice trembling softly. "I don't know why I'm here. I just felt drawn to this place. And now that I know you're here, I realize it was you that I was drawn to."

Darius smiled. "Do you even know my name?"

She looked him up and down. It didn't bother her that he wasn't wearing any clothes. For some reason, his nudity seemed completely normal to her.

Darius stood up and closed the distance between them. "Do you even know who I am?"

"I'm ashamed to admit, I don't recollect your name. Survey courses are always packed with so many fresh faces, most of whom drop out mid-term, that I honestly hadn't given you a second notice. Not until yesterday, that is."

Darius circled Anderson, batting her hair lightly as he walked behind her. "My name is Darius Reid. You'd be wise to remember it."

"Yes," she answered. "I will."

"Again," he said, stepping back in front of her and making eye contact. "Why did you come here?"

"I-I don't know. I felt drawn to you. I want you to..." She slowly got down on her knees, tossed her hair to one side, and, reaching up, tugged on the collar of her shirt. She pulled it down to better expose her neck, but also exposed her breasts in a sexy display for him to see. "I want you to bite me again."

Darius smiled. "All you had to do was ask."

Settling to his knees, he took Anderson in his arms, leaned over her, and sank his teeth into her neck. There was a squelching sound as he suckled on her vitality, the smell of cherry blossoms filled his nostrils, and her taste got his heart racing. Pulling his fangs out, he gasped and said, "You taste so good. I can't explain it, but you're..."

Anderson quickly began undressing, stripping her clothes off as fast as she could. Down to her underwear, she got up and sat on the bench near the bowling ball return. "I want you to bite me here," she said, touching her pelvic region. "And here," she added, touching the tender part of her inner thighs.

Darius smiled and approached her. Getting on his knees, he bent over her midsection and slowly sank his fangs into her waist, near her hip. Anderson let out a deep, sensual sigh. As Darius drank from her, she squirmed and rubbed her hands over her body. Squeezing her breasts, she said, "More. More!"

Velma smacked her tongue against the roof of her mouth in annoyance. "Come on, ladies, let the Master have peace as he plays with his pet here."

Jealous, Velma spun around and stormed off. Sophie and Amber ignored her and drew closer to Darius. He nodded for them to join him, and Sophie bit into the woman's calf. At the same time, Amber took Anderson's arm, raised it over the woman's head, and then buried her face into her pectoral region, biting the tender area where the shoulder connects to the breast.

Stacy Anderson let out another moan, this one bordering on the licentious. All three vampires fed on her, but only until Darius signaled for them to stop. Both Amber and Sophie rose to their feet, dabbing the blood away from the corners of their mouths. Darius stood above Ms. Anderson, who was panting heavily, her body fighting to hold on to life.

Scooping her up in his arms, Darius walked her into the back office and set her down on the old sofa the manager kept for lounging on while getting stoned. They called it the "Old Green Stoner Couch." Biting his wrist, Darius cut his arm open with his fangs and then held it to Anderson's mouth. She resisted at first, but then she began to drink.

Darius infused her with his vampire blood, and her wounds gradually began to mend themselves. Soon, her vitality returned, and she looked up at him. "Why do I feel so sleepy?"

"Because," he said, climbing onto the sofa with her, "you're now bound to me through blood." Darius wrapped his arms around her, and she planted her head on his shoulder. After a few minutes, she fell asleep in his arms, her head resting on his chest as he stroked her hair.

Velma stood out in the parking lot, kicking rocks and cursing under her breath. That's when she heard a diesel engine sputtering to a halt and noticed a combine parked in the cornfield across the road.

A smile crept onto Velma's lips as she watched the old farmer climb out of the combine, take off his straw cowboy hat, and fan himself. Today was sweltering hot, and this gave her an idea.

She crossed the road, entered the corn, and walked toward the old farmer. As she approached, he noticed her and waved both hands to warn her that it wasn't safe. She ignored him and continued walking straight toward him.

"Miss, it's not safe in the cornfield when we're cutting!"

Velma knew little about farming, but she had heard of double cropping, where corn is grown, harvested, and immediately followed by the planting of barley. She assumed that harvesting this early in the season must somehow be related to that.

The farmer gave up warning her and just watched as she approached. Velma didn't even hesitate but walked straight up to him, bared her fangs, and stuck him. The man staggered back, hands reaching out for help that wouldn't come.

"*Ack~*" He gurgled as she clutched his throat tightly with her hand. She sucked his vitality out of him to within an inch of his life, and then, biting into her wrist, she grabbed his face with her other hand and forced open his mouth.

Pouring her blood down his gullet, she made him drink. If Darius could create vampires, then so could she.

The old man lurched away from her, clutching his throat, coughing, and spitting. "W-What in God's name is wrong with you?"

He continued hacking up the blood, and then, like a cool Autumn breeze suddenly dying out, his fit of coughing ceased.

He stood up, looked at her with a confused expression, and then combusted into flame.

He began screaming and ran through the field, flames leaping off his body and threatening to catch the entire cornfield on fire.

"Fucking Hell!" Velma shouted, chasing after the flaming human.

She ran up and shoved him hard, careful not to catch on fire herself. He stumbled forward and then biffed it, crashing to the ground face-first.

Velma started stomping on him, not to put the flames out but to terminate him. She couldn't have anyone find out about her failure. Even as his crispened body was starting to go out, revealing a charcoal-coated human barbeque, she raised her boot high and then brought it down with a resounding *crunch*, flattening his skull.

The man's body stopped writhing and became still. His skin still smoldering in the sun, Velma looked down at her handiwork and mumbled, "Shit."

Darius was right in calling them Ash-heads, as their skin would instantly turn to ash upon contact with sunlight.

Why could Darius make vampires, but she couldn't? Were there unspoken laws to this shit? Or was it because he'd slept with them all? Ew, gross, she thought, realizing that to turn the old farmer, she likely would have had to sleep with him or something equally as depraved.

She'd try again when things were less conspicuous, but for now, she needed to figure out how to dispose of his body. It would be too coincidental, she felt, for another bizarre murder to make headlines directly across the path from the previous one. The media would be all over her in a heartbeat if she left this old farmer to be dug up by the bowling alley. Also, Darius would be furious with her. So, she decided to move the body as far away from here as possible.

Dragging the man's burnt corpse by his feet, Velma pulled him further out into the field. About a quarter mile up the way, the Wood River butted up against this farmland. She'd dump the body in the river and hope that it would wash downstream.

After dumping the body, she'd need to figure out what to do with the tractor. If anyone found the body, they'd put two and two together. She couldn't risk it coming back to her or Darius. So she knew who to call.

Jesse would do anything for her. She could tempt him with the promise of sex, and he'd lick the mud from her shoes for her. She'd have him move the combine and park it in a random field far away, and then she'd torch that field to make it look like the scene of the crime.

Yeah, she thought. That ought to work.

After she finished covering up her mistake with the farmer, Velma went straight to Darius's house. She found herself caring for him more and more and wanted to ensure he was okay.

Walking up his front steps, she rang the bell and waited. When Stacy Anderson answered the door, Velma wanted to scream.

"Is he here?" she asked.

"Yes. Come in," the woman said. "He's been expecting you."

She stepped into Darius's home and took a look around. It seemed like any regular family home to her. Then she came around the corner to find Darius and his mother sitting at the kitchen table.

Stacy returned to her seat and then sat down with her back to the kitchen windows, Darius and his mother sitting at either end of the table.

"There's one more spot available, sweetie," Darius's mom said, gesturing to the available chair.

"Um, thank you," Velma replied, slowly sitting down at the table.

"Velma is one of Darius's girlfriends," his mom told Miss Anderson. She's over here almost every day."

"Mom!" Darius said, feeling embarrassed. "She's not here every day."

"I said almost every day, didn't I?" his mom shot him a sharp look, and he lowered his gaze.

"Yes, ma'am."

"I think it's sweet that he respects you so much, Mrs. Reid." Anderson reached across the table and touched Mrs. Reid's hand. "And your son is a diligent worker. One of my top students."

This pleased Mrs. Reid to no end, and she scooted back and stood up from her chair. "Who wants pie? I made some fresh peach cobbler pie this afternoon."

"I'd love a piece," Miss Anderson said, still trying to impress Mrs. Reid.

Velma looked at Darius as if to ask, "What the fuck" is she doing here?

Darius shook his head as though to say, not now.

Velma looked over her shoulder and called out to Mrs. Reid. "I'd also love a piece," she chirped. "You know I love your cooking, Mrs. Reid."

Darius's mother chuckled as she pulled the pie out of the stove warmer and brought it to the table. Drawing a knife from the kitchen drawer, she handed it to Velma.

"Will you do me the favor of cutting everyone a slice? My

arthritis in these old hands is acting up, and I'm afraid I'll make a mess of things."

"No problem," Velma said, taking the knife. She pointed it at Miss Anderson and said in a somewhat sarcastic tone, "Anything I can do to help."

"What a sweet girl," Mrs. Reid said, shooting her son a look. "Don't you think so, Darius?"

"Yes, ma'am. Velma is the best," he replied.

Velma looked at him, stuck out her tongue, and began politely cutting everyone a slice. She made sure to cut Miss Anderson an oversized piece. Let those calories inflate the stupid cow into a Goodyear blimp for all she cared.

After taking just one bite, Anderson moaned in pleasure and quickly covered her mouth. "This is the best-tasting pie I've ever had," she said, crumbles spilling down her chin as she talked with her mouth full.

"Suck up," Velma whispered. Anderson heard her and smiled in reply as if to say, game on bitch.

"It's my favorite, too," Darius said, stuffing his face.

Shooting Darius a sharp glance, Velma said, "Can I talk to you for a moment? In private?"

"Yeah, sure," he said between two large bites of peach pie.

"Now?" she insisted.

She got up and headed up the stairs to Darius's room. Darius finished off his plate, grabbed her untouched plate, and took Velma's pie with him up the stairs.

"Excuse me, Miss Anderson, I need to speak with her." But feel free to stay as long as you'd like."

"I appreciate that, Darius," Miss Anderson said, smiling up at him as though she had a school girl crush.

After Darius disappeared upstairs, Mrs. Reid sat down with

a kettle of tea and poured a nice cup of lemon tea for herself and Miss Anderson to accompany their peach cobbler.

Upstairs, Darius shut his door and looked over at Velma, who was sitting on his bed. She buried her face in her hands and began crying. "I messed up, D. I fucking messed up."

"What are you talking about?" he asked, crumbs falling out of his mouth as he spoke.

"I tried to turn someone today. But it didn't fucking work." She looked up at him, her mascara bleeding down from her eyes. "He fucking ignited like a goddamn firework and went up in smoke."

"Yeah, about that..." he said, rubbing the back of his head as he set his plate down on the corner of his dresser. "The same thing happened to me my first time with Billie Bobby Brown."

"Billie?" she asked. "Shit, I thought she was out on maternity leave."

"Well, I guess I came out here the night I was turned. I don't remember much, but she was here, and I fed on her. Then, I thought, fuck it, I'll turn her like my Maker turned me. But I missed a step."

"She burned up?"

"Like a mother-fucking bonfire," he said. "It was terrifying. She turned to ash right before my eyes."

"So, do you have to sleep with them to turn them?"

"It's more than that. You must bond yourself to them, both emotionally and spiritually. They won't last until the next daybreak if there's no connection. They either combust or wither away into gray husks of the undead. Everyone I know calls them Grays."

"I see," she said, sounding saddened by the fact that she didn't have any friends other than the Slayers and Darius. She wouldn't be forging any strong connections anytime soon. As for Jesse, sadly, she had to dispose of him along with the combine and the rest of the evidence, tying her to the murder of that farmer.

Jesse was tied up in his apartment, a heroin needle stuck in his arm, and a suicide note on his bed explaining the guilt he'd felt for murdering that poor old farmer. But Darius didn't need to know about any of this.

A knock on the door forced Velma to wipe her eyes as Darius went over to answer it.

Stacy Anderson was standing at the entrance and smiled when Darius answered. "Your mom wanted me to check on you."

"That's my mom for you, a perpetual worrywart."

Anderson stepped into his room and looked around at Darius's things, almost entirely ignoring Velma. "So, this is your room?"

"That's the rumor, anyway," Darius teased.

"You're so funny." She laughed with more emphasis than seemed natural, showing how funny she found him. Anderson closed the door behind her, looked at Velma, and then back at Darius. "Don't you think he's to die for?"

Velma leaned back on the bed and just stared at Miss Anderson. "What are you even doing here?"

"She's tethered to me," Darius said.

"We have a bond," Ms. Anderson replied. "I'm never leaving Darius's side ever again."

Velma laughed aloud at that. "You can't be serious?"

"She's not," Darius replied. "She's my thrall. Watch this." Darius turned toward Miss Anderson and said, "Take off all your clothes."

Velma watched in amazement as Miss Anderson stripped to

nothing. Kicking off her panties and letting her bra drop to the floor, she stood before them, completely exposed.

Darius walked over and lit a scented candle that Velma had brought over the last time they were intimate in his bedroom. He lit it, let the wax melt, and then handed the candle to Miss Anderson. "Put this on your chest," he said.

Again, Miss Anderson did exactly as he asked. There was no hesitation, no questioning her Master, just blind obedience.

"Cool, right?" Darius asked, turning to Velma.

"What else can you make her do?"

"Anything I desire," he replied.

"May I offer a suggestion?"

"Tell her to walk home and leave us for the evening."

Darius shrugged as if he were okay with it.

"Miss Anderson...I mean, Stacy."

"Yes, Darius?" She batted her eyes and smiled at him vacantly, unaware of their scheming.

"Go home."

"Yes, Darius," she answered. And with that, she turned and exited his room, leaving her clothes on the floor where she'd shed them. After all, he hadn't told her to get dressed again. All she could do was obey his direct commands.

Stacy Anderson went down the stairs and into the main room. She paused at the kitchen entrance and said, "Thank you for the wonderful evening, Mrs. Reid. But I must be getting home now."

Mrs. Reid was washing the dirty dishes from dinner and, without looking over her shoulder due to her early onset rheumatoid arthritis, said, "My pleasure, Miss Anderson. Feel free to visit anytime."

Stacy opened the front door of Darius's house, stepped out,

and exited. She walked down the stairs, across the yard, and to the sidewalk, where she casually turned and headed up the street toward her apartment, eleven blocks away. And she did so bare naked, not a single fiber of fabric anywhere on her entire body.

Darius and Velma poked their heads out of his second-story bedroom window and watched Miss Anderson pass an evening jogger who nearly tripped over himself as he did a double-take. A subtle smile spread across the jogger's lips, but he shook his head, quickly refocused, and continued on his way.

"I have to admit, she is pretty fucking fit for a forty-year-old teacher who sits at her desk all day."

"Isn't she, though? She must do yoga."

"Yoga and Pilates," Darius informed Velma.

"Yoga and Pilates," she confirmed with a nod.

Darius and Velma laughed, then ducked back under his windowsill and stood in his room, gazing into one another's eyes.

Velma brushed a tuft of hair behind her ear and nervously chewed on her tongue stud. "I'm sorry if I've been acting like a jealous bitch. But I think I might be in love with you." She looked at him, her eyes on the verge of tears, dreading what he might say. She would literally die if he didn't like her back.

Darius just stared at her for what seemed like an eternity.

Unable to take the suspense, she snapped at him. "Well, aren't you going to say something?"

"I'm in love with you, too," he replied.

Velma's eyes lit up, and she threw her arms around his neck, beginning to kiss his face. "Oh, thank God. I was so worried that you weren't into me."

"Oh, I'm into you," Darius answered.

Velma took his hand in hers and then sat him down on the

bed. He watched as she sat down next to him. "I hope your mom doesn't mind if I spend the night?"

"It's fine. She knows we're dating."

"She does, does she?" Velma quizzed, shooting Darius a skeptical look.

"I told her that we were an item."

"So, what are you saying? That I'm your girlfriend?"

"Yes!" Darius laughed. "What's with the twenty questions? You're my girlfriend."

Velma squealed and pounced onto Darius, and they fell back onto his bed together. She kissed his lips and then looked him straight in the eyes. "I have to admit, I fucking like the sound of that."

Before he could reply, she smothered his mouth with another sultry kiss and rolled on top of him. Straddling his thighs, she sat up and reached underneath the back of her shirt, folding her arms around herself to unfasten her bra. Letting the girls out, she let Darius reach up and grope her breasts, letting out a sensuous sigh.

After everything that had happened, Velma wanted him to be hers and only hers. She would make this night a night that Darius would never forget. Because he was her King, and she was his Queen, and she'd do anything to make him happy. Absolutely anything.

LOVE PRICKS LIKE A THORN

MADELINE ELIZABETH MICHAELSON SAT at her kitchen table, waiting for Jaclyn to walk through her front door. She'd been waiting nervously for the past half an hour and fidgeted with the small, gift-wrapped box in front of her.

Wrapped in blue foil paper with a purple ribbon, Maddie was nervous about taking the next step in her relationship with Jaclyn. And even though she'd lost one of the most remarkable men she'd ever known, she couldn't let that stop her from living her best life.

Maybe she was being selfish. Most people grieved for months, even years, before moving on. She'd moved on after a couple of rough weeks. What did that say about her?

She didn't care what others thought, though. She was positive that Jackie was her person. She only prayed that Jackie felt the same way about her.

The door lock clicked, alerting Maddie that Jaclyn was returning home. She sat up, straightened her posture, and then brushed her hair back with her fingers, fluffing it out to try to add some volume.

Jaclyn entered the kitchen and looked over to find Maddie sitting at the table. "Um, hi," she said, uncertain about what was happening.

Maddie patted the seat next to her and offered Jaclyn a chair. "Please, sit. I need to talk to you about something."

Jaclyn smiled, went over, and sat next to Maddie, taking her hands in hers and glancing down at the present sitting on the table. "What's all this about, babe?"

"I know we've been through a lot over the past month. But you've been right by my side through it all. You're my lighthouse. My beacon in the dark. And, well, I was just wondering..." She paused as if she were fishing for the right words. I was wondering if you'd like to...I mean, if you'd like to..." She gave up trying to say whatever it was she was trying to say and slid the present over to Jackie. "Open it."

Jaclyn smiled at her as she accepted the gift and began unwrapping it. Peeling off the decorative paper and ribbon, she found a clamshell case for a ring inside. She held the box in her hands and looked up at Maddie, who nodded encouragingly. Jaclyn obliged, slowly lifting the lid to peer inside.

"I don't understand," she said, making a curious face. Then, opening it the rest of the way, she found a freshly made key to the apartment.

"It's a key to the apartment."

"I see that," laughed Jackie. "But I already have a key to this apartment." She drew out her key and dangled it in front of

Maddie for her to see. Maddie reached up and snatched that key out of Jackie's hands.

"No, you don't understand. This key," she said, holding up the confiscated item, "is Mike's spare key. That key," she added, nodding at the key Jackie now held, "is your key to *our* apartment."

"I see."

"I don't think you do, Jackie. I'm asking you to move in with me. Permanently."

"*Ohhh,*" Jackie said, letting out an elongated sigh of relief. "That makes so much better sense."

"So, what do you say? Live with me?"

Jackie placed the key back in the box and closed it. Resting her hand on the box on the table, she stared at it for the longest time, thinking about her answer. Anything she said, though, would be the wrong answer.

She knew that if she said yes, Maddie would unwittingly be letting her husband's killer into her home. She'd be sleeping in bed with a monster and not even know it. If she said no, Maddie would be crushed by her rejection, and their relationship would likely be over.

She knew she had to do the unthinkable and make Maddie hate her. It would be the only way to break things off and let Maddie move on with her life. A life free of having to learn that the person you think you love is the person you hate with every fiber of your being.

"I love you," Jackie began, "you know this. But I always want us to be honest with one another, no matter what." She had to make her lie count, believable enough that Maddie would eat it up hook, line, and sinker.

"All right," Maddie said in a long, drawn-out manner, her

voice wary, revealing that she didn't know where all this was going.

"During that week after the funeral, where you ripped into me, berated me, and told me you never wanted to see me again...I was hurt. And, well, I'm not proud to admit this, but you deserve to know the truth. I slept with Layla Harker."

"You did what?!" Maddie drew her hands back from Jaclyn's, not wanting to touch her any longer. She stared at Jackie for the longest time, then, shaking her head, said, "No. I don't care. We can work through this. We can..."

Jackie reached out to take Maddie's hands in hers, but Maddie pulled away again. They looked at each other. The silence magnified the awkwardness and discomfort of that moment.

"So, what? Are you calling it off?" Maddie asked.

"Call it off?" asked Jackie.

"Are you going to call it off with Harker?"

Jackie sat back in her chair and sighed in annoyance. "She doesn't mean anything to me. It was just meaningless sex."

"Sex isn't just meaningless. Not to me," she said, her face growing red with anger even though she tried her best to suppress it. "Who initiated it?"

Jaclyn knew that if she told Maddie Harker had initiated it, she'd be clear. However, if she said that she had come on to Harker, they were over. But Jackie wanted Maddie to live a good life. A life free from the demons that haunted her. Free from a life with a fucking vampire. It was the easiest decision she'd ever had to make.

"I did," she lied, diverting her eyes, trying her best to look guilty as all sin.

Furious, Maddie stood up and pointed at the door. "I think

maybe you should see yourself out."

Jackie merely replied, "Yeah," and slid the gift back across the table to Maddie.

Without so much as another word, Jackie turned and left Maddie, who sat sobbing torrential tears.

Jaclyn got in her Challenger, revved the engine angrily, and drove straight to the nearest bar. It was called *The Wicked Rabbit* and had an image painted on the entryway glass of Alice from *Alice in Wonderland* being chased by a wild-eyed rabbit. Parking by the curb on the opposite side of the street, she cut across traffic, ignoring the cars honking at her, and stormed inside.

Upon entering the pub, she looked over at the bar to find the last person she expected to see sitting there...Layla *fucking* Harker.

Jackie went over and sat down next to her partner. She made eye contact with the barkeep and held up two fingers, signaling him to bring her over two shot glasses. As if reading her mind, he brought over the glasses, and she grabbed the bottle of Jack Daniels sitting in front of Layla and poured herself and Layla a shot. They downed them together and let out satisfied sighs.

Jackie slammed the shot glass back onto the counter and let it all out. Not holding anything back, she spilled her personal life story for Layla to dissect. "So, Maddie and I just broke up."

Layla looked over at her but didn't say anything.

"I had to...you know? She doesn't know how dangerous I am. People around me get hurt. I can't let her be the next casualty of my shit life. She deserves better."

Layla grabbed the bottle and poured them both another round. They downed those shots, too.

"Layla, I'm telling you, if you knew the half of it, you

wouldn't be sitting here with me right now. You'd likely be arresting my ass and tossing me in jail. My life is a total mess right now. You have no idea."

A quiet calm fell over them as Layla continued to refuse to speak. Instead, she nodded at the bottle, notifying Jackie that it was her turn to pour. She obliged.

Another six shots went down like water, and Jackie felt buzzed while Layla tottered on her barstool as though she could tip over at any moment.

Jackie hiccupped and let out a fiery whiskey-laden belch. She tried pouring another set of shots, but the bottle was empty. "Fuck. We're out. This bottle is bone dry."

Layla hiccupped, *hic*, and then answered, "We can't have that now, can we." *Hic* Layla slid her arm across the bar, held up her hand, and said, "Barkeep, a bottle of your finest brandy!" *Hic*

"Brandy sounds good."

"You sound good," Layla laughed. Her laughter was interrupted by another hiccup.

Jackie shot Layla a warm smile. This was the first time she'd seen this side of Layla. But her amusement quickly melted from her face, and she grew serious.

"What is it?" Layla asked, noticing something was wrong.

"I had to lie to Maddie to get her to dump me."

"I'm listening," Layla said in a slurred voice. *hic*

"I told her that you and I..." She pointed a thumb at herself and then aimed a finger at Layla, getting the order of her gesture completely backward from what she'd said. But she was drunk, so fuck it. "I told her we, you know, did it."

"Did what?" Layla asked, blushing. *hic*

"I told her you and I had sex."

Layla gasped and sat up straight, then slumped to the side. Resting her head on her palm, she smiled at Jackie. "You told her *that?*"

Jaclyn folded her arms across the bar counter and buried her face in her arms. "Yesh," she replied, her words slurring. She was so fucking embarrassed that she'd just outed herself. But what else could she do? Layla was so disarming, and more importantly, she needed someone to talk to right now.

Layla leaned forward and whispered into Jackie's ear. "You know those panties of mine you like?" *hic* "They're yours if you can get them off me."

Jacklyn raised her head and looked at Layla's beat red cheeks. It was clear she was doing her best to flirt with her. "Why are you so plastered?" Jaclyn asked, letting out a laugh. "I'm the one having a bad day."

"Oh, I wouldn't be too sure about that," she said. Just then, the rum bottle arrived, and she picked it up to admire it. "*Ahhhh,* yes. Sweet spirits whisk us away to happier times." She poured them both a shot, and they raised their glasses. With a clink, they said cheers and then downed their rum with unfettered haste.

"Seriously, though," Jackie insisted, "tell me what's so terrible that it has you washing away your troubles in a place like this?"

"You wouldn't believe me even if I told you," Layla said.

"Try me," Jackie countered, placing her hand on the counter so that her pinky finger brushed up against Layla's.

Layla glanced down at Jackie's hand, which was touching hers, and smiled affectionately. Then, she set her smartphone on the counter and slid it across the bar top for Jackie to look at.

Jackie looked down at Layla's phone and saw a video of some

security footage. It was in night vision, so everything looked almost like a negative, but she braved it and hit the play button. She instantly regretted doing so.

Playing on the video feed was a fully fanged-out version of her biting into Darius Reid's neck under the park bypass. The short clip ended with her looking up, her eyes reflecting in the moonlight like a wild animal, blood dripping down her chin, chest, and breasts. She looked terrifying.

"It's not every day you find out your partner is a vampire," Layla said, eying Jacklyn suspiciously. Her inebriated giddiness had melted away, and now she stared at Jaclyn with a somber look that demanded answers.

Jaclyn's face sank, and she looked up at Layla, who no longer seemed drunk. Layla's gaze burned with suspicion and a million other questions that Jackie had no defense against. The only thing she could do was admit the truth. "I can explain," she said.

"Please do," Layla answered, reaching out and taking her phone from Jackie's hand cautiously.

They stared at each other for the longest time, then Jackie muttered, *"Fuuuck me."*

Thirty-seven minutes later, Jackie and Layla were back at Jackie's apartment, lying on her bed, sweaty and out of breath.

"I didn't see that coming," Jaclyn said, gasping for air.

Layla laughed. "I knew I'd go home with you sooner or later."

"You did, did you?"

"I felt the attraction from the moment I saw you."

"When I bumped into you and was rude to your face?"

"People mistake strong for bitchy when it's a woman. I knew you were strong. That made me want to know you more. And then Ackhurst paired us up, and I was low-key flirting with you the whole time." She brushed her bangs behind her ear. I just wasn't sure if you were picking up on my signals. Knowing you had a girlfriend, I didn't want to push things."

"Ex-girlfriend," Jaclyn corrected.

"Right. Ex-girlfriend," Layla repeated. Rolling onto her side, she grasped Jackie's chin and gently guided her face toward her own. "I want to see them."

"What?" laughed Jackie.

"Your fangs," Layla said. "Show them to me."

"Are you sure?"

"No," Layla replied. "Yes. I don't know." She leaned in and kissed Jackie's lips, sliding her fingers into Jackie's mouth. Then, probing and prodding, she started searching for the mythical vampire inside.

"*Staaahp,*" Jackie laughed, grabbing Layla's hands and pulling her fingers out of her mouth. "Fine. I'll show them to you."

Layla smiled at her and held her gaze until Jackie grew self-conscious.

Opening wide, she hooked the inside of her cheek with an index finger and pulled her lips back. Then, she let her fangs slowly grow to their full three centimeters.

"Can I touch them?" Layla asked, reaching out her hand like Sleeping Beauty reaching for the loom's needle.

"No," Jackie said, clutching Layla's hand. "If you prick yourself, I might lose control and hurt you."

"I get it now. You keep everyone at arm's length because you don't trust yourself."

"I'm a monster, Layla. How could I ever trust myself, let

alone allow anyone else to?"

"Because," Layla said, lying on top of Jaclyn's chest and bringing her lips so close to Jaclyn's that they brushed up against one another. "I trust you."

Layla kissed Jaclyn long and hard, her tongue sliding into Jackie's mouth and delicately dancing around her razor-sharp fangs. Flirting with danger never felt so good.

"Why did you break up with Maddie?" Layla asked. "The truth this time."

"Like I said," Jackie informed her, sitting up in bed. "I'm dangerous."

"You'd only say something like that if you hurt someone. Did you hurt someone, Jackie?"

Jaclyn closed her mouth and stared at Layla, debating whether she should come out with the truth. Then she turned her face away, refusing to divulge that bit of information. Hurt someone? No, she thought. She'd done worse. She'd killed. And not just once, either.

"Look, I'm not here to judge. Six hours ago, I lived in a normal world with everyday mundane criminals. Now, I live in a world with supernatural creatures that drink blood and walk among us in plain sight. In addition to this, I have had several murder victims drained of their blood. I don't even know what the ethical logistics are behind allowing vampires to eat people or denying vampires their food source and starving them to death. Either way, it sounds like a lose-lose situation for you."

"If I told you that I allegedly had killed people, then what?"

Layla sat up, rising on the bed and settling back onto her heels. She placed her hands in her lap and stared at Jackie for a long time, thinking about her response. "If that was true–"

"Allegedly," Jackie reiterated.

Layla smiled and nodded. "If true, I'd have no choice but to arrest you."

Jaclyn turned her head and looked out the window of her apartment. Layla's eyes stayed fixed on her. She watched as Jaclyn debated whether to reveal everything or keep everything safely locked in the closet with the rest of her secrets.

"So, if I offered you my blood, would you drink from me?" asked Layla after a long, drawn-out silence.

Jackie looked at her with a shocked expression. "God, no."

"Why not?"

"Because I'd get your memories. I'd see your most intimate thoughts. It would be the literal rape of your mind."

"Only if it's not consensual," she corrected.

"I beg your pardon?" Jacklyn shot Layla a somewhat perplexed look.

"It would only be rape if you stole my blood and memories from me against my will. If I offer it freely, I'm giving you my consent." Layla reached over and grabbed Jacklyn's fingernail file from off her bedside stand. It was the only thing sharp enough to test her theory.

"What are you doing?" Jaclyn asked, a startled expression crossing her face.

Layla took the nail file and pressed it into her left breast.

"I wouldn't do that," Jaclyn said.

"Do what?" Layla pressed harder until it looked like she might break the skin.

"I'm warning you, Layla. Nothing good will come of this."

Jaclyn felt her fangs growing in anticipation of a freshly tapped spring. "Please, Layla," she said, tears welling up in her eyes. "Don't do this. I don't want to hurt you."

Another tense few seconds ticked by before Layla let up and

tossed the nail file to the floor. She began panting heavily, letting out all her nervous tension. "I'm sorry. I had to know."

"Know whether I'd tear you apart? Make you into a vampire? What?" asked Jaclyn. She struggled to mask her anger, but she was irate. She didn't like being toyed with.

"Whether or not you like killing," Layla answered. "But I can tell that you genuinely care for my safety. And someone whose instinct is to save an innocent victim can't be the cold-blooded killer we're searching for. There's good in you, Jaclyn Benoit. Don't let anybody tell you otherwise."

A single tear trickled down Jaclyn's cheek. "I killed my partner, Layla." Jaclyn held out her arms and turned her wrists up, offering herself to Layla. "So, now you know what kind of monster I am. You'd best get it over with and arrest me now."

Layla slid off her heels and settled onto the bed. She let herself dive deep into Jaclyn's blue eyes as if she were diving into the great, vast ocean.

"I'll make you a deal," Layla said. "After we find the serial killer, *then* I will arrest you for the murder of your partner. Until that time, however, I need you by my side to work on this case.

Jaclyn turned her face away as she continued to lean against the headboard. Layla crawled toward her and gently placed her hands on Jaclyn's knees, drawing her attention back to her. "What are you doing?"

"I like you," Layla replied.

Jaclyn laughed. Then she opened her mouth wide as if she were at the dentist and flashed Layla her fangs. "Then you're a misguided little girl."

"You know what we need?" Layla asked, her eyes lighting up with excitement.

Jaclyn merely shook her head, not knowing where she was

going with this.

"Ice cream!" exclaimed Layla, sitting up and bouncing off the bed. "Do you have any?"

"I think so," Jaclyn said, smiling at Layla, who never ceased to amuse her.

Layla grabbed an AC/DC shirt off Jaclyn's armchair and threw it on. She found Jaclyn's bathrobe hanging on a wall hook and tossed it to her. Having dressed, she dragged Jaclyn into her kitchen and began rummaging through her freezer.

"Jackpot!" Layla chirped excitedly, drawing out a large tub of mint chocolate chip ice cream. She ripped off the lid and tossed it aside. Then, grabbing a spoon from the drying rack by the sink, she scooped up a large spoonful of the green minty ice cream and told Jaclyn to "Open wide."

Jaclyn laughed and opened her mouth, letting Layla feed her a spoonful of mint chocolate chip. Layla helped herself to a bite, and as Jaclyn let the ice cream melt down her throat, she quietly said, "Why is this so fucking good?"

Layla leaned in and kissed Jaclyn's mouth, both swapping minty-sweet kisses. "*Mmm,*" Layla moaned as she kissed Jackie's lips. When Layla tasted the salt, she drew back, finding tears streaming down both of Jackie's cheeks.

Layla set the ice cream aside and opened her arms. Jackie fell into her embrace and held her tight. Layla hugged her back and let Jackie sob into her shoulder for as long as she needed. "*Shhh,*" Layla hushed in a consoling manner. "Everything will be alright."

After a long cry, Jackie dried her tears and apologized. "I'm sorry. I know this has been a weird night."

"You're telling me," Layla said in a playful tone. "I just found out my best friend is a vampire."

"Did you just refer to me as your best friend?" asked Jackie, batting her lashes as she smiled at Layla.

Layla blushed. "I don't have many friends," she replied. "I hate to admit it, but you're my only friend in my sad workaholic life right now."

"Ditto," Jackie said, letting out a sigh of disappointment. If it hadn't been for Maddie, she would have had no one in her life. Hell, she couldn't even begin to express how thankful she was for having Maddie in her life. But that was a bridge she needed to keep burned to the ground. If only to protect Maddie from monsters like her.

Layla grabbed a second spoon and handed it to Jackie. They placed the tub of ice cream between them and clanked spoons.

"Bon Appétit," Jackie said, smiling as they drowned their sorrows in a large tub of mint chocolate chip ice cream.

13

SOPHIE AND AMBER
DINE OUT

SOPHIE AND AMBER STEPPED off the Greyhound bus, its hydraulic brakes hissing as it decompressed. Their feet crunched through the fresh snow, and they waited for the bay doors to open so they could retrieve their luggage. March was the last month they'd have snow up in Aspen, and they wanted to get their snow bunny on.

"I'm slipping into my bikini and hitting the outdoor pool as soon as I can," Sophie said, bending down to grab her limited-edition hot-pink Rimowa suitcase. Sliding out the handle, she swung her leg over the suitcase and mounted it rodeo style. With an electric *whir* of her motors, she drove off.

Dragging her old-fashioned Gucci bag out from under the storage compartment, Amber turned around and held it with both arms as she lumbered after Sophie. She called out to her travel companion. "Hey, wait for me!"

Sophie was filing her nails when Amber, huffing and puffing, finally arrived at the resort entrance. She was practically dragging her bag and dropped it in front of Sophie. "Right, now," *pant* "I can catch," *pant* "My breath."

Sophie looked at Amber, got up from her suitcase, grabbed the handle, and wheeled it inside the Four Seasons Aspen resort lobby.

"Oh, for Pete's sake," Amber grumbled as she sat on her luggage to catch her breath. Instead, she found herself trying to catch up with Sophie again.

They checked in at the front desk and admired the massive ceilings and multiple fireplaces. The hotel was enormous. She couldn't wait to see their suite. At nearly two grand per night, it was fully equipped with a full-sized kitchen, fireplace, living room, two bedrooms featuring king-sized beds and their own bathrooms and walk-in closets, and a balcony jacuzzi.

When they arrived at their rooms, Sophie slid the keycard through the reader, and their door was unlocked. Both girls entered the suite with big eyes and jaws agape as they took in the luxuriousness of the estate.

"I've never seen anything so big," Amber said, running around from room to room like an excited child. She then flopped back onto her bed and sank into the plush covers.

Sophie went to her room, leaving the door open so she could see Amber's room. She began peeling off layers of her clothes. "I don't want to be late to the pool party," she informed Amber, laying a yellow bikini on her bed.

"Right," Amber said. "What pool party?" she asked.

The men's Olympic snowboarding team is here for practice this weekend. Why do you think I chose this date?"

"Honestly, I didn't have a clue."

"You know, all of them are as fit as fuck from their steady diets of Sushi and Redbull. It will be like an all-you-can-eat buffet!"

"Ah, I get it now. We're here to dine out for a change."

Having put on her bikini, Sophie sauntered into Amber's room and sat on the edge of her bed. "Dress as slutty as you want, babe. Tonight's goal is to get as many hot men as possible to our suite and party like it's nineteen ninety-nine all over again."

"We were three in nineteen ninety-nine," Amber said.

Sophie laughed. "It's just a phrase. You know, the last year of the millennium?" She could see by Amber's confused look that she wasn't following. "Before it turned two thousand?"

Amber shrugged and then pulled out her forest green bikini. It complimented her red hair and pale skin nicely. She stripped right in front of Sophie, who merely responded with an eye roll. Amber wasn't the brightest bulb in the box, but where she lacked in smarts, she certainly made up for in sheer beauty.

In terms of sheer beauty, she was a mix between Karen Gillan and Bella Thorne. She was also fun, had a childlike wonder, and was game for anything. And she meant *anything*. Amber was the perfect wing-woman to have at your side when you wanted to party or get into trouble. She was the kind of friend who would gladly spend a night in jail alongside you to enjoy the moment together.

Although she could be a bit of a ditz sometimes, Amber was as loyal as they came. Her smile was downright infectious. Sophie still hadn't met a man who could resist Amber's charms.

Not even ten minutes later, they returned downstairs, splashing around in the main pool, giggling, and acting ditzy.

Only a couple of the star athletes had arrived, but when they saw a couple of attractive women having fun in the pool, they quickly texted their buddies.

Soon, the pool was filled with frosted-tipped blonde men, their rippling six-packs and perfectly sculpted chests and arms on display.

Sophie managed to convince about seven of the guys to get in the pool with her, and Amber went out to flirt more one-on-one with the five guys who were too shy to join the game, Marco Polo.

"Drinks in my room!" Amber shouted. All the young men cheered with excitement.

Sophie pulled herself out of the side of the pool and said, "Listen up, gents. We're in room seven-oh-eight. Be there in twenty, and we'll get this party started! Woo!"

The guys cheered, and Sophie and Amber grabbed their towels, dried off, and, not taking the time to dry their hair, raced to the elevator.

Sophie repeatedly mashed the button and informed Amber of the battle plan: "You make sure the standing bar is fully stocked. I'll order some special items from the dispensary. If you don't see a guy with a drink in his hand or who's high, you help them get there by offering some weed or an alcoholic drink."

"Got it," Amber replied. She squealed with glee and then turned to Sophie, "I'm going to have so much sex tonight."

Sophie laughed. "And then we feast!"

Twenty minutes later, on the dot, there was a knock at their door. Sophie and Amber had managed to change into their evening dresses, although their hair was still a little damp. Amber opened the door and found five of the athletes standing there, all of them looking nervous.

"Hi, guys!" she chirped. "Come on in."

They entered, and Sophie shot them a disappointed look. "Where are the rest of you?"

"Oh," said one of the snowboarders, "the others have girlfriends or are taking the night off to recoup. We partied hard the last three nights, so, you know."

"Their loss," Sophie said, grabbing two of them by hand and drawing them inside. She led them to her bedroom and began unfastening her dress right away. The two men she'd chosen looked at each other and then high-fived.

The remaining three looked at each other and then at Amber. "Don't look at me," Amber said. "My roommate is a slut. It will take a few drinks for me to loosen up."

Two of the men stumbled over each other as they rushed to the bar, fumbling to get their drinks made. The remaining man, a brunette with kind eyes, looked over at Amber with a shy grin.

"What's your name?" asked Amber.

"I, uh, I'm Erik Masters," he said.

"Are you a snowboarder too?"

"Yeah," he said, rubbing the back of his head nervously. Looking around the room, he said, "Nice room. I bet your family is loaded if you can afford one of the top suites here."

Amber shook her head. "No. We paid for everything ourselves. We both work. And we're roommates, so we save enough each year to treat ourselves to a nice vacation."

"I see," he said. "In that case, may I say there's nothing more attractive than a working girl who gets it done."

Amber laughed. He wasn't much of a conversationalist.

"Why don't you sit over by the fire and relax? Is there anything you'd like?"

"A Coke," he answered.

"Got it. A Coke and Jack Daniels."

"No," he corrected. "Just the Coke. I don't drink."

"Oh, all right," Amber said, walking over to the bar to make his drink. "I've got edibles."

"I'm afraid I won't do any of that either. I'm Mormon."

Amber shot him a worried look. "Well, that's no fun. Don't you ever want to throw caution to the wind and let loose?"

Erik shook his head. "Not really. Snowboarding is my life. Recreation, women, everything else comes in a distant second."

"Well, maybe I'll be able to change your mind." Amber batted her eyes at him and flirted shamelessly. With a little effort, she knew she could get him to bend to her will. But cracking him would be half the fun.

One of the other men handed her a Blue Lagoon cocktail that he'd made. She sipped it and hummed with delight. "It's sooo good!"

"Erik, there is still a virgin. We're trying to get his cherry popped, but we haven't had any luck so far."

"Is that so?" Amber brushed a tuft of red hair behind her ear and looked over at Erik, who was blushing. Sipping from her straw, Amber drained the entire glass, grabbed Erik's hand, and towed him to her bedroom. His friends hooted and hollered as they cheered him on.

Amber kicked her door closed with the heel of her foot and pointed at the bed. "Strip and get on the bed."

"I appreciate the thought, but I'm saving myself for my future wife."

Amber peeled off her dress and revealed she wasn't wearing

anything underneath. Standing before him in nothing but her birthday suit, she replied, "What makes you so sure that I'm not going to be the future Mrs. Masters?"

She walked up to him and placed her hand on his chest. His heartbeat increased, and she could feel the blood course through his body. Amber looked up into his eyes, and then, grabbing his hands, she forced them onto her hips and pulled herself into him. She gently kissed him on the mouth, and the cool, sultriness of her lips caused him to melt into her.

Soon, she was teasing him with flicks of her tongue. Little teases turned into mouth-to-mouth dalliances with tongue-on-tongue action. And before either of them knew it, they'd fallen back onto her bed, his arms racing to tear off his clothes.

Amber made sure to make him feel as good as he'd ever felt. Helping him, she guided him inside her and smiled, their hips grinding with a steady rhythm as she stared deeply into his hazel eyes. After he came, she rolled off, and they lay on the bed panting. Their bodies were dripping with sweat.

"I'm sorry," Erik apologized. "I'm no good. It's my first time and—" he failed to finish the sentence. Instead, he just stared into her eyes.

Amber finished for him. "Amazing. Right?"

"Yeah," he replied. He laughed softly to himself and then added, "I'm glad we did this. " You're so amazing."

"Are you hungry?" she asked, sitting up.

"Not really," he answered.

"All right," she said, sliding off the bed. "But I'm famished. So, I'm just going to step out for a bit and grab a bite. I'll be back soon."

He smiled and watched her open her door and walk out of her room stark naked. She didn't have a care in the world about what anyone thought. He had never met a woman like that in his life. Beautiful. Bold. He liked her boldness and was confident that the moment she returned to the room, he would ask her to marry him. After all, they'd just had sex.

Amber shut the door behind her and looked over at the two guys she'd left behind earlier. "Oh, hi, guys. Is it hot in here, or is it just me?"

They looked at one another and then began stripping as fast as they could. She began to walk over to them, her fangs already growing in anticipation of the meal.

When they looked back up, Amber had already pounced on the white boy nearest to her. They crashed to the floor as she ripped into his jugular. The other man jumped back, covering his junk with his hand and yelling, "What the fuck?"

She snapped her head to the side and eyed him from over her shoulder. Blood dripped from her chin, and his friend made gurgling noises as he bled out.

Terrified, the man dashed toward the hotel room door, but she moved so fast he practically ran into her. He slid to a halt on the smooth wood floor and looked at her, blood trickling down her bare chest.

"Fuck this shit," he said, then spun around and made a B-line to the balcony. Reaching it before her, he threw open the doors and ran outside. Looking over the railing, he realized they were too far up for him to jump. He wouldn't survive the fall.

He turned just in time to see Amber coming at him. She tackled him, and they tumbled into the hot tub with a violent splash. Although he tried to climb back out, she dragged him back under, where he thrashed around, desperately attempting to break free.

It was no use, though. Amber was too strong, and soon

enough, the hot tub turned pink with the young man's blood. Amber climbed out of the hot tub and walked back inside, the water diluting the blood on her, making her look as though she was splashed with pink watercolors.

As she approached her bedroom door, it opened, and Erik was caught standing at the entrance in only his boxers. He looked at her, his eyes slowly settling onto the dead body lying on the floor behind her.

Just then, Sophie's door opened, and Sophie was covered head to toe in thick crimson. Chunks of meat dripped down her chin and her naked body. She grinned, flashing her fangs, and Erik slowly backed up. Behind her, the white bedspread had been stained burgundy, and blood splatter dappled the walls like a Jackson Pollock painting.

"What the fuck is going on here?" he shouted, his volume trying to mask the underlying fear.

"Oh, sweetie," Amber said, "I forgot to tell you. The thing we're hungry for isn't sex or a fun time. It's your blood."

Erik turned and ran back into the room. Amber and Sophie just looked at each other.

"Where do you think he thinks he's going?" Sophie asked in an amused tone. "There's no way out of there."

Amber shrugged. "Beats me."

The women entered the room together and heard the latch on the bathroom door.

"Oh, isn't that cute," Sophie said sarcastically. "He's locked himself in the bathroom."

"What will we ever do?" asked Amber, clasping her hands together and throwing them to her shoulder like a damsel in distress.

Both women laughed as they approached the door.

Amber sank to her knees, realizing Erik was probably already leaning against the door to brace it.

"Erik, I know you're there. I can hear your heart racing."

"Go away!" he yelled. "Leave me alone."

"I'm sorry, babe. But I can't do that. After all, we've grown so close during our short time together. In fact, I've come to realize that I might genuinely like you."

There was no response. Amber looked back up at Sophie, who stood there looking annoyed. "Are you just going to play with your food?"

Amber stuck her tongue out at her. "They taste better when they're properly scared. I like to marinate my food. I don't just gorge myself on every Tom, Dick, and Harry that comes my way."

"Are you calling me fat?" Sophie said, eyeing Amber with a suspicious look.

They both laughed at the inside joke between them, both understanding that as vampires, they'd never get fat. They'd always be just as they were.

Amber turned back to the door. Reaching up, she let her fingers grow into claws and then dragged her nails down the door, making large scratch marks. "Please, let me in."

"No!" Erik growled defiantly.

"Pretty please?" asked Amber.

"No! Go away."

"You're hurting my feelings, Erik," Amber said, her voice turning serious. She stood up, and then, with inhuman strength, she punched through the door and tore it away from the wall. Tossing it to the side, she looked down to see Erik sliding back on his hands to try and get away.

He backed his way up to the large four-person jacuzzi

bathtub, and Amber followed him into the room.

"Please, don't hurt me."

"I wasn't lying," Amber said, getting on all fours and crawling up to him. Coming nose to nose with him, she reached up with her hand, causing him to flinch, and then reached past him to turn on the tap.

He opened his eyes, looked up at the running water, and then back at her. Amber held up a loofa and said, "I'll need you to scrub my back. I think I have blood on it."

She grabbed Erik's arm and hoisted him up, forcing him into the bath with her. Sophie just smiled as Amber made Erik clean her.

"I don't know if this is the most morbid or most erotic thing I've ever seen," Sophie said, laughing.

Amber waved Sophie over, beckoning her to join them. She nodded and climbed into the tub with them, sitting directly behind Erik, who gulped nervously.

"You won't be needing these," Sophie said. Reaching down, her hands sinking below the surface of the water, she ripped Erik's boxers off and tossed them across the room, where they landed in a wet wad by the toilet.

Sophie began running her hands across Erik's back and shoulders. At the same time, she began kissing his neck with soft lips and feathery, light kisses.

"W-what is going on?" he asked.

Amber glanced over her shoulder and smiled at him. "Have you ever been with two vampire women before?"

Erik gulped again. Amber laughed and then said, "Keep scrubbing."

Sophie whispered into his ear. "You're hers now. You're her thrall."

"Thrall?" he asked, nervous to learn what that word even meant.

"You're her slave. Her pet. Her plaything to do with as she pleases. And if you're a good boy, you might one day be made into her Familiar."

Amber turned around in the tub and then popped her fangs. Sophie did the same, and they both sank their teeth into opposite sides of Erik's trapezius. He winced in pain and let out a small yelp, but as they fed on him, a sudden rush of euphoria overwhelmed him.

The rest was all a blur. Bits and pieces of the evening flashed across his memory. He remembered being in bed with both women. He remembered drinking from more than one bottle of expensive brandy and laughing and falling over himself as he passed from one woman to the other. He remembered Amber rubbing her fingers through his hair as he vomited his guts out into the toilet.

Erik cracked his eyes open to find himself lying in bed alone. Sunlight was already beaming through the curtains and flooding the room. He groaned and held his hand up to block out the searing light. He slowly rose from the bed and, stretching, walked into the room. There wasn't a trace of blood and no bodies, either.

Had he dreamed it all? He yawned as he tried to reason through the haze of a hangover.

Slowly, he reached up to his neck and felt the puncture wounds from where the vampire woman had bitten him.

"*Fuuuck,*" he said, realizing that everything he had thought was a bad dream had truly, irrefutably, and undeniably happened.

Although he was alive, he was now a thrall, bound to a

Master who owned his heart and soul. A red-haired girl he didn't know, but whom he was bound to through a blood curse for the rest of his life.

Without warning, the door to the room burst open, and Amber marched back inside. "I change my mind," she said.

She reached up with a claw-like hand and slashed Erik across the throat, ripping out most of it in one fell swoop.

Erik collapsed to his knees and tried to mumble, "Why?"

Amber knelt on one knee, leaned in, and kissed him on the lips. "I'm not ready for anything long-term at the moment," she informed him, his life draining from his face. "And I don't think I can go long distances. It's so passe. But look on the bright side. At least you got to experience a small taste of life before you went."

Amber reached up, gently touched his cheek, and kissed him one last time.

Then, without so much as a second's hesitation, she stood up, marched out of the room, and didn't look back at Erik as his lifeless, blood-soaked body tipped over and fell into a bloody heap on the floor.

As Amber exited the suite, Sophie leaned against the side of the elevator, waiting for it to come to pick them up. "Did you finish it?"

Amber let out a sigh. It sounded sad. "Yes. But I really hated doing it. I liked him."

"Well, there's always next year."

"Yeah," Amber said, nodding in agreement. She began to perk up a bit. Brushing her dress down, she stood beside Sophie as the elevator chimed.

They waited for the elevator doors to part, and then both stepped inside. Turning at the same time, they both stared out into the hall. The hotel suite door remained ajar, and they could see Erik's lifeless hand and growing pool of blood.

Sophie smiled a fang-toothed grin, and Amber remained melancholy, still feeling her loss when the elevator doors clamped shut again.

14

VAMPIRE LOVE AFFAIR

LAYLA STRETCHED OUT HER leg, bubbles falling off in foamy clumps as she rested her thigh on the edge of the fabulous porcelain tub. She leaned back, took a deep breath, and slowly exhaled. The scented candles she'd lit all over the room simultaneously filled the air with a flowery and woody aroma.

Maybe she could have used fewer scented candles, but she wanted to relax. After her tumultuous entanglement with Jaclyn Benoit, to put it that way, she needed some quiet time to clear her head and gather her thoughts.

In her mind, she knew she should be furious at Jaclyn for keeping her real nature a secret. At the same time, Layla understood that the world wasn't ready for the revelation that vampires were real. Heck, half the world still felt that gay people and other queer folk were abominations. They weren't prepared for vampires. Of that, she was sure.

For Layla, there was no love lost on the bigoted, anti-gay propagandists who peddled right-wing radicalism without a care in the world. All of the naysayers, including her religious father, pretended to be virtuous and morally superior to the abhorrent gays when, in fact, it was quite the opposite as far as reality was concerned. Instead of being morally superior, he was prejudiced. And instead of being virtuous, he was bigoted. Instead of loving his daughter, he'd shunned her and turned her out as if she were more meaningless than a piece of dryer lint.

At least, that's how it had felt when he slammed the door in her face after telling her never to come back—there was no longer a loving home for her to return to. And why? Because Layla had chosen to express that small part of her that she'd kept secret for so long. And for that little outburst of daring to be herself, the people who should have loved her the most cut her off.

Imagine telling these kinds of people that vampires are real, she thought. She'd bet her bottom dollar that they'd lose their shit.

Although she had her fair share of resentment, she didn't resent being raised in a strict Muslim household. It taught her to respect her parents and elders, to be disciplined, and to keep her secrets hidden from the rest of the world, lest she be judged unfairly.

Now, she kept Jaclyn's secret too. And she was okay with it because she was starting to have genuine feelings for Jackie. Feelings she'd likely also have to hide from the world, not because they were gay, but because they were vampire and human. But she wasn't going to hide her feelings from Jackie. If they were meant to fall madly, deeply in love, then who was she to stand in the way of the Fates?

It was strange. She'd expected the existence of vampires to bother her, but it didn't. Instead, she jumped into bed with the first sexy vampire she saw. What did that say about her?

Of course, that probably had more to do with the fact that she had already had a crush on Jaclyn when she discovered the whole vampire thing. Although it was a shock, for sure, Layla could take a step back and put it all into perspective.

People had shunned her for the better part of her life simply because she liked women. She never wanted to force such a small-minded, bigoted position onto anybody else lest she become a hypocrite. So, after learning that Jackie was a vampire, she went to *The Wicked Rabbit* bar, drowned out her intrusive thoughts in a never-ending sea of bourbon, and hoped for the best.

Little did she expect Jaclyn Benoit, of all people, to walk through the front door and find her sitting there, half drunk. It was almost as if destiny had thrust them together. Oh, boy...did it ever. And they came crashing together, hard.

She let out a sigh of frustration as she reflected on their evening together. Layla desperately wanted to see Jackie again. But that was how it always was when you met someone with whom you had a genuine connection. You never wanted to be apart. But she was still a U.S. Marshal, and her first duty was to catch Danielle Pruette's killer.

A loud crash rang out from her living room, and she sat up in her bath. Glancing over at her Glock sitting on the chair next to her sink, she slowly rose out of the water, soap suds slipping off her brown skin and melting back into the bath. Stepping out of the tub, she retrieved her sidearm from the chair and slowly drew it from its holster.

Holding her gun at the ready, she looked in the mirror to see her glistening, wet body and shook her head. No, she thought. You don't want to fend off burglars in your birthday suit. She grabbed a teal Egyptian cotton towel off the shelf and wrapped herself in it. Then, picking her gun back up, she carefully unlocked the safety and called out, "Who's there?"

There wasn't any reply, but she could hear someone or something shuffling around, bumping into furniture in the dark. She cracked the bathroom door and peeked out, holding her gun at the ready. "I can hear you out there. To clarify, I am armed and a Special Agent with the U.S. Marshals Service. I won't hesitate to shoot you."

She pushed the door open and cautiously stepped out of her bathroom and into her studio apartment. It was too dark to make anything out, but she heard some movement back by the kitchen and trained her focus on the dark corner by the entrance.

"I don't want to hurt you, but I will defend myself."

"She can't be trusted," a voice said. Darius Reid, the lead suspect in the Pruette case, stepped out of the shadows and into the light.

"You're the kid that everyone has been looking for. Darius, right?"

"I didn't come here to talk about me, Ms. Harker." I came here to warn you about Detective Jaclyn Benoit. She's not who you think she is."

Layla had a good hunch she knew precisely who Jaclyn was. Darius, however, didn't know that she knew who Jaclyn was. Layla decided to feign ignorance. "What are you talking about?"

Darius took another step toward her. She raised the gun and widened her stance as she steadied her aim and got ready to shoot.

"Jaclyn Benoit is a monster. Maybe worse than this is that she's a mother of monsters." He reached up, hooked his cheek with his pointer finger, and pulled it back, revealing a fang.

"You're a vampire," she said, without the least bit of surprise. After all, she'd seen the footage of his assault.

"You don't seem surprised," he said, taking another step forward.

"Don't come any closer," she warned, keeping her sights fixed on him.

"Ah, I get it now. She confided in you so that you would take her side," Darius said. "But you need to know something, Agent Harker. She's killed more than just her partner."

"How do you know about that?" Layla asked.

"You mean, how do I know about Michaelson's murder? Because I was there. I saw it."

"Shit," Layla cursed under her breath. With an eyewitness to Michaelson's murder, this changed everything. Now, she'd be forced to arrest Jaclyn sooner rather than later.

"She also killed those poor unsuspecting souls at Mel's Diner."

This caught Layla's attention. Until now, she assumed that it was part of a random serial killing. She had evaluated Jaclyn's moral fortitude and found it as solid as a marble statue. If what Darius was saying was even remotely close to the truth, she'd have to rethink her assessment of Jaclyn. And, sadly, she'd have to rethink their relationship.

"Say I believe you," Layla said, stepping to the side to get a better view of Darius. "What do you intend to do with me?"

"Oh," he grinned, his smile stretching wide. "I intend to make a statement with you. But don't worry, I won't kill you. I need you alive long enough to pass on a little message to Detective Benoit for me.

"What message would that be?"

"My message is simple...Mind your own business!" he hissed. Charging forward, he dashed across the room so fast that Layla barely had time to react.

She fired off a shot, and Darius smashed into her shoulder first. She flew back and hit the wall, the sheetrock and paint fracturing under her weight. She fell to the floor, winded, leaving an indent in the wall.

Darius looked down at his shoulder and began to pick at the hole in his hoodie. "You shot me," he said, surprised she managed to get a shot off. "You fucking shot me."

Layla staggered to her feet, coughing as sheetrock dust fell out of her hair and coated her wet skin. Looking over, she saw that she'd dropped her gun about five feet from where she stood. Darius was the same distance away. They each looked at the gun and then at each other, a tension growing as to who would make the first move.

Layla lunged forward, reaching out for her gun. But Darius was too fast. He cut across the distance and flew into her at breakneck speed. Smashing into her with his full force, Layla felt her ribs crack as he sent her flying across the room. She hit her glass windows and fell to the floor.

Coughing up blood, she stood up to find Darius standing directly in front of her. "Send Jackie my warmest regards."

Before Layla could react, he shoved her back, and she hit the glass with such force that it shattered all around her. The last thing she could remember before everything went dark was that five stories up might not kill her, and before everything went out like a light, she heard the crunch of steel wrenching under her body and thought, I hope it's not my car that I'm crushing.

Layla's eyes popped open, staring at the night sky. Stars blurred in and out of focus as she regained her vision. It was clear outside, and she could see various constellations.

Groaning, she fought against the pain and turned her face to the side. Luckily, a parked car had broken her fall. The wail of ambulance sirens could be heard in the distance, and she saw a couple of middle school-aged kids standing next to their bikes, looking at her in shock, their jaws hanging open.

That's when she realized her towel slipped off during the fall. She turned her head to the other side, found her towel had fluttered down, and landed on the car roof alongside her. With a painful grunt, she managed to grab the towel and pull it over herself, covering up her more sensitive bits.

"Are you all right, lady?" one of the kids asked.

The other boy, probably about twelve years old, hit his friend's arm. "Don't talk to her."

"Why not?" the kid asked.

"She might be one of those killers," he said nervously.

"Killers don't try to kill themselves," the first boy said.

"I didn't try to kill myself," she said, her voice raspy.

"See?" the first boy said.

Layla tried to sit up, but a pain shot through her side like a red-hot poker piercing her ribcage, and she groaned so loudly she thought she'd wake the neighborhood. Crashing back onto the roof of the car, she waited until the paramedics got there before attempting to move again.

"Is she going to be all right?" one of the kids asked the medic.

"Well, she'll live," the paramedic replied.

"My friend took a picture of her boobs," the boy said, pointing at his friend standing next to them.

"Hey!" the other boy squeaked, shocked that his friend would rat on him so easily. "She doesn't need to know that!"

"It's fine. Keep it," Layla groaned. It's not like she could do anything about it. She was a wreck, and luckily, those kids had been there to call nine-one-one. She owed them something more than just gratitude, and a few shots of her boobs wouldn't be the end of the world.

"Really?" the kid asked. "Thanks, lady!"

With that, the two kids sauntered off, their faces buried in the phone as they swiped through the images, two giant smiles on their faces.

"Speaking of covering up, we're going to move you onto this stretcher, ma'am, and may need to readjust things."

Layla nodded, giving her consent, and two paramedics lifted her off the crushed car and set her onto a stretcher.

"We'll get you inside the ambulance and make you as comfortable as possible for the ride to Wood River General. But before that, I need to check for broken bones and any possible hemorrhaging."

Layla nodded again, and the paramedic felt around her body, gently squeezing her all over and asking if it hurt. She shook her head no, even though every part of her hurt like a motherfucking son-of-a-bitch. Still, if something were broken, she'd let them know by screaming to high heaven.

Two men hoisted her up into the back of the ambulance with another medic from the firetruck and secured her inside. As he was hooking up the I.V. drip, she heard a voice arguing with the ambulance paramedic.

"Sorry, ma'am, I can't let you pass this spot."

"I'm Detective Benoit, and this is my partner. So, you can be assured that this is precisely where I need to be right now. I suggest you step aside lest I be forced to arrest you for impeding an active investigation."

Layla craned her neck to get a look, but it hurt too much. She groaned and let her head fall back onto the pillow that the paramedic had given her to help try to make her a little bit more comfortable.

Jaclyn hopped up into the ambulance and sat down beside Layla. Taking her hand, Jackie whispered, "Don't worry, I'm here." I'm here now."

"Do you think I taste better bruised?" Layla asked. She laughed at her joke, but her laughter turned into a cough and a groan.

"It's the drugs talking," the medic said, looking up from what he was doing to address Jaclyn. "The Norepinephrine was out, so I put her on morphine to help with the pain. She may have a couple of broken ribs, but her heartbeat is as strong as an ox's. Although I wouldn't recommend letting her move around too much until we can get her back to Wood River General for an MRI scan."

The medic shut the ambulance doors and then sat at the front of the cab, monitoring Layla's vitals. The driver looked back at everyone, nodded, and shifted the ambulance into gear.

Jaclyn held Layla's hand for the entire ride back to the hospital. As the ambulance came to a stop at the emergency doors of Wood River General Hospital, a flock of nurses arrived to collect Layla.

She had difficulty letting go of Layla's hand as they pulled her away on the stretcher, but her attention quickly affixed itself to a doctor who strolled up to her. Introducing himself, he said, "I'm Doctor Cary Wallace. Do you think you could fill out her paperwork?"

"Yes," Jaclyn replied.

"Are you her wife?"

As if it were the most natural thing in the world for her, Jaclyn answered, "Yes."

The doctor nodded and gestured for her to enter through the Emergency doors. Once inside, he handed her off to a black nurse with bright red cornrows.

"Hey, I know you," the nurse said, handing Jaclyn a clipboard with paperwork.

"I don't think so," Jaclyn replied, not looking over at the woman. She kept her eyes on the ER doors through which they'd wheeled Layla.

"No, I know you," the nurse insisted.

Jaclyn looked at her. It took a second, but then she remembered her face.

She was a drug addict from Chicago. A woman she'd crossed paths with when she'd gone to the slums to feed. She hated feeding on druggies, as she called them. They always tasted so bitter and left a horrible aftertaste in her mouth. But nobody ever asked questions if a few heroin addicts disappeared by a seeming overdose. The needle marks already covered up the vampire bite.

"Wait," Jaclyn said, brushing back her jacket and flashing her badge. "I think I do recognize you. Were you in rehab up at Vernon Hills? I worked security there before transferring out here to Wood River."

"Uh, yeah," the woman replied, now uncertain about her recollection. Also, seeing that Jaclyn was a police officer made her recoil a little.

"It's so wonderful to see you get your life back on track," Jaclyn looked down at the woman's name tag, "Octavia."

Octavia leaned forward, put her hand to her mouth, and whispered, "Please don't tell anybody about my past addiction. I could lose my job."

Jaclyn placed her hand on Octavia's and smiled. "I wouldn't dream of it. Us women need to stick together." She winked at Octavia, went to the furthest corner, and sat down to finish the paperwork.

After scribbling down Layla's information, Jaclyn put the pen down and covered her face with her palm. She didn't want to cry publicly, but she genuinely liked Layla and didn't want to lose her. The tears came on their own.

Rubbing the tears from her cheeks with her thumb, she got up and handed in the paperwork. She then found herself a cup of coffee and returned to her seat. She wasn't leaving this hospital without Layla.

Sitting in her chair, which was far more uncomfortable than it had any right being, Jaclyn watched the clock on the wall. It ticked by so slowly that she felt she might be losing her mind. At the same time, however, her eyelids grew heavy, and she found herself dozing off only to snap awake again. Soon enough, it became clear to her that she couldn't fight the drowsiness, and she slowly drifted away.

Someone clearing their throat jolted her awake, and she looked up to find Doctor Wallace, who had greeted her at the ambulance, standing over her. She slumped in the chair, pushed herself up, and asked, "What time is it?"

"It's half past three in the morning," he replied, checking his watch. He looked at her and said, "I have good and bad news. Which would you like first?"

"Don't beat around the bush, doc," Jaclyn said. "Give it to me straight."

"Bad news, your partner will be out of commission for a week or two. Her glenohumeral joint was torn up badly from the fall, and she has a severe concussion. The good news is she'll make a full recovery."

"Jaclyn let out a sigh of relief. "Thank you," she said.

"There's one more thing that you should know as her wife," he said, rapping his fingers on the chart he held. "I don't know how much Layla has told you about her medical condition, but seeing as she said I could share any updates with you, it's best to be informed so you can both plan for a better future together."

Jaclyn didn't correct him. She was curious and liked the sound of being called Mrs. Harker. All fantasies aside, however, she knew it would be wrong to listen to Layla's personal medical information. Before she could speak up, however, the doctor cut to the chase and spoke over her.

"Layla has a rare blood condition called Myelofibrosis."

Jaclyn stared at him blankly. "Myelofibrosis? What's that?"

"Her body produces too many red blood cells. There are numerous treatments, many of them evolving chemotherapy and radiation. If that's too invasive, it's easy to regulate using less invasive techniques."

Jaclyn nodded along as Doctor Wallace continued sharing his diagnosis of Layla. "The easiest way to regulate Myelofibrosis," he informed her, "is to have a pint of blood removed once a month. If she did that, then she wouldn't need fancy or expensive treatments and would go on to live a comfortable, everyday life."

Jaclyn stood up, a smile forming on her face. This was too good to be true. Her girlfriend needed Jaclyn to bleed a pint out of her every month. She could most certainly manage that.

"I'll discuss it with her the moment we get home. Thank you, doc." She took his hand in hers and shook it enthusiastically. As he left, she played with her hair, twirling it around her finger and making coils.

Serendipity had brought them together. How often do vampires find a perfect partner, especially one who has a blood ailment of producing excess blood that can be fatal if not removed?

It felt like the universe was sending her a clear message to be with this woman. Who was she to argue with the universe?

She'd already warned Layla about the side effects of blood-sharing. She would gain all of Layla's memories, the good and the bad. Likewise, Layla would gain hers too. It was a very intimate affair, and she would have to be absolutely sure that this was what she wanted before proceeding.

Still, if it meant saving Layla's life or giving her a better quality of life, Jaclyn was more than willing to do it.

15

NEVER A STORY OF MORE WOE

PICKING UP MIKE'S THINGS at the station was the thing Maddie dreaded the most. She knew Jackie would be there with her new pet, Layla Harker. She wanted to call Layla a girlfriend-stealing whore, but she didn't know the woman. It wasn't Layla's fault that Jackie omitted crucial details when she slept with her.

Details like the fact that Jackie already had a girlfriend with whom she was already sleeping with. Maddie shook her head and tried to calm herself. It wasn't just men who cheated, after all. Women could lie and cheat with the best of them.

She parked her blacked-out Lincoln Aviator in front of the station and entered through the side entrance. She signed in at the counter and tried her best not to be seen by anyone who would recognize her. She was about to make it to Mike's desk when Jackie stepped out from behind the corner of the room.

"Oh, hey," Madeline said. Jackie brushed her hair back over her shoulder and smiled at her with the fucking amazing smile. It wasn't fair, Madeline thought. Breaking up over a one-time fling when they weren't even married. Hell, she didn't know what they were.

"Hey there," Jackie replied. "How–"

"I–"

They started to speak simultaneously, accidentally cutting each other off.

"You go first," Madeline insisted.

"How are you?" Jackie asked, reaching out and touching Maddie's arm.

Madeline didn't know whether to pull away or melt right there on the spot. "I'm good. Still not great. But you know...better."

"I bet you're here for Mike's things. I already have them packed and ready to go for you."

"You do?"

"Yeah, of course," Jackie replied, smiling at her. They stared at one another for a moment, and Jackie grabbed her jacket off the back of her chair and said, "Come on, I'm taking you to lunch."

"I don't know if that's a good idea," Madeline replied.

"I won't take no for an answer," Jackie insisted.

Madeline debated taking her up on the offer. She knew it would end in make-up sex or some other ridiculous things like her asking Jackie to move in again. No, she wasn't ready for anything like that. Jackie needed to figure out what she wanted in life.

Reluctantly, she agreed to go to lunch. "All right. But just lunch and nothing else. I'm not going to let you break my heart again."

There was a prolonged silence as Jackie turned and looked at Madeline with sad eyes. "Fair enough," she said, then waved her hand for Madeleine to go on ahead.

They had almost made it to the exit when Layla Harker, wearing an arm sling, walked through the door. Practically running into each other, they all stopped in the middle of the hallway.

"Hey, babe," Jackie said, leaning forward and giving Layla a peck on the cheek. "I'm taking Madeline out for lunch. I hope that's okay?"

"It's fine with me," Layla said. She turned to Madeline and said, "I'm so sorry for your loss." Then she shot Jaclyn a sharp look as if to say *you better know what you're doing.*

Madeline insisted on driving, so she drove them downtown to her favorite Italian place, Lucali Bianco's. It only seated about twelve, but they had the best carbonara sauce she'd ever tasted, and their garlic bread sticks made Olive Garden's taste like greasy cardboard by comparison.

She ordered a couple of glasses of red wine, and they talked about their past week. To Madeline's surprise, Jackie was upfront with her about what happened to Layla.

"Yeah, she was in the hospital almost two full weeks. Yesterday was her official first day back on duty," Jackie informed.

"Well, I hope she's doing better now. You look good," Madeline said.

"That's the wine talking," Jackie teased.

"You always look good," Madeline insisted. "It's almost as if you never age. I'm already starting to get wrinkles and finding rogue gray hairs. You look as new as the day the stork dropped you on your parents' front doorstep."

"It was the back doorstep," Jackie corrected.

Madeline laughed, which also prompted a laugh to slip out of Jackie's lips. Soon, they were talking as if it were old times.

Madeline placed her hand on Jackie's, letting her giggles subside, then took a breath and came out with it. "I've been diagnosed with breast cancer, Jackie. I'm scheduled for a double mastectomy this time next month. I know we're not on the best of terms right now, but I want you by my side."

Jackie took both Madeline's hands in hers. "Of course, I'll be there for you. One-hundred percent. All you need to do is ask."

"You talk as if you still love me," Madeline said, her gaze sinking to the table with sadness.

Jackie gently placed her fingers under Madeline's chin and raised her chin up until their eyes met. "I do love you. I never stopped loving you, Maddie. It's just with everything, Mike, the murders, Layla, things were getting too complex. At one point, it felt like I was with you because you were like this forbidden fruit. I had to have you. But you were better than anything I could ever hope to find in a hundred lifetimes. And I got scared. I messed up and lost the best thing I ever had."

"My offer still stands," Madeline said. You're welcome to move in with me if you'd like. I don't even care if you're still seeing Layla. We can be roommates or whatever you'd like."

Jackie smiled. "I appreciate that. And if rent in this town gets any fucking higher, I'll take you up on that offer. But, right now, I think I'm good."

Madeline nodded, feeling that she wanted to tell Jackie she was still head over heels for her and that she'd do anything to win her back. But the pasta arrived, and Madeline decided to bite her tongue, keep her gushing sob story to herself, and drown her woes in freshly baked bread and cheesy goodness.

Holding up her wine glass, Madeline said, "To us!"

Jackie clinked her glass against Maddie's and, with a smile, replied in kind. "To us!"

They downed their glasses in one long swill and ordered another round.

By the time they'd finished dessert and were stumbling drunkenly to the car, they'd put the past squarely in the past.

"You sure you don't want to come over?" Madeline asked.

"I would, but Layla is waiting for me back at the office. But I promise I'll be there tomorrow and every day afterward to help you through this tough time."

Madeline flung her arms around Jackie and hugged her, squeezing as hard as she could. Jackie buried her face on Madeline's shoulder and took in her scent. She still smelled like a summer breeze.

Madeline leaned forward and pecked Jackie on the cheek. Then she got into her car and told it, "Home." The car started and began to drive her to her destination. Madeline looked out of her rearview mirror to see Jackie waving goodbye as she stood in front of the restaurant.

The Aviator pulled into Madeline's driveway and parked itself. When the motor turned off, she opened her car door and slid out. Still a bit tipsy, she began making her way to her front steps when she heard something and spun around.

A figure stood on the sidewalk, directly under the streetlamp. He wore a dark hoodie, and Madeline's heart nearly skipped a beat from fright.

"Oh, shit," she said, rummaging through her purse, searching for her mace.

"Jaclyn Benoit can't be trusted," the man in the hood said.

"Jaclyn?" asked Madeline, feigning ignorance.

"Don't pretend like you don't know her. I saw you both at the funeral exchanging words. It looked like she wronged you. And you'd be right."

The man reached up and pulled down his hood, revealing the face of a twenty-something black kid.

"How do you know Jacklyn?" she asked.

"Oh, that's the thing, Mrs. Michaelson. I know her in passing. I know her from the night she and your husband interrogated me for the murder of Danielle Pruette. Don't look so worried. I'm walking free, so clearly, I didn't do it. But I saw the person who killed your husband."

"You what?" she asked, her voice growing stern as if she didn't appreciate being lied to.

"I'm not lying. I saw who killed your husband, Mrs. Michaelson. I'd be happy to testify if you'd like. Until then, here's my card." Darius reached into his pocket, drew up a business card for West Side Bowling Lanes, and handed it to her.

"Meet me here, and I'll tell you everything I know."

Madeline took the card and looked it over. After reading it, she had so many questions and looked back up to ask a few follow-up questions, but the kid was gone. She stepped out into the street and looked up and down the boulevard, but he wasn't anywhere to be seen. It was as if he had vanished into thin air.

She looked down at the card again. "Screw it," she said. And with that, she drew out her car keys and got back into her SUV.

Madeline sped the whole way out to the West Side Lanes and parked her car. The parking lot was dark, but it was filled with approximately two dozen vehicles. It was the first time since the murder of that girl that she'd ever seen the bowling alley full.

She got out and locked her car using her key fob. Cutting across the lot, she entered the bowling alley.

Inside, techno music was thumping, and people were dancing as if they had nothing to lose because it was the end of the world. They even had a giant disco ball casting beams of light all over the room as it spun to the rhythm of the music. She navigated a sea of college kids until she found the black kid from earlier sitting with two lovely women.

"Mrs. Michaelson, glad you could make it." My name is Darius. Darius Reid. This is Sophie and Amber." He stood up and shook her hand, and then offered her a seat next to them. "I wasn't sure you'd come."

"If you know who my husband's killer is, of course I needed to come."

"Do you want anything? Something to drink, perhaps?"

She shook her head and then leaned forward. "All I want is the name of the person that I need to report to the authorities."

"I see," Darius said. "You're not messing around."

"Damn straight." This elicited nods of admiration from the two girls.

Darius leaned in. "I'll tell you. But you're not going to like the answer." When she didn't reply but merely held his gaze, he could tell she was determined to find out. "That night, I was leaving the station, and I saw Jaclyn Benoit cutting Detective Michaelson's throat."

Madeline stood up, her eyes burning furiously as she didn't believe him. "What is this, some sick joke? Did you find out Jackie and I were in love and seeing each other, and decide it would be fun to mess with the old widow?"

"It's no joke, lady," Sophie said. Darius raised a hand,

gesturing to her to hold off from commenting for now.

Madeline wagged a finger in his face and scolded them even more. "I don't know what you and your friends are up to, but Jaclyn Benoit is a good woman." And you should be ashamed for even suggesting something like this. It's sick. You're all sick!"

Darius didn't respond as she expected. Instead, he merely slid his cell phone across the table. "You might want to take a look at this."

Madeline picked up the phone and saw what appeared to be Jackie kissing Mike. She was necking with him in the alley behind the precinct, her hands all over his body. It only dawned on her then that maybe she was seeing him, too, which was why he was fine with her and Jackie being together. Perhaps they were a messed-up trio.

Madeline screamed and almost dropped the phone when Jackie turned around. But clutching it tight in both hands, she brought it close to her face and then paused the image. Jackie's mouth was covered in thick crimson, and Mike's throat was spurting blood. Without a shred of remorse, she'd ripped out his throat.

Dropping the phone, Madeline slowly backed up and pointed down at it. "What the fuck is that?"

"It's proof," Darius said. Proof that Jaclyn Benoit isn't what she appears to be. How much do we really know about Detective Benoit? She appeared five years ago, and subsequently, people began to go missing. Not many at first. Just every other month or so. Then, almost overnight, the killings increased. Five are murdered at Mel's diner. Then Danielle Pruette turns up dead. And, less than a week after that, there's a massacre at the community college. It's like the Blood Drive murders all over again, but ten times worse."

Darius pinned the college massacre on Jaclyn, but it only made sense. She's the one who made him, and so shared some of the blame. None of this would have happened if she had left him alone that evening.

"I still can't believe it," Madeline said.

"Oh, believe it, sister," Amber chimed in. "The bitch is a grade-A, bona fide psycho."

"Why did you wait till now to tell me all this? Why didn't you come forward earlier? My husband's killer has been walking free all this time. I mean, Jackie and I, we…"

Madeline stumbled forward and reached out to grab the back of the booth. Darius jumped up and caught her in his arms, helping her sit back down.

"Mrs. Michaelson, believe me when I tell you that I wanted to come forward earlier. I did. But who do you think they'll believe? Some black kid from the poor side of town or the beautiful white cop who busted her ass to climb the ranks to become a detective?"

"I see your point," Madeline said. Sophie brought her a glass of water, and she drank it. After calming herself, she turned to Darius and asked, "What now?"

"Now, we make the bitch pay."

She nodded and looked over at the two girls, who were smiling ear to ear. Madeline almost did a double-take because it looked like they had vampire teeth. "How do you propose we do that?" she inquired, turning back to face Darius.

Darius rose and began walking toward the dance floor. As he stepped out onto the dance floor, the music died, and everyone parted as though he were their king. He walked to the sound stage, where Velma was tuning her guitar. He wrapped his arms around Velma and kissed her. "How do you think we should make the bitch detective pay, babe?"

Velma smiled. "We take what's most important to her."

Madeline nodded along with that idea. Suddenly, the two girls sat on either side of her and ran their hands over her. Leaning uncomfortably close, they began smelling her hair and skin. This made her feel a little awkward, but she tolerated it. That's when she realized that Darius and the entire group of young people were all staring at her. Now, it was getting freaky.

"Don't worry," the red-headed girl said, stroking her hair. "We'll make it painless."

"What?" Madeline asked.

"You silly girl," the blonde said. "Don't you see? *You're* the thing Jaclyn prizes most in the world. It's not your fault. You'll just be another victim of her reign of terror."

Scared, Madeline tried to stand, but both women pulled her back down and pinned her to her seat. "Let go of me," she demanded. I'm the wife of a police officer. You can't..."

The blonde pushed a finger to Madeline's mouth, silencing her. *"Shhh."*

Darius shot both of his consorts an affirming look, and then they turned and hissed, their fangs growing. Madeline tried to fight them off, but before she could reach out for the gun in her purse, they sank their fangs into her. She screamed.

As they drank, she thrashed and fought and cried. A couple of days ago, she had resigned herself to the fact that the cancer would likely take her. But now, knowing what she knew, she couldn't let them kill her. Not until she had her revenge.

"I beg you, please don't kill me. Not yet. Not until I get my revenge on that two-faced slut."

Darius raised a hand, and both women stopped feeding and drew back.

"If I make you into a vampire, there's no going back. So, you need to think this through."

"Oh," Madeline said, her voice practically a growl, "I've thought it through. That bitch needs to pay for what she did to Mike. For what she did to me. To you. All of us."

Darius thought about it for a long time and then, smiling, replied, "Nah." We're good."

The blonde and the redhead looked at each other and smiled. Then they piled onto Madeline, sinking their fangs into her. All she could do was scream as they bit into her. Worse than that, she felt them clawing at her skin.

Somehow, she managed to break free, staggered forward, and stumbled into the crowd. Running up to people at random, she begged them for their help: "Please, you have to help me. Can't you see what's happening? Please call nine-one-one. Call somebody! Anybody. Please!"

Madeline bumped into one person after another but always managed to find herself falling back to the center of the dance floor—the one place she didn't want to be.

She slowly stood in the middle of the dance floor, surrounded by about forty or fifty young people. Getting caught up in the ebb and flow of the crowd caused her to panic, and she spun around, looking for a way out.

She noticed something wasn't quite right as she did a full circle. They smiled at her with razor-sharp fangs protruding from behind lips stretched too tightly across their pale faces. They weren't normal college kids. They were vampires.

The group gathered around her and began hissing like venomous snakes. Slowly, they closed in on her, tighter and tighter, until she knew there was no possibility of escape.

Her heart sank in her chest. Darius had offered her the one

thing she'd wanted—her husband's killer. But in an ironic twist of events, the one thing the vampire killer wanted was her, because he knew killing her would hurt Jackie more than anything.

She was the sacrifice. And like a fool, she took the bait. She'd walked right into the vampire's den. She sank to her knees as the circle of hissing vampires closed in on her.

She looked up at the disco ball gleaming on the ceiling. Then, with a splatter, it was coated in a red spackle, and she felt herself start to fade.

Staring up at the ceiling, the black fringes at the edge of her vision blended with the crimson wash that flooded her sight, and she realized that the blood was her own and that she was already as good as dead.

16

THE VAMPIRE KING'S BROOD

JACLYN CUPPED HER HANDS on Maddie's window and peered into her house. She rang the doorbell, but there was no answer. It was right about now that she kicked herself for giving up that spare key.

The inside of the house was dark. Where could she be, Jackie wondered. She said she'd be home. They agreed to let Jackie come at 7:00 AM sharp, have breakfast together, and talk about, well, Maddie's unfortunate diagnosis.

She contemplated kicking in the door and was almost about to think of reasons to justify breaking into her ex-girlfriend's home without coming off like a stalker creep when her phone rang.

"Detective Benoit," she said, without even glancing at the caller. When she heard Layla's voice, she felt a sense of relief.

That is, until Layla told her the reason for the call.

"Come again? Where exactly are you?"

Jaclyn's face went blank, and she jammed her phone in her pocket, leaped down the stairs, and ran to her car. She peeled out and turned on her police lights. Speeding through every stoplight and intersection in town, she got the Hellcat up to 137 mph as she raced out of town.

Skidding to a stop at the edge of the road, she flew out of her car without bothering to close her door. Two other squad cars were on the scene, and she saw Layla standing down near the river. Right next to the Wood River bridge.

Layla saw her coming and intercepted her, grabbing her shoulders and holding her back. "No, Jackie. Listen to me. You don't want to see this."

"Let go of me," Jackie shouted, pushing Layla out of her way. She ran forward, nearly bowling over one of her fellow officers. She broke down into tears when she looked down at the spot – the same spot she'd been standing in weeks prior.

In the exact spot where Danielle Pruette had been dumped lay Madeline Michaelson. Her body wasn't pristine. It was shredded as though it had gone through a butcher's meat slicer. Many of the lacerations were still wet with fresh blood.

Jaclyn screamed at the top of her lungs and collapsed to her knees. Layla was there and dropped down alongside her and threw her arm over her as Jaclyn grabbed Layla's shirt and wrung it tightly in both hands, sobbing uncontrollably.

Every inch of Madeline had what appeared to be claw marks on her. It was as if she was mauled by a long procession of wild animals who all decided to take turns attacking her. Only her face was left relatively unscathed, with only one or two minor cuts.

That's how she knew it was a statement—a message. The killer wanted her to know he knew who she held dear. They wanted her to see that they knew who and what she was and that they could reach out and snatch the ones she loved right out of her arms.

Maddie's body looked like one of those poor college students who had been murdered a few weeks earlier. Deep in her undead gut, she knew that it was Darius's doing. He was the only one who knew what she was from the beginning. He was the only one who could enact such savagery in a state of blind rage.

What had she done? Jaclyn had created Darius. She'd created a monster. A monster who hadn't stopped at one victim. Or even two or three. The mayor was already calling for nine o'clock curfews due to the number of missing people, most of them young people. What had Darius been up to these past several weeks? What twisted Machiavellian machinations had he concocted?

Unable to look at Madeline's mutilated body any longer, Jaclyn stood up and started back up the hill toward her car. Layla reached out and grabbed her sleeve, but she jerked it away and kept going.

"What are you planning to do?" asked Layla, following Jaclyn up the hill. Layla was doubly concerned because, unlike the rest of the town, she knew Jaclyn's true nature. She knew that she was perhaps the most dangerous thing in Wood River—even more dangerous than the killer they'd been hunting.

"I have a date with my hellspawn," Jaclyn answered.

"Your hellspawn?" That's when Layla realized she meant the kid, Darius. Knowing that Jaclyn Benoit was not stopping when she was determined, all she could do was call out to her and wish her luck. "Stay safe, babe."

She wasn't sure Jaclyn had heard her over the rumble of the car's V8, which sounded as angry as she was. The engine roared to life, and Jaclyn raced away in her Hellcat.

Smoke from burned rubber wafted toward Layla, creating a smoky haze all around her. She turned around and looked down at Madeline's body lying in the grass by the bank of the river, and put her hands on her hips. "Well, this sucks."

Racing out of town to West Side Bowling Lanes, Jaclyn slammed on the brakes, bringing her car to a screeching halt in front of the building. She nearly tore her door off its hinges as she exited and marched through the front entrance.

It was morning, so she didn't expect any patrons to be at the establishment. However, to her surprise, the place was packed with young people lounging about. The entire establishment smelled like marijuana, and she could see the ones who were awake were huddled together, passing blunts around. Others sprawled out, passed out on the floor. Some were naked and having sex in random places in the bowling alley. She recognized Nightwisps when she saw them.

Darius had been busy making vampires. She was amazed that he was smart enough to keep them weak. Keep them Nightwisps – vampires that had to cling to the dark lest they burst into flames by the slightest touch of daylight. That way, he had power over them. But right now, she didn't care what kinds of trouble they were up to. They couldn't leave the bowling alley until nightfall. Right now, she only wanted Darius.

Weaving between slumbering bodies, careful not to step on

anyone, she went over to the back booth, where two women sat staring vacantly out across the dance floor with maudlin eyes. Their backs to the bowling lanes, the two women seemed to be in a daze, their eyes half open. As she drew close, she noticed how bloodshot their eyes were and knew they were stoned out of their minds.

"Where is he?" Jacklyn growled.

"Where's who?" the redhead asked.

Jaclyn slapped the girl who sat up, startled by the uncalled-for violence. "Hey, that was uncalled for.

"I'll ask you one more time. Where is that little prick, Darius?"

The girl leaned forward. "Darius?" She laughed. "He's probably at home with his mommy. He's such a spoilsport. He never wants to join in on the fun."

"Why do you want to talk to Darius?" the blonde asked. She tapped a cigarette out of a pack and then licked it. She flicked the cigarette around with her tongue, twirled it in her mouth, and then slid it the right way out. Bridging up a lighter, she lit it and blew the smoke directly at Jaclyn.

Jaclyn waved her hand in front of her face, breaking up the smoke. "I don't just want to talk to him, I want to tan his no-good hide."

"Why so angry?" the redhead asked. "It's not like you found your best friend murdered like he did. Oh, no, wait. You did, didn't you?"

Jaclyn shot the girl with an icy glare and asked, "What do you know about Madeline's murder?"

"We know that it's been a month, and yet, Danielle Pruette's murder is out there somewhere, walking free. For all we know, she could be you. After all, you have no problem killing innocent people like that partner of yours. Who's to say you didn't kill Ms. Pruette, too?"

"If that's what he told you, it's a lie."

Both girls stood up and began to walk around Jaclyn like wolves circling their prey. "Come now, detective. We know what you are. We're all the same here." She swept her hand across the sea of writhing bodies, gesturing to the brood of vampires that had taken over the bowling lanes like a terrible plague.

"I'm nothing like you, soulless, gutless, little whelps."

Popping their fangs, both girls hissed at Jaclyn. Instinctually, she popped her fangs and hissed louder. They were but pups. She was an experienced vampire, over one hundred and eighty years old. Most of these baby-fanged vampires weren't even a week old.

"You'd be wise to put away those fangs, lest I tear them from your skulls and make necklaces with them."

"Oh, so vicious. Darius told us to be careful with this one," Sophie laughed.

"True, sister. He did warn us of her bloodlust," Amber answered.

Jaclyn felt she was wasting her time. These fledglings only wanted to toy with her. But they were merely distractions. Darius was who she wanted. She turned to leave but felt a hand reach out and grab her arm. She looked down at the hand on her arm and then slowly raised her eyes to find the blonde holding her back, the girl's nails biting into Jaclyn's flesh.

"We didn't say you could leave yet."

Jaclyn grabbed the girl by her throat and, moving so fast they both blurred out of sight, they flew across the room. Smashing into the bar and the numerous shelves of fine liquors, they shattered all the glass, along with the reflective mirrors that added depth to the bar display. Crashing to the floor, Sophie coughed up blood.

The entire bowling alley came to life, and everyone looked up to see Jaclyn's demon wings fully extended. She glanced over her shoulder at them all, and they crawled back, retreating to the depths of the bowling alley with fear.

"Are you going to kill me?" the girl wheezed, her hands rubbing her throat.

"No," Jaclyn replied, standing over the girl and glancing back to ensure none of the Nightwisps tried anything funny.

Amber, the redhead, stepped forward. "I think you should leave, Detective Benoit," she said, her voice turning sincere. "He's not here."

Jaclyn looked at all the faces, realizing they were all Darius's progeny. As such, they were her grandchildren. My God, she thought. He's been creating an army. But for what purpose? What was he planning?

Storming out of the bowling alley, she retracted her wings and got back into her car. With a rumble of the V8, the Hellcat roared to life, and she peeled out of the parking lot.

Six minutes later, she stood at Darius's front door and talked to a lovely old lady.

"No, Mrs. Reid. Your son isn't in any trouble. I need to ask him some follow-up questions regarding the Pruette case."

"Well, he's not here right now," she replied. "I think he might've had a class today."

"Class?"

"At the community college. My son is now a college student.

"I bet you're proud of him."

"A mother's love knows no bounds, but it warms my heart

to see he's trying to make something of himself. Since losing his father, Darius hasn't come out of his shell. But he seems to be a new man over the past few weeks.

That was the understatement of the century, Jaclyn thought. But it wasn't her place to butt into family affairs. "Thanks for your time, Mrs. Reid. Maybe I'll catch up with your son another time."

Jaclyn smiled and then turned down the steps. College had started again, as she knew it would, but for Darius to return to the crime scene was bold, even by his standards.

She decided it would be best to walk there. It was six or seven blocks away, but she needed to calm herself and collect her thoughts. If she killed him for murdering Madeline, she wouldn't be any better than he was. She needed to talk to him and figure out what his end game was.

When she arrived on campus, it looked strange. It was all cleaned up, and there wasn't a trace of the bloodbath that had stained the campus just a few weeks ago. It felt peaceful and calm somehow.

She noticed some students giving her nervous glances, and she looked down to see her badge prominently displayed. With everything that had transpired, she didn't blame them. It's best to be aware of your surroundings and take notice when something doesn't belong.

Finding her way to the main lecture hall, she saw about a dozen students waiting for the teacher to get there. But Darius wasn't among them.

"Hey," she asked a student sitting close to the back entrance, "Is this the accounting course?" He was tapping his pencil on the edge of his desk as though he were keeping the beat to some epic drum solo.

"Yeah," the young man answered. He looked up at her and then smiled. "Whoa, you're hot. Do you want to get some drinks later?

She tapped a finger on her badge. "I'm flattered, but no, thank you. You're a little young for my tastes." The kid shrugged and then resumed tapping his pencil on the side of his desk.

The instructor was late to the lecture, so she consulted the campus map and located the business department. Luckily, it was in the same building, but down the hall and to the right, then down another hall, and finally, at the end of the East Wing.

She entered the accounting department offices, but no secretary was at the front desk. Most of the offices were dark, as the professors were probably all currently teaching their courses, all but one. She went over to the door and knocked twice, but not hearing any reply, she decided to open it.

Jaclyn opened the door and leaned in to find Darius balls deep in Miss Anderson's ass. Her skirt riding up on her hips, her blouse completely open, Darius's hands reached around her body and groped her chest.

Having unexpectedly appeared at the entrance, they both looked at her with shocked faces, and Anderson gasped, her libidinous breath masking an orgasm, *"Detective Benoit?"*

"Oh, shit. I'm so sorry," Jaclyn said, quickly closing the door. At a loss for words, she stepped back and just laughed away the awkwardness.

What would she even say? They were both consenting adults. Nothing illegal was going on. At most, they were maybe breaking some arcane campus policy found in an outdated school handbook somewhere.

To her relief, she didn't have to wait for long. Half a minute later, the door flew open, and Miss Anderson walked out of her office, hastily tucking her buttoned-up shirt back into her skirt.

"How may I help you, detective?" she asked, looking up at Jackie with big eyes and what Jaclyn could only assume were false lashes. The sweet scent of sweat dappled her chest, and Jackie's heightened senses could detect trace amounts of Darius's semen on her breath.

"Actually, I'm here to see Darius Reid," she said. "His mother said I'd find him on campus." Jutting a thumb over her shoulder, she added, "Yours was the only room with a light on. I'm sorry to have barged in like this."

Miss Anderson's cheeks went flush with embarrassment. "Right, well, he'll be out in a minute. He's just...getting..." She paused to check her watch and then quickly changed the subject. If you don't mind, I'm running late for class. Please excuse me."

Jaclyn nodded and stepped to the side to allow Miss Anderson to go teach her class. When she looked over her shoulder at the office, Darius was standing in the doorway, nonchalantly leaning on the frame, his face creased into a crooked grin.

"How can I help you, Jaclyn? You don't mind if I call you Jaclyn, do you?"

"I prefer my friends to call me Jackie."

"Are we friends?" he asked.

"No," she said. "I suppose we have a different dynamic." She looked up and down the hall and then said, "We need to talk."

"It took you long enough," Darius replied.

She shot him a puzzled look. "What does that mean?"

"It means what it means. You turned me into a monster. But it only took you a month to want to talk about it."

"We're not monsters," she said, even though she knew that she didn't believe it herself. They were monsters, but they also retained remnants of their humanity. All they could do was try to forge a new identity, one where both the good and the bad hybridized into something new—hopefully, something better.

"You don't sound so certain," he said, catching her in the lie.

"Maybe not. But I do know we're more than that, monsters or not. Don't let the monster define you, Darius. Don't give up your humanity. Because once you let go, there's no going back. The monster is all that will remain."

Darius strolled past her and covered a yawn. It was almost as if he were bored by her pontificating. "Is that what you wanted to tell me? That I'm better than the total sum of my experiences?"

"We are the total sum of our experiences," she replied. "How you choose to use the lessons from those experiences is what defines you."

She followed him even though she didn't know where he was leading her. They walked out the back exit, across a small Japanese-style garden behind the university replete with a coy pond, and then to the very edge of campus.

The campus sat on the cusp of town, and, other than the access road they built behind it, it looked out onto the cornfields. They stood together, looking out at the corn gently swaying in the breeze.

"How long have you been a vampire?" he asked.

"Almost two hundred years," she replied.

He glanced at her. One eyebrow was raised in curiosity. "Really? That long, huh? Interesting."

"Why's that interesting?"

"Because it means that I have time."

She stared at him for the longest time, waiting for him to finish that thought.

"Look, detective, from monster to monster, Wood River is mine. You can move on and find another town where you can play cop. But this one is going to be my domain. All I ask is that you respect that."

"Play cop? I am a cop. Or does this badge no longer hold any meaning for you?"

Darius shrugged.

I don't understand why you're being territorial. What are you saying, Darius, that you're some self-proclaimed king? King of the Vampires?"

"What's wrong with having dreams, detective?"

"Let's cut the bullshit and get to brass tacks. Did you kill Madeline Michaelson or not? If not, we're fine here. If so, then I'll have no choice but to take you into custody. And I know that would break your poor mom's heart."

Darius looked her straight in the eyes and answered, "No. I didn't kill the cop's wife."

It was such a definitive answer that she was almost taken aback. "No?"

"I didn't kill her," he reiterated. A subtle grin began to form on his face as he continued, "My acolytes did."

"You're admitting it then?"

"I admit only that a rogue group of vampires killed both Detective Michaelson and his wife. Shall we take it to the authorities?" He looked her dead in the eye, and she turned away.

Her brow tightened, a crease forming at the bridge of her nose as she turned and glowered at him. "You're not going to get away with this. I will expose you."

"Not without exposing yourself, I'm afraid, *Jackie*." Now that they were so familiar with one another, he emphasized her name.

She glowered at him even more, but it didn't faze him. He smiled in return, his bright white teeth showing. His fangs gleaming in the daylight. Darius was formidable, that was for sure.

"I lost so many over the years I've lost count. So many slipped away into the afterlife. After a while, you become numb to it. Indifferent. Being a vampire isn't always easy, and your only companion is death. There's been enough death in Wood River to last us more than a lifetime. So, I'm asking you, as a favor, please, no more murders in Wood River.

"A favor, huh? And if I refuse?"

"If you refuse, then I will bring the full weight of the law down on you. Do I make myself clear?"

Darius smacked his teeth in annoyance and grumbled, "Crystal."

He wasn't intimidated by her anymore, and she needed to know who the new King in town was—the King of the vampires. Turning toward her, he grabbed her face and kissed her lips, pulling her into him.

Jaclyn drew back, pushing Darius away with her hands. Wiping her mouth, she looked at him and said, "What the fuck, dude?"

"Isn't that how you made me? If I recall, you had to sleep with me for me to gain your powers. You poured your blood down my throat and then sealed it with a kiss, no?"

"It's called the vampire's kiss," she informed him. "If you bite someone to turn them into a vampire, you must drink all their blood. After that, you share yours with them to revitalize them. It's at this point that you can choose which sort of vampire to make. If you let them on their way, they will turn into

Nightwisps."

"Nightwisps?" he asked. "I've just been calling them Ash-Heads because they always burn up." He laughed. "It took me about five tries before I figured it out with Velma. You must fuck the ones you want to be your equal."

"If you sleep with them, in the Platonic sense, the transference of their soul and yours will bond in the dream world, where you usually have visions of mating with them as your partner. The visions are primal, animalistic, and sometimes obscenely graphic. Somehow, this mating ritual tethers them to your curse in the real world. It's all about vampiric mysticism, and I don't fully understand how it works. Like me, though, you figured it out on your own."

"Yippee-kai-yay for me," Darius said sarcastically. "Do I get a gold star?"

"Darius," she began. Then stopped and looked away. "Would it even matter if I said I was sorry?"

He looked at her and smiled. "Probably not. I mean, it's already too late for an apology, don't you think?"

She looked at him again. Then, as she walked out into the street, she turned around. Throwing out her arms, she spread her wings five feet in either direction, showcasing her impressive ten-foot wingspan.

"Holy shit!" Darius said. "That's fucking awesome. Why don't I have wings?

"Because," she replied, "the only way to get wings is to take them from your Master."

"You mean I have to kill you to get them?"

"That's how it works. But you couldn't kill me even if you tried."

"I guess we shall see."

She pointed at him and narrowed her eyes. "No more killing. I mean it. Next time, I'll have no choice but to arrest you and any of your so-called Ash-Head acolytes."

With the flap of her giant wings, Jaclyn crouched down, leaped up into the air, and flew away into the night sky.

Darius stared up at her, watching her in awe. "I want those wings," he muttered, envious of her special abilities.

17

THE SLAYER'S REPRISE

SOARING THROUGH THE SKY in broad daylight was risky. But as the alpha vampire, she needed to put the pup in his place. Darius wouldn't stand a chance if it did come down to an altercation between them. What did bother her, however, was the army he was creating. If she let that go unchecked, it could become a much bigger problem down the road.

A few minutes later, she touched down on the roof of her apartment. Folding her wings up, she turned to the rooftop hutch and opened the door. She walked down the stairs to her landing and then entered her apartment.

Once inside, she shut her door and leaned against it, letting out a loud sigh.

"You home?" a voice called out from her bathroom.

Jaclyn smiled. She wasn't expecting company, but Layla's

voice put her at ease. It was nice to have someone she cared for so deeply. And their relationship, which had been growing over the past three weeks, continued to deepen.

Even when she was with Maddie, as badly as she wanted a future with her, she knew it would never have been possible. There had been too many secrets between them, not to mention all the things that threatened to pull them apart rather than build them up.

The death of Michaelson was the inevitable wedge that would drive them apart and destroy their relationship. And the truth was, she had loved Madeline so much that she knew the best thing was to let her go, to let her move on with her life.

"Uh, yeah, babe. "I'm home," Jaclyn answered, tossing her car keys into the bowl on the console table by her entrance.

Layla stepped out of the bathroom, brushing her teeth. She was wearing tight, yellow shorts with pink trim that drew attention to her long, slender legs, and a black spaghetti-strap tank top as her nightshirt.

"What time is it?" Jackie asked.

"It's a quarter after eight. I just hopped out of the shower."

"I must have lost track of time."

Pulling out her toothbrush, Layla looked at Jackie with heavy eyes. "Did it go okay?"

"The thing with Darius? You'll be happy to learn I didn't tear his head off."

"You didn't kill him? I'm impressed."

"We talked. He made a pretty solid argument. I created him. One monster has inevitably created another monster, and in this act of creation, I'm culpable. If I come for him, he'll expose me for Michaelson's murder."

"So, Madeline was just a pawn in his twisted game of chess,

then?"

"Essentially, yes. It was his way of hurting me for turning him. And by killing her, he hoped to provoke me enough to out myself as the monster of Wood River."

Layla put her toothbrush back in her mouth. She didn't know what to say. Sure, Jaclyn had killed in the past. How many had she killed over her approximate two hundred years as a vampire? She didn't want to think about it.

However, the fact remained that Jackie was an apex predator amongst all apex predators. The lion kills the gazelle for food. The tiger stalks the water buffalo from the nearby foliage. The wolf hunts white-tailed deer through the snow-covered mountains. And vampires prey upon humans.

Jaclyn just happened to be at the top of the food chain. That wasn't her fault.

It was hard to judge someone for their basic nature—something they had no control over. People had judged Layla for being gay her whole life. Would she simply be making the same mistake by judging Jaclyn as a cold, cold-blooded killer? No, she was more than that.

But the Lady Justice whispered to her conscience, letting her know that Jaclyn's murders couldn't be ignored forever. Eventually, Layla would have to fulfill her promise to arrest Jaclyn for her crimes. Then, vampire or not, it was open season on Detective Jaclyn Benoit.

After all, Layla Harker hadn't gotten the nickname the Pied Piper of the Marshal's Service for no reason. They called her that because she always came for you, no matter what. Usually, it came with the acknowledgment that she'd drive the criminals out of town, just like the Pied Piper of Hamelin, driving the rats over the cliffs.

Criminals always run. Apply enough pressure and turn up the heat in the kitchen, and they bolt. That's how she always caught her perps. Wood River was different, however. Things weren't so black and white in this town.

Maybe Jaclyn was a monster in the literal sense. At the end of the day, though, perhaps the adage was correct. Sometimes, you need to fight fire with fire. And sometimes, you need to fight evil with evil.

"I can't out Darius and his brood of vampires without outing myself," Jaclyn continued. "He made it painfully clear that if he was going down, he was taking me with him."

"That sucks," Layla mumbled, toothbrush dangling from the corner of her mouth. "I definitely wouldn't want to be in your shoes."

Jaclyn sighed. "Yeah."

Layla went over to the kitchen sink, drank from the faucet, gargled, and then spit. Setting her toothbrush in the drying rack for the utensils, she turned toward Jaclyn and gave her an almost sorrowful look.

"I think it's time," she said, her voice delicate. She tugged at her shirt collar and pulled it down over her shoulder.

"Oh," Jaclyn said, realizing it was time to take Layla's pint of blood. It would be the first time she had drunk from Layla. It would be the first time she gained Layla's memories. "Are you sure? We can draw your blood the old-fashioned way and fill up some blood bags. I don't *need* to bite you, technically speaking."

"I know it sounds strange, but I want you to do it. Oddly enough, it feels like a way we can be more intimate together."

"I know we've discussed this a thousand times, but I need you to be certain." Once I drink from you, I'll know everything there is to know about you. I'll see your deepest, darkest secrets and fears. All your trauma, too."

"But you'll see my happy memories too. You'll gain a comprehensive understanding of who I am as a person. If you still love me after all that, I'll know I've made the right choice."

"Do you think I love you?" Jaclyn asked, catching her in the act of baiting her.

"But you do," Layla teased, smiling at her.

"Am I so transparent?"

"Only when you stand in front of a mirror," Layla teased.

"Hey!" Jaclyn said, raising a finger in protest. But before she could say anything else, Layla grabbed her by her shirt, drew her in, and silenced her lips with a kiss.

"What I'm saying, Jaclyn Benoit, is that I'm in love with you."

They kissed again, and Layla took Jaclyn's hand, guiding her to the bedroom. She settled onto the bed and then looked up at Jackie. "So, do I just lie here, or...?"

Jaclyn settled onto her knees by the side of the bed and popped her fangs. Slowly, she bent over Layla and ran her hands up and down Layla's legs as if she were giving her a light massage.

Unexpectedly, she grabbed Layla's thigh and spread Layla's legs apart. Layla leaned back on her elbows and peered down at Jaclyn as she dappled her inner thigh with a myriad of wet kisses.

Each kiss sent a tingling sensation through Layla's body. She wanted to scream out in pleasure, but held her breath instead. Right near the upper part of her thigh, Jaclyn sank her teeth into the softest area of her flesh. Layla let out an unexpected moan so sensual she thought she might orgasm. "Oh, fuck that's hot. I thought you were going to bite my neck."

After sucking for a while, Jaclyn pulled back and touched her finger to her temple.

"What is it?" Layla asked, a tinge of concern in her voice.

"Nothing. It's..." Growing overwhelmed by the flood of memories, Jaclyn began to cry. "It's just...I got flashes of Kandahar."

Layla sat up in bed and hugged Jaclyn. "You're the only person I've ever told."

Jaclyn sobbed into Layla's shoulder as they sat in bed holding one another.

"It'll be all right," Layla whispered, stroking Jaclyn's blonde hair. "I survived."

Jaclyn wiped her eyes and stood up beside the bed. "I'll kill them. I'll kill them all."

Layla gasped when she saw Jaclyn's eyes turn black. Then, biting her bottom lip, she rose to her knees, reached up with a gentle hand, and touched the side of Jackie's cheek.

"Look at me. Those memories are so distant to me now that they seem more like a bad dream I once had. I don't want to dredge up the past, especially about having been tortured. My healing journey has brought me to you. That's all that matters."

Leaning in, Layla kissed Jackie's lips when, suddenly, a loud crash came from the kitchen, startling both women.

"What was that?" Layla asked, clutching her chest. Springing into action, Layla went over to the dresser and fetched her gun. Holding it in front of her, she motioned for Jaclyn to head out into the hall first.

Following her out, they looked up and down the hall, but there were no signs of a break-in, at least not on this side of the apartment.

Another bang rattled about in the kitchen, followed by a whisper, "Oh, shit."

"Keep your voice down, or she'll hear us."

"Too late," Jaclyn said, stepping into the kitchen. "She's already heard you."

"See," the blonde from the bowling alley said, "I told you."

"It wasn't my fault," the redhead replied. "That lamp wasn't supposed to be there."

"What are you two doing in my kitchen?" Jaclyn asked, her eyes still a vampy black.

The blonde grabbed a knife from the knife rack on the kitchen counter and waved it threateningly. "Oh, you know. The Master wanted us to come teach you a lesson in manners."

"You do realize he sent you to your deaths, right?"

"Tsk, tsk," the blonde woman said, swaying back and forth as she continued to swipe the knife menacingly. "Slinging threats already, detective?"

"Sophie, what do you think...should we cut out her tongue?"

"Amber, shush. We shouldn't use our real names."

"Sophie and Amber, is it? Well, let me teach you what happens to uninvited guests."

Jaclyn moved so fast that they didn't have time to react. A smack echoed off the walls, followed by a gust of wind that seemed to come out of nowhere, and Amber flew across the room, crashing into the living room sofa. Tumbling over it and onto the hardwood floor, she smacked her head on the wood and then pushed herself up.

"Fuck my tits," Amber cursed. "The bitch hit me so hard I think I swallowed a tooth."

Sophie looked behind her shoulder to find Jaclyn's taloned claws reaching out for her. She was barely fast enough to evade the lacerating swipe. Leaping backward, she crashed into the kitchen counter and hissed at Jaclyn, warning her to stay back.

Jaclyn hissed back, louder and more forceful, and walked toward Sophie. This didn't deter Sophie, who lunged forward, thrusting her knife in front of her. "I'll kill you, you vamp whore!"

The muzzle of Layla Harker's gun spat flames from the kitchen doorway as she fired off two rounds at the blonde vamp.

Sophie stopped midway between her and Harker and, stunned, looked down at her shoulder. She'd been shot. Two slugs were now lodged in her shoulder, and they burned like a mother-fucker.

Enraged, she threw the knife at Harker, which embedded itself in the door frame next to Harker's face. It wobbled there briefly, and Harker looked at it with shock. "You missed."

"Fucking bitch!" Sophie growled, snapping back into the moment. "Of course, I missed! You fucking shot me!"

"You know what? I wish I could say that I'm sorry," Layla retorted. "But I'm not."

"Fuck you, you slu–" Before Sophie could finish slinging another insult, a hand grabbed her shoulder and yanked her back.

Sophie's feet lifted off the floor, and to her surprise, she flew across the kitchen, smashing into the opposite wall with a resounding thud. Then, she crumpled to the floor, and the wind knocked her out.

Rising from behind the sofa, Amber looked over at Sophie, who was already pushing herself back to her feet, and then over at Layla. "That wasn't very nice," Amber said. She then hissed at both Layla and Jaclyn, baring her fangs.

Distracted by Amber's hissy fit, Sophie leaped onto Jaclyn's back, clawing, scratching, and doing everything she could to gain the upper hand. At the same time, Amber looked over at

Layla, who promptly spun around and dashed into the hallway, making a quick retreat.

"Oh, no, you don't!" Amber said, chasing after Layla. "I'm not finished with you!"

Stepping into the hall, Amber looked down to see Layla aiming her gun at her.

"Shit!" Amber said, ducking just in time. The shot rang out, and the slug impacted the wall above her, shattering a painting frame of James Dean at the diner by Edward Hopper.

Rising back to her feet, Amber hissed again and then threw out her arms, extending her claws; she stared at Layla with a carnivorous intent. "I do like Indian food," she snarled.

"I'm Arabic, you fucking twat."

"Whatever. That's not the point. You're ethnic. And after I skin you alive, I'll suck the marrow from your bones! How's that sound?"

Amber lunged forward, and Layla dodged Amber's first swipe, but she couldn't evade the second. Screaming out in pain, Layla felt Amber's claws tear into her back. She stumbled to the ground and, placing a hand on the wall, was already pushing herself back up.

Amber paused to lick the blood from her fingers, allowing Layla enough time to get back onto her own two feet.

"*Yum*...tasty. I wonder how good the rest of you taste," Amber said, sliding her tongue between her two fingers and doing some mock cunnilingus in a lewd fashion.

Thrusting her shoulder into Amber, Layla slammed into her and propelled her into the hallway wall. Rebounding off the vampire girl, Layla flew backward, crashed into the bathroom door with full weight, and tumbled to the floor.

Landing on the soft shower mat on the floor, she rolled onto her back and aimed her gun at the door. She didn't think the redhead would be stupid enough to step into her sights, but she was proved wrong three seconds later when Amber suddenly appeared in the doorway.

"Sorry, but I'm already spoken for," she said, her finger squeezing down on the trigger.

A single shot drilled into Amber's head, forcing her to stop dead in her tracks. She reached up and touched the hole in her head. It took her a moment to process what had just happened. Gradually, a pleasantly surprised grin formed on her face.

"I thought that shot would have killed me," she said, sounding relieved. "But, since I can't be killed that easily, I'm going to tear you apart!" She hissed again and dove for Layla.

Layla didn't hesitate. The moment Amber lurched toward her, she squeezed down on the trigger, firing three more shots into the vamp's head.

Amber's body fell onto Layla, nearly knocking the wind out of her. Grunting, she rolled the vampire corpse off her and crawled on her elbows, scooting to the back of the bathroom. She kept her gun trained on Amber just in case those final shots didn't do the trick.

Most of Amber's head was completely missing, except for a piece of her lower jaw, which was hanging onto a strand of neck meat. The rest of her skull was blown to bits. Little more than a gooey stump of red gore, thicker than strawberry jam, remained. Most of her brains were splattered across Jaclyn's bathroom wall.

Layla hugged the toilet and then, with a pain-laden grunt, hoisted herself up. She fell back, her ass hitting the edge of the tub, and then sat there for a moment as she caught her breath. Once she was good, she forced herself to her feet, her legs shaking with adrenaline. She stepped over the body and, pulling back on the slide of her gun, loaded a fresh shot into the chamber as she darted into the hall and raced to help Jackie.

More crashing and banging rang out from the kitchen. Padding down the hall on tiptoes, she slipped into the kitchen undetected and found Sophie pinning Jaclyn against the kitchen island at the center of the kitchen area. Holding another knife to Jaclyn's throat, it looked as though things were about to get messy.

That's when Sophie's face went blank, and she staggered back. Slumping over onto the counter next to the sink, she looked up in shock as Jaclyn held her blackened heart in the palm of her hand. She'd torn it right out of Sophie's chest.

"You cock-gobbling whore-bag," Sophie said. "My goddamn heart...you tore it out of my fucking chest!"

"You weren't using it," Jaclyn said, tossing it over her shoulder. It landed with a wet-sounding splat on the floor. "Figured you didn't need it."

"*Hilarious*," Sophie said with droll sarcasm. She tried to take a step forward but fell back onto the counter again, the cabinet drawers rattling. "What did you do to me?"

"It will take your body a few hours to adjust to not having a heart. But you'll live. Well, technically, you're already dead, so you'll survive. But you get what I mean."

"I thought a stake through the heart would kill a vampire," she said, thick blood dribbling over her bottom lip.

"A stake through the heart won't stop a vampire," Jaclyn laughed. "You have to destroy the entire skull to kill a vampire."

"Good to know." Sophie opened the nearby drawer and pulled out a meat mallet. "All I need to do is batter in that little head of yours, detective. I hope you're ready to dance."

Mustering up enough strength to make one final assault, she raised the mallet high above her to bring it down on Jaclyn's head and was about to attack when another gunshot rang out.

Stunned, Sophie's eyes grew wide as she collapsed to her knees. Struggling to turn her head, she looked behind her to find Layla standing in the doorway, the barrel of her gun exhaling small gray wisps of smoke.

Jaclyn went up to Sophie and gently removed the hammer from her hand. Then, raising it high above her, Jaclyn grunted and brought the tenderizer down as hard as she could on Sophie's skull. There was a crack, the sound of her skull breaking open like a walnut, and then a wet slosh as the hammer pulverized her head.

Sophie's shoulders slumped, and her body tottered. Then, she fell onto her side. Her two eyes stared in opposite directions; her head cleaved in two.

Layla looked down at Sophie's mangled face, and she was relieved that they'd managed to fend off the intruders. Exhausted, she sank to her knees and slumped over.

"You're hurt," Jaclyn said, running up to Layla and putting her hand on her shoulder. Jaclyn inspected the fresh lacerations on Layla's back. It looked bad. It looked as though some psychopath had taken a blade saw to Layla's skin and cut her up terribly. Of course, that analogy wasn't too far from the truth.

"It's just a scratch."

"Rather nasty ones, at that," Jaclyn added, peeling back the strands of shredded cloth.

Jaclyn turned and grabbed a white mug from the mug-rack on the wall by the sink. She then pressed a sharp thumbnail into the tender bottom of her wrist and cut her wrist open. As the blood trickled down, she held it over the mug and filled it about halfway full of her blood.

"What are you doing?" asked Layla, shooting Jaclyn a timid glance.

Handing Layla the mug, Jaclyn replied, "Drink this. Your body will heal instantly."

"I won't become a vampire, will I?"

"Not if I leave you alone tonight."

Layla reluctantly took the cup and, holding it in both hands, looked at Jaclyn one more time before drinking. What she wasn't expecting was to get all of Jackie's memories in return. She groaned in pain as a hundred-and-eighty-seven years' worth of memories seared her mind like a branding iron, threatening to burst blood vessels as new neurons formed like webbing across her brain. Clutching her head in her hands, Layla collapsed to her knees.

A hundred and eighty-seven years was a lot to absorb in a single instant. Unlike the thirty-eight years that Jaclyn acquired with ease, Layla was overwhelmed by the sheer amount of information that she had received.

Even though she wanted to stay present and talk with Jackie about a million different things, the flashes wouldn't stop coming. Each vision burned itself into her memory in milliseconds before she could even process its meaning. Her brain felt like it was on fire.

All her mind could do was shut down, and her eyes rolling back in her head, she passed out and fell forward. Jaclyn rushed over and caught her before she hit the cold marble floor of the kitchen.

"Rest," she whispered. Then, picking Layla up in her arms, she carried her to her bedroom and set her down on her bed.

After tucking Layla in, Jaclyn went over to the window and

placing a foot on the windowsill, looked back at the woman she was falling for. "I'll see you in the morning."

Jaclyn's wings unfurled as she stepped away from the window of her apartment. Her wings caught the wind, and with a couple of powerful flaps, she sent gusts of air downward that rattled the trash cans on the south-facing side of her alley.

Darting upward, she climbed high into the evening sky and did a barrel roll, her wings curling around her like a protective cocoon. She shot above the clouds, wispy trails of vapor following her ascent. Her wings opened again, stabilizing her, and her vampiric silhouette formed against the backdrop of a blood moon.

RAYMOND ACKHURST RETURNED HOME and hung his navy blazer in the entryway closet before heading to his bedroom. As he walked down the hall, he was already loosening his yellow necktie.

Stripping down to nothing but a white undershirt and boxers, he tossed his dirty clothes into the bedroom hamper and then returned to the hallway, following his nose to the kitchen. Something good was cooking.

The house smelled of spices, shrimp, and all kinds of goodness. "It smells delicious," he said, wrapping his arms around his wife's waist as she stirred a big pot with a wooden spoon.

Brushing her hands off on her white apron that she wore over a yellow summer dress that complemented her brown skin, she leaned back and kissed him. His bushy mustache tickled her upper lip, causing her to let out a giggle.

"Tonight's my famous Louisiana gumbo," she said, picking up her wooden spoon to stir the pot some more.

"Where are the girls?" Raymond asked.

"Rubi has volleyball at the high school, and Samantha is at Matthew's house."

"I'm not sure how I feel about our daughter dating some white boy."

"It's fine," his wife said. "Matt is a sweet kid."

"Mmm-Hmmm," he answered, his tone bordering on sarcastic.

She rolled her eyes at him. "Go take a shower and get dressed for dinner. The girls should be home within the hour, and we'll eat as soon as they get back."

Ackhurst spanked his wife's booty, and she giggled as he backed away, doing a happy shuffle, rolling his shoulders, and swaying his head like the Shaquille O'Neil meme.

"Mmm-hmm," he said again, but this time it sounded sultry and sensual. "That's what I'm talking about... mama's got back."

She laughed and threatened to wallop him with her wooden spoon. "Go on, get," she said in good humor.

After his shower, Raymond put on a pair of blue jeans and a navy-blue police t-shirt with a golden police badge embroidered on it, featuring the ceremonial date of his promotion to captain. The shirt was a big, snug fit on him since he'd put on some weight in the past ten years, but it was his favorite lounge-around-the-house shirt.

Ackhurst sat himself at the table and then, looking all around, asked, "Tina, where's today's paper? I can't find it."

"I set it on the chair over by the telephone," his loving wife replied.

He looked back over his shoulder and spotted it. "Ah. You're right."

"You know I'm always right," Tina said, glancing over her shoulder and winking at him.

By the time his girls walked through the front door, he was on page seven of the paper, reading an article about the housing crisis in the United States. There had always been a housing crisis in America because corporations that continued to buy up land would rather price-gouge the average American than create affordable housing for everyone.

He set the paper down, waited for his girls to come over to him, and gave them his mandatory peck on their cheeks.

"Hey, Daddy," Sam said, giving him a big hug.

"Is that cologne I smell on you?" he asked sternly.

Sam grew pink in the cheeks. "Daddy!"

Rubi sat at the table and rested her face on her palms. "Ask her about the foundation she's wearing to cover up all those hickeys that Matt gave her."

Raymond folded his paper and slapped it onto the table with a *thwump*. "What's this about a hickey?"

"I am not covering anything up," Sam gasped. "Matt and I haven't even..." Sam said before stamping her foot. She turned toward her sister and practically jumped across the kitchen table to lay hands on her. "I'll beat your fat ass!"

Raymond reached out and grabbed her by the wrists, gently pulling her back. "Let your sister alone, now. She's just teasing. And I don't care if you have a hickey. Your mom vouches for Matt, and that's good enough for me."

"I love you, Daddy," Sam said, hugging him again. After she was done hugging him, she stuck her tongue out at Rubi and took a seat.

"And for the record," Rubi said, "My ass looks *fiiine!*" She snapped her fingers and added an *"Uh-huh!"* for good measure.

"Wash up, girls," their mom said as she brought the pot to the table and set it down on a couple of potholders.

"Yes, mamma," Rubi said. She raced Sam to the sink, and when they got there at the same time, Rubi bumped Sam out of the way with her hips. As the older sister, she couldn't let Sam get one up on her.

Sam gasped aloud, exaggerating her shock. "Did you see that?"

"No," Raymond said, poking his nose back into his newspaper. His wife walked around the table and snatched the paper from his hand.

"You know what my rule is about reading a paper during dinner. Before and after, but never–"

"During," he sighed, saying it along with her. He chuckled to himself and then snapped his fingers at his children, who were engaged in a water splash fight. "What's gotten into you two tonight?" he asked. "You're acting like a couple of bratty children, not the independent and well-educated young women your mother and I brought you up to be."

"We are children, Daddy," Rubi informed him.

"Rubi, you're a senior in high school, and your sister still has two years left. You need to set a better example. Be a leader. For the rest of the night, I would like you both to stop antagonizing each other and get along. If not for me, for your poor deer mother who looks like she's about to have an aneurysm."

"Yes, Daddy," they said in perfectly harmonized unison.

Tina laughed and looked at Raymond with a big ole smile. He smiled back, thankful that he had married the most beautiful woman he'd ever seen.

Everyone took their seats and, linking hands, Raymond Ackhurst said grace. After their dinner prayers, Tina dished everyone up as the girls passed the garlic bread around.

"I love garlic bread," Rubi said.

"I love it more," Sam retorted, shooting Rubi a large smile as if to rub it in that she managed to get the last word in.

"Dad, she's doing it again."

"So what? You both love garlic bread. Just leave it at that."

"Oh, how I miss eating garlic bread," an unfamiliar voice said. "These days, it burns the roof of my mouth something fierce."

Everyone's heads snapped to the back of the kitchen, near the back door, where they saw a punk rock girl with black hair, fishnet stockings, a torn black t-shirt with an image of Hello Kitty on it layered over a white tank top, and pink highlights standing in their kitchen.

That wasn't the only strange thing. A baseball bat wrapped in barbed wire was slung over her shoulder, and she had leather wristbands with metal spikes on them. Her body had about half a dozen tattoos and about twice as many piercings, and she looked particularly dangerous.

Raymond couldn't put a finger on why he felt she was dangerous. She just was. He glowered at her and asked, "Who the Hell are you? And what are you doing in my house?"

"Relax. I'm just a messenger," she said. Raising her bat, she brought it down on the ceramic pot of gumbo, shattering it, and the gumbo splashed everywhere.

"What the fuck?!" Rubi shouted out as Sam screamed.

"Language!" their mom chirped as she jumped up and grabbed the towel hanging on the stove's handle. She quickly began dabbing up the gumbo splashed across the table, pushing the larger chunks back into a central mound.

When Tina turned back around, she saw that the intruder had placed the barbed bat up against Sam's neck. "I don't want to hurt anyone, but I will if you push me. So, sit your fat ass down and hear me out."

"We're listening," Raymond said, eyes locked onto Sam's. He noted the tears trickling down her cheeks, and he hated how scared she looked. He never wanted his kids to experience the horrors he had to face as a police officer. But he wasn't expecting a literal horror to walk through his back door. "Let's just take a breath and listen to what this young lady has to say."

"I have a message from the King of the Vampires–"

"Vampires?" Rubi scoffed.

The punk rock chick let out a deafening hiss, and they all covered their ears and watched in horror as fangs grew from her mouth. "Silence!" she roared, backhanding Rubi across her face. The slap left a red welt on Rubi's cheek, who, deciding to bite her tongue, glared back at the vampire girl.

"You've got something you want to say?" the vamp asked.

"No," Rubi replied, turning her icy gaze away and pouting. She didn't want to cause another outburst that could endanger her family.

"That's what I thought," the vampire said. Next, she raised a slender white arm above her head and, curling her tongue in her mouth, let out a shrill whistle. The high-pitched kind you reserved for calling a dog.

Suddenly there were four gray, baldheaded, Nosferatu-looking mother-fuckers standing all around them. Raymond wanted to know how they got there. All his doors were locked, yet somehow, they just manifested in his dining room as if out of thin air.

"Where the fuck did these creeps come from?" Rubi cried out.

"Language!" her mom scolded. "I won't have foul talk like that in my house. Do you hear me?"

Velma laughed but still held the bat to Sam's face. Slowly, she let Sam go and drew back. Then, with a wave of her hand, she gestured for the creatures to help themselves. *"Bon Appétit."*

The vampires leaped onto each family member; the girls shrieked so loudly that their screams could be heard three blocks away. Tina screamed, too, while her husband, Raymond Ackhurst, threw an elbow. The moment his vampire hit the ground from a busted nose, Raymond charged the punk rock girl.

She swung the bat, hitting him squarely in his temple with a resounding *thwack*. Raymond dropped to the ground, his vision blurring in and out. Mustering all his strength, he fought through the fog and slowly rose to his feet.

He couldn't give up. His family depended on him. Just as he stood up, she heard the vampire girl clear her throat. "Heh-hem." Raymond spun around, and another blow to the head sent him crashing to the ground.

When he came to, blood was drizzling down his temples, and he realized that the woman who'd broken into his home was crouched over him, sucking on his neck. Looking over at his family, he saw that the vampire that he'd knocked to the floor had crawled over to his wife so that she had two creatures leeching her blood.

Both of his daughters were pinned to the ground, too. Rubi was lying on her back, her legs kicking and squirming as she struggled in vain to throw the monster off her. Sam was in the same situation, but she'd managed to roll onto her stomach and was trying to claw her way out of the kitchen, a vampire clinging to her back.

Mustering up all the strength he had in him, he slowly rose to his feet, pried the succubus from his neck, and slammed her down on the kitchen table so hard it split in half. She let out a grunt as they collapsed onto the ground together.

Raymond was the first to his feet. Not wasting any precious time, he leaped over his wife and dashed into the living room. Opening the living room closet, he quickly found his gun belt and gun.

Drawing his weapon, he spun around. The woman vampire was already standing in his living room, smiling at him from behind burgundy lips. Using her thumb, she dabbed the corners of her mouth and wiped away Ackhurst's blood. "You're stronger than you look, for an old man," she said, smiling a cruel and slightly manic smile.

Raymond raised his gun, pointing it at her chest, and pulled the trigger. *CLICK* *CLICK*

Nothing. Damn, he thought. The gun was empty.

The vampiress smiled at him and held out her hand. "Looking for these?" Opening her hand, palm facing up, she revealed she had his missing bullets. Her smile grew even wider as she dumped them onto the floor. They tinkled against the hardwood like metallic rain.

A forlorn look settled across his face, and, under his breath, he mumbled, "I'm getting too old for this shit."

The vampire girl hissed, leaped onto the coffee table, and

jumped into the air to try to tackle him. As she leaped up, Raymond twirled the gun around in his palm and caught it so that he was holding onto the barrel. Using the butt of his weapon as a makeshift bludgeoning tool was as good as a blackjack or slapper, and he took a swing at her.

Even though he swore he should have clocked her across her jaw, somehow, the vampire girl dodged it. He spun around, swinging his gun like Thor's hammer, but he missed her again. "Are you going to dance all night, or are you going to fight me?" he asked, his eyes burning with intensity.

She toyed with him for a few minutes before reaching up and catching one of his punches, her tiny hand palming his enormous fist. His eyes widened when he realized her strength was more than that of a normal human. If this were true, perhaps her speed was far superior, which would at least explain how she could move about undetected.

"My name is Velma Lorren Chadwick, by the way." Just thought you should know who's going to hand you your ass."

She tossed Raymon Ackhurst into the living room wall. He hit the ground with a thud and crashed along with a mirror that shattered, scattering like jagged diamonds across his living room floor.

Making a split decision, he grabbed one of the more significant shards and cut his hand. His heart pounding in his chest, he jumped up and stabbed the jagged glass into the vampire girl's abdomen. She hissed at him and then staggered back. Slowly, she pulled the shard out of her side and then growled, "I will bleed you like a sacrificial pig."

"Bring it, snaggletooth," he said, raising his fists as he readied himself for round two. Blood trailed down his cut hand, but it didn't hurt since he had so much adrenaline coursing through his veins.

Raymond threw the first punch, his knuckles cracking against her skull. It was a solid hit, and she staggered back, grabbing the edge of the wall to steady herself.

"Fucking hell," she said, rubbing her jaw. "Who are you? Fucking Muhammad Ali?"

"Three-time collegiate boxing champ of Brown University, Rhode Island."

Raymond tucked himself into a ball, dropped, and rolled across the floor, snatching a handful of bullets in one fluid motion. He ignored the jagged pieces of broken glass that got stuck in his back as he popped back up to his feet. Sliding the cartridge out, he inserted the bullets into the cartridge with his thumb and, once finished, slapped it back into the gun with the palm of his hand.

When he raised the loaded gun, pointing it directly at Velma, she dove out of the way. Little did she know he wasn't aiming at her in the first place. Firing off two shots in quick succession, he blew the head off of the closest gray Nosferatu mother-fucker—the one attacking his beloved wife, Tina.

Startled by the gunshot, the others looked up and hissed at him. Captain Raymond Ackhurst didn't hesitate. With precision aim, he took them out one at a time—each one of the ashy bastards receiving a complimentary two bullets to the head.

Once the gray vampires were down for the count, he remembered he wasn't alone and turned to find the young vampire girl army crawling down his hallway.

He walked up behind her, and when she looked up at him, he said, "I ain't never shot at someone who didn't first shoot at me. But even though you didn't technically pull the trigger, you did assault *my* family. *My* wife. *My* children. So, it made me think. There ain't nothing wrong with shooting someone, so long as it's the right people getting shot."

With that said, he pulled the trigger. It only responded with a disheartening click.

"Well, shit," he said in a discouraged tone. The gun was out of ammunition, and he was fresh out of reloads.

"Oh," she said despondently, "that's too bad."

Leaping up to the ceiling, she clung to the corner crevice where the wall met the ceiling. In the dim hallway, she looked like a vicious spider, staring at him with an upside-down smile. An ill-boding smile.

Before he could back away and make a hasty retreat, she leaped down and tackled him to the ground. Landing on top of his chest, Velma began slashing at him with her claws. Raymond screamed out as she tore into him, mauling him like a wild animal.

"Get off me, you crazed, b–"

She clocked Raymond across the jaw with a left-hand cross so hard he almost blacked out. Then she hit him with a right hook that was equally as vicious. Her knuckles were covered in blood, but he had a suspicion it wasn't hers.

Dazed by her relentless pummeling, he was too stunned to move as she bent down and bit into his ear. *Arghhh!* he screamed as she tore off a chunk of his right ear.

Spitting the wad of flesh out, Velma got up and placed a heavy boot on Raymond's chest. "My message is this. This town now belongs to the Vampire King. If you care for your family, you will do well to leave Wood River and never come back.

Anyone who stays beyond this weekend will be made a subject of the Vampire King, Darius Reid."

Velma looked back at her dead cohorts and the group of sobbing women who'd huddled together out of fear. Turning back around, she caught Ramond crawling toward the living room phone, which sat on the side table between the couch and one of the recliners.

Velma gave a swift kick to Raymond's skull, and he went out like a light. Ackhurst's body collapsed onto folded arms, and the side of his head trickled blood. His left eye was black and blue, swollen, and half-shut. His bottom lip was cracked open and bleeding, and there was already bruising on his neck from where she'd bitten him.

Yawning, Velma placed a hand over her mouth and looked down the hall. Her head tilted to the side, she stared down the hallway as if caught in a daydream and then asked, "Do you mind if I use your bathroom? I really gotta take a piss."

Velma looked back at the sobbing trio of women who, reacting to her gaze, cried out in distress and began to sob even harder and, in Velma's opinion, more obnoxiously. Why did people who were always about to die either become stoic and silent or ugly cry as though it would change the course of their unfortunate destinies?

Bored with their hysterics, Velma ignored them and sauntered down the hall. She checked each door until she found the bathroom. She pulled down her fishnet stockings and panties, sliding them over her knees and letting them fall to her ankles as she plopped her bare, white cheeks down onto the toilet seat.

As she pissed, she hummed a little ditty–one of her songs– one of the songs of *Velma and the Slayers*–to help mask the embarrassingly loud tinkling sound. She pulled off a piece of toilet paper, folded it, and wiped her undercarriage. She flushed the toilet and then checked herself out in the bathroom vanity mirror. She dabbed some blood off her lip and chin and smiled at herself when she looked presentable again.

That's when she heard a crash in the living room, followed by the dial tone of phone buttons being pushed.

"For fuck's sake," she said, rolling her eyes.

She peeked out into the hallway and decided she didn't want to risk another altercation with the police captain. The man wouldn't give up. Even though she was faster and stronger, it just wasn't worth the trouble.

She turned back around, opened the bathroom window, and climbed out. Once outside, she could hear the fleet of sirens approaching her location. She picked up her pace as she cut across the backyard and headed into the nearby trees.

Disappearing into the night, she had one more thing to do before she could meet up with Darius again. Now that the police chief had been warned to stay out of their business, she was off to kill the mayor and his wife.

She contemplated whether she should make it quick or messy. *Definitely messy,* she thought. A foreboding grin spread across her lips, her fangs poking out as she merrily skipped through the woods to continue with her bloody rampage.

THE MASTER AND THE MARGARITA

COME MORNING, JACLYN BENOIT found herself sitting at a French diner in Quebec, a city she hadn't been to in ages. It was here, in Quebec, that she'd first met Emile de La Boetie. And although he wasn't her creator, he was her Master. He took her under his wing and taught her everything he knew about their kind.

Jaclyn remembered what *Emile de La Boetie* had told her about how to make a vampire. He taught her about the Nightwisps, vampires that couldn't tolerate light. He also told her about the dhampir half-breeds and the purebreds that could walk in the sun.

But transference was the only way to make a true vampire. And only a purebred could make other vampires. Nightwisps could bite you, but the only consequence would be lacerations from their bites and the loss of blood from their feeding.

"Drain them of their vitality, replenish it with your own, and take them into your bosom as a mother would her beloved child. Sleep with them until dawn the next day, and when you both awaken, the vampire curse will have spread to your chosen one. Emile de La Boetie explained the process and how to make vampires should she ever wish to.

Emile had warned her that the link between master and creation was so strong that one could hear the other's thoughts whenever they were near. She'd never heard Darius's thoughts, but she had been having terrible nightmares recently, and she couldn't help but wonder if that was related somehow.

Her thoughts shifted back to Layla. She didn't want Layla to be transformed. She was madly in love with her, so she flew long and far. Her passion was so strong that she didn't want to risk being in the same town, let alone the same state as Layla Harker.

If she had stayed the night with Layla, then come morning, Layla would have become a vampire. The only way to ensure she didn't turn was to get as far away as possible. Jaclyn didn't know the exact range or even fully understand the metaphysics of transference.

How could one soul tether another? How could an undying anchor any soul, for that matter? Why did vampires stay animated rather than decaying like zombies? There were still things that she didn't have the answers to.

So, she flew all night, weathering the frigid winds and inclement temperatures. She flew until she was optimistic that Layla Harker would be safe from the vampire curse.

Although she'd researched more about vampires on her own, Emile's words still echoed in her mind. What he had said about purebred vampires, Nightwisps, and another kind that he referred to as Grays. Little cherub-like vampire babies spawn whenever a mother vampire, impregnated by a human male, is killed before she can give birth.

Grays were mindless little monsters that only fed. They clawed their way out of their mother's womb, like a velociraptor breaking through its shell, and then gorged themselves on anything and everything with a pulse. According to Emile, Grays were extremely dangerous.

On the other hand, she and Darius were what Emile referred to as purebred vampires. These sentient vampires possessed autonomy and were regarded as the nobility among the vampire races. Only the Ancient Masters, vampires who had lived for over 1,000 years and were believed to be nearly extinct, held a higher status than they did.

According to legend, purebred vampires are created with romantic intent. In that intimate realm of romance, where affection blooms into love, a vampire can bond their undead soul to that of a living mortal or to another vampire they have created.

Darius was spawning countless minions, but this process didn't produce purebreds, as there was no intent to bond with them. This lack of connection explained why he couldn't create more beings like the girls who had attacked her and Layla in her apartment. It was likely that he had been romantically involved with those girls and, on some level, genuinely felt for them, which facilitated a smoother bonding process.

Currently, all Darius could create were Nightwisps. However, if they were neglected and not fed for too long, they would deteriorate into ravenous monsters—ugly, gray motherfuckers—the kind you might find in a Richard Matheson novel. Their human features would fade, and they would become hideous creatures of the night.

Emile explained the rules to her. If you fed partially on a victim, they could easily survive. They'd remain human and have enough bad dreams to fill a lifetime. But if you drained someone of all their blood and they died in your presence, they would become Nightwisps and would be forever chained to the darkness. The slightest touch of the sun would burn them up.

Nightwisps lurked in the shadows and typically resided in large cities, where they could retreat underground. They lived in subways, underground shopping malls, and basements, emerging only at night to feed.

What Darius was creating was dangerous. Because Nightwisps were unpredictable, the Red Rage could take them at any moment, and it was only the fear of the Alpha that kept them in check.

Jaclyn leaned back in her chair and exhaled, letting out a long, slow breath. She stared out the window at the people walking between the local shops and finished her espresso. She placed the cup down on the saucer and then drew out a twenty from her cleavage, the place where she always kept a secret stash of cash for emergencies. Then she got up and headed for the door.

She remembered what she was wearing when she caught the young man at the register grinning at her with flushed cheeks.

During her flight, the wind and sleet had tattered her clothes so severely that she was practically standing in her underwear when she landed in Quebec. The only place open in the middle of the night was a twenty-four-hour adult toy store.

To make matters worse, the only article of clothing they had in her size was a sexy dominatrix leather leotard. Naturally, she picked the leotard. At three hundred dollars, it was a little pricey, but it was genuine leather. And it came with a French tickler, which she opted to leave behind with the transgender store clerk.

Jaclyn stepped out from under the veranda and walked into daylight. The sun's intensity caused her eyes to feel its sting, like a thousand hot needles pricking her retinas. She threw up her hand to blot out brightness. Squinting beneath its burning hot radiance, she turned her eyes away and noticed small wisps of steam rising off her bare shoulders.

Fuck, she said in her head. This was a bad sign. She was due for a feeding whenever her skin began to steam. If she put it off too much longer, the Red Rage would take her, and she'd leave only death and carnage in her wake. Right now, she couldn't risk causing an international incident by losing her temper and tearing up half the town. Whether she wanted to or not, she knew she had to feed. And she had to feed as soon as possible.

Spinning around, she put a smile on her face and headed back inside the restaurant. Walking up to the waiter, who was still standing by the register, she cleared her throat and leaned on the counter—making sure to show off her cleavage—which, coincidentally, looked fucking fabulous in this getup.

The young man looked at her with a cheeky grin as she leaned in. "Meet me in the women's restroom in five minutes," she whispered. She then turned around, tossing her hair like a model, and sashayed to the back of the restaurant, where she paused at the restroom door to glance back at the waiter.

His eyes were fixed on her, and she playfully blew him a kiss before ducking inside the women's room. As predicted, he arrived early, and she began kissing him.

Things grew heated as his hands squeezed her ass, and he

picked her up, moving her over to the sink, where he set her back down. His hand slid down to her waist and thighs as he kissed her neck, slowly moving down to her chest. Jaclyn threw her head back and let out a sensual sigh as he dappled the top of her breasts with light, feathery kisses.

He couldn't have been more than twenty. Most likely working his way through college. Squeezing her thighs, he slid his hands down to her knees and pried her legs apart. She felt the heat of his groin press into her, and she let out a little chirp excitedly as he gave her a hickey on the top of her breast. She reached around him and, taking his tight ass in her hands pulled him into her and moaned lightly as she signaled that she wanted him—all of him.

That's when he looked up to gaze into her eyes, only for his eyes to trail off to the side, locking onto the image of himself in the mirror. Himself and no other, that is. He suddenly froze with fear as he stared past her head.

His face drained of color, and it appeared as though he'd seen a ghost. He looked at her, then at the mirror, and back at her again as he slowly drew back.

"What's the matter?" she asked, confused as to why his mood had suddenly shifted from hot and bothered to terrified. Following his gaze, she turned toward the bathroom mirror, and then it dawned on her as to what had frightened him so badly. Instead of two bodies in the reflection, there was only his. "Oh, yeah. That."

She'd almost forgotten about the lack of reflection. More specifically, she could manifest a reflection if she were fresh from a feeding frenzy. The human blood was enriched with life-affirming vitality that allowed her to see herself for short periods, usually two to three hours, give or take. But, having not fed in two weeks, she was as though she didn't exist, and she'd gone entirely invisible.

She turned back around, but the young man was already backing away from her, his hands trembling with fright. Slowly, his back pressed up against the restroom stall. Unexpectedly, the bathroom stall door swung open, and he tripped over his own feet, falling back into the stall.

"*Aide!*" he shouted in French. "*S'il vous plaît aidez-moi!*"

Jaclyn pounced on him fast, covering his mouth with her hand. "*Tais-toi et tu vivras peut-être,*" she whispered. *Shut up, and maybe you'll live.*

He nodded, his eyes growing large with fear.

Jaclyn gently removed her hand from his mouth and then, noticing that he was going to behave, popped her fangs.

"*S'il vous plaît, mon Dieu. Aie pitié de mon âme,*" he prayed as she sank her fangs into his neck. Yelping lightly, his body suddenly went limp as euphoria overtook him.

Careful not to drain him completely, she gently set him down and propped him up between the toilet seat and the stall. He wouldn't remember much when he woke up, but this wasn't her first rodeo either. She could see by absorbing his memories that he'd just recently broken up with his girlfriend.

Jaclyn unfastened his belt, fished out his phone from his pants pocket, propped his head up, and carefully placed his face onto her abundant cleavage.

Holding up the smartphone for a selfie, she stuck out her tongue between her vampire fangs and flipped the bird. She even kissed the unconscious kid on the lips and snapped another photo. She set him on the toilet, his pants slipping down around his ankles, and then gently propped him against the side wall of the stall.

If Jaclyn knew anything about French girls, she knew they were the most jealous breed of woman on the planet. Seeing her boyfriend's face buried in a mature dominatrix's breasts with a vampire kink would spark some jealousy in any hot-blooded French girlfriend. Maybe even enough to force her to take him back.

Scrolling through texts, she found his ex-girlfriend's last few text messages and promptly sent her the risqué photos. Not even ten seconds later, a message calling him an ass but telling him to come over popped onto the screen. Jaclyn smiled.

"You're welcome," she said as she tossed his phone onto his stomach.

As she exited the restroom, the waitress cleared the things from her table and looked back at her. Jaclyn wiped the corners of her mouth to make sure there was no blood giving her away, but to the server watching her salacious tongue play, it conjured up a more sexually explicit image.

"You might want to check on your mate back there," Jacklyn said. "Poor thing is all spent. Tasted great, though." She winked at the girl, who stood there, unsure of what to think, and then sashayed to the restaurant's front entrance and stepped outside.

This time, when she stepped into the light, nothing happened. She let out a relieved sigh and then flagged a taxi to take her to the airport. There was no way she'd risk an international flight in broad daylight.

Jaclyn arrived back in Wood River around 6:30 p.m. She landed at Wood River Airfield, which was more of a cornfield converted into a landing strip for crop dusters and other small aircraft. It sat about a quarter mile from Mel's Diner. Hopping out of the single-engine prop plane, she thanked the pilot for the lift and then walked to the diner.

Pickup trucks honked every time they passed as she was still wearing the dominatrix outfit. She merely responded by flipping the bird and continued on her way. Once she'd arrived at the diner, she asked to borrow someone's cell phone and called an Uber.

A Toyota Prius pulled up, and a middle-aged man wound down the window and asked, "You, Jackie? Jackie Ben-Noit?"

"I am," Jaclyn answered. "And it's pronounced *Ben-wah.*"

"Shit, sorry 'bout that." He unlocked the door, and she got in. I'm not very good with names. I never forget a face, but names, that's a different matter entirely."

She looked up to catch him adjusting the mirror to get a better look at her more feminine features, so to speak. She tensed up, realizing he might not be able to see her reflection in the mirror yet, but she let out a pent-up sigh when she caught a glimpse of her reflection. She hadn't even realized she was holding her breath.

"So, what are you supposed to be? Some sex person?"

"Undercover," she said, crossing her legs and arms.

"I bet," the guy responded, shifting the car into drive. He chuckled to himself as he pulled out of the parking area. Glancing back up into the mirror, he asked, "So, how long have you been a call girl?"

"No. Not that undercover. I'm a cop," she answered.

"I bet you are," he said, winking at her. It was clear he didn't believe her. "A naughty stripper, cop? So, how much do you charge per hour?"

She rolled her eyes and then said, "Two grand."

"*Yowzah!*" he gasped. "That's a bit out of my price range. Don't make much of a living driving people around out here. But I don't have much in the way of smarts or technical skills either, so this will have to do for now."

She was surprised Darius hadn't gotten to this one yet. It seemed he was targeting all the blue-collar workers and turning them into grays, the equivalent of his own army of worker drones. Or maybe it was a sign that Darius wasn't as powerful as she'd imagined. Perhaps there was still hope that she could turn the tide and prevent any further death and destruction. *Knock on wood,* she thought to herself.

She told the driver to drop her off at the police station, and he gulped, realizing she wasn't kidding about being a police officer. Without any more intrusive questions or glances in the rearview mirror, he drove her straight there.

When she arrived, she paid him with another twenty from her cleavage, and he smiled as he tucked it in his shirt pocket and patted it.

"Thanks for the lift," she said, shutting the car door behind her. "You can keep the change."

"Any time," he said, nodding at her. He gave her a two-finger salute, let his foot off the brakes, and slowly eased away.

As his Prius pulled away, Jaclyn noticed that her Hellcat was parked across from her in the police parking area. She muttered, "What the hell?"

"Hey, you," a familiar voice called out to her from over her shoulder. She turned around to find Layla standing behind her, a smile stretching from one ear to the other. She was wearing a dusty blue suit that almost seemed gray, and tossed something to Jaclyn.

Reflexively catching the item, she looked in the palm of her hand to find her car keys.

"I took the liberty of bringing your car here," Layla said. "Figured it would be safer in the middle of a police station lot than a college parking lot."

"Good thinking," Jaclyn said. "You look good."

Layla laughed. "So do you. But, if you don't mind my asking, what on Earth are you wearing?"

"It's a long story for another time," Jaclyn said.

Layla shrugged it off. It wasn't that important anyway. She was just more curious than anything.

Jaclyn turned toward the station and was about to head toward the back entrance when Layla reached out and grabbed her by the arm, stopping her.

"We have the afternoon off."

"I beg your pardon?" asked Jaclyn.

"Imagine my surprise when I woke up to find two dead bodies in your apartment with absolutely no recollection of why or how they got there. Of course, I called it in. How could I not?"

"Ah," Jaclyn said. "I see."

"So, now I'm off duty until they can determine if it was a clean shooting, and you are off duty because it happened at your place right before you disappeared for twenty-four hours. I covered for your hot ass, so you better take the day off with me and debrief me on where the hell you've been for the past twenty-four hours and what you've been doing."

"Yeah, I get how that looks bad."

"Looks bad?" Layla laughed. "You look fucking guilty. I lied more in the past eight hours than I have in my entire life. You owe me big time, sister."

Jaclyn nervously bit her lip. "So, what'd you tell them?"

Unexpectedly, a catcall rang out, and Jackie and Layla looked over to find two officers walking to their patrol car.

"Looking fine, Benoit!" one of them shouted.

"Just ignore them," Layla said.

Jaclyn smiled and flipped them the bird. They laughed again and climbed in.

"A couple of things," Layla said, changing the subject. Yes, she lied to protect Jaclyn. And she'd do it again without hesitation. But that wasn't what was important right now. Covering for the one you love is a given. What she was most concerned about were the memories Jaclyn had acquired. Traumatic memories. Life-altering event.

"You were never supposed to learn about Kandahar. So, I'm going to say this once and only once. I don't ever want to talk about it. It took six years of therapy just to come to terms with the trauma I endured in that prison camp. That's as much as I care to say about that. That chapter of my life is over, and I'm moving on."

"Understood. And what's the other thing?"

"When were you going to tell me that you're one hundred and eighty-seven years old?" Tapping the side of her temple with her finger, she added, "Remember, I have your memories now too."

Jaclyn's cheeks flushed, and she whispered through her teeth, "Keep it down. Nobody can know."

"Okay, *Grandma*," Layla teased. "Your secret is safe with me."

Layla nudged Jaclyn with an elbow and then started toward the car.

"Hey, since my place is now a crime scene and your place is still in disarray, where are we going?" she asked, catching up to Layla.

"A motel. There's one out on old Crestwood Avenue just down from Mel's Diner, where we can lay low for a day or two. Who knows, maybe you can bite my thighs again?"

"When you put it that way," Jaclyn laughed. "How can I

possibly refuse?"

They both got into Jaclyn's car and slammed the doors shut. Before she pressed the red start button, however, she turned to Layla and said, "Thank you for having my back. I mean that."

"I'm your partner. Of course, I have your back." She yawned and then laid back in the seat and closed her eyes. "I'm beat. Wake me when we get there, okay?"

Layla opened her eyes again and found Jackie's face staring down at her. She looked down as Jaclyn swung her leg over Layla's thighs and settled onto her lap.

Their intensity was so hot when their eyes met again that Layla thought her heart would burst inside her chest. Before she could say anything, Jaclyn's lips came crashing into hers. The touch of her skin on hers was electric, and shivers ran down her spine as they kissed.

"You need to stay awake for at least twenty-four hours after a vampire bite, just to err on the side of caution. Better safe than sorry."

Layla nodded. "In that case, you better find a way to keep me wide awake."

"I have an idea," Jaclyn said, gazing into Layla's sultry brown eyes with her ocean blue ones. Their lips brushed one another, their heated breath passing to one another as though they were sharing one soul. Their passion for one another overwhelmed them, and their mouths crashed together again, their hands frantically peeling layers of clothes off.

"Right here in the parking lot?" asked Layla, raising her arms for Jackie to pull off her shirt.

"Yes," Jackie whispered, taking off Layla's shirt and tossing it into the driver's seat. "I want you. Right here. Right now."

Layla arched her neck and raised her face to accept more of

Jackie's kisses. At the same time, she reached behind her back and began unfastening her bra. Just then, the precinct doors flew open, and eleven or twelve officers poured out of the precinct's side exit. They jumped into their squad cars, and with a rumble of half the fleet starting up, the sirens and the lights came on.

"What the hell is going on?" Jaclyn said.

Layla fastened her bra and popped open the door. Jackie slid off her lap and stepped out into the street. She was still wearing her dominatrix outfit, but didn't care.

Throwing her shirt on, Layla stepped out of the car and stood behind Jackie as she quickly buttoned her shirt. They turned to watch the procession of squad cars tear out of the parking lot, lights flaring and sirens blaring in flashes of red and blue.

"Jackson," Jaclyn shouted over the blare of sirens, catching the attention of the officer closest to her. "What the fuck is going on?"

"The captain called in a 10- 62 B. All units are *en route* there now."

"Shit," Jaclyn said. She looked over at Layla, who was tucking her shirt back into her gray dress pants. "I have a bad feeling about this."

"A 10-62 B? Who would be bold enough to break into the police captain's home?" Layla asked, but she realized the answer before she even finished the question. "Darius," Layla said, shooting Jackie a worried look as her thoughts aligned with Jaclyn's. "We killed his consorts, so he's going to take something from us now."

"Let's just pray he didn't hurt Captain Ackhurst's wife or kids."

Jaclyn jumped back into her car and revved it to life. Layla followed her lead, and with seven hundred horsepower going to the rear wheels, she mashed the pedal. The Hellcat's ultra-wide tires squealed like banshees as she burned rubber.

The back end of Jaclyn's murdered-out Hellcat swung wide as the car did a total one-eighty burnout. As she peeled out of the parking lot, the Hellcat fishtailed back and forth as if it were about to lose control. Then, Jaclyn's tires found purchase on the city street's asphalt, and the car pulled away from the police station, large white plumes of smoke rising in its wake.

Like a bat out of hell, the car tore down the road. Weaving in and out of traffic, Jaclyn soon took the lead of the police procession. She pulled out ahead of all the other squad cars as she raced to save the captain and his family from the Darkness that had descended upon the small town of Wood River.

20

BLOOD HARVEST

PREGNANT WITH LIGHT, THE moon hung heavy in the night sky—a giant swollen orb glowing against an inky void. The wind seemed to rustle the trees, but the night was calm, and the breeze was too faint to cause any natural disturbance. Still, the trees and thickets swayed and rustled until, out of the shadows, a dozen Nightwisps stepped forth.

More gray-skinned atrocities emerged from the shadows as the sun began to set. Their gray skin, bald heads, and black eyes made them look like hideous demon children. Their human features had morphed into emaciated, sinewy physiques like those of mentally ill anorexics. No longer were they fleshy and warm-blooded. All their hair had fallen out over the past several weeks as Darius had deliberately kept them weak and starving so that their bloodlust would be at its most when he unleashed them onto the city.

In addition to their emaciated physiques, their fingernails had grown into thick black claws, and their human teeth had fallen out, only to be replaced by two rows of densely packed fangs, which gave them menacing, needle-like smiles. Any humanity that they may have once had was all but lost to them now, leaving only undead creatures of the night.

As with the worst viral diseases, they had a deep-seated urge to propagate themselves. At the instinctual level, feeding and sex were the same thing for the mindless creatures. If they fed to completion, draining their victims fully, they'd propagate themselves and create new Nightwisps.

Nevertheless, in their blood-frenzied minds, they rarely fed until they had completed the task. Their hunger pangs force them to attack everything in sight, taking a bite from one victim and quickly moving on to the next. They caused more damage than anything and left bloody carnage in their wake.

Mature, purebred vampires were more deliberate in their feeding. They didn't succumb to the Red Rage as quickly as the Nightwisps. They could regulate their feeding and mood and even choose when to propagate their kind, just as Jaclyn did when she created Darius.

It wasn't her intent to turn him. Not initially. However, the circumstances had left her with no choice but to act. Little did she suspect he'd rage out the very same day he was created. Usually, it took a week for the vampire's bloodlust to take hold. But occasionally, some extra voracious vampires were born into the ranks of the undead.

These vampires couldn't control their urges as well as they'd like and would often lose control, wreaking havoc on everything around them. The Elders tolerated them, however, because their acts of violence kept the vampire legends alive.

Darius was, according to Jaclyn's letter, one such vampire. A voracious feeder type. The kind that lacked control.

"Fuck," Darius cursed, crumpling up Jaclyn's letter and throwing the wad across the room. It landed on the floor next to the trash bin.

Velma rolled over in bed, sleeping naked next to Darius, and, sitting up, raised her arms above her head, stretched, and yawned. "What's wrong, babe?"

Darius stood up and paced the floor next to his bed. "It's that fucking whore detective. She keeps writing me these cryptic letters about the history of vampires as if I give two shits. This time, she wrote a pseudo-apology. What the fuck am I supposed to do with that? Sorry, I turned you into a fucking demonic creature? Hope you have a nice life."

"I thought you liked being a vampire," Velma said, strolling over to the mini frig in Darius's bedroom and grabbing a Heineken from it. She slapped the cap off using her vampire strength, causing it to fly across the room, pinged against the wall, and ricocheted into a nearby trash can. "Score!" she said, proud of herself for making the shot.

After downing half the bottle, she offered the rest to Darius, who waved the offer off with a shake of his head and an unspoken, *no thanks.* Velma shrugged and finished it off in front of him. Kicking her head back, she arched her back to take in every last drop. At the same time, her perky breasts jutted out, her dark pink nipples standing erect on her chest. After finishing the entire bottle, she burped, wiped her mouth, and tossed the bottle over her shoulder—missing the trash can completely this time.

"I do," he replied. "I do enjoy being a vampire. It's just that she acts so superior. And I'm not talking about her hypocritical righteousness of being a killer who wants to uphold the law. I'm talking about the way she walks, the way she talks, the way she sucks the air out of the room every time she enters it. She's fifty shades of fucked up but acts like she's God's gift to humanity."

"If you want, I'll track her down and kill her for you."

Darius hung his head low, a sadness weighing on him. "We lost Amber and Sophie because we underestimated Jaclyn Benoit and her partner, that Fed, Layla Harker."

"You think the Fed knows about Jaclyn?"

"I mean, after what went down with Sophie and Amber, I'm sure of it. The question is, why isn't the Marshal arresting Detective Benoit? What unnatural sway does Jaclyn hold over her?"

"Maybe they're in love?" suggested Velma with a shrug. Velma found one of Darius's old Dr. Dre t-shirts and slipped it on. She pulled the stretched-out collar down her left shoulder to expose her white skin, giving her that added sex appeal. Meanwhile, the t-shirt was long enough for her to wear like a miniskirt, the short length making her legs look longer than they were.

Darius plopped down onto the edge of his bed and pressed his fingers together under his chin. After a moment's reflection, he smiled and said, "Love, you say? If that's the case, I have an idea."

Velma smiled and licked her fangs. "Do tell, Master."

"I want you to take twenty of our Nightwisps and track down the girlfriend, Ms. Harker. When you find her, I want you to terrorize her. Chase her into the woods and send the Nightwisps after her. Let them feast on her meaty bones."

"What if she manages to come out alive?"

"I don't care so much if she lives or dies. I want her to feel the terror that comes with being a vampire lover. I want her to see that Fear is what we are made of. Our legends should not be taken lightly. The world must learn to fear us again. And we can start with her. Maybe after we're done with her, she'll have second thoughts about being a vampire lover."

"Consider me on it," Velma replied. She grabbed Darius by his hand and reeled him in. Kissing him long and hard, she broke away, licked her lips, and skipped out of his bedroom.

Still only wearing his Dr. Dre t-shirt, she'd only put on her fishnets and thick goth boots with spiked toes to match. Grabbing her spiked bat from the umbrella holder next to the front door, Velma stepped out into the night, slung her bat across the back of her shoulders, and looked up at the full moon. It looked so big and heavy as it hung in the sky.

Putting her fingers to her lips, she whistled, and a pack of Nightwisps emerged from the shadows all around her. The gray monstrosities materialized from between parked cars and nearby trees all along the length of the street. As they gathered around Velma, she made hissing noises, communicating with them in tones and utterances that only their primitive vampire minds could understand while pointing toward Wood River.

The Nightwisps nodded at her orders before darting into the trees, hissing like vipers as they raced to find Federal Agent Layla Harker. Their fangs dripped with eager anticipation of fresh blood.

Surrounded by a team of a dozen Nightwisps, Velma leisurely strolled down the downtown streets, her trusty razor wire-wrapped baseball back slung over her shoulder. A night jogger came around the bend and quickly turned and sprinted the opposite way upon noticing her army of undead vampires.

One of Velma's Nightwisps hissed and stepped forward, willing to take chase, but she held up a hand and hissed at them to fall back into line. They did as they were told, and she started whistling one of her band's songs as she continued up the road.

Not more than a block and a half later, a police car came tearing into the four-way intersection, its brakes squealing as it slid sideways and came to a stop. The door flew open, and a black male officer with a narrow mustache stepped out and aimed his gun at Velma.

"Stay where you are."

"What's the matter, officer? Did I break any laws?"

"Apologies, miss. But a BOLO with your description has come down from headquarters. You fit the description of the woman who terrorized the police captain and his family. I'll have to ask you to peacefully come in for questioning."

"Hssssk!" Velma hissed, her gray Nightwisps racing forward at a full sprint. Startled, the officer fired off two shots before getting taken to the ground by three Nightwisps. His screams rang out as their claws and fangs tore into him.

The pack of Nightwisps finished him off as quickly as a swarm of piranhas leaning only a bloody splotch on the ground next to the patrol car.

Velma smiled and casually walked by the police car, its lights flashing silently in the night. Red and blue hues washed across the pale faces of the undead Nightwisps as they strolled on by. Over the radio, dispatch was asking the officer if he needed any backup. When there was no reply, they stated they'd send a cruiser out to his last known position.

Overhearing dispatch's warning, Velma smiled and hissed again, pointing at an apartment up the street. "That's where the Fed lives, my pets. Seek her out and bring her to me."

Velma stood in the street looking up at Layla Harker's windows. Sure enough, not long after her Nightwisps had entered the building, gunshots lit up the windows in flashes of fiery orange.

Layla's apartment door smashed under her weight as the Nightwisp tossed her through it. She collapsed to the floor in her hallway and coughed up blood. Luckily, she still held fast to her gun and one extra magazine in her other hand. The bad news was that she wasn't wearing anything but her maroon-colored lingerie, which she'd bought as a surprise for Jaclyn. Needless to say, she was way underdressed for a vampire brawl at 3 AM.

With her back up against the hallway wall, she fired off two shots, taking out some gray vampires that had attacked her. She looked over at her broken window, the one she'd just fucking fixed a week ago, and saw three more of the deranged creatures climbing into her apartment.

"Perfect fucking night to decide to sleep in my place and get a fresh change of clothes," she griped. She looked over at her phone on the coffee table by the sofa and then at the monsters streaming into her apartment. She wanted to get her phone and call Jaclyn, but she wasn't entirely sure she could take on three of the creatures at the same time.

The gray vampires began sniffing the air, looking for her, when her phone lit up and vibrated on the coffee table in the black stillness of her apartment. The distraction was enough to draw their attention. They turned and hissed at the noise, then slowly gathered around the table, looking at the bright light.

Layla didn't waste any time and pushed herself to her feet. She slid the extra magazine into the waistband of her panties and hobbled her way toward the stairwell. Before entering the stairs, she hit the elevator up button, ducked away, and took the staircase to the lobby.

Cringing from the pain of the lacerations on her arm, she leaned against the cold concrete wall of the staircase. She could hear the snarling and hissing of the vampires stalking her, but then the elevator dinged. She looked up at the center of the stairwell and glanced at the flight above her. The elevator dinged again and began heading to the top floor. It would take a couple of the beasties with any luck.

She limped down the next five flights of stairs before entering the hallway on the ninth floor. She poked her head down the corridor and looked both ways, checking for any possible threats. No monsters. She sighed and walked more confidently toward the elevator. She pushed the button, and the elevator lights indicated that it was rising from the third floor. She raised her gun and, holding it steady with both hands, aimed it at the elevator doors. When the chime rang, and the doors slid open, she let out another sigh of relief. It was empty.

Riding the elevator to the ground floor, Laya waited for the doors to open fully, keeping her gun aimed squarely at the wide-open lobby. She peeked out and quickly scanned the room. There were no signs of monsters, and it was void of movement or life.

Jogging over to the front desk, she picked up the phone and tried dialing. When she picked up the phone, however, the signal was dead. "Shit, someone had cut the landline."

She knew it wasn't the grays, as they weren't intelligent enough to execute advanced tactics. Someone higher up on the vampire food chain was aiding them.

Layla walked over to the wall, pulled the fire alarm, and headed toward the lobby doors. Hopefully, the white noise would function as another layer of distraction for the monsters. At the same time, it would alert the authorities, and soon enough, both the police and firefighters would respond to her call. That's when the other elevator dinged.

Slowly turning toward the opening doors, Layla found all three creatures standing in the elevator, staring out at her, their eyes fixed on her.

They raised their heads and began sniffing the air, and when they caught her scent, they all began hissing and attempted to lunge forward, jamming each other up as they tried to exit the elevator at the same time. This gave Layla the opportunity she needed, not to escape but to send the bastards back to whatever Hell they came from.

Quickly, she raised her gun and fired with carte blanche.

She dropped all three of them with precision headshots.

Vampire blood started filling the lift, and as it coated the elevator floor, their blood began dripping in the crack between the doors, the lobby, and down to the basement level. Shrieks began to echo up from the basement as the vampires down below caught the scent of their brethren's blood. It sent them into a wild rage.

Clanging and clunking rang up from the depths of the building's sub-basement, and Layla looked over at the stairwell doors. They rattled violently as though a whole host of creatures were flooding the narrow stairwell as they clambered up the stairs to ground level—to the lobby.

"That's a hard pass," she said, quickly making her way to the lobby entrance. She checked her gun's chamber and then the magazine and did a quick ammunition count. Eight rounds left, including one in the chamber.

Stepping out of the building, she walked into the street only to pause and slowly turn her gaze to her right. Velma stood half a block away with a host of about twenty gray vampires behind her.

"Ah, there you are, Special Agent Harker."

"Shit," Layla cursed, raising her gun and firing off two shots.

Both vampires on either side of Velma dropped to the ground, and Velma looked down at them both, then looked back up, her eyes meeting Harker's. "You missed me."

"I won't miss a second time," Layla replied.

"Oh, but I'm willing to bet I have more friends than you have bullets."

"What do you want?" asked Layla, keeping Velma trained squarely in her sights.

"I want my little beasties to tear you apart. And once they've had their fill, I'll shove this razor wire bat where the sun doesn't shine and make you pay for killing my sisters. By the time I'm finished with you, you'll be the sorriest piece of ass in all of Wood River."

Although the fire alarm was blaring in her building, Layla noticed no sirens to answer her call, no emergency vehicles to rush to her aid, just the kind of unnerving silence you get with the calm before the storm.

"Ah, do you hear that? The sweet sound of silence. I hope you weren't expecting someone to rush to your rescue. Nobody is coming, I'm afraid. They're all too busy dying."

"In that case," Layla said, raising her gun. "Maybe you should join them."

A gunshot rang out, and Velma leaped out of the way, narrowly dodging the bullet. Without her vampire speed and strength, she would have been killed.

A Nightwisp standing directly behind Velma absorbed the headshot and dropped out of sight. Velma let out a disappointed sigh as she looked back at her murdered pet. Looking back up, she glowered at Layla and then pointed her bat at her. "Get her, my babies. Suck the meat from her bones and feast until you've had your fill!"

Layla turned and raced up the street as the hissing only grew louder behind her. The soles of her feet clapped along the black asphalt street as she ran. "How about you bloodsucking leeches suck on this instead."

Layla reached back and fired off her remaining rounds without looking, emptying her cartridge, and either through luck or muscle memory, she managed to take out one additional vampire.

Upon depleting all her rounds, her gun's slide caught, showing that it was empty. With a flick of her wrist, she ejected the spent cartridge, flinging it away from her. She slid the refill into the gun in one smooth motion. Slapping the fresh cartridge into place, she ran up the street, her adrenaline masking the pain of her lacerations and sore feet.

Once she arrived at the city park, she turned immediately right and cut through it, dashing past picnic tables and a children's playground as she made her way toward the woods at the other end.

The soft grass felt soothing beneath her feet as she ran. Approaching the tangle of dark branches and shadows of the forest's edge, she knew it would provide enough cover for her to play a game of cat and mouse.

Obviously, she'd need to make every shot count. She only had what was in her gun, and once she ran out, it would be hand-to-hand combat, whether she liked it or not. She needed to find a sharp branch, rock, or something to defend herself with.

The gray creatures were closing in on her, but she stopped at the edge of the tree line to glance back and do a head count.

"Damn," she thought to herself. There were twenty-two vampires and only seventeen rounds of ammunition in her magazine. Layla wasn't sure she could handle five vampires bare-handed, but she wasn't ready to give up. Until then, she'd need to make every shot count.

Shrieking their way up the street, the monsters came for her. She turned back toward the cover of the woods and cocked her gun. Without rushing, she casually walked into the thicket of trees, every step a taunt saying, *Come and get me if you dare.*

It was by plan that Layla Harker let the monsters see her disappear into the dark, tangled branches of the forest. As they funneled into the trees moments behind her, she quickly ducked behind one of the thick trunks that blotted out the moon's light.

The gray monsters may be creatures of the night, but they never faced anything like her. In fact, she was going to show them why she had been given the nickname "The Djinn of Kandahar." A nickname that she'd always resented until now.

The monster's wild hisses filled the woods, and she quickly found a secure location and spun around, raising her gun.

WHY WON'T YOU ANSWER your phone, babe?" Jaclyn asked as she stared at her phone screen.

She redialed Layla for a third time, nervously chewing on her bottom lip. It wasn't like Layla to dismiss her calls. The pit of Jaclyn's stomach sank, and she worried that something terrible had happened to Layla. She needed to find her and fast.

Off in the distance, sirens wailed, and gunshots rang out. Jaclyn was already grabbing her red leather Jacket off the back of the kitchen chair and heading out her door when the emergency alert came across her smartphone.

EMERGENCY ALERT: CURFEW ADVISORY!

City-wide alert: A mandatory curfew has been implemented for Wood River County. Please stay inside your homes or at a friend's house. Repeat: stay safely indoors. Do not go outside.

"That can't be good," Jaclyn said to herself as she walked out into the street. She heard a loud blast and looked to her right to see that looters were already at work raiding the local shops. Under normal circumstances, she'd make an arrest, but a state of emergency had been declared, which meant the protocol was to regroup at the police station and get new orders. It will be all hands on deck tonight.

She was about to head to her car when she heard screams of terror ring out behind her. She turned back around to find the looters getting swarmed by a throng of Nightwisps. The monsters leaped up into the air and pounced onto the looters, clinging to their backs like vicious bloodworms with their barbed fangs.

"You've got to be fucking kidding me," she said, drawing out her gun.

Jaclyn walked casually toward the chaos, and when she was within fifty feet of the bloodbath, she drew on the grays and fired six clean shots. The vamps dropped to the ground one by one, and the looters lay moaning, clutching at their open wounds.

"You've gotta help us," one of the looters said since Jaclyn was a police officer.

"You'll live. Right now, though, I suggest you get off the street, board up your windows, and lock your doors. The night is only going to get worse."

Taking her advice to heart, they staggered to their feet and limped away. She turned back to her car when she heard more Nightwisps descending on the two looters from behind. She knew it was over for them. Their screams only lasted a few seconds before their throats were ripped clean out of their bodies.

Arriving at her black Challenger Hellcat, Jaclyn got in, revved her engine to life, and pulled away from the curbside. Tires squealing, she floored it and roared up the street.

The ear-rattling noise of her 700-horsepower beast drew the attention of a pack of Nightwisps standing in the street. Without so much as tapping the brake pedal, she mowed down five of the vamps like they were bowling pins, their bodies thumping against her car as she cut through the pack.

"Sorry, girl," she said, apologizing for the damage she was inflicting on her baby.

One of the Nightwisps managed to leap onto the roof of her car and was hissing at her through her sunroof. She swerved left and right, but it managed to hang on. Flooring it, she drifted a hard right, her car skidding around the corner, its tires kicking up large plumes of smoke behind it.

Luckily, it was enough to shake the Nightwisp loose, and it tumbled to the ground, rolling away. She then raced up the street at sixty-eight miles an hour.

Glancing out her driver's side window, she saw Rick Bernthal and some of the regulars camped out in front of his sporting goods store, their hunting rifles and several buckets of ammunition in hand. They were the stereotypical end-of-the-world Doomsday prepper types, having the time of their lives picking off Nightwisps as if they were overgrown voles.

Slamming on the brakes, she skidded to a stop across the street from them and rolled down her window. "Heads up, boys, there's a whole pack of these creatures hot on my ass. About a dozen or so more, so be ready."

"Well, shit, if you'd have told me it was gonna be Christmas early, I would have brought the big guns," Rick said, cocking his twelve-gauge shotgun. "I guess that'll have to do."

He nodded at her, and she nodded back. Then she peeled out and tore away again, leaving them in the haze of her burnt rubber.

When the sound of gunfire erupted behind her, she glanced into the rearview mirror to see muzzle flashes lighting up the smoke. She felt relieved when the gunfire didn't stop. This meant they were holding their own.

As soon as Jaclyn's eyes met the road again, a woman clinging to a child appeared directly in front of her. "Jesus Christ!" she shouted, slamming on the brakes and swerving so she didn't wipe them out.

Her car flipped onto its side, caught air, and rolled four times before sliding on its roof, sparks shooting out behind it. The Hellcat came to an abrupt halt when it crashed into a yellow Jeep Wrangler and a silver Prius parked across the street.

Parked upside down, Jaclyn unbuckled herself and climbed out of the shattered window. She dusted herself down and checked for any injuries. Surprisingly enough, she remained unscathed.

The woman and child looked over at her, their faces filled with terrified expressions. Jaclyn merely raised a hand and asked them, "Are you all right?"

The woman was too shocked to speak and responded with a subtle nod. Jaclyn motioned for them to come over to her.

"It's best if you get off the street," she said, waving them to her. When they approached her, the creature stalking them emerged from behind one of the parked delivery trucks. If she hadn't called them over when she did, they would have run smack dab into the hideous thing.

"Get behind me," Jaclyn said, stepping before them and taking aim. She fired off a singular shot and put one between the eyes of the creature, the back of its skull blowing out in gory detail. It hit with a thud and flopped onto its side. Making sure it was dead with an additional shot to the chest, she turned back around and faced the mother and child. "We need to get you to a safer location. More of these things will be coming soon."

The mom nodded and pointed over at the Presbyterian church up the street. Its lights were lit up, and she could hear prayers and hymns from the building as they pleaded to their absent God to protect them from the very real monsters.

"Right," Jaclyn said, a hint of sarcasm in her voice. "In about twenty minutes, that place will be a literal death trap. How about..." she paused and glanced around the street, spotting a nearby Seven-Eleven that had drawn down its security blinds. She ushered the two across the street and over to the convenience store.

When they approached the doors, she saw that the lights were off and the doors were locked. She tapped on the glass sliding doors with the barrel of her gun. Flashing her badge, she said, "I'm a police officer. Open up."

The owner, a short, balding Indian man, looked hesitant but eventually came over. He quickly unlocked the doors and let the mother and child in.

Keep them safe and lock the doors behind me." Oh, and get the kid something to eat and drink."

The store owner nodded and then asked, "You're not going back out there, are you?"

"I'm afraid it's in my job description. Serve and protect. You know the drill." She winked at them and then turned, beginning to march up the street. A cacophony of gunfire rang out in the distance. North, South, East, and West—it was utter chaos across town. Wood River was at war.

Jaclyn trekked across town on foot toward the Wood River Police Station when she came across the city park. She stopped in her tracks when, out of the corner of her eye, she caught sight of a woman sitting on one of the children's swings. The metal chains of the swing creaked gently in the evening breeze as she swayed back and forth in her seat.

Stopping dead in her tracks, Jaclyn looked over at the woman. She wore maroon-colored underwear and was covered in blood. As she swayed gently back and forth in the swing, Jaclyn couldn't help but notice the bloody pipe resting in her hand that dragged on the ground, carving little lines in the sand beneath the swing.

"Layla?" A flood of relief rushed over her as she ran to her girlfriend. Dropping to her knees, she looked up at Layla's face and placed her hands on her legs. "Babe, it's me. Jackie. Are you hurt?"

Layla looked down at Jacklyn's worried expression and smiled. "I've been better," she said.

"My God, Layla. You look like you've been through Hell. "I've been worried out of my mind about you," Jaclyn said, reaching up to touch Layla's face. "When you weren't answering my calls, I assumed the worst. What are you doing out here?"

"Darius and his bitch acolyte Velma have declared war on Wood River. I just took out over twenty of those things. And there's no end in sight."

Jaclyn helped Layla up, gently holding her waist. She looked her straight in the eyes. "Are you okay to keep going?"

"I'm just getting my second wind," she said, tossing the pipe away. Layla reached back, pulled her gun out from her back waistband, and shot Jaclyn a determined look. "You wouldn't happen to have any extra ammunition by any chance, would you?"

Jaclyn laughed. Reaching into her jacket, she pulled out a fresh magazine and handed it to Layla. "You know something? I think I just might."

Layla gladly took it and promptly slipped it into her gun, cocked it, and loaded one into the chamber. When Layla's eyes met Jaclyn's, she caught her girlfriend looking her up and down. Feeling slightly self-conscious, she asked, "What?"

"I was just thinking," Jaclyn said, "you look exactly like the woman of my dreams. Fine as can be and holding a gun."

Layla laughed and rolled her eyes. "If you say so."

Jaclyn took off her Jacket and handed it to her. "Here. You must be freezing."

"Honestly, I've been too busy killing vampires to even think about it. My adrenaline is at an all-time high." She accepted the red leather jacket that complemented her blood-stained skin and underwear and slipped it on.

"The whole city is under siege," Jaclyn said, looking back down the street the way she'd come. "Right now, we need to regroup at the station. Hit up the armory and arm ourselves to the teeth. Then we'll take this fight to Darius and his army of vampires."

Jaclyn turned back around and, without warning, Layla grabbed her by the nape of her neck, drew her in, and kissed her long and good. Gently pulling away, Jaclyn looked into Layla's big brown eyes and asked, "What was that for?"

"I know this shitshow must be hard on you. Seeing as it's open season on vampires in Wood River, I felt you needed... my support. I don't know what I'm trying to say."

"I do," Jaclyn said, brushing Layla's face with her thumb. "I love you, too."

Layla blushed. "I know it doesn't make sense. We've only known each other for a short three weeks. But I do. I do love you, Jaclyn Benoit."

"I'm sensing a but in there. Let me guess, I'm a killer and that doesn't sit well with you, right?"

A seriousness settled across both of their faces. "I thought I could brush it aside. I was so into you, I let my emotions override my common sense. At the end of the day, though, I will have to arrest you and bring you to justice."

"Agreed," Jaclyn said. "Until then, however, let's try to reach headquarters and then save whatever is left of this town."

Layla laughed. "I'd settle for just making it through the night, to be honest."

"You and me both, babe."

Layla cocked her gun and smiled.

"Here they come," Jaclyn said, turning toward the hissing sounds that were coming from all sides. Every shadow seemed to be taunting them with the threat of something terrible lurking just out of view.

"Holy shit!" Layla yelped, ducking out of the way as a Nightwisp flew out of nowhere and lunged at her. She ducked its attack, and it flew over her, tackling Jaclyn instead.

Layla watched with chagrin as Jaclyn and the creature collided and tumbled to the ground, landing in a bone-bruising heap. Layla peeked through her fingers and whispered, "Oh, fuck. Sorry about that."

Jaclyn's fangs popped, and she hissed back at the creature. Grabbing the Nightwisp's head, she snapped its neck, practically tearing it from its shoulders, and tossed it aside. She quickly stood up and looked over at Layla with her feral gaze.

Her eyes had turned pitch-black, except for a red halo that circled her irises. "It's fine," she said. "I've dealt with these things for over a hundred years. It doesn't take much to put them down. Permanently."

As she looked over at Layla with a demure smile, the creature began to twitch and shift as though it wanted to come back to life. Jaclyn drew her gun and fired two shots into the back of its skull, putting it down for good.

"Did I ever tell you," Layla said with a coy grin, "that a woman with a gun is one of the sexiest things in the world to me?" She hit back with Jaclyn's own medicine, her smile growing even more expansive.

Jaclyn took Layla's hand and pulled her in close. In vampire form, she bent down and kissed Layla's mouth. Both of their pink tongues danced around her protruding fangs in a sensual pirouette.

Sensing something wasn't quite right, Jaclyn eased up and held Layla by the shoulders. "What's the matter?"

I think it's a blood problem. I'm feeling lightheaded."

Jaclyn nodded, and then, taking Layla in her arms, she dipped her like a dancer and pushed her fangs out even longer. With a deep breath, she tossed her platinum hair over her shoulder and then bent down and sank her fangs into Layla's left breast. Layla let out a small chirp but then relaxed as Jaclyn drank.

Several Nightwisps came around the corner and froze, watching the act of an Alpha feeding. It seemed as if something instinctively prevented them from interrupting. Jaclyn looked up and hissed at them, and they turned and lumbered up the street, looking for easier prey. Once they'd gone, she went back to feeding, this time biting into Layla's right breast.

Jaclyn slid her hands down Layla's thighs, squeezed, and drew Layla up. Holding her in her arms, Layla's legs wrapping around her waist, she pressed her up against the brick wall of the local hardware store.

Aroused by the rough foreplay, Layla gasped sensually as Jaclyn slid her hands up and down her body. Letting her down gently, Jaclyn slowly sank to her knees and spun Layla again so that she was facing the brick wall. Hands spread out as though she were about to get frisked, Layla looked down at Jackie and nodded, giving her permission to bite her.

Jaclyn slowly ran her slender fingers down Layla's sides, bringing them to rest on the edges of Layla's hips. Biting down, she sank her fangs into Layla's right hip, just above her buttocks, and proceeded to drink. As she did, she gave Layla's ass a squeeze which enticed a moan from her lips.

When she was about finished, she pulled out, but to Jaclyn's surprise, Layla slowly turned around and placed her hand on Jaclyn's head, forcing her to stay on her knees. Layla rested her back on the cool brick wall as her girlfriend kissed the top of her thighs.

Jaclyn looked up at Layla as she very gently drew Jaclyn's face into her crotch. Jaclyn wrapped her arms around Layla's thighs, embracing her in a hug and resting her face against the warmth emanating from her panties.

Taking a deep breath, Jaclyn sighed and then kissed Layla just below her belly button. As she slowly stood up, she kissed Layla's abdomen, chest, and neck. When she finally reached

Layla's lips, she kissed them as well, pulling her in and tightly wrapping her arms around her. Embracing the woman she loved, Jaclyn felt as though she never wanted to let her go.

It took everything they both had not to tear each other's clothes off and make love right there in the middle of the street like a couple of sex-starved animals. Instead, they just breathed heavily and took in the memories of each other's scent, the softness of each other's skin, and the sweet taste of one another's lips.

A rapid series of pops broke their reverie, and they turned their heads in the direction of the gunfire. More sporadic pops, followed by a loud bang that could have been a grenade going off, rang out, but this time it was far closer than before.

"We'd better check on that," Layla said.

Jaclyn nodded and then smiled at her girlfriend one last time. They turned and walked up the street together just as another series of shots echoed into the night.

Coming around the bend of the hardware store, they saw five patrol cars encircling the main entrance of the police station two blocks up. Between them and the station was a horde of Nightwisps. Maybe sixty in total.

The creatures hissed like angry cats as they clawed at the barricade. Standing at the center of the horde was none other than Velma, a vicious smile spread from ear to ear.

"Isn't it my favorite two lovebirds?" Spinning and dancing and making a show of how much fun she was having, Velma stopped fifteen feet in front of Layla and Jaclyn and bowed reverently.

"This one is mine," Layla said, unamused by Velma's antics. She raised her gun and took aim at the girl, who didn't seem to care in the slightest as she went back to dancing and twirling again as if she were a carefree ballerina.

Jaclyn nodded and supplied backup, covering Layla's six. "Just be careful. She's unpredictable."

"Unpredictable? Oh, I don't think I'm unpredictable. Ultimately, I still have only one goal. To taste the blood of my enemies as I tear their throats out." Velma smiled, twirling her bat, and she started walking casually toward Layla and Jaclyn. "You know," she continued in a somber tone, "I've been meaning to repay you two for what you did to Sophie and Amber." Sure, they were a couple of the dumbest cunts that ever walked the Earth, but I loved them like sisters."

The Nightwisps parted, making way for their queen, as Velma stepped out into the middle of the street, still twirling her bat.

"So, are we doing this?" asked Layla, raising her gun and pointing it at Velma.

"Give me your best shot," Velma sneered.

"I thought you'd never ask." Layla fired off a couple of rounds, but Velma moved so fast she was able to dodge both gunshots. The two Nightwisps standing behind her dropped to the ground, but Velma charged forward, her barbed wire bat raised as she unleashed a terrible scream.

Layla fired three more shots, managing to clip Velma's right arm. This didn't deter her assailant in the least, and Velma leaped into the air, launching a vicious knee attack.

Ducking and rolling out of the way, Layla narrowly avoided Velma's strike. The sound of the bat clanking on the pavement echoed, and Velma looked up to find Jaclyn leaning against the lamppost, arms folded.

Velma raised her bat and pointed it at Jaclyn. "Stay right there, you vamp-cunt. When I'm done with your little girlfriend here, I'm coming for you."

Jaclyn didn't say anything in reply. It would be a waste of her breath. Instead, she just raised her hand and pointed at Velma's blind spot.

"Huh?" Velma asked, turning around just in time to meet Layla's fist in her face.

A crack rang out as Layla made contact, hitting Velma as hard as she possibly could. Velma staggered back and then looked up with surprise. Her jaw was dislocated. She grabbed her chin, grunted, and popped her jaw back into place.

"Ugh! That fucking hurt," she growled, massaging both sides of her jaw.

"How about we make a deal?" Crouching down, Layla set her gun on the street, keeping her eyes fixed on Velma. Slowly rising back up, she raised her hands, showing that she was unarmed. "You keep those fangs stowed, and we settle this woman to woman."

"It won't be a fair fight for you, but fine," Velma said. "No fangs. Simply good old-fashioned violence." She tossed her bat to the ground and then charged Layla. "I'm gonna suck the marrow from your bones and drink you dry like a fine Chianti!"

Layla took the first swing, but Velma blocked it with her forearm. Responding in kind with a powerful right gut punch, Velma sent Layla flying into the air. Layla crashed down onto someone's Ford F-150; the impact of her body crashing onto the hood set off the truck's alarm.

Layla quickly slid off and fell to her hands and knees, hacking and coughing up blood. This caused Jaclyn to be concerned, and she took a step forward, debating whether she should jump in and help, but Layla halted her with a raised hand.

Managing to catch her wind, Layla took a deep breath and

said, "You pack quite a punch." She stood back up and wiped the blood from her bottom lip with the back of her hand. "Let's see you try it again."

"Oh," Velma replied, cracking her knuckles, "I could do this all night long."

The two clashed in the middle of the street, the throng of Nightwisps holding back as if commanded to watch and not interfere.

Velma threw another powerful punch, but Layla, her military training kicking in, dodged it expertly. She then leaped up and clung onto Velma's arm like a wet cat. Using Velma's momentum against her, Layla swung up onto her arm, threw her legs up, and hooked them around Velma's torso, putting her in an arm lock.

Using her weight to lean back as far as she could, Layla pulled on Velma's arm until she lost her footing. Both women tumbled to the ground, landing in a tangle. Layla scrambled to secure Velma in a more effective armbar, locking her forearm and wrist together so that Velma couldn't break free, no matter how strong she was.

With a grunt, Layla wrenched Velma's arm and threatened to snap it at her elbow if she didn't yield.

Screaming out in frustration, Velma tried her best to break free. But even with her newfound strength, Layla had leverage. Physics was physics, and she couldn't escape its grasp.

Unable to get the upper hand, Velma popped her fangs and hissed. But Layla wasn't having it, and with a loud cartilage-popping crunch, she snapped Velma's arm and quickly rolled away.

Screaming, Velma stood up, her right arm limp at her side, torn out of its arm socket and dangling like a wet sock. She huffed and puffed with rage and spat as she screamed at Layla.

"You fucking bitch. I'm going to rip your heart out!"

"I warned you. The moment the fangs come out, I stop playing nice. You brought this on yourself."

"I'll kill you!"

"Tsk, tsk," Jaclyn said, smacking her teeth and shaking her head in disappointment. Looking up, she met Velma's hateful gaze and let out a regretful-sounding sigh.

"What?!" snapped Velma, standing hunched over as she held her wounded arm and glowered at Jaclyn Benoit.

"You do realize you're tussling with the two-time world Judo champion in the women's lightweight division, don't you?" Jaclyn asked, still leaning against the lamppost as though she didn't worry about the world. Not to mention Special Agent Harker's extensive military training. You best quit while you're ahead lest she tear you apart limb from limb."

Layla brushed her nose and hopped around to keep her muscles warmed up.

"Ooh, I'm so scared," Velma hissed. Then, she lunged forward with incredible speed, her claws and fangs fully extended. Layla only had time to raise her arms to block the brunt of the attack. She screamed out as lacerations opened across both forearms.

She turned in time to find Velma licking the blood off her fingers. "You taste fucking good. I've never tasted anything like you before."

"I have a clotting disease. My blood runs thick. So thick that it will kill me if I don't siphon it off every couple of weeks. I'm told it's enriching."

"*Mmm...*I can't wait to drink you up like a fucking Cherry milkshake," Velma answered, licking her lips.

"Suck my dick, bitch," Layla growled, dashing forward. They charged one another again, and Velma took a wild swing, attempting to slash Layla's neck open.

Layla saw it coming and leaned back, narrowly avoiding Velma's long black claws. Velma took another swing with her good arm, but Layla quickly ducked out of the way.

Before Velma could regain her footing, Leyla kicked out her left knee and dropped her to her knees. In a fluid maneuver, Layla grabbed Velma's hair and then kneed her straight in the nose, breaking it with a vicious cartilage-shattering crack.

Falling onto her ass, Velma sat dazed as she wiped the blood from her nose and looked down at her blood-coated hand. Eyes wide with rage, her head snapped up, and she shouted, "I'll kill you, you fucking bitch!"

Velma slapped the ground with her good hand, stiffening her body like a plank, and rose to her feet as though she were emerging from a coffin. Hissing at Layla Harker, she leaped into the air, claws slashing Layla's right shoulder.

Layla screamed out as Velma cut her again, but she still managed to slide out of the way, avoiding any follow-through.

Both women's eyes met, and then Layla looked over at her gun lying in the street. Velma followed her gaze and smiled as they darted toward the weapon.

Layla dove for the ground first, reaching for her gun but falling short. Before she knew it, Velma was on top of her, clawing at her back. She screamed out as Velma's razor-sharp nails slashed their way through her flesh, shredding Jaclyn's nice leather jacket in the process as she clawed at her like a mountain lion.

Reaching out again, Layla managed to grab her gun and quickly rolled onto her back, firing as Velma was about to strike again.

Velma's eyes went wide, and then a trickle of blood oozed out of her mouth and dribbled down her chin. She slowly looked down to find Layla's gun pressed against her ribcage, a smoldering hole where her heart should be.

"Bitch," Velma hissed, the last of her air passing over her lips before she toppled over. Her body landed with a thud on top of Layla. Knowing that Velma could heal, though, Layla pressed her gun to the temple of Velma's head and, turning her face away, pulled the trigger.

Skull fragments blew out of the side of Velma's head, and pushing her body off her, Layla sat up, chest heaving, as she gasped for air.

Slowly getting to her feet, she looked over at Jackie apologetically. "Sorry about the jacket."

Jaclyn waved it off. "Don't worry about it. I can always find a new jacket. I can't find a new you, though."

She walked toward Jackie, a prim smile forming on her lips as she allowed herself to enjoy the small victory. But she slowed up when she noticed Jaclyn's face had drained of color.

Before Layla could turn around to see what it was, she felt Velma's nails pierce her side from behind.

Layla screamed out as Velma plunged her elongated nails into her backside. She staggered forward as Velma tore them back out, her blood splashing across the pavement. Collapsing to one knee, Layla looked over her shoulder to see Velma, skull half blown off, standing over her with a vicious grin.

The force of the rushing wind blew Layla onto her backside, and she watched as Velma's head flew off her shoulders, spiraled through the air, and then hit the pavement with a wet-sounding thump.

Layla, gripping her side, grunted as she rose to her feet. Turning around, she watched as Velma's headless body sank to its knees. It tottered momentarily before Jaclyn gently nudged the shoulder of Velma's body with her foot. They watched it fall to the ground.

"Now what?" Layla asked, turning around to face the horde of Nightwisps that was slowly closing in on them. Without their Master to keep them at bay, they slowly inched toward Jaclyn and Layla. All of them hissed like feral cats as they drew closer.

Jaclyn looked down, noting that Layla's side was severely injured. They both were running low on ammunition, and Jaclyn had the sinking feeling that they were outnumbered three to one.

I'd say we run, but you're in no condition to run, let alone walk. You need a doctor."

"I'll live," Layla said, limping toward the Ford pickup truck from earlier. "Right now, though, we need to take cover."

Realizing her plan, Jaclyn pried open the truck's dented door. "It's not much, but it'll have to do."

They were nearly surrounded by the time they were ready to climb into the truck. Feeling defeated, Layla sighed and said, "What's the point?"

She turned back toward Jaclyn, and the two women looked at each other, acknowledging that this could be the end.

They were about to embrace for one last kiss when the whirr of an engine came from down the street. The Nightwisps began hissing and screeching and dashed up the street, leaving both women alone. Jackie and Layla shared a confused glance, then looked up the street to find an armored SWAT vehicle plowing through the gray Nightwisps as if they were bowling pins.

The Nightwisps tried to swarm the vehicle, but it was too heavy, and they merely battered themselves as they bashed their bodies against it.

Not slowing down, the vehicle mowed down a group of about seven or eight of the gray stragglers and broke away from the pack. It skidded to a halt next to the detectives, its hydraulic brakes letting out a hiss of air as if proclaiming its victory. The back hatch flew open, and Captain Ackhurst poked his head out.

"You two done playing slap and tickle with these gray ballsacks out here or what?"

"Boy, is it good to see you, Captain," Jaclyn said, a relieved smile cracking on her face.

With the Captain's help, she hoisted Layla into the armored vehicle and climbed in after her. Slamming the door shut, gray hands pounded against the back door almost as soon as she'd closed it.

"Let's get you two back to base," Ackhurst said, leaning back on the bench seat. He had a double-barrel shotgun resting by his side, and then, plucking out a cigar from under his bulletproof vest, he flicked out a lighter and lit it up. "Before we do, however, I have one question for you, gals."

"Sure, what is it, boss?" Jaclyn asked.

"Why are your eyes all black like that?"

Layla and Ackhurst both turned to Jaclyn and peered into her black eyes. She looked back at them, shock and dismay setting in as she realized she'd forgotten to transform back into her human self.

"Well, shit," she muttered. "I guess the cat's out of the bag."

"She's a vampire, Captain," Layla quickly informed, jumping in on Jaclyn's behalf.

"I can very well goddamn see she's a vampire. What I want

to know is, are you on our side, Jackie, or theirs?"

"I'm not on their side, I can promise that much."

"She means that she's on our side, Captain."

"That's what I said."

"No," Layla corrected, shaking her head. That says nothing with respect to whether you're on our side. But I know that you're good. And I know you're on the side of justice. So..." Layla turned back toward the captain, still flustered, and tried desperately to help Jackie save face. "I think you should give her a break, Captain Ackhurst. She's good. I know it in my heart. She's on our side."

"Yes, Raymond, I'm a vampire. And a lesbian. But above all, I'm a goddam proud police officer, and I'm not about to let a bunch of, how did you put it? Oh, yeah. A bunch of wrinkly gray ballsacks, overrun my town." Jaclyn took a deep breath and then turned to Layla. "And you're a good kisser, babe. I thought I'd toss that out there while I was at it.

"Thanks," replied Layla in a cheerful tone. "I feel the same way about you."

Puffing on the cigar, Ackhurst nodded in agreement. "No need to get all mushy on me, ladies. Everyone already knows you two are porking. And right now, that's the least of our worries." He puffed a few clouds of smoke and then added, "And if you say she's one of the good guys, Special Agent Harker, then I'm inclined to take your word for it."

Layla and Jackie looked at each other, laughed, and hugged.

Pounding the side of the armored vehicle with his hand, Ackhurst signaled the driver to get going, his cigar sliding to the corner of his mouth as he continued puffing on it.

A few minutes later, the armored vehicle pulled into the back of the police garage, and the garage doors rattled shut behind it, sealing it safely inside headquarters. As the officers stepped out of the vehicle, a round of applause greeted them.

Stunned by the unexpected greeting, Jaclyn and Layla glanced around at all the familiar faces. It felt like they'd come home from the front lines, and everyone rejoiced.

The sad truth of the matter, though, was that half the precinct was either missing or lying on stretchers. Layla looked around at the wounded and felt it seemed as though they'd been waging an uphill battle for the past several hours.

Ackhurst put his cigar out on the fender of the armored SWAT vehicle and then cleared his throat. "Listen up, folks. It's a sad day for Wood River. Our beloved town is under siege. Evil has descended upon us and threatens our town, our loved ones, and our families. I, for one, am not having it. I say, screw these ugly mother-fuckers!"

"Hurrah!" the gathering of Wood River's finest shouted. "Hurrah!"

"We're the last line of defense, ladies and gentlemen. If these fanged-fuckers beat us tonight, there's no telling what kind of damage they'll do as they spread across this country like a scourge. Well, I'm here to say that ain't going to happen. Not on my watch."

"Hurrah!" They cheered again, giving Ackhurst their undivided attention.

"So, arm yourselves and be vigilant. Because tonight, we make our last stand here in Wood River! Let our town be remembered for something other than the number of its slain victims. Let it be remembered for the day we stood up to evil and sent these mother-fucking vampires back to Hell!"

"Hurrah!" the police officers shouted as the captain finished his rousing speech.

After the captain's rousing speech, Jaclyn overheard how bad it was out there. According to everyone's accounts of the past few hours, the entire city had been overrun.

"Come on, Harker," Jackie said, looking over at her girlfriend, "Let's get you cleaned up. And from the looks of it, you'll need some stitches, too. Maybe I can find you a fresh set of clothes in my locker while we're there."

"Fuck, I forgot what I was wearing." Layla looked down at herself in embarrassment and then backed up as Jaclyn escorted her down the hallway toward the station's small clinic. Have you ever had that dream where you go to school and everyone's staring at you, only to look down and find that you're naked?

Jaclyn nodded and looked over at Layla, who stopped in the middle of the hall and gestured at herself, brushing her hands along her body as if to show off her attire. "This. This is that dream."

"Don't worry about it. I can honestly say that most of those people have other things on their minds at the moment. Besides, there's no way in Hell you could ever look bad. You're too goddamn beautiful."

Layla smiled and then, reaching her arm around Jaclyn's neck, pulled her in and kissed her cheek. "You're too sweet."

"I mean it, Layla Harker. I love you. I love you now, and I'll love you when you're wrinkly and old."

"If you plan on staying with me that long," she quipped sarcastically.

"I plan on fucking marrying you, Layla."

Both women stopped in their tracks and, standing in the precinct hallway, stared into each other's eyes.

"You better not be joking about that, Jaclyn. As madly in love as I am with you, I don't think my heart could take being hurt."

"I'm dead serious, Layla. I want to marry you. I want it more than I've wanted anything in my life."

Layla and Jaclyn stared at one another for the longest time. Then, as if they had read each other's minds, they came crashing together, their lips virtually melting together as they kissed.

Once the passionate embrace ended, Jaclyn pulled away and looked at Layla curiously. "So, Layla Harker, what do you say? Will you marry me?"

"Yes," Layla replied with a laugh. She broke into a smile and promptly jumped into Jaclyn's arms. "I will marry you, Jaclyn Elizabeth Benoit. I'll marry you in a heartbeat."

The Unfortunate Murder of Danielle Pruette

THE FLICKERING LIGHTS OF the precinct clinic buzzed overhead as Jaclyn finished stitching and bandaging Layla's shoulder and abdomen. After mending Layla's clothes, she retrieved the extra items she'd stored in her locker.

"These should fit you," she said. "Sorry, I didn't have an extra bra." When Layla started undressing right in front of her, Jackie turned away to let her have a modicum of privacy.

"You don't have to do that," Layla said. "We've seen each other naked a dozen times. If not more."

Jacklyn turned around and smiled, her eyes moving up and down her girlfriend's body. Layla was tucking the blouse top into the black slacks. Although Jackie was slightly taller, Layla's hips were wider, forcing the pants to look spectacularly tight on her.

Jaclyn eyed Layla up and down, nodding with approval. "You look…"

"I look like you," Layla laughed, finishing Jaclyn's sentence, but perhaps not in the way she intended. They both laughed.

"What are you saying?" Jaclyn asked as she gathered Layla's dirty clothes in her arms, walked over to the garbage bin, and tossed them in. "That I don't have good taste?"

Layla laughed. "God, no. Your fashion taste is terrible, babe." Layla gestured at herself, wearing Jaclyn's attire. "I look like a secretary."

Jaclyn stuck her tongue out at Layla and then reached forward and snapped off Layla's top button, allowing her blouse to fall open, revealing her ample cleavage. "Well, now, you look like a sexy secretary."

Layla rolled her eyes. They looked at each other and, after a short pause, broke into another fit of laughter.

"After this is all over, remind me to take you shopping for proper clothes," Layla said.

Jaclyn laughed. "Oh, most definitely. I'd like that."

A few seconds later, a woman poked her head in the doorway. She looked around with a lost expression on her face.

"Can I help you?" Layla asked her, giving her a comforting smile.

"I'm looking for the U.S. Marshal. Ms. Harker."

"That would be me. What can I do for you?"

The woman stood there looking nervous and then timidly stepped into the room. "My name is Alicia Pruette. Danielle was my daughter."

Jaclyn nodded as she made her way toward the exit. "I'll go get you both a cup of coffee."

"Oh, you don't need to do that," Alicia said.

"It's no bother," Jaclyn insisted, turning and exiting the room before Alicia could protest any further.

"I'm so sorry for your loss," Layla said, walking over and taking Alicia's hand in both of hers. "But it's nice to meet you finally."

"I don't know who I'm supposed to talk to about this, but it's probably better if I just show you."

Alicia reached into her arm bag and pulled out a purple notebook with glitter and butterfly stickers on it. "I found this in my daughter's room. She took it everywhere with her. I'd always see her jotting things down in it."

She handed the notebook to Layla and then gave her a sorrowful look. "After the funeral, I was such a mess. I wasn't ready to go through all her stuff yet. It was painful and emotionally draining, but I managed to pack away Danielle's things. And I found her journal under her bag. It was just sitting on her vanity chair. It was almost as if it had been calling to me. And when I read what was in it…Well, I think you should read it for yourself. I know it's not much, but I hope it can help solve the case of my daughter's murder."

Layla could see tears welling up in Alicia's eyes. Still feeling overwhelmed, Alicia Pruette spun around and, dabbing her eyes with a tissue she plucked from her purse, scurried out of the room and disappeared around the corner as quickly as she had appeared.

Layla looked down at the notebook in her hands. What secrets did it contain, she wondered.

She carefully unfastened the rubber band that held it secure and slowly opened it. Thumbing through the pages, she stopped on a random page and whispered, "Holy fucking Christ."

She began fanning through the pages more eagerly until she

came to the most recent set of entries and started reading.

May 2nd, 2023

Michael and I met in secret again today. It was just as great as I remembered it from when I used to babysit his kids for him, when we first started seeing each other. We fucked out back of the Bowling Alley after my shift. He's so tender and sweet. He told me he was going to leave Madeline and that he'd marry me. He even showed me the ring he'd picked out for me as proof. I asked him if he was having second thoughts, but he told me that his whore of a wife was fucking his lesbian partner, and as long as she had a girlfriend, he didn't see why he couldn't be allowed the same.

May 10th, 2023

I'm so fucking stupid. The last time we had sex I let him cum inside me. I missed my period this month. I might be fucking pregnant. If my family finds out, they'll expect me to introduce them to the boyfriend. I don't have a fucking boyfriend. I'm seeing a married man. A cop, no less. What's wrong with me?

May 16th, 2023

It's no joke. I'm pregnant. I'm going to tell Michael today. I don't want to make his life any more difficult than it already is, but eventually, he will have to choose between me and her. But I'm starting to realize he's never going to leave that cheating whore of a wife of his. She's too in love with that fucking lady cop, Jaclyn.

May 20th, 2023

It's not fair. I can't stop crying. It took me a week to find the courage to tell him. I invited him to the bowling alley. We had sex in the back office, and then I told him I was with child. His child. He grew furious and blamed me for being reckless and not using birth control, even though I totally did. He told me he didn't want to see me again and that I was too much of a strain on his marriage. I laughed and asked if he was sure about that. His partner is the actual strain on his fucking marriage. I told him he needed to grow a pair and either stop treating me like his side chick, leave his wife, or call it off. He stormed out. I'm still crying.

May 23rd, 2023

It's my 21st birthday tonight. I invited the band, The Slayers, along with Amber, Sophie, and Velma, to the bowling alley. We're going to get drunk after my shift and smoke a ton of weed. I invited Darius, too. He's been so sweet to me the past couple of weeks. Spring break is almost over, but Michael has been ignoring my texts. I invited him to see me tonight. If I'm stoned and wasted, I may be able to take his rejection and not want to fucking kill myself. Doubt it. But here we are.

May 24th, 2023

It's 2:00 a.m., and Darius has just driven off. I'm waiting in my car. I got a text from Michael that he was coming to see me. He wanted to wish me a happy birthday in person, he said. I have a feeling he's coming here to wish me goodbye. The storm is finally dying down, so I'll wait in my car until he arrives. Oh, I think I see him now. A patrol car just pulled into the parking lot.

"Holy shit," gasped Layla, realizing that she held the missing puzzle piece in her hands. Her face went blank as she fell into deep contemplation, piecing everything together.

Everything from the murder of Danielle Pruette, the Blood Drive Killer, the death of Detective Michaelson, and all the rest fell into place like cards being shuffled back into a deck. All the information was there—she just needed to place it in the correct order.

Clasping the diary tightly, she raced into the hall and practically jogged to her computer. Settling into her seat, she set the diary on the corner of her desk and logged onto the crime network. She brought up the GPS data for every cruiser in the shop. Scrolling through, she found the cruiser registered to Michaelson on the night of May 24, 2023.

Its GPS placed it at West Side Bowling Lanes at 2 AM that night. Danielle's body was found at 2:15 AM just up the river. This placed Michaelson at the crime scene between the time Darius had left and the time Danielle Pruette was murdered. This made him the lead suspect in the murder case.

The only problem. He was already dead. Jaclyn had ripped his throat out. She told Layla that it was because of the Red Rage. But now she wasn't so sure.

If Jaclyn had found out about Michaelson's infidelity... If she had learned the coroner's report about the sexual assault on Danielle Pruette the night of her death... If she'd learned that Michaelson had raped and killed Danielle to keep her quiet, that would be incentive enough for Jaclyn's brutal attack. It would explain everything.

"She was pregnant, you know."

Layla was startled, a shiver creeping down her spine, and spun around in her chair to find Detective Jaclyn Benoit standing directly behind her, holding two white Styrofoam cups of piping hot coffee.

Jaclyn held out one of the coffees, and Layla gladly received it, taking a quick sip.

"So, it would seem," Layla answered, cupping her hands around the warm cup. "I read the entries leading up to the night of her disappearance. It places Michaelson at the crime scene that same night. Nobody was searching for a police officer, though. Everyone was looking for the Blood Drive boogeyman."

"Michaelson wasn't the Blood Drive Killer, but his obsession with the case led me to suspect he might be a copycat. During my off time, I investigated cold cases that all seemed to have one thing in common. He was always the detective assigned to the case of the missing or murdered women. I couldn't prove it. I couldn't tie him to any of the victims. Not until now, that is," she said, nodding at Danielle's diary.

"Did you know? Did you know that he had killed her?"

Jaclyn nodded a solemn yes. "I was walking back from Mel's diner after what had been my worst blackout in ages. Gradually, I began regaining my awareness, and by the amount of blood and gore covering my body, I knew that I'd done something terrible. Something unspeakable. But I was too scared to go back. I just walked back into town, the rain washing the blood from my hands, slowly erasing the evidence along with it.

When I arrived at the bowling alley, I hoped to use their phone before they closed. Call a cab, you know. Just get out of the rain. When I arrived, it was too late. They'd already closed for the night.

"That's when I heard arguing. I stood by the roadside at the edge of the cornfield and watched my partner, Michaelson, get into a domestic dispute with Danielle Pruette. Things got heated, and then Michaelson showed his true colors and bashed Danielle Pruette's head in with the butt of his gun. I watched him unbuckle his pants and have his way with her before tossing her in the trunk of her car.

"The worst part of it all was, with my heightened fucking vampire senses, I could hear the baby's heartbeat fade away to nothing in its mother's womb. She was pregnant."

"My god," Layla gasped, covering her mouth. "That's terrible." She leaned back in her office chair, contemplating everything. Then, raising her eyes, she met Jaclyn's gaze.

"I know that look," Jaclyn said. "It's the look you get when something weighs on your mind. So, feel free to send it my way."

"It's just…If I recall correctly, the medical examiner's report said there was DNA evidence. Semen, to be exact. How did Michaelson dodge that bullet?"

"Probably exactly how you'd expect. He had access to the evidence room, the lab, and everything a detective needs in investigating a high-profile case like this. With unrestricted access, he could have easily changed the charts, tampered with the samples, or falsified reports."

Layla shook her head in solemn disbelief. "I still can't get over the fact that he thought he could get away with it. All those women?"

"There are many kinds of evil in the world, Layla. There's supernatural evil like me. Like Darius. Then there's natural evil, like droughts, earthquakes, tsunamis, and hurricanes. And then there's a more perverse evil. An evil that exists only in those rotten to their core. It hides in broad daylight and dresses itself as people you trust. Michaelson was that kind of evil. The worst kind. Of all fifty shades of gray in the world, he was pitch black."

"I'm so sorry you were betrayed like that."

Jaclyn smiled briefly, showing her appreciation to Layla. Even so, her smile quickly faded away to a more serious face—a face marred by the horrors of having witnessed real evil.

After the incident at Mel's Diner, I went home and took a shower. Like Lady Macbeth, I tried to scrub that damn stain off me," Jaclyn informed her. "But the sin of what I'd done had stained my very soul. It was never going to scrub clean. I'm a fucking vampire. I walk amongst the human world like a wolf in sheep's clothing. What I did was wrong, but at least there's a reason and rhyme behind the things wolves do. Michaelson was something worse. Something evil."

"Something profane," Layla added. "He had to be a sociopath of the highest order to hide that side of himself from you so well. You're not a bad detective, Jaclyn."

"Even if that's true," she said, deflecting, "I still should have picked up on it sooner." Jaclyn took a long, drawn-out breath and pinched the bridge of her nose. "While interrogating Darius, I realized Michaelson was behind me, taking mental notes. I knew that when Darius left the station, Michaelson would go after him and question him. Pry any information he could out of him that might tie him back to Danielle Pruette's murder.

"Darius was our lead suspect given the time frame, and eventually, Michaelson being the piece of shit he was, would have planted evidence and tried to pin the whole thing on him. I couldn't let that happen. So, after releasing Darius from questioning, I caught up to Michaelson during one of his cigarette breaks and approached him. I feigned interest in him, pretending to have used his wife as a means to get closer to him. Being the self-absorbed prick he was, he bought it. And while we were necking, I bit in, and the rest is history."

"You tried to save Darius."

"But then," Jaclyn laughed, "he saw me. Darius saw me fully vamped out and feeding on my partner. I knew that if I let him go, eventually, his story would be investigated, and who do you think they'd pin the recent string of murders on? My dick partner or the blood-sucking monster?"

"So, you tried to scare Darius away?"

"It would have worked, too, but then he tripped. He hit his head, and his blood was so enticing. I began to lose control of myself." Jaclyn's eyes welled up with tears, and she wiped a sniffle away with the back of her hand. "If I hadn't turned him…maybe all of this," she pointed toward the barred windows at the burst of gunfire going off outside as armed police defended the station from the Nightwisps, "then, maybe all of this would have never happened."

Layla stood up, firmly clasped Jackie's neck, and pulled her close, touching her forehead to Jackie's. Layla wrapped her arms around her and whispered, "You were trying to help him. You stopped a killer, and you tried to save the kid."

"I messed up, Layla. I didn't know what Darius would become. I couldn't foresee how voracious his appetite would be."

"How could you? "You're a vampire, not a fortune-teller."

Jaclyn chuckled, wiped her runny nose, and sniffled again.

"So, what do we do now?" asked Layla. She knew the proper procedure for filing new evidence; she just wanted to confer with Jaclyn, since she was also at the center of this mess.

"File the journal and the police log into evidence. You've closed the case."

"You could have closed it without my help," Layla said, reaching up to brush a tuft of Jaclyn's blonde hair behind one of her ears.

"No. It had to be you. It always had to be you."

"The Blood Drive in the 90s wasn't…" Layla deliberated whether she should even finish her thought.

"Me?" Jaclyn asked, finishing her sentence for her. "No. It was some vampire named Charles Bennington. An actual douche type, if you know what I mean. It was his murders, the Blood Drive murders, that had initially caught my interest.

Believe it or not, it was the whole reason that I transferred to Wood River, Iowa, in the first place.

"I wanted to see if there were other vampires like me. His kills fit the vampire M.O. like a glove. When I arrived, he'd already moved on. Last I heard, he'd moved up to Livingston, Montana. But I was new in my career, and I didn't have the power or authority to chase after would-be serial killers."

"So, you hunkered down here and made a life for yourself." Layla sat back in her chair as Jaclyn sat on the edge of her desk.

"I think I'm ready for a change, though. I've grown weary of this small-town life. I might like to move to Rome. Try a stint abroad."

Layla shot Jaclyn a hurt look. "So, you no longer want to get married?"

Jaclyn pinched her nose again and shook her head. "No, it's not that. I do. It's just...I need a vacation." She looked back up into Layla's brown eyes with her clear blue ones. "What do you say we make Rome our honeymoon destination?"

"I've always wanted to vacation in Italy," Layla replied, leaning back in her chair. A reserved smile formed on her lips as she ruminated about all the places she'd like to visit in Italy. The Vatican. Rome. The countryside with its green rolling hills and lush vineyards. She'd love to rent a villa in Tuscany and stay for six months.

The distinct smell of cigar smoke lingered in the air, and both women turned to find Captain Raymond Ackhurst standing in the bullpen entrance, chomping on a cigar. "You two chatty Katherines about finished, or is there something I need to know?"

Jaclyn cleared her throat and slapped a firm hand onto Layla's shoulder. "Special Agent Harker just cracked the Danielle

Pruette case."

"It's about Goddamn time," Ackhurst said. He sucked back on the cigar, the tip lighting up ember orange before disappearing behind a cloud of smoke.

Captain Raymond Ackhurst stood off to the side of the room, tilting his head back, and blew a couple of smoke rings toward the ceiling. As the rings wobbled away, slowly expanding, he shot out a third, which passed through the center of the first two rings.

Impressed by the feat, both women watched in appreciation of such a lost art form. Not many people can string their smoke rings these days. Ackhurst took another couple of puffs and jutted a thumb over his shoulder.

"All right, here's the plan. I want you two to hit up the armory and gear up. Kevlar, rifles, shotguns, fully automatic machine guns, stun grenades…it's all there. Pack as much heat as possible, and then meet me at the front of the station in twenty."

"Yes, Captain," Jaclyn said. She stood up, straightened her posture, and saluted him. With a final puff of smoke, he saluted her back and then turned, disappearing into the gray haze of his own devising.

"I didn't take Ackhurst to be a cigar man," Layla said, swiveling back and forth in her chair.

Jaclyn settled back down on the end of the desk and smiled. "Every year he quits, and every year some stressful bullshit gets him to start up again."

Gunfire erupted out front, and they knew that the army of Nightwisps had descended upon them like a swarm of insects. Jaclyn reached out a hand and smiled at Layla. "The enemy is at the gates. Shall we?"

Layla took Jaclyn's hand in hers and was hoisted to her feet. "We shall," Leyla replied as they headed to the armory together. It was game time.

23
DEATH'S SHADOW

SCREAMS RANG OUT ACROSS town as Darius walked down the central avenue, his hood up, hands in pockets. He ignored the chaos erupting all around him and casually walked down the street toward home. He hadn't been back in days, having been preoccupied with preparing his army.

Since he no longer needed to eat human food, he deliberately avoided places that reminded him of his never-ending hunger. A bloodthirst that would never leave him. A single paper cut could cause him to feel light-headed. And would send him straight into a Red Rage.

Although he despised Detective Jaclyn Benoit, he was starting to feel that he should probably take some of her letters to heart. He needed to learn to control his vampiric urges lest he devolve into a mindless monster like the grays he'd created.

Perhaps it was simply because he was feeling down. With the deaths of both Amber and Sophie still weighing on him, he felt less whole somehow. At least he still had Velma. At least he still had his mom.

Arriving on his block, he looked up to find the front door of his house hanging partway open. It appeared as if someone had broken in and just left the door ajar. Growing nervous, he pulled his hands out of his pockets and ran to his house.

"Mom!" Darius shouted. Mom, are you there?" He burst through the door, looking left and right, searching for signs of intruders. It was unusually dark. His mom usually kept a few lights on in case he returned in the middle of the night. "Mom, where are you?"

He rushed into the kitchen, the most likely place she'd be. His mom spent hours in the kitchen. She'd sit at the table and read, or make some of her famous Southern gumbo or a fancy food dish for her church's bi-weekly potluck.

When she wasn't to be found, he raced upstairs to her bedroom. She wasn't there either. Panic began to set in, his chest feeling heavy, and he leaped down seven or eight stairs at a time, hit the landing, and dashed over to the basement door.

The cozy basement had a washer and dryer, his old entertainment setup, an Xbox, and a videogame collection. There was also a large beanbag chair, in which he would sit and spend hours playing games. On a school night, he'd play until one or two in the morning, pass out in the chair, and get up at seven-thirty to rush to class.

Darius typically enjoyed showering at school. Gym class was second period, so he could get his morning shower and be fresh for the rest of the day.

The basement was dark, so he went over and flipped on the

switch. The room lit up, but there was nothing but his stuff –
just the way he'd left it. The utility closet was empty, too, apart
from a basket of dirty laundry that appeared to have been set
aside for washing later.

Where could she be, he wondered. Racing back up the
stairs, he popped into the kitchen and looked around. He took a
deep breath and slowed his heart. Gathering his thoughts, he
focused and scanned the room again. That's when he noticed it.
The kitchen trash bin was missing its garbage bag.

"Shit, shit, shit," Darius cursed as he flew out of the back
door of his house. The screen door flew open, slapping against
the house, and then slammed shut behind him. He leaped off the
porch and ran toward the wooden fence at the end of their yard.

When he reached the fence, he noticed the gate was ajar.
"Mom!" he shouted, realizing she'd stepped away to take out the
trash. Of course, it was the worst possible night to be outside
the safety of one's home.

Flying into the alley, he turned toward the trash cans and
looked down to see his mom's legs sticking out from behind
them. "Mom!" he hollered. That's when he heard the squelching
noises.

Coming around the bend, he found two gray Nightwisps
hunched over his mother, feeding on her. Her face was blank,
her eyes staring out in fear. But it was clear she was gone.

"No!" Darius screamed. The Nightwisp, closer to him,
looked up and hissed. Darius threw out his arms, popped his
fangs, and hissed three times as loudly. His eyes turned black,
and the red halo around his iris glowed red with anger.

Both Nightwisps backed away, but Darius flew into a rage
and pounced on them. He ripped the first one's head clean off
and slashed the second one across the chest with his claws,

wounding it badly. It screeched like a scared animal, ran into the neighbor's yard, and disappeared into some nearby hedges.

Darius crouched down next to his mother and placed his hand on her neck, desperately hoping for a pulse. There wasn't so much as a murmur of a heartbeat.

Breaking down, he began sobbing uncontrollably. If only he'd been home. If only he'd been there to take out the garbage when she asked, his mom would still be alive.

All of this was his fault because she was dead. He'd created the Nightwisps. He'd set them on the city like a rabid junkyard dog, allowing them to tear up the town with abandon.

He should have asked Velma to watch over her, he thought. He reached into his pocket and pulled out his phone. Quickly dialing her number, he let the phone ring. It rang until her voicemail picked up. He hung up and redialed immediately.

"Come on, come on," he whispered impatiently. "Pick up your phone."

Still, when there was no answer, he shouted, "FUCK!" and threw his phone at the tool shed. It hit the shed and shattered into a thousand pieces.

Darius took another deep breath, collected himself, and slowly stood up. He had been hasty in blaming himself earlier. He hadn't been home much, and, indeed, he'd created the Nightwisps. But it was Jaclyn Benoit who'd made him. She was the real villain in all this.

If she hadn't created him, none of this would have happened. His mother would still be alive. Hell, Amber and Sophie would still be alive. Everyone in Wood River would be going about their mundane daily lives.

Ignorance truly is bliss, he thought.

But now, he was furious. Jaclyn Benoit was the cause of all

his pain and misery. And tonight, he swore to himself that he'd hunt her down and end her reign of terror once and for all. Someone had to stop her. It might as well be him.

"Oh, shit!" a voice cried out.

Darius spun around to find a group of high school kids cutting through the alley to escape a group of Nightwisps.

"Shit, I know you, man. You're that guy who works out at the bowling alley," the tall, blonde kid said.

Darius recognized the muscle-bound ringleader behind which the two girls and nerdy-looking kid cowered. His name was Brian Cranston, star quarterback of the Wood River Senior High Honey Badgers.

"Hey, number eighty-seven," Darius said, smiling and trying to act friendly. He was never the best socialite, but needed this guy to buy into his charm.

"Yeah, that's me."

"You're like the star quarterback, aren't you?"

Brian looked at his friends and smiled. "I told you I was famous." They groaned and rolled their eyes.

Darius walked up, put his arm around Brian, and walked him away from the others. "Hey, let me talk to you in private for a second."

"Uh, yeah, sure," Brian said hesitantly. He wasn't sure why this strange kid wanted to talk to him, but when they'd stepped aside, Darius revealed his dead mother to Brian. The others looked over and screamed in fright when they saw the body lying there, and both girls, along with the nerd, ran away.

"Just ignore them," he said, his fangs growing longer.

Brian turned to see Darius staring at him with red eyes. "What the fuck, man! Are you one of them?!" he said, trying to turn and run. But Darius's grip was too firm.

He reeled Brian in and sank his teeth into his neck. Brian screamed out, his voice echoing down the alley and spurring on his classmates who didn't dare look back.

Once Brian was drained, Darius dropped his pale body to the ground. After a few moments, his pale skin turned a medium gray color, like that of an Elephant. Lying on the ground, Brian's dead body began to jolt and spasm like an epileptic person. After the violent seizure, Brian slowly stood up, his vampire form taking hold.

Transformed, he shook his head, his hair falling away until he was bald. Unexpectedly, he screeched as if in immense discomfort and began tearing off all his clothes. Dropping his shredded shirt onto the ground, he looked down at Darius and hissed.

Darius hissed back, but Brian was larger than him, with muscles like a bodybuilder, and towered over him. As he had learned, most Nightwisps were primal. They reacted instinctively, behaving more like animals than sentient creatures.

Given this, Brian would need to be put in his place; otherwise, being the biggest of the grays, he'd think he was the alpha. Darius would have to bring him down a peg and make him fear him; otherwise, Brian would be more trouble than he's worth.

Brian swung his clawed fingers as if on cue, but Darius reached up and caught the blow, holding Brian's wrist in place with little effort.

"My turn, asshole," Darius said with a smile.

With a grunt, he threw the newly formed Nightwisp into the air, tossing him like a rag doll. Brian's bulky body crashed into Darius's tool shed that sat in the backyard, bringing the whole thing down on him.

Brian's large, hulking body disappeared beneath the crumbling shed. This only angered Brian even more, and from beneath the debris, Darius could hear him snorting and snarling. The rubble of the shed shifted, and Brian shot up. Throwing out his arms, he hissed even more loudly than before—a direct challenge to Darius.

"Yes. That's the fury I want from my subjects," he said, a twisted smile contorting his face into something more frightening—into an evil grin that is both manic and sinister all at the same time.

Brian leaped from the rubble, landed in the backyard, and charged Darius. Seeing the tackle coming, Darius slid forward, cutting their distance in half in a split second, and threw out his elbow. Darius hit Brian dead center on the bridge of his nose and dropped him.

Rendered unconscious, Brian crumpled to the ground like a ton of bricks. Darius stood over Brian's gray, leathery body and grinned victoriously.

When the vampire formerly known as Brian woke up, he'd be better behaved. Now that he knew he couldn't take Darius in a fight, he'd fall in line and do his Master's bidding. And Darius had something specific in mind for Brian the Gray.

Bending down, Darius grabbed Brian's arm and began dragging him down the alley. "Now that you know who the real alpha is here, I have a job for you. I need you to kill Jaclyn Benoit for me."

24

Vampire Slaughterhouse

BY THE TIME MIDNIGHT rolled around, Wood River was in flames. Being your stereotypical Midwestern town located in rural America, most people had guns. And the townsfolk were armed to the teeth.

This allowed them to gather into small militias that took on the vampires. They demonstrated a surprising amount of resilience as the battle continued. Still, the subsequent bloodbath was unavoidable, and both sides took massive casualties.

Jaclyn Benoit stepped outside the police station and tugged on her Kevlar vest, ensuring it was snug. It was a standard navy-blue vest with "Police" written in bold white letters stamped onto the breastplate.

Layla followed Jackie out, her tan vest contrasting with

Jackie's navy blue one. Layla's was a military vest, light tan to match desert camouflage, and had "U.S. Marshal" written in black on the front. Either way, they were armed to the teeth. Layla grabbed a grenade belt and armed herself with an M320 grenade launcher attached to an M4 Carbine assault rifle.

"Did I ever tell you that a woman with a gun is about the sexiest thing in the world?" Jaclyn teased, winking at Layla.

Layla laughed. "You know, I've heard something along those lines."

Captain Raymond Ackhurst blew on a coach's whistle, drawing everyone's attention to him. "All right, people. Beyond this barricade over my shoulder, there is a horde of gray *Voyage of the Demeter*-looking mother-fuckers. Aim for their heads. Anything else has proven ineffective against these resilient gray ballsacks. Blast them to Hell. Good luck, and stay alive out there!"

"Hurrah!" the thirty well-armed police officers shouted in unison. With that, the barricade gates opened, and the officers charged out into the dead of night. Gunfire immediately erupted, and Layla took a step forward to follow their lead when Jaclyn reached up and touched her arm, urging her to hold back.

"What is it?" Layla asked.

"Something isn't right with this. The swarm we faced earlier was twice as large. Where did they all go?"

"Oh, that little fucker. He's smart."

"You're referring to Darius?"

It's clear that Darius has honed his strategic skills by playing a significant amount of Call of Duty. He's luring the police with a scattered trail of his gray minions, creating a false sense of victory as the police pick off their numbers. By the time they realize it's a trap, he'll ambush them with his entire vampire army."

"We have to warn them," Layla said, and Jaclyn nodded in agreement.

Jackie approached one of the officers at the front gate and said, "Hey, Peralta. Where's the captain? I need to speak to him about something."

"He ran back inside. He said something about not wanting to go to Hell without his stogie.

"Thanks," Jaclyn said, turning around. Looking at Layla, she said, "Stay here with Peralta and continue providing cover fire. I'll be back as soon as I can."

With that, she quickly returned to the front entrance of the precinct and disappeared inside.

Captain Ackhurst was digging through his desk drawer for his box of Cuban Cigars. They were once illegal imports, but now that the border with Cuba had reopened, they were regular imports. And he imported them quite frequently.

"Bingo," he said, pulling up the box and opening it. Only two cigars remained. He tucked the first one into his pocket, clipped the second one with his cigar cutter, and lit it up with the old Zippo he kept in the box for emergencies.

Lighting up, he inhaled deep, sucking back on the cigar, and after holding it in, let out a few puffs. Just as smoke escaped his lips, he heard a scream. Realizing the scream came from inside the precinct, he promptly drew his Colt .45 revolver and stepped out of his office, gun held at the ready.

A female officer, whom he recognized as Jannet Rodriguez, came racing around the corner. He waved her toward his office, and she began to run toward him when a gray skin came out of nowhere and tackled her to the ground.

"Jesus H. Fucking Christ!" Akehurst cursed as he stepped out of his office and into the bullpen. He aimed his gun, but he didn't have a clean shot. The creature was perched on top of her, fangs drooling in anticipation of the kill. "When did the ninth gate to hell open up?!" asked Captain Ackhurst.

"Help me!" Jannet cried out. She clawed at the ground, her fingernails leaving scratch marks on the hardwood floor as she desperately tried to drag herself away and break free of her attacker. But he was too strong and moved too fast.

She winced in pain and yelped as the gray monster sank his fangs into her neck with a wet-sounding squelch!

Captain Ackhurst flipped over a nearby table and took cover. Aiming his revolver at the creature's head, he growled, "Eat lead, you blood-sucking leech!"

Ackhurst fires his revolver two times. The first shot missed and embedded itself in the wall. However, the sound of the bullet whisking near its ear caused the Nightwisp to look up and hiss just in time for the second bullet to split its head open.

Vaulting over the table, using his arm as a brace, and swinging his legs over, Ackhurst rushed over to Jannet Rodriguez. She was gurgling up blood and trying to speak.

"Don't talk. Just save your breath, kiddo," he said, pressing his hands to her neck to try and stop the bleeding. But it was no good. The vampire had ripped half of her throat out, and before he knew it, she wheezed her last breath, and her face went blank as her body fell silent.

"Goddammit," he grumbled, removing his hands as he sat on his knees, feeling defeated. "You were a fine officer, Rodriguez. A damn fine officer."

Captain Ackhurst grunted as he pushed himself to his feet. Before he could stand up, however, a gray vampire burst into the room and darted toward him. He reached for his gun, but his hands were covered in Rodriguez's blood, and his revolver slipped out of his hands and fell to the floor with a solid thud.

"Shit," he growled, throwing up his arms in time to brace himself from the full-on body tackle. The vampire collided with him, and they rolled over the table he'd used as a makeshift barrier. Tumbling to the ground, Ackhurst grabbed the gray monster's throat and held its snapping jaws at bay.

His other hand clutched the monster's wrist so it wouldn't claw him. The creature's right arm supported its weight as it pinned the captain to the floor with its left arm.

Through a clenched jaw and gritted teeth, Ackhurst growled, "Get off me, you wrinkly old cock-bag!"

The vampire hissed in return, its drool dripping in glistening strands of saliva which landed on the captain's shirt, staining his collar. Without warning, the creature's head burst like an overripe melon, and blood splattered everywhere.

Captain Ackhurst reflexively turned his face as chunks of vampire meat dappled his face. Tossing the body to the side, he sat up and wiped the gory remains from his face, but only seemed to smear things. Opening his eyes, he saw Jaclyn standing in the doorway, the barrel of her Glock 17 smoking, white tendrils of wispy smoke climbing up toward the ceiling.

"They got Rodriguez," he said, pushing himself back up. Walking over to where he dropped his piece, he bent over, picked up his revolver, and tucked it back into his underarm holster.

Jaclyn didn't know how to respond. She could only look over at Rodriguez's lifeless body and shook her head with a sunken gaze.

"Thanks, by the way," the captain added. "For saving my ass back there."

"You would have done the same," she replied.

"So, um, how long..." he hemmed and hawed, trying to find the right way to broach the subject of her vampirism. Supposing there was a proper way. He'd never known any vampires before. She was his first.

Anticipating his question, Jaclyn answered, "Almost two hundred years."

Ackhurst chuckled lightly. "Well, *shiiit.* I bet you've seen some stuff."

"I saw the expansion of the West. I lived through the Gunslinger era. I saw America industrialize. I lived through both World Wars. But I'm still quite young in terms of vampires and how long we can exist."

"You don't...um...sparkle, do you?"

"You mean like in the *Twilight* books?" She laughed and shook her head. "No, I don't sparkle."

"But you can walk in the daytime?"

"I'm what we call a purebred vampire. These creatures we're fighting are just the monster version of us. Mindless. Bloodthirsty. Dumb as a bag of rocks. Then you have the ancients. These vampires are over a thousand years old. We call them the Elders. I've only met one of their kind. Anyway, daylight harms the Nightwisps or Grays, as you call them."

"I see," he said, still trying to process the information. Learning that one of your finest was a vampire wasn't something that happened every day. Not knowing how to react, Ackhurst decided it was probably best to change the subject. He asked, "So, you and Layla are...um..."

BWA-FOOM!!!

A loud rumble shook the station before Captain Ackhurst could finish his sentence. It was clear a grenade had gone off just outside. Jaclyn and Ackhurst exchanged a stunned look.

"Layla," Jaclyn said, her voice heavy with worry.

They jogged to the entrance and headed outside. When they got outside, they found the gate, and both officers guarding were blown to smithereens. Jaclyn was relieved to discover that Layla was not among the casualties.

"Stay with me, son," Captain Ackhurst said, checking the officer's pulse furthest away from the gate. It was Peralta. Noticing that Peralta was trying to tell him something, Ackhurst leaned down and listened closely. "What is it, son? Spit it out."

"He took her," Peralta whispered. He winced with pain and let out a low groan. Captain Ackhurst propped his head up so he wouldn't choke to death on his own blood.

"Layla?" Jaclyn asked. "Who took her?"

"That black kid. The one you're investigating," informed Peralta. "I don't remember his name."

"Darius Reid?"

"Yeah. That's the one," he said in a gruff tone.

"Fuck," Jaclyn hissed and took off running down the street.

"Goddammit, Jackie!" shouted Captain Ackhurst, calling after her. "Now is not the time to play hero." But it was no use. She was faster than a regular human and was already too far down the street for his words of caution to reach her.

A couple of officers came running out of the precinct, grabbed their comrades in arms, and dragged them inside. Meanwhile, Captain Ackhurst pulled out his revolver, popped open the chamber, and gave it a spin. He had three rounds left and two cartridges on his belt. He replaced the bullets, loading the revolver fully, and then popped the chamber back in and tucked his gun into its holster. Bending down, he picked up the pump-action shotgun that the dead officer was no longer using and cocked it.

Puffing on his cigar, he pulled the smoking stogie out of his mouth and exhaled a cloud of smoke. "I'm ready for you mother-fuckers. Bring it!"

As three grays ran toward the gate, trying to get in after the explosion, Ackhurst started unloading shotgun rounds into them, blowing them four feet backward with the sheer force of each point-blank blast.

When his shotgun ran out, he tossed it aside and used his Colt .45. The blasts from the .45 were nearly as powerful, and he took down two grays with one shot.

Finally, the hammer on his Colt clicked, signaling it was empty. He pulled up a fast-load clip with six new bullets and, flicking his wrist, popped open the chamber, let the shells slide out, and then popped in his reload.

He stepped out from the safety of the barricade and began blasting Nightwisps left and right. Running out of ammo even faster than before, he reloaded his remaining rounds and, using the palm of his hand, slapped the chamber back into place and gave it a spin.

Captain Ackhurst could see four more creatures running up the street, all their fingers and arms reaching out for him like the tangled and knotted limbs of withered branches.

"I am getting too old for this shit," he grumbled. Then, as he stood his ground, he slowly raised his revolver, cocked the hammer back, and aimed his weapon. As he held his gun steady, he drew out his last cigar and lit it up.

Gun in his right hand, smoking stogie in his left, Captain

Ackhurst opened fire and unleashed Hell on the horde of Nightwisps racing toward him.

"DARIUS!!!" Jaclyn screamed at the top of her lungs. "Darius! I'm here! You hear me?! I'm right here!"

She stood atop an SUV tipped over onto its side in the middle of the street. Behind her was a car fire, and in front of her, more Nightwisps. Most of them seemed to ignore her since she was fully vamped out.

Mostly, they ignored their own, but occasionally, a random gray would turn and come at her, hissing and screeching like a banshee—a type of primal challenge, she imagined. She picked off these pests like a farmer picking off black-tailed prairie dogs.

The barrel of her gun smoked as she shouted again. "Darius! I'm the one you want. Let her go, and I'll give myself willingly."

Laughter seeped out from the dark alleyways and from all around. The more laughter there was, the more menacing it seemed. Stepping out from behind a wrecked car, Darius held Layla by her neck and made himself known. "Imagine my disappointment when, on my way over here, I found Velma's corpse lying in the middle of the street. It seems you can't help yourself, Jackie. You're just stuck in one gear—kill or be killed."

"Darius, listen to me–"

"No!" he shouted, cutting her off. "You listen to me. I was a nobody in this town. Then you turned me into a bloody vampire! I became popular. Girls started to like me. Other men felt intimidated by me. I was finally coming into my own. And I was just about to forgive you for turning me into this monstrosity." He gestured at himself with his free hand, his other hand still tightly clasped to Layla's throat. But then you systematically had to destroy everything I ever cared about. Amber. Sophie. Velma. My mom."

Realizing Darius was distracted, Layla used her leverage to springboard off the side of the broken car, do a backflip, and break free of his grasp. The moment she was free, she ran toward Jaclyn, who drew out her gun and pointed it straight at Layla.

Their eyes met, and Layla knew what to do. Diving forward, like a baseball player diving into first, Layla hit the dirt. At that exact moment, Jaclyn fired three rounds from her gun and shot Darius, who was in pursuit of Layla.

Taking three to the chest, Darius staggered back and looked up. "Bitch," he snarled. Then, raising his hand, he snapped his fingers, and the car behind him shot across the street, scraping on the pavement and shooting up sparks before crashing into the flower shop on the other side.

A massive gray Nightwisp stood in place of the wrecked car and hissed loudly. It was large and muscular—a former athlete of some kind—and about the size of the freakin' Incredible Hulk.

Darius simply glowered at Jaclyn and then, pointing his finger at her, growled, "Kill her."

The creature charged forward, passing Layla, who rolled out of the way just in time to avoid being trampled by the monster. She watched it pass by and tried to tackle Jaclyn.

Jaclyn's wings shot out, and she used them to counter his velocity by flapping herself forward. She braced herself against the brunt of the head-on assault. Her feet skidded back on the pavement, and they came to a standstill.

The supersized gray hissed at her, and Jaclyn popped her fangs. They pushed off from one another, the creature hunching low, throwing out its arms, and hissing more. In response, Jaclyn fanned her wings to increase her stature and hissed back.

Layla crawled over to another car. Pushing her back against the silver Chevy Tahoe on the opposite side of the street, she drew her rifle and pointed it at Darius.

Darius didn't wait around to find out who the victor of this battle would be. For him, it was just enough that Jaclyn would have to suffer. Before turning away, he looked over at Layla.

"See you later, Agent Harker."

"Not if I see you first," she said, standing up and firing off a couple of bursts of automatic fire from her M4 Carbine.

Darius was fast, though, and vanished without a trace.

She suspected it wasn't the last they'd see or hear from him. But right now, they faced a different kind of threat.

Layla quickly spun around and aimed her rifle at the massive gray in case Jaclyn needed any backup. Fixing her rifle sights on the Nightwisp's gray bald head, she centered him between her crosshairs and waited for Jaclyn to give her permission.

Layla heard hissing coming from all sides as she held her target in her sights. She glanced around to see about a dozen Nightwisps seeping out of the dark crevices between buildings and dark alleyways.

The fires from burning cars lit up their gray skin, casting orange hues. She noted their black demonic eyes looked darker somehow in the contrasting light.

Standing back-to-back, a throng of gray vampires manifested all around Jaclyn and Layla, surrounding them from nearly every direction. With no hope for escape, Layla glanced over her shoulder at Jaclyn and said, "If things go south, I just want you to know that I love you."

"I love you, too, babe," Jacklyn replied. Then, striking her

Glock 17 across her chest, Deadpool style, she cocked it one-handed.

Layla followed her lead and drew back her slide one-handed, John Wick style, did a quick check of the loading chamber, and then let it click back into place—fully cocked. If they were going to go down, they'd go down in a blaze of glory.

25

No Salvation for the Wicked

"FUCK THIS BULLSHIT!" LAYLA shouted. She stood up and, drawing the M320 grenade launcher off her back, she cocked it and let loose and sent a volley of projectile grenades at the throng of gray monsters rushing toward her.

With a hollow-sounding thump, the grenade launched out of the M320. It sailed through the air and promptly crashed down between half a dozen grays. They all looked down at the shell as it rattled on the ground, and then – *BOOM!*

The fiery explosion sent vampire body parts flying everywhere. The remaining Nightwisps ran to the other side of the street and regrouped. Layla merely launched another grenade, which was followed by another massive explosion. This time, the blast accidentally destroyed part of the local coffee shop, *The Broken Mug.*

"Shit! Oops, sorry," she said, squinting at the destruction she'd caused. Her cheeks turned rose-pink with embarrassment.

She turned just in time to see the big guy bullrush her. She raised her rifle and blocked his razor-sharp claws. But he hit it with such force that she flew back into the Chevy Tahoe. Its side crumpled with her impact, and having the wind knocked out of her, she slid to the ground, coughing and gasping for air.

Layla mustered up enough strength to sit up and raise her rifle. She found it broken into two parts. Luckily, the damn thing absorbed the brunt of the blow and likely saved her life. She unfastened the M320 grenade launcher, which was still fully functional. She loaded her last grenade and cocked it.

The hulking gray mass jumped through the air and tackled Jaclyn to the ground. They tumbled several feet before Jaclyn managed to kick him off. He flew back, crashing into a mail truck.

As he impacted with the side, it crumpled in, and envelopes and other mail shot out. Filling the air, mail fluttered to the ground like autumn leaves falling from an autumn tree. The big gray vampire grunted, claws scraping the caved-in sides of the van, climbed out of the crumpled-up vehicle, and howled at the moon.

After yowling and fussing, he turned to bullrush Jaclyn again, but Layla wasn't about to have any of it. She fired off her last grenade, and it exploded just short of his left shoulder. The explosion sent him flying into the glass of the flower shop window across the street, and he disappeared inside.

"Nice shot," Jaclyn said. Layla nodded and, realizing she was out of ammunition, tossed the grenade launcher and drew out her sidearm.

Both women inched up to the broken window of the

storefront, keeping their eyes fixed squarely on the black void that filled the shop's interior.

"Do you think it's dead?" asked Layla.

Jaclyn raised her hand, gesturing for her to hold back. Cautiously stepping up to the shattered window, Jaclyn's shoes crunched down on the broken glass, which crunched beneath her feet like freshly fallen snow.

"HIIISSSSK!" The gray Nightwisp leaped out of the darkness, grabbing Jaclyn's wing as he flung her into the adjacent brick wall. Jaclyn hit hard and coughed up some blood, then looked up, the red halos of her black eyes flashing with rage.

The two charged one another again, but the gray kneed Jaclyn squarely in her gut, and she collapsed to the ground. The monster grabbed both of her wings, taking one in each hand, then placed a foot onto her back and leaned back as he began to pull.

Jaclyn screamed in agony as the monster tried to tear her wings off her back. Layla didn't like hearing the person she cared about shriek in pain, so she quickly began to unload an entire clip into the gray's back, hitting it with everything she had.

The gray raised a charred and blackened arm, damaged by the grenade blast, and absorbed her bullets.

It turned and swatted at her, hissing a warning for her to keep her distance. She backed up several steps, released her spent cartridge, and quickly slapped in a new one.

Her little diversion had worked. Jaclyn twisted around and broke free of the creature's grasp. She flew up into the air, grabbing the gray's head as she flew upward.

A gust of wind caused Layla to shield her eyes, but she could make out Jaclyn carrying the gray high into the sky. Once they were about a hundred and twenty feet up, she dropped the fucker.

He smashed into the pavement, leaving a small crater as the blacktop crumbled in around his unconscious body. Not wasting a beat, Layla cocked her gun and walked up to the gray monster. Blood oozed out of its eyes, ears, and mouth, but it wasn't dead.

It was still breathing shallowly, but she could tell its bones were shattered into a thousand pieces as it tried to move, to reach out and grab her, but it couldn't. It yowled in pain, and some small part of her felt sorry for the creature, its yellow eyes staring helplessly at her.

Raising her gun, she fired five shots at its face and put the wretched thing out of its misery. Jaclyn landed ten feet away, looked over at Layla, and down at the creature. She raised her eyebrows, showing that she was impressed.

Clapping echoed up the street, and they both turned to see Darius standing in the open. "Bravo, ladies. Bravo."

"Call off your foot soldiers, Darius," Jaclyn pleaded. "You've lost this fight."

"The fight isn't over yet," he replied.

"You don't understand, Darius." I'm giving you the chance to turn this around. Walk now, and you'll live to see another day."

"It's you, detective, who doesn't get it. Everyone I ever loved is dead – because of you, my mom, Velma, Sophie, Amber, and Danielle. Even your partner and his wife got entangled in your dark web of blood and malice.

Jaclyn and Darius walked toward each other, surrounded by half the town that was burning around them. When they came within two feet of each other, they stopped and stared at each other, like two cats locked in a showdown.

"It's not going to end well for you, Darius."

"Funny, I was going to say the same thing to you, Jackie."

Both vampires phased in and out, becoming little more than a blur as they moved too fast for human eyes to see. Layla squinted, aiming her gun at one spot and then another. But each time she thought she had a lock on them, they blurred out of sight and reappeared in another location.

Suddenly, Jaclyn's body crashed down in front of her, and before Layla could react, Darius was sitting atop Jaclyn, his legs straddling her waist as she lay on her back.

Pinned to the ground, Jaclyn looked up at him, her black eyes burning with rage. She was sorry she'd ever created him.

Layla held off, choosing not to fire as she knew Jackie needed to finish this fight herself.

Raising his hand, his claws glistening with her blood, Darius smiled down at her. "Any last words, detective?"

"I'm done fighting. I don't want to kill you, Darius."

"Suit yourself," he said with a light shrug. Then, bringing his sharp nails down, he dug into her vest and ripped it off her. Underneath, she had on a black tank top.

Tossing the vest away, Darius raised his claw-like fingers again, this time to try and rip out her heart. But a single gunshot rang out, and a bullet pierced his right hand.

"Fuck!" he shouted, clutching his hand with his other one. His head snapped to the left, and he glared at Layla Harker with a burning fury that caused her to take a step back. "I was going to let you live, Agent Harker. But you just sealed your fate."

Jaclyn's hand shot up and grabbed Darius by the throat. Rising, she stood up and hoisted him above her as though he weighed nothing and squeezed his windpipe.

"Ack!"

"Did you say something?"

"Gack!"

"It doesn't matter," Jaclyn said, shaking her head disappointedly. I've given you more than enough chances to fall in line, but you seem determined to exact revenge. An eye for an eye, is that it? Revenge is meaningless when it's divorced from justice. I wish you could see that."

Darius reached down and took Jaclyn's throat in his hands and began to squeeze. Each of them is trying to kill the other.

Slowly, Jaclyn sank to her knees, still clutching Darius's throat. His eyes began to roll back in his head, but suddenly, they popped back open, revealing his black obsidian gaze.

He pried Jaclyn's fingers off his throat. Then, with his razor-sharp fingers, he thrust his hand into Jaclyn's gut. His fingers penetrated her abdomen, and she groaned in pain.

"Just die!" Darius screamed in her face, spittle from his mouth splashed across her cheek. "Just fucking die, already!"

Blood dripped over Jaclyn's lip, and she coughed a wet cough. Darius pushed his hand into her body even further, causing her to groan in agony once more.

"Please," he said, tears swelling in the corners of his eyes like the ocean waves, "Just die. And it will all be over."

The mechanical click of the gun cocking caused him to look to his right. The temple of his head ran into the muzzle of Layla Harker's gun, and she pulled the trigger.

Darius's body fell to the ground, and Jaclyn fell along with him. Hitting the pavement, Jaclyn held her abdomen and rolled onto her back. She looked up at Layla, eyes thankful but still in a bit of shock.

"I had to," Layla said. "He was never going to stop. He was never going to quit killing."

Kneeling next to Jaclyn, Layla pulled up her sleeve and extended her wrist. "Drink. You need to heal yourself."

Jaclyn shook her head, knowing it was too dangerous. Layla put her wrist to Jaclyn's mouth and then gently placed the muzzle of her gun against Jaclyn's temple.

"Drink. I'll stop you if you get out of control."

Gun to her head, Jaclyn took Layla's wrist and bit into it. She drank fast and hard, and Layla whined lightly as the pain was unpleasant, to put it mildly.

"All right, that's enough," Layla said, mustering the strength to pull her arm away. They would have been in trouble if Jaclyn had lost control.

Jaclyn growled at her as she continued drinking and pulled Layla's arm back to her mouth.

"I mean it," Layla said. "Don't make me kill you, Jackie. Please. Choose life."

She was growing fainter by the second and could feel herself slipping away. As she began to feel the darkness encroaching around her vision, she began to squeeze down on the trigger.

A split second before she was about to fire, Jaclyn pulled back and, gasping for air, relinquished her hold on Layla's arm.

"I'm sorry," Jaclyn said, apologizing for almost taking it too far. Sitting next to Layla, panting, Jackie's chest heaved as she fought to catch her breath.

"Feel better now?" Layka asked, massaging away the bruise left from the bite mark with her thumb.

Jaclyn wiped Layla's blood from her mouth with the back of her hand and whispered, "Yeah. Thanks, love. I needed that."

Layla drew back and let out a massive sigh of relief. Jaclyn pulled her shirt up, exposing her abs, and showed Layla she was fully healed.

"What now?" Layla asked.

Jaclyn got up first and helped Layla to her feet. "With Darius dead, his coven will scatter. The Nightwisps won't survive long without their master."

"I'm sure Wood River's finest will hunt down the rest."

"Still," Jaclyn said, looking over her shoulder in the direction of gunfire. It was a good sign since it meant people were still fighting off the vampire scourge. "The secret is out. Because of what happened here in Wood River, the whole world will know that vampires exist."

"Is that such a bad thing?" asked Layla. "Not all vampires are evil, after all." She smiled at Jaclyn and reached out to touch her.

Jaclyn pulled away and then turned to face Layla. Her face was sad. "Are you sure about that?"

Nobody in this world is entirely good or entirely evil. We're made up of all the colors of gray. Humans are complex, messy creatures with intricate emotions. But, deep down, I know there's still good in you, Jaclyn Benoit."

"I wish I could believe that," Jaclyn replied, brushing her long platinum-blonde hair behind her ear. "But I think it's better if I disappear for a while. Let things cool down."

"Where will you go?"

Jaclyn shrugged. Then she took Layla in her arms and kissed her long and good.

A laugh escaped Layla's lips; drawing back, she smiled at Jaclyn. "So, I guess this is goodbye?"

"I'll miss you, Layla Harker. You are the love of my life. However, I'm unable to be around you right now. It's too dangerous. Dangerous for you. For me. For everyone in Wood River."

"I understand," Layla said, turning her head and taking in a deep breath as she stared down the empty street behind them. "Will I ever see you again?" When Jaclyn's reply didn't come, Layla turned back around, only to find that Jaclyn was already gone.

She was a creature of the night and had returned to the night from whence she'd come. She was a dark angel, the savior of Wood River. However, most would likely disparage her and call her a monster. They could only see the bloodsucker, the succubus, the thing they called vampire.

Regardless of what the world thought, though, Layla knew better. Jaclyn wasn't evil. She was cursed, but she fought it the best she could. She resisted the temptation to succumb to evil and became something else—something new, something noble rather than profane.

She was unbridled like the wild stallion, feral and free like the gray wolf of the mountain forests. She was just another force of nature to contend with.

Layla wiped a tear from her cheek. Although this may be goodbye, she was positive this wasn't the last she'd see of Jaclyn Benoit.

With love in her heart, she muttered one final thought aloud. Hopefully, it was loud enough for Jaclyn to hear it.

"I'll miss you too, my love," she whispered. "Stay good."

WOOD RIVER CEMETERY SAT cradled in a misty clearing beneath a phosphorescent moon that hung in the vast Midwestern sky. The moon's soft white glow blanketed the landscape, highlighting the rows of gravestones and Christian crucifixes.

Large spruce trees surrounded the main burial site, and their green pines were sculpted into perfect cones that dotted the perimeter like green tin soldiers—soldiers who guarded their loved ones. It was the most peaceful Wood River had been in weeks.

The gravestones, carved with the names of those buried beneath the earth, cast eerie shadows across the finely manicured grass. The sweet scent of freshly planted flowers lingered in the air, and the nearby trees wavered ever so gently in the evening breeze.

The number of newly sunken caskets would make even the most ironclad individuals feel uneasy. A reminder of how the denizens of Wood River had met their gruesome demise. Many of whom died in the recent vampire attacks.

The outbreak had spread across the sleepy town like a medieval plague. It was only because of a handful of brave police and militia that Wood River managed to end the terrible infestation.

Unsurprisingly, though, many of the creatures had fled and disappeared into the night. They were most likely hiding in barns, sheds, and abandoned trailer homes. Although infestation persisted, it was far more manageable now.

As things slowly began to return to normal in Wood River, the news reports couched the unexplained events in terms of a nearby prison break. For most, that was as good an explanation as any. And so, it came to be known as the Wood River Prison Break Massacre.

The murders weren't attributed to just one psycho killer but many crazed individuals who escaped a maximum penitentiary in the neighboring county of Fredrickson. The road to Mel's Diner cuts right through Fredrickson County and back again.

This explanation, conjured up by local news outlets, accounted for the diner massacre and the strange happenings at the West Side Bowling Lanes, a little further up the road.

Wood River, it was said, was the refuge for the Fredrickson convicts. The news warned that if you happened to see anything strange out that way, you were to report it immediately. Convicts were still at large, after all. All this, to cover up the small fact that vampires existed.

Even armed with the truth, most weren't willing to accept

the fact that vampires were real. However, supernatural monsters walked among them regardless of what people wanted to think. A fact that the good folks of Wood River, Iowa, found out the hard way.

In the distance, several plots down in Wood River Cemetery, the soft grass rustled in front of a gray tombstone. Unexpectedly, the earth undulated, and the ground began to swell. A mound gradually formed and grew larger and larger until, like a spider's egg sac, it was ready to burst.

Once it had grown to the size of a soccer ball, the freshly laid sod split open, and a pallid hand tore out of the green grass and soil and reached into the moonlit sky.

The hand grew into an arm, and the arm grew into a torso as a naked woman with ivory skin clawed her way out of the bowls of the earth, prying herself free from the dirt and muck.

She struggled to her feet and looked around, swaying on wobbly legs. Her naked body was stained with dirt and the residue of dew from the early morning grass.

"What the fuck?" she spoke aloud, her throat parched and her voice gravely and rough. Was it the cemetery? What was she doing here, she wondered.

Although she had a vague recollection of the past week, she wasn't entirely sure how she came to find herself buried alive. Turning around, she looked down and read the name chiseled onto the tombstone: *STACEY ANDERSON. 1992-2024.*

"Fuck me," she said in a raspy voice, her eyes fixed on her own grave. She was way too young to have died. Except, she wasn't exactly dead. She wasn't quite alive, either. She was one of what the kids called "undead."

She only knew romanticized types of undead, such as vampires and zombies, and things that wouldn't give up the ghost because they had unfinished business on Earth.

Stacy's eyes grew wide as her memories slowly returned to her. She recalled that she was in the middle of fucking one of her students, Darius Reid, when they were rudely interrupted by that nosey detective Jaclyn Benoit.

After that embarrassing encounter, she went on to teach her class. Still obsessed with Darius, she wanted to meet him again after work and make love to him all over again. She craved his touch. His presence. She needed him inside of her and all around her.

She'd become obsessed, unable to shake her libidinous urges. After he'd slaughtered everyone on campus but spared her life, she couldn't stop obsessing. He'd chosen her. For whatever reason, he decided to gift her with life, and she swore she'd use that gift to serve him in any way possible.

She was utterly his to do with as he pleased. And she meant *anything*.

Once the class had finished, she immediately rushed back to her office to call him and set up a date. She wanted to be his so badly. So badly, in fact, she'd kill to keep him. But when she returned to her office, she found a strange man waiting for her.

The stranger caught her attention for a few reasons. First, his striking silver hair was long and beautiful, cascading over his shoulders. Second, his attire appeared old-fashioned, reminiscent of styles from a couple of hundred years ago.

Aside from his silver hair, his only distinguishing feature was the ruby-red spectacles he wore. They were circular and reminded her of the ones Elton John was famous for wearing.

OH, GOD. Her breath caught in her chest as she remembered him slipping off his sunglasses as he introduced himself.

His eyes were as red as the ruby lenses he wore. He was a

vampire. *What was his name again? Why couldn't she remember it?* It was on the tip of her tongue, but it felt like something was preventing her from recalling any key details.

"*Ow,*" she said, wincing from a sharp pain. It was the first time she had been aware of the pain in her arm. Looking down at the underside of her forearm, Stacy found a brand stamped on the soft part of her flesh—a symbol of some kind.

It was some Egyptian design—an all-seeing eye of sorts. The eye of Ra, perhaps? She didn't know what it meant or why it was burned into her flesh, but she had a strong suspicion that the mysterious vampire she'd met in her office had something to do with it. No, more than that. She *knew* he had something to do with it.

Stacy Anderson felt the mud drying on her skin as the breeze picked up. She brushed off the loose soil from her naked body and then looked around the cemetery. It was quiet. Peaceful.

Looking up at the moon, she realized something was amiss with her. The orb glowed with a radiance she'd never noticed before. But more than that, it made her feel electric. It made her desire physical touch and sex.

Stranger than the moon's soothing properties, however, was the fact that she didn't feel cold. Her skin didn't bristle in the cool night's air. No chill ran down her spine. She felt fine. She felt fucking fantastic. That was saying something for a woman who'd just crawled out of her grave.

No way, she thought. How was it even possible?

Reaching up with her fingers, she gently ran them across her lush lips, and, opening her mouth just a crack, she touched the sharp points of a set of perfectly formed fangs.

"Holy fuck," she said, a twinge of excitement surging threw her. She'd been turned into a vampire.

She pinched the bridge of her nose and groaned as the memory of her murder came back to her. That two-faced snake, Velma, had tricked her into coming to the bowling alley, promising that Darius wanted to see her. Stacy arrived around midnight, and Velma greeted her, but Darius was nowhere to be found.

Velma came onto Stacy and tried to finger her, but she wasn't into it, so she brushed the girl aside. This made her mad, and Velma jumped her, slicing her throat and then bleeding her dry. Stacy remembered being dumped in the back dumpster, where she stared up at the night sky, bleeding out.

Moments from her final breath, the man in the ruby glasses appeared. He stared down at her for a while, then bit his wrist and extended his arm, holding his wound above her mouth. She remembered the drops of blood dappling her lips when fading fast, and everything went black.

But here she was—a vampire. So, putting it all together, she knew that the stranger was her savior.

Stacy let out a groan as her back began to itch terribly. It came upon her like a fit, and the itching only grew more intense. She collapsed to her knees and, reaching behind herself, began scratching and clawing at her flesh. She wanted to tear it all off so badly.

Her fingernails dug deep into her back as she clawed at her skin. Blood spilled out from the gashes, and Stacy screamed out in agony. She clawed more and more until, to her dismay, she began to pull pieces of her shredded skin off in large patches.

Unexpectedly, two wings sprouted from beneath her shoulder blades, and, ripe with blood, like a newborn fetus, she slowly expanded them, letting herself, wings and all, bask in the moonlight.

It was at that moment that she knew. She wasn't just any run-of-the-mill vampire. She was a full vampire. Replete with wings and an insatiable sexual appetite. She thought *how glorious* it was to be such as she fanned her wings, letting them harden beneath the moon's nourishing and healing light.

Sitting on her knees in the cemetery, she arched her back, threw out her arms, extended her wings, and screamed up at the sky.

Spawning from something as terrible as it was beautiful, she inherited an ancient curse. She didn't feel any pain, and the evening chill didn't bother her. If all she knew about vampires was true, she was practically immortal.

She gazed up at the golden orb in the sky and took a deep breath. The cool air filled her lungs, and she smiled. Exhaling, she allowed herself to accept her fate. She had become something as powerful as it was awful.

Rising to her feet, Stacy ran her hands down her bare skin and started dancing erotically in the cemetery. She danced beneath the full moon, her hips swaying seductively, her body moving in a hypnotic rhythm.

She raised her arms above her head and twirled like a ballerina, dancing above her final resting place. She felt the soft grass slip between the toes of her bare feet with every step. Her orchid-pink nipples stood erect on her breasts while her hips swiveled, rocking in a sensual manner that would arouse anyone with a warm-blooded pulse.

The passionate essence of her dance was a celebration—a wild Bacchanalian revelry. She felt revitalized. However, she felt that Stacey Anderson was too ordinary a name.

Stacey, the vampire, however, seemed laughably mundane. As a rejuvenated queen of the night, she needed a new name, a better name—one that would be as potent as it was alluring.

Arcadia? Yes, she thought to herself. *You shall be known as Arcadia from now on and forever more.*

Stacy Anderson was no more. The timid human with co-dependency issues had been stripped away, leaving only the raw presence of a much more powerful being.

Arcadia felt that the birthplace of the gods of antiquity was the perfect name for her because, like them, she had been born again, not as a weak and fragile human, but as a powerful and beautiful goddess—a vampire goddess.

THE END

Jaclyn Benoit
January 19, 1809

OTHER WORKS BY TRISTAN VICK

NOVELS

The Scarecrow & Lady Kingston
The Chronicles of Jegra 1-6
Valandra 1-3
Bitten 1-3

COMICS

The Astonishing Adventures of Alicia Carter & Robot

The Viking Berserker ZARNA
Daughter of Wolves
Animal Woman
The Profane

www.regolithcomics.com

**REGOLITH
PUBLICATIONS**